*The Best from
Fantasy
and
Science Fiction
22nd Series*

The Best from

Fantasy
and
Science Fiction

22nd Series

Edited by

EDWARD L. FERMAN

DOUBLEDAY & COMPANY, INC.
GARDEN CITY, NEW YORK
1977

The editor hereby makes grateful acknowledgment to the following authors and authors' representatives for giving permission to reprint the material in this volume:

Harold Matson Co. for *The Hertford Manuscript*, by Richard Cowper, copyright © 1976 by Colin Murry.
Scott Meredith Literary Agency for *A Case of the Stubborns*, by Robert Bloch
Algis Budrys for *Books: Where We Are and Where We Came From*
Joanna Russ for *My Boat*
John Varley for *In the Bowl*
Liz Hufford for *This Offer Expires*
Baird Searles for *Films: The Fantastic Ten*, copyright © 1977 by Baird Searles
Robert P. Mills Ltd. for *The Women Men Don't See* by James Tiptree, Jr.
Manly Wade Wellman for *The Ghastly Priest Doth Reign*
Harvey Jacobs for *Dress Rehearsal*
Tom Reamy for *San Diego Lightfoot Sue*
Harold Matson Co. for *Out of Dickinson by Poe*, by Ray Bradbury
Edward Wellen for *Sanity Clause*
Isaac Asimov for *Science: Thinking About Thinking*
Robert P. Mills Ltd. for *Mute Inglorious Tam*, by Frederik Pohl and C. M. Kornbluth
R. Bretnor for *Old Uncle Tom Cobleigh and All*

Copyright © 1973, 1974, 1975, 1976 by Mercury Press, Inc.

ISBN: 0-385-12451-1
Library of Congress Catalog Card Number 76–56287
Copyright © 1973, 1974, 1975, 1976, 1977 by Mercury Press, Inc.
All Rights Reserved
Printed in the United States of America

First Edition

Dedication

For Emily

CONTENTS

INTRODUCTION

Why this book is different from all others in the series

The Magazine of Fantasy and Science Fiction is mainly in the business of publishing fiction of almost infinite variety and length. And we are proud to present, in this twenty-second volume in a series, a dozen of the best stories from the last three years, ranging from Harvey Jacobs' funny 1,600-word sf piece "Dress Rehearsal" to Tom Reamy's tragic 16,000-word award-winning fantasy "San Diego Lightfoot Sue."

However, regular readers of *F&SF* know that there is somewhat more to the magazine than the fiction. We are talking about the "back-of-the-book" material, the regular features that we publish under the heading "Departments."

About 15 per cent of every issue is devoted to these popular and respected departments. They are absolutely essential to the personality of the magazine; they are not in any sense detachable parts, and we've concluded that they correctly belong in an anthology titled THE BEST FROM FANTASY AND SCIENCE FICTION. We refer specifically to Isaac Asimov's long-running science column, Algis Budrys on books, and Baird Searles on films. We have also included a poem by Ray Bradbury and a sampling from the *F&SF* Competitions, which have increased in popularity to the point that 500 to 1,000 entries are not uncommon.

And so we have here for the first time a completely representative BEST FROM F&SF, a book that will give you the feel of the total magazine and, we think, add to your pleasure.

—*Edward L. Ferman*

The Best from
Fantasy
and
Science Fiction
22nd Series

Richard Cowper is the pen name for John Middleton Murry, Jr., an Englishman who lives in South Wales and says of himself: "I was born in 1926 in the eclipsing shadow of an illustrious father. I took to writing as a young bird takes to flight—by reason of heredity. I regard science fiction as one of the few literary forms which are able to satisfy that appetite which Dr. Johnson identified for all time as 'the hunger of the imagination which preys upon life.'" Mr. Cowper's sf novels include *Clone* and *The Twilight of Briareus*. He has written several extraordinary stories for *F&SF*, including "The Custodians," "Piper at the Gates of Dawn," and the piece you are about to read: a gripping tale of time travel to the grim days of the Great Plague.

The Hertford Manuscript

by RICHARD COWPER

The death of my Great-Aunt Victoria at the advanced age of 93 lopped off the longest branch of a family tree whose roots have been traced right back to the 15th Century—indeed, for those who are prepared to accept "Decressie" as a bonafide corruption of "de Crècy," well beyond that. Talking to my aunt toward the end of her life was rather like turning the pages of a Victorian family album, for as she grew older the England of her childhood seemed to glow ever more brightly in her mind's eye. In those far-off days it had been fashionable to accept the inevitability of human progress with a whole-heartedness which is almost impossible for us to imagine. In the 1990's life presented *Homo sapiens* with a series of "problems" which had to be "solved." It was as simple as that. The Edwardians merely gilded the roof of that towering pogoda of Victorian optimism which collapsed in smithereens in 1914.

James Wilkins—Great-Aunt Victoria's husband—died of trench fever in the Dardanelles in 1916. They had no children and she never maried again. I learned later from my aunt that James had been a keen member of the Fabian Society. He had also been an active partner in the antiquarian book business of Benham & Wilkins which owned premises off Old Bond Street.

Shortly after James's death, and much to her family's astonishment, Victoria announced her intention of taking over her husband's share of the business. She very soon proved herself to be an extremely capable business woman. She made a specialty of English incunabula, and throughout the 20s and 30s she built up a thriving trade with countless museums and university libraries all over the world. When the vast Hertford Collection was sold off to pay death duties in 1938, Great-Aunt Victoria had her seat reserved in the front row of the auction gallery throughout the two weeks of the sale, and in the price register published afterward the name Wilkins was prominent among the list of buyers.

In October, 1940, a direct hit from an incendiary bomb destroyed the premises and much of the stock of Benham & Wilkins overnight. She was close to sixty at the time, living alone in Hampstead, and I remember receiving a letter from her in which she told me that she had decided to sell out. She did not sound particularly regretful about it. "No doubt it had to happen," she wrote, "and I consider myself fortunate that it did not happen to me too." I discounted the unfamiliar note of fatalism in her words as being due to shock.

She lived on in her house in Well Walk, growing preceptibly frailer as the years advanced, but with her mind still alert. I used to make a point of calling in to see her whenever I was up in town and was invariably offered China tea and caraway-seed cake for which she had a lifelong passion. On one occasion, in the late 50s, she told me she had once been "propositioned" by H. G. Wells.

"I had no idea you knew him," I said. "When was that?"

"Oh, at about the time he and Shaw and the Webbs were squabbling over the future of the Society."

"The Fabian Society?"

"Yes, of course. 1907, I think it was."

"And what was the proposition?"

She laughed. "The usual one, I gathered. He said he wished me to help him with a book he was writing on the emancipation of women." She paused and gazed out of the window. "He was a strangely attractive little man."

"But you didn't accept?"

"No. Perhaps I should have done. Of course I had met him before that—at the Huxley's. Everyone was talking about him." She paused again and seemed for a while to lose herself in reverie, then she remarked, "Did you ever read a story of his called 'The Chronic Argonauts'?"

"I can't recall it," I said. "What was it about?"

"About a man who invents a machine which will carry him through Time."

"Oh, you mean 'The Time Machine,' Aunt."

"Indeed I don't. I'm quite sure that was the title. I'd never seen 'chronic' used in that way before. It was a serial he was writing for a magazine. He showed me a copy of the first installment. You see we both knew the man it was based on."

"I'm surprised it was based on anyone," I said.

"Oh, yes," she assured me. "A Doctor Robert Pensley. He lived in Herne Hill. Like all of us in those days he too was a great admirer of Professor Huxley."

I helped myself to another slice of seed cake. "And what did the doctor make of young Wells's portrait of him?" I asked.

"As far as I know he never read it."

"Oh? Why not?"

"He disappeared."

I blinked at her. "Just like that?"

She nodded. "It created quite a stir at the time. There were rumors that he had skipped off to America."

"And had he?"

"*I* don't think so. And neither did Wells." She chuckled—a strangely youthful sound from lips so old—and added: "I remember H.G.'s very first words to me when he learned what had happened: 'By God, Vikki, don't you see? He's done it!'"

"And what did he mean by that?" I asked.

"Traveled in Time, of course," said Aunt Victoria in the matter-of-fact tone she might have employed in saying: "Caught the 10:15 to Portsmouth."

I am ashamed to say I laughed.

She gave me a darting, sidelong glance from her clear, gray eyes. "You think it quite impossible, of course."

"Oh, quite," I said, setting down my tea cup and wiping the cake crumbs from my fingers with my handkerchief.

"Wells didn't think so."

"Ah, yes," I said. "But then he wrote science-fiction, didn't he?"

"I don't see what that has to do with it."

"Well, I presume he'd just appreciated that he had the material for an excellent story. After all, he wrote it, didn't he?"

"He wrote it *down,*" she said.

"Well, there you are then. And no doubt Doctor Pensley's descendants are living happily in America to this day."

Aunt Victoria smiled faintly and let the subject drop.

I was in Melbourne, Australia, right on the other side of the globe, when I received a letter telling me that Aunt Victoria had died. The news did not come as any great surprise because I knew she had been in poor health ever since catching a severe dose of flu in the early spring, but the sense of loss I felt was real enough. Her death seemed to nudge me appreciably nearer to my own grave.

When I returned home to England, some six weeks later, it was to discover that my aunt's mortal remains were nourishing the rose bushes in Highgate cemetery and the house in Well Walk had already been sold. I also discovered a letter awaiting me. It was signed by her bank manager, who, it appeared, was the executor of her will, and it informed me that I had been left a legacy of a thousand pounds together with "a particular token of the regard in which the late Mrs. Wilkins held you."

I lost no time in traveling up to town from my house in Bristol and presenting myself at the bank manager's office. After the formal exchange of polite regrets for the sad nature of the occasion, I was handed a brown paper parcel, securely tied and sealed, with my own name written upon it in Aunt Victoria's quite remarkably firm hand. I signed the official receipt, was presented with an envelope containing a cheque for 1,000 pounds, and stepped out into the street. I was not consumed by any overwhelming curiosity to discover exactly what "token of regard" the parcel contained. From the shape of it I guessed that it must be a book of some kind, and I had a shrewd suspicion that it would prove to be the photograph album which Aunt Victoria and I had often looked at together when I visited her in Well Walk.

There being nothing further to detain me in London, I took a taxi to Paddington and caught the first available train back to Bristol. Having decided to invest a modest portion of my windfall on a first-class ticket, I had the unfamiliar luxury of a whole compartment to myself, and seated there, relaxed and extremely pleased with myself and the world, I finally got round to untying the string which, I did not doubt, Aunt Victoria had fastened with her own capable hands.

I soon realized that I had been mistaken in my previous assumption. The book which emerged from beneath the layers of brown paper and newsprint in which it was wrapped had certainly been old long before the invention of photography. It measured roughly 12 inches by 9, was bound in dark brown leather, and had a heavily ridged spine of the kind which I believe is known in the antiquarian book trade as "knuckled." There was no tooling of any kind either on the covers or on the spine, in fact nothing at all on the outside of the book to indicate what its contents might be. For the life of me I could not conceive why Aunt Victoria should have left it to me.

As I turned back the front cover, I found, lying inside, a sealed envelope, inscribed with my Christian name and bearing at the bottom right-hand corner a date—June 4th, 1958.

I laid the book down on the seat beside me, slit open the envelope and extracted two sheets of the tinted notepaper which my aunt had always favored. I put on my spectacles and read the following:

Wednesday evening

My dear Francis,

There was a point during our conversation this afternoon when I was sorely tempted to march upstairs and fetch down this book. Though I am sure you don't realize it, there was something about the way in which you dismissed the very idea of time travel as being 'Quite impossible!' that struck me as almost unbearably smug. However, second thoughts being, as usual, better than first impulses, I have decided instead that I shall leave you the book in my will. So by the time you read this letter I daresay you will already have become accustomed to thinking of me as your late Aunt rather than your Great Aunt! I confess that it makes me smile even as I write it.

From the ex-libris plate inside the front cover you will see that this book comes from the Hertford Library which was sold up in 1938. It was part of a lot consisting of some half a dozen miscellaneous 17th Century Registers which I obtained for the proverbial song simply because no one else seemed interested in them. It was

*not until I was going through them to make out entries for our Over-
seas catalogue that I noticed that one of them had stitched into the
back of it about twenty flimsy sheets of paper which were quite
different in texture from those which make up the rest of the volume.
Since the binding itself was indisputably 17th Century workmanship
and all the other entries concerned the years 1662–1665, I started to
examine these odd pages with some interest. I discovered, to my astonishment, that they constituted a sort of rough journal or diary,
written in pencil, and covering a period of some three weeks in August and September, 1665.*

*I will not spoil my own pleasure in imagining your expression as
you read them by telling you what I believe them to be. All I will say
is that the Register was entered in the Hertford Catalogue in 1808
as having been purchased along with two others 'from the Estate of
Jonas Smiley Esq.' To the very best of my knowledge they lay there
in the library of Hertford Castle gathering dust for the next 130
years.*

I trust you will find it as interesting and as instructive as I did.

Yours most affectionately,
Victoria.

I re-read the letter from beginning to end in total bewilderment. At
first, I confess, I could only assume that I was the victim of some extraordinary practical joke she had chosen to play upon me, but it was
so unlike Aunt Victoria to do anything of the kind that, in the end, I
simply shrugged and picked up the book. Sure enough, pasted inside
the front cover was an engraved bookplate depicting two remarkably
well-developed mermaids holding aloft a shell in which reclined a
grinning skull, a quill pen and an hourglass. Circumscribing this
somewhat ill-assorted gathering was a fluttering banner emblazoned
with the legend EX LIBRIS HERTFORDENSIS. So at least there
seemed to be no doubt about that part of Aunt Victoria's story. I
turned over the stained flyleaf and found myself contemplating an
ornate sepia script which informed me that this was ye Register
opened on November 20th 1662 for ye Hostel of Saint Barnabas in
ye Parish of Wapping of which ye Recording Clerk was one Tobias
Gurney. The first entry on the next page read: *Decd. at the 4th hr.
Agnes Miller, fem. age indet. of ye fev. quot. tert.*

I ran my eye down the column which appeared to consist almost
entirely of records of deaths and then flicked on through the

yellowed pages till I reached those leaves which Aunt Victoria had spoken about. I saw at once why they had caught her attention. For one thing they measured little more than 6 inches by 4, and the paper, besides being badly faded at the edges of the sheets, was ruled with faint lines. But even more striking was the difference in the handwriting. These pages were covered in a minute, cramped, cursive script quite unlike the hand of the recording clerk. If I had to select one adjective to describe it, the word would be "scholarly." In fact the tiny writing put me immediately in mind of that of J. E. Lawless, my erstwhile tutor at St. Catherine's; there were even some of the identical abbreviations—"tho." for "though"; "wd." for "would"; "shd." for "should"—which I remembered he had favored. Settling myself firmly into the corner closet to the window, I raised the book to catch the maximum amount of daylight and began to read.

Some twenty minutes before the train was due at Bristol I had reached the last entry. I find it quite impossible to describe accurately my precise state of mind at that moment. I remember becoming conscious of an acute headache, the onset of which I had, presumably, ignored while I was engrossed in my reading. I remember too that as I unhooked my spectacles and gazed out of the window I experienced a most extraordinary sense of disorientation —perhaps "displacement" would be the better word—as though the green fields and cosy Wiltshire farms beyond the tract had become mysterious, insubstantial, illusory things; mere tokens of stasis in some fantastic temporal flux. The moment passed quickly enough— the discipline of a lifetime's ingrained habit of thought soon reasserted itself—but I was left with the same excessively unpleasant sense of inner quivering that I had once endured after experiencing a minor earthquake in Thessaloniki. To say that I doubted what I most firmly believed would be putting it too strongly; to say that my philosophical foundations had been temporarily shaken would not be putting it quite strongly enough.

It will, I am sure, be maintained that I am either the instigator of —or the victim of!—some elaborate hoax. The first contention I shall perforce ignore, since, knowing it to be untrue, it does not particularly concern me. To the second I am forced to return a reluctant verdict of "Not Proven." I have had the Register examined by two separate experts in such matters and both have assured me, to my own total satisfaction, that the notebook pages which have been incorporated within it were stitched into the binding at the time when the book itself was bound up, i.e., not later than the middle of the 18th Century and, in all likelihood, a good half-century earlier. *Yet the paper of the notebook itself is, indisputably, of a type not manufactured before 1860! Ergo,* either somebody is lying or the notebook is genuine.

If we assume that some person (unknown) had wished to perpetuate such a hoax, when could it have been done? From the internal evidence certainly not before 1804. Therefore this anonymous hoaxer must have had access to the Hertford Library, have inserted his spurious material into the Register, have replaced it on the library shelf and then *done nothing at all to draw attention to it.* Since, presumably, the whole point of a hoax is to deceive as many people as possible, this strikes me as just about the most pointless hoax ever devised.

That leaves, as far as I am concerned, only my Great-Aunt Victoria. She had custody of the Register from the time of the sale in 1938 until the day of her death—ample opportunity certainly in which to have "doctored it" to her heart's content. Furthermore she, with her professional connections, would have been ideally situated to carry out such a plan had she wished to do so. This would have entailed forging the whole "diary" itself on suitable paper, having the Register broken down and the forged diary incorporated, reassembling the whole and restoring it to its original condition in such a way as to totally deceive two vastly experienced and disinterested professional experts. She would also have had to insert (or have caused to be inserted) two completely spurious entries into the Register proper, doing it in such a way that there was no observable discrepancy between those false entries and the ones which preceded and followed them. The only way in which this could have been done would have been by removing two of the original sheets, obtaining two blank sheets of the identical 17th Century rag paper, forging the entries to correspond *exactly* with those in the rest of the book, and then reassembling the whole. I am prepared to admit that all this *could* have been done, but nothing will ever succeed in convincing me that it was. Nevertheless, since such a thing is conceivably possible, I must to that extent accede to the verdict of "Not Proven" on the second of my two counts.

Having said that, all that remains is for me to transcribe *in toto* the contents of this extraordinary document and to add, by way of an appendix, the relevant entries from the Register itself together with a few concluding observations of my own.

Although the transcript is a faithful word-for-word copy of the original text, I have taken the liberty of expanding the author's abbreviations, inserting the paragraphs, and tidying up the punctuation where I think it is called for. The diary commences at the top of the first page, and it is possible that a preceding page or pages were lost before the others were incorporated in the Register.

It is, of course, utterly pointless to go on cursing myself for my idiotic complacency, yet has there been a single waking hour in the last 48 when I have not done so? To assume, as I did, that the Morlocks* had done no more than carry out an investigation of the superficial structure of my Machine was an inexcusable indulgence in wishful thinking, bolstered, unfortunately, by my successful onward voyage and return. Yet even now I am by no means certain that the Morlocks were responsible for that microscopic fracture of the dexter polyhedron. Could it not equally well have occurred during that final frenzied battle within the pedestal of the White Sphinx? Indeed it seems more than likely. What is utterly unforgivable is that I should have failed to detect the flaw when I carried out my detailed check on Friday. Well, few men can ever have paid more dearly for wanton carelessness.

I knew that something was amiss the moment I had recovered sufficiently from my initial vertigo to scan the dials. Instead of circling smoothly around the horologe the indicator arm had developed a perceptible and disquieting lurch, first slowing and then accelerating. I realized at once that two of the quartz pillars in the quincunx were out of phase and I suspected some minor fault of alignment which it would be but the work of a moment in the laboratory to correct. Although the dials on the fascia showed that I was already well back into the 17th Century, a glance at my pocket watch informed me that my journey was less than two minutes old. Very gingerly I coaxed the right-hand lever toward me and was much alarmed to observe that the pulsation of the needle at once became far more pronounced. This, together with that indescribable nausea which is seemingly an unavoidable concomitant of Time travel, produced in me a sensation that was uncomfortably close to panic. Nevertheless, I kept my head sufficiently to observe that I was not about to enter

* *For this and similar references see* The Time Machine *by* H. G. Wells. *—Ed.*

into conjunction with some massive external object and, very gently, I brought the lever back into the neutral position.

The machine was resting on the bare hillside, its brass runners buried in grass and buttercups. Above me the sun was blazing down out of a cloudless sky, and from its position relative to the meridian I judged the hour to be early afternoon. Some way down the slope of the hill below me two brown and white cows were grazing placidly, flicking their tails at the flies. As I glanced away I saw one of them raise its head and regard me with mild curiosity. So much for the 17th Century, I thought, and with a silent prayer on my lips I thrust forward the left-hand lever which would send me winging forward through the centuries to 1894. *And nothing happened!* I tried again and even risked further pressure on the right-hand lever. The result was exactly the same.

My emotions at that moment were all but identical with those I had experienced when I first looked down from the gazebo on the hillcrest above the Hall of Eloi and found my Machine was no longer standing where I had left it on the lawn before the White Sphinx. It is the fear that grips the marooned mariner when he sees the topsail finally dip below the horizon. For a minute or two I surrendered to it cravenly and then, thank Heaven! reason reasserted itself once more. I had successfully surmounted the earlier crisis: I should survive this too.

I climbed out of the saddle, stepped down into the grass, unclipped the aluminum cover and peered into the womb of the quincunx. One glance was sufficient to tell me what had happened. Of the four polyhedral quartz prisms, the second dexter one had *fractured clean in two along its plane of cleavage!*

For a long moment I simply stared at it in disbelief while the full implication of the disaster gradually dawned upon me. With it came an overwhelming awareness of the grotesque and inescapable irony of my predicament. There, a mere ten paces from where I was standing, lay my workbench, and lying upon that workbench were no fewer than *four identical quartz polyhedra,* any one of which could have been fastened into place within a matter of moments! Ten paces or two hundred and thirty years! Compared with my previous voyage it was hardly a hairs-breadth of Time, and yet, for all that, those vital components might just as well have been engulfed in the swamps of the Jurassic.

I reached into the quincunx, unscrewed the two halves of the broken rod, withdrew them and examined them. I thought I could detect a minute scratch ending just where the fracture began. "Ah, fool," I castigated myself bitterly. "Crass, unmitigated fool!"

I sat down in the grass with my back resting against the framework of the Machine, and tried to marshal my fragmented thoughts. It was plain enough that my only hope of escape was to obtain a replacement for that broken prism. I even derived a mite of consolation from the wry reflection that had it been the neodymium dodecahedron which had shattered I should have been lost indeed since that—chronically speaking—essential element had been discovered only in 1885! But how to set about obtaining a replacement?

I rose to my feet and consulted the fascia dials once more. A brief calculation told me that I was now in the year 1665 A.D. The date did indeed touch some faintly disturbing chord in my memory, but I was too concerned with finding a solution to my immediate problem to spare any time on tracking it to its source. Reaching into the pannier below the saddle, I next drew out the canvas knapsack and my kodak. Then, mindful of my experiences with the Morlocks, I unscrewed the two control levers, thus still further immobilizing my already impotent Machine. That done, I carefully removed the second of the dexter prisms, reasoning that, if a replacement were ever to be obtained, a complete artifact would provide a more satisfactory pattern than a broken one. These practical actions, small enough in themselves, did much to help me take that first imaginative step on the far side of the gulf, which is imperative if a traveler in Time is to preserve the full effectiveness of his intellectual faculties.

My next move was to take stock of my useful possessions. I was, it is true, somewhat better equipped than when I had first launched myself so impulsively into the Future, but since I had planned for a brief expedition into the early Holocene, it was open to question whether a patent pocket compass, a kodak, a specimen case, or a notebook and pencils would be of very much service to me in my present predicament. Far more to the point was the handful of loose change, which, by a fortunate oversight, I was still carrying in one of the thigh pockets of my knickerbockers. It amounted in all to two sovereigns, three florins, a sixpence and some assorted coppers. Apart from my fob watch, the other pockets surrendered little more than a small tin of licorice cashews, my tobacco pouch and pipe, a box of lucifers, a twin-bladed penknife and a brass-sheathed pocket lens. This latter I put to immediate use by verifying what I had already suspected concerning the microscopic cause of the fracture in the prism.

The warmth of the summer sun was striking full upon me. So I loosened the belt of my Norfolk jacket, hoisted the knapsack over my shoulder and, after bidding my Machine a truly heartfelt *au revoir,* settled my cap square on my head and set off, striding out through the buttercups across the flank of the hill in the direction of the Camberwell.

The plan of action I had settled upon was simple enough—to get to London as soon as I possibly could. It was there, if anywhere, that I might hope to find a skilled lapidary artificer whom I could prevail upon to fashion me a 4-inch polyhedral rod of rock crystal sufficiently accurate for my needs. An exact replica was obviously too much to hope for, but I reasoned that I had already sufficiently demonstrated how even a flawed rod would serve its purpose long enough to enable me to effect my return to the 19th Century.

Ten minutes brisk walking brought me within sight of the Thames basin, though the river itself I could perceive only as a tremulous silver flickering in the distance toward Rotherhithe some four miles to the northeast. I was astonished by the amount of woodland which clothed the south bank of the river from Battersea to Greenwich. Although it was largely dispersed in the form of small coppices and outgrown hedgerows, the spaces between those closest to me were filled by others yet more distant so that the general effect was to screen the city from my sight. Had I chosen to ascend to the crest of Herne Hill, I would doubtless have obtained a view of the whole panorama, but time was too precious. Leaving the hilltop windmill on my left, I descended by means of a dry and rutted cart track toward the untidy huddle of houses which I guessed must be ancient Camberwell.

The track led me down into the road, which I recognized as connecting Camberwell with Dulwich, and so I turned to my left and headed in the general direction of Walworth. As I rounded the corner which brought me in full view of the hamlet, I was surprised to observe that a rough stockade had been erected across the road. The centerpiece of this makeshift barrier was formed by a large hay wain, on the top of which were seated three men, one of whom appeared to be shouldering a musket. I paused for a moment to take stock of the situation; then, able to make nothing of it, I approached and called out to ask whether I was on the London road. "Aye!"

shouted one of the men, rising to his feet. "And keep a-going, stranger! We're all sound bodies here and by the Lord's grace will stay so."

Perplexed in the extreme, I continued moving steadily toward them, whereupon the same man shouted again, "Not one step further upon thy life!"

I halted in my tracks and stared at him—or rather at the musket which he was now pointing directly at my head!—and raised my hands to show that I carried no weapon. "I wish you no harm, good people," I cried.

"Nor we you, mister," responded the spokesman. "So get ye gone."

"But this is most uncivil," I protested. "I have urgent business to transact in London."

"Aye, and the Angel of Death likewise!" cried one of the others. "Four thousand souls been culled at last week's billing."

This extraordinary remark did what nothing else in the exchange had so far achieved. The significance of the final figure registered upon the dials of my Machine reverberated through my stunned mind like an electric alarm bell. *1665. The year of the Great Plague!*

My hands dropped to my sides as though paralyzed, and I stood transfixed, wonderstruck, staring at the three men. One of them raised his fingers to his lips and whistled shrilly. A moment later I caught the excited yelping of dogs. There was an urgent cry of "Sic him! Sic him!" whereat I spun about and fled precipitately with a pack of eager curs snapping at my flying heels.

No sooner had I regained the sanctuary of the cart track than the dogs, with a few backward looks and admonitory snarls, trotted off toward the village, leaving me with a painfully racing heart and the realization that my predicament was far worse than even I could have imagined. My historical knowledge of the effects of the Plague was woefully sketchy, though I did recollect from a childhood reading of Pepy's Diary that commercial life of some sort had continued in the city throughout the visitation. My longing to be quit forever of this benighted age increased a hundredfold. I resolved to strike out at once across the fields in the general direction of Southwark, avoiding, as far as humanly possible, the vicinity of any of the scattered farms or hamlets I might encounter on the way.

An hour (and several wearisome detours) brought me within sight of the Old Kent Road, along which I perceived a number of covered carts and several head of cattle being driven in the direction of London Bridge. I skirted around the edge of a cornfield, thrust my way through the hedge and, having gained the highway, set off at my best pace in the wake of this motley caravan. I soon came up with a young cattle drover, who eyed me somewhat oddly, no doubt on account of my dress, though in truth my tweed knickerbockers were perfectly recognizable descendants of his own leather breeches and woolen hose. The most obvious anachronism was my checkered cloth cap (all the men I had seen so far had been wearing either the broad-rimmed "wideawake" or the high-crowned "steeple" style of headgear favored by the Puritans). So on the pretense of wiping the sweat from my brow I removed the questionable article, stowed it away in my pocket, and gave the youth a good day. He returned my greeting civilly enough and enquired what I was traveling in. My look of perplexity led him to say, "Are ye not a pedlar?"

It seemed prudent to agree that I was, and I asked him whether he knew of any jewelers or instrument makers still trading in the city.

He shook his head and said he supposed they must all have fled if they had the means to do so. Realizing I should get no useful information from him and anxious to push on with all possible speed, I wished him a good journey and strode off in the wake of the carts.

I was by now within plain sight of Southwark Cathedral and the Old Bridge, and for the first time since setting foot in this grim century I found myself gazing about me with real curiosity. The great river—sparkling, green, and clear in a manner all but unimaginable in 1894—was crowded with vessels of every conceivable shape and size from tiny skiffs to quite substantial merchantmen. Indeed, further down stream below the Tower I counted no fewer than 23 large craft moored out in midchannel, while a host of small rowing boats fussed around them like water beetles. As to the city itself I think what struck me most forcibly was, firstly, the grisly row of several heads adorning the battlements of the Bridge Gatehouse and, secondly, the gaiety and brightness of the waterfront houses, each decorated individually to its owner's whim. The sight of those bright reflections shimmering on the sunny water affected me so strongly that it was with a real sense of impotence and loss that I suddenly realized how, within a mere twelvemonth, the ravages of the Great Fire would have destroyed forever most of what I was now seeing. That it must be so I acknowledged, but it caused me none the less a pang for that.

As I approached the Gatehouse, I observed a group of watchmen armed with pikes and muskets examining the contents of the incoming carts and questioning the drivers. Since pedestrians did not appear to be attracting the same attention, I strode on purposefully, only to be halted by one of the guards demanding to know my business. I told him I was a pedlar-mechanician seeking out instrument makers in the city and added that I would be obliged if he could assist me with directions.

He looked me up and down, scrutinizing my woolen necktie and my stout Highland brogues with obvious suspicion. "And whence come ye, master pedlar?" he asked.

"Canterbury," I replied glibly, offering the first likely name that came to mind.

"Be ye of sound health?"

"Indeed I am," I said, "and hopeful to remain so."

"Aye," he muttered, "with God's blessing, so are we all. Be advised by me, master, and look to peddle your wares elsewhere."

"I have no choice in the matter," I replied. "My trade is too rare." So saying, I slid my hand into my trousers pocket and jingled my coins meaningfully. "Would you happen to know of any jewelers still trading in the city?"

He squeezed his nose thoughtfully between his finger and thumb. "Ludgate's their common quarter. But the sickness lies heavy thereabouts they say. More I know not."

I thanked him for his help, drew out a penny from my pocket and handed it to him. As I hurried onto the bridge, I glanced back and saw him turn the coin doubtfully between his fingers before tapping it against the steel blade of his pike.

I crossed the river without further incident, picked out the gothic spire of Old St. Paul's soaring high above the roofs to my left and knew that Ludgate lay immediately beyond it, hidden from my view. I passed through the gate at the north end of the bridge and stepped down into the city.

No sooner had I done so than the waterside breeze died away and I was assailed by a most terrible stench from the heaps of garbage and human ordure which lay scattered all down the center of the street, baking in the sun and so thick with flies that the concerted buzzing sounded like a swarm of angry bees. I felt my stomach heave involuntarily and clutched my handkerchief to my nose and mouth, marveling how the other pedestrians seemed able to proceed about their business seemingly oblivious to the poisonous stench.

I had covered barely 200 yards before I came upon a house, securely shuttered and barred, with a clumsy cross daubed upon its door in red paint and the ominous words *Lord, have mercy upon us* scrawled above it. Dozing on a stool beside it was an old man with a scarlet wooden staff resting across his knees. I observed that my fellow pedestrians were careful to give the area a wide berth, and at the risk of fouling my shoes I too edged out toward the center of the street, glancing up as I did so in time to see a small white face peeping fearfully down at me from behind one of the high leaded windows. In spite of the heat I shivered and quickened my pace, taking the first available turn to the left and hurrying down what is still, I believe, called Thames Street. As soon as I saw the cathedral spire rising to my right, I turned again and headed toward it.

As I made my way along the narrow alley, I scanned the signboards on either side and eventually saw one which bore a representation of a pair of compasses. I hurried toward it only to discover that the shop was locked and barred. I squinted in through the leaded window at the selection of terrestrial globes, astrolabes, hourglasses and astronomical rings and felt my heart sink. What earthly hope had I of finding anyone capable of supplying my needs in an age which was only just beginning to emerge from the shadows of the mediaeval? As I turned dispiritedly away, I saw an elderly gentleman emerging from a door further up the street. I waited until he came abreast of me and then accosted him politely and asked whether he knew of any instrument maker or optician still working in the neighborhood.

Perhaps something in my manner of speech or my dress intrigued him because he peered at me shrewdly from beneath the broad brim of his hat and asked me if I would care to specify exactly what it was I was looking for.

Having nothing to gain by not doing so, I told him I had urgent need of some skilled artificer capable of fashioning for me a small rod or cylinder of rock crystal.

"Why, sir," he said, "if you seek a lens grinder, then Master William Tavener is your man. His shop lies hard by St. Anne's in Carter Lane." He indicated with his cane the direction I should take, adding that he could not vouch for it that the man had not fled the City, though he believed not.

I thanked him warmly for his assistance and made haste to follow his directions. Ten minutes later I had found the shop, exactly where he had described it, with a large gilded spectacles frame hanging above it for its sign. I glanced briefly at the small display of reading lenses in the window, realized that this or nothing was what I had been seeking, and with a painfully racing heart reached for the door latch. To my inexpressible relief the door opened and I stepped over the threshold into the shop.

A small brass bell was standing on the wooden counter, and, after waiting for a minute or so, I picked it up and rang it briskly. I heard a door bang somewhere in the back regions of the shop and the sound of approaching footsteps. Finally a young woman appeared holding a baby in her arms. She stood gazing at me somberly for a moment then asked, "What is it ye seek, master?"

"Is Mr. Tavener in?" I asked. "I have some urgent business for him."

A distant voice called out: "Who is it, Bessie?"

"Robert Pensley," I supplied. *"Doctor* Robert Pensley."

I thought I detected a faint quickening of interest in her face as she passed on this information. "He'll be down to you in a minute, sir," she said.

"Does he work alone, then?"

"Th' prentices have flown this month past," she said. "I warrant I'd have followed them had it not been for father. Plague or no plague, he'll not budge."

"Have you any rats in your house?" I enquired.

"Aye, some I daresay. What house hereabouts hasn't? They swarm up from the fleet like black heathens."

"Their fleas are the plague carriers," I said. "Rid yourself of the rats and you'll be safe."

She laughed. "Lord, sir, the beasts are dying without any help from us! I found two lying stiff in the jakes this very morning."

"You didn't touch them?"

"Not I," she said. "Father hoisted them with the furnace tongs and flung 'em over the wall into the ditch."

"On no account handle them whatever you do," I said. "One bite from an infected flea and that could well be the death of you. Believe me, I know."

"They do say as it's the foul air," she said. "There's orders posted abroad for the watch to burn night fires at every street crossing—and all day long in the open yards. But father says the London air's always been as foul even when there was no plague."

"He's right," I insisted. "So do as I say, Bessie, and promise me you'll touch no dead rats; then you and your babe will both live through it safely."

She smiled. "Me, I hate the ugly brutes. Hark ye, here comes father now."

A middle-aged man with a bald crown to his head and sparse brown hair touched with grey came shuffling out of the passage at the back of the counter and nodded to me. "We've not met before, I think, sir," he said. "What is it ye seek?"

I lifted my knapsack on to the counter, unbuckled it and drew out the complete prism and the two broken pieces. "I want you to cut me an eight-faced crystal prism to these identical dimensions, Mr. Tavener," I said. "Can you do it?"

He took the whole crystal from me and held it up, twisting it this way and that as he squinted at it. "May I asked who fashioned this for ye, sir?"

"I had it cut in Italy."

"'Tis fine workmanship. I've seen none better." And with that he handed it back to me with a smile.

"But you must keep it, Mr. Tavener," I insisted. "It is to be your pattern. The dimensions are vital, I do assure you."

"I'm sorry to disappoint ye, Doctor," he said, "but seemingly that's what I must do. Single-handed I'm so tardy in my work that it would be the best part of a three-month before I could even consider it. Why, I have grinding in hand upstairs for Master Hooke, due last month, that bids fair to keep me till the middle of next."

"Mr. Tavener," I cried desperately, "I have not traveled all this way to find you, only to be denied! Will you tell me how long it would take to cut such a prism?"

He lifted the rod again and turned it over speculatively between his fingers. "Cut *and* polish?" he inquired.

"Of course."

"Two or three days. Depending on how fine ye wanted it."

"And what would you charge?"

"A guinea a day for the skilled labor."

"I'll pay you ten," I said, and the words were no sooner out of my mouth than I realized what I had said.

He peered up at me quizzically over the crystal. "Ten guineas?" he repeated slowly. "Ye'd pay me *ten gold guinea pieces?*"

I nodded. "I will. Providing you'll put the work in hand for me at once."

He looked down again at the prism and traced its beveled contours with his fingertips. I could see he was wondering what kind of man I was to have brought him such a proposition. "D'ye mind telling me why the matter is so urgent, sir?"

"You'd not believe me if I did, Mr. Tavener," I said, "but I assure you it could well be a matter of life or death. Time is of the essence."

"Well, there again, sir," he said, "I know not whether I even have such a blank to suit. Like all else, good crystal's hard to come by in these black days. But perhaps you'd care to step up into the workshop and see what there is."

"Then you *will* undertake it?"

"If I have no satisfactory blank, sir, then no amount of willing on my part will make ye one," he said. "So you'd best come up and see for yourself."

I followed him through the shop, up some dark stairs and into a long, low-beamed workroom which must surely have been cantilevered on to the back of the house. Windows ran round three sides and two of them looked out over the graveyard of the church next door. The early evening sunlight was slanting in through a dusty drapery of cobwebs. An antique wooden treadle lathe stood against one wall. Suspended above it was a rack of tools. Instead of a fireplace there was a charcoal oven-furnace and a glass-making crucible. The whole place was depressingly reminiscent of a Dürer engraving of an alchemist's glory hole, but while Mr. Tavener was routing in the depths of a cupboard, I examined two lenses I found lying on a bench and discovered them to be of astonishingly high quality.

Tavener emerged clasping a chunk of quartz which he brought across to the bench and laid before me. "That's Tintagel pebble," he said. "Would it do?"

I picked up the crystal and held it to the light. As far as I could tell, it was flawless. I handed it back to him and expelled my breath in a long sigh. "It will do perfectly, Mr. Tavener," I said.

At that very moment the clock in the church began to sound a chime, and without thinking I pulled my watch from my fob pocket, intending to set it by the prevailing time. I had just clicked open the gold face-guard when I noticed that Tavener's gaze was riveted on the instrument. I smiled. "You will not have seen a watch like this, I daresay, Mr. Tavener?" I detached the chain clip and held the instrument out to him.

He took it from me and turned it round wonderingly in his fingers, rather as the guard at the bridge gatehouse had turned over the penny I had given him. Then he lifted it to his ear and a look of the most profound astonishment suffused his face. It is, in truth, a fine timepiece, made by Jacques Simenon of Paris and given to me to mark my 21st anniversary by my dear mother and father. I took it back from him, opened the case with my thumbnail and showed him the jewel precision movement within. "Why, sir," he breathed, "that is a true miracle! God's truth, never in my life did I dream to see such a thing."

"I warrant it is the only one of its kind in the world today," I said.

"That I can well believe, sir. I doubt the King himself hath such a treasure."

"Mr. Tavener," I said slowly, "would *you* like to own that watch?"

He looked at me as if I had gone clean out of my mind and said nothing at all.

"I mean it," I said. "So anxious am I to have the prism cut that I am prepared to give you my watch in exchange for it. It is worth far more than ten guineas. Make for me a perfect copy of that prism, put it into my hand, and I will put the watch into yours. See, here is my hand in pledge of it."

Tavener looked down at the watch ticking away merrily on the bench with the yellow sunlight winking from the jeweled balance. It almost seemed to have hypnotized him. "Well?" I said. "Isn't it a fair bargain?"

"Aye, sir," he agreed at last. "I must suppose ye best know what ye are about," and with that he joined his palm to mine and we shook upon the contract.

"And when can you start?" I asked him.

"Tomorrow, God willing. But I shall have to ride to Edmonton first for pumice powder and rotten-stone. I'm clean out of both of them."

"How long will that take?"

"All day, most like. 'Tis ten mile there and no less back."

"And those things you must have?"

"Aye. For cutting pebble. 'Tis not like your whoreson glass. The other grits I have enough of."

"It's not for me to teach you your business, Mr. Tavener," I said. "All I can do now is to wish you God speed."

◆ "Believe me, I'll not tarry, sir. As it is, the lass won't care to be left."

I picked up the watch and clipped it back onto its chain. "I am just newly arrived in London, Mr. Tavener," I said, "and as yet have no lodgings. Could you perhaps recommend me to some inn close by?"

He scratched his chin. *"The Three Keys* in Lower Wharf Street is a clean house," he said. "It's just down alongside Paul's Steps. I daresay that would suit ye. The air is more wholesome by the water."

So I took my leave of him with my heart feeling a good deal lighter than it had for many hours. I soon found The Three Keys and prevailed upon the landlord to rent me an attic room overlooking the river, paying for one week's rent and board in advance with the first of my two sovereigns. I told him that the coin was a Polish *thaler*—Henderson the numismatist once told me that this coin bore a superficial resemblance to our modern sovereign—and he accepted it cheerfully enough, no doubt on account of his having frequent dealings with sailors from foreign ports. I drank a mug of ale with him and ate an excellent mutton pasty while he regaled me with horrific stories of the ravages the "visiation" was wreaking upon the city. He also told me that the ships I had seen drawn up in mid-stream were filled with wealthy citizens who had embarged their wives and families and would permit no one else to set foot aboard, all their daily needs being supplied by boatmen who purchased food on shore, rowed out with it, and loaded it into baskets which were then hauled up on deck.

Soon after this I retired to my room intending to take a short nap, but whether from the unaccustomed effect of the strong ale or by simple reaction to the day's exertions, I fell deeply asleep and did not wake until the next morning, though I seem dimly to recall having my dreams invaded by the sound of a handbell being rung in the street below and the jarring clatter of iron-shod cart wheels upon cobble stones.

Apart from a brief excursion this morning along the waterfront, during which I purchased for myself a less anachronistic hat with one of my three florins and a plain-fronted, linen bib shirt with another, I have spent the whole day closeted in my attic writing up this record of what must surely be one of the most extraordinary days ever spent by a 19th Century gentleman.

August 28th.

To Tavener's early, only to find the shop locked up. I waited for over half an hour hoping that at least his daughter would put in an appearance but saw nobody. I made my way round to the back of the premises and peered up at the workshop windows. The whole place seemed utterly deserted. The rest of the morning I spent wandering about the city in an agony of apprehension. Finally I returned to Carter Street, knocked on the door of the house adjoining the shop and inquired whether they knew anything of the man's whereabouts. The woman told me that Tavener, accompanied by his daughter and her child had set out early the previous morning in a small pony cart and had not been seen since. Telling myself they had been delayed at Edmonton and would surely return that afternoon, I wandered into the cathedral and despite my own anxiety, was deeply moved by the sight of hundreds of people all kneeling in silent prayer. I read a printed proclamation which I found nailed up in the cathedral porch. It was signed by the Lord Mayor and the Sheriffs and gave a series of orders to the citizens, some of which explained the odd noises I had heard—handbells, horns blowing and the rest. Nothing more desperately ironical than the directions *to kill all dogs and cats!*—the one slender hope of keeping some of the rats out of the houses! Returned to Tavener's three times more, then finally back here feeling thoroughly depressed.

August 29th.

Spent a wretched night lying awake listening to the melancholy cries of the bellmen—*Bring out your de-a-a-d! Bring out your de-a-a-d!* Resolved to try to speak to the Mayor or the Sheriffs and attempt to persuade them to at least rescind the order for the destruction of dogs and cats. Heard the squeaking of mice—or rats!— behind the wainscot and broke out into a cold sweat of pure terror. Would I not be better advised to seek lodgings south of the river?

(later)

Still no sign or word of Tavener. Wrote him a note which I thrust under his door, urging him to contact me immediately he returns. Found another lens grinder in Cheapside, but lacking the prisms which I had left with Tavener, I could only give him a rough description of what I wanted. Since he had no suitable crystal anyway, it

was so much wasted effort. However he told me that William
Tavener was "a true man of his word" and that my business could
not be in better hands. Consolation of a sort, I suppose, if only I
could be sure that my business *was* in his hands!

A thoroughly unnerving encounter in a street (Bread St.?) linking
Cheapside with Watling Street. Saw a man I took for a drunkard
staggering toward me. Just before he reached me, he pitched over
and fell full length on the cobbles. I hurried up to him—he was lying
on his face—turned him over and saw to my horror that he had all
the signs of the plague, gross swellings at the sides of his neck and
dark blotches under his skin from internal bleeding. There was a
trickle of blood running from the corner of his mouth, though this
may well have been a result of his fall. He was still breathing—a
throaty, rasping sound—and as I bent over him, he vomited up a
black, evil-smelling bile—shuddered once, violently, and lay still. I
looked up and saw that the narrow street, which had been busy
enough when I entered it, was now completely deserted. All round
me I heard the staccato sounds of doors and window shutters being
clapped to. I felt for the poor devil's pulse and found nothing. I left
him lying there in the street and hurried away.

When I had recovered something of my composure, I made my
way straight to the Mansion House and asked if I could speak to one
of the Sheriffs or some other person of authority upon a matter of
great urgency. Finally I was granted an audience with a Mr. Robinson, the Private Secretary to Sir Charles Doe. He listened patiently
while I poured out my reasons for at least rescinding the order for the
destruction of cats and dogs. Having heard me out, he thanked me
politely and then told me that I was mistaken since it had been
proved quite conclusively that the plague was transmitted by the
"evil miasma" which was inhaled by these very animals and then
breathed out upon their unsuspecting victims! Besides, he added with
a charming smile, did I really suppose that such a tiny creature as a
flea could carry all the monstrous weight of such appalling infection?
Furthermore, if extra proof were needed, could any man deny that
fleas had been skipping around London for years before the outbreak
of the present calamity? "Bubonic plague," I said, "is carried by the
black rat in the form of an invisible bacterium, *bacillus pestis*. When
the rats die of the infection, their fleas seek out other hosts and by
sucking their blood transmit the infection to them. Would you be
so good as to record that fact and see that it is conveyed to Sir John
Lawrence? If the authorities act promptly, thousands of innocent

lives may yet be saved." Mr. Robinson smiled and nodded and scribbled something on a piece of paper. "I will see that your message is conveyed to His Lordship, Doctor Pensley," he said. "And now I really must beg ye to excuse me, for I have a great deal of most pressing business to attend to." And that was that.

August 30th.

It is now three whole days since I spoke to Tavener and still nothing. Last night, for the first time, I found myself the victim of a most dreadful depression, which I could not shake off. All day long a heavy pall of cloud has hung over the city, and my eyes are still red and inflamed from the sulfurous smoke of those infernal bonfires they light *to sweeten the air!* This afternoon I was assailed by an ungovernable panic fear that my Machine had been discovered and removed. I ran down to the waterside, paid a boatman sixpence to ferry me over to Southwark and made my way back across the fields to Herne Hill. My relief at discovering my Machine still standing exactly where I had left it—and, apparently, untouched—quite overwhelmed me. I sank down in the grass beside it and wept like a child. While I was making my return, a violent thunder storm broke, and by the time I eventually got back to the inn I was soaked to the skin. The landlord persuaded me to drink a stiff tot of hot Hollands punch, which, though it may not be the universal specific he claims, certainly seems to have done something to lift my leaden spirits.

August 31st.

Tavener is returned!! The serving maid who attends on me in my room brought up my clothes, which had been drying overnight in the kitchen, and told me that Tavener's daughter had brought word to the innkeeper. My spirits soared like a sky lark. I was out of bed, had dressed, and was on my way to Carter Street within minutes of hearing the news. Bessie came to the shop door herself and told me that her father was already at work upstairs on my commission. Not wishing to delay him still further, I asked her to tell me what had happened. Whereupon she invited me through into their parlor and told me how they had been stopped at Stanford by a barrier across the road, similar in all respects to that which I had encountered at Camberwell. Unable to persuade the villagers to let them through, they had been forced to make a detour as far westward as Palmer's Green before they could circle back by a maze of by-lanes toward Edmonton. They had spent that night under a haystack and, on resuming their journey next morning, had reached Edmonton around noon only to find to their dismay that there a similar barricade had been erected. Her father had spent most of that afternoon parleying with the constables and had eventually prevailed upon them to allow him through. But their troubles were still not over. The dealer who normally supplied him with materials had shut up his works for the duration of "the visitation" and gone to lodge with his sister in Newmarket! Having got so far, the resourceful Tavener was not to be denied. He forced an entry into the store shed, helped himself to whatever he wanted, left some money to pay for it together with a note of explanation and, next morning, the three of them were on their way back to London.

All had gone well until, while they were descending Stanford Hill, the axle of their hired pony-cart broke. Tavener was somehow able to effect a temporary repair which enabled them to crawl back to Wood Green where they had spent the rest of that day finding a wheelwright and persuading him to replace the broken axle. This meant still further delay, and by the time the job was finished it was too late to continue to London. They spent that night in Wood Green and had set out the following day, arriving back at Carter Lane at about the same time as I was on my way back from Herne Hill.

I have recounted here briefly what Bessie Tavener spent an animated hour in describing, painting a remarkably vivid word picture of the pathetic bands of fugitives from the city whom they had encountered roaming the forest round Woodford—"living like gypsies, poor souls, with nary a scanthing of provender to keep their bones from rattling." I was moved to ask her whether she regretted having to return to London, but she said there were already many cases of plague in the outlying districts and if she was fated to die of it she would rather draw her last breath in her own house than lost among strangers. I repeated my stern warning about the rats and extracted a solemn promise from her that she would keep well clear of any place where fleas might be caught. She gave me her word readily enough, but I suspect it was more to humor me than because she believed me.

I looked in briefly upon Tavener before I left and told him how inexpressibly relieved I was to see him back. He merely nodded, gave me a shy grin, and returned to his lathe. As I stepped out into the street, which smelt mercifully sweeter for the deluge yesterday eve-

ning, I felt as though a huge and suffocating burden had been lifted
from my shoulders.

Sept. 1st.

The soaking I received in the thunderstorm seems to have left me
with a chill. Hardly surprising. However, I have before me one of the
landlord's excellent "Hollands tonics," which is a great source of
comfort. Shortly before noon I called round at Tavener's to see how
the work was progressing only to find him engaged in packing up a
box of lenses for a little hunchbacked fellow in a grubby wig.
Tavener introduced him to me as Master Hooke. As I shook him by
the hand, I thought, by way of a joke, to say: *"ut tensio sic vis,* Mr.
Hooke." He gave me a most extraordinary look as if to say: "Who is
this madman I have by the hand?" and the thought crossed my mind
that perhaps he had not yet formulated that shortest of all Physical
Laws which posterity would link to his name. Thereafter we chatted
in a desultory way about the plague until he hobbled off with his box
of lenses under his arm.

After he had gone, Tavener showed me how the work on the
prism was progressing. The blank is already two-thirds shaped in
rough, and he hopes to have that part of the work completed by this
evening. Then the labor of polishing begins. In spite of my pressing
him he would not give me a definite date for completion on the
grounds that Tintagel pebble was notoriously slow to take a fine polish, being "hard nigh unto diamond." He is certainly a most meticulous craftsman, who obviously takes a profound—though somewhat
inarticulate—pride in the quality of his work.

Sept. 2nd.

A violent bout of sweating in the night left me with a feeling of
great lassitude and a severe headache. I arose late, dressed myself,
went out into the street and was overcome with a fit of giddiness not
unlike the vertigo I have experienced while Time traveling. I have no
doubt at all that it is an unwelcome aftereffect of the chill, but I
could well do without it. On my returning to the inn the landlord
made my blood run cold with a story of some poor pregnant girl in
Cripplegate who was nailed up in her house when one of her sisters
contracted the plague. All the rest of the family were stricken down
one after the other until finally, when only she was left alive, she
gave birth and, with no one on hand to help her, died, not of the
plague, but of a hemorrhage! With her self-delivered infant in her

arms! The sheer, wanton cruelty of this policy of sealing up houses is almost beyond belief. No phrase sickens me more than the pious: " 'Tis God's will," and I must be hearing it in one form or another twenty times a day.

Sept. 3rd.

Little doubt in my mind but that I've caught a really nasty dose of influenza. I have passed all the day lying in bed, and despite the sun beating down on the tiles overhead making this attic as hot as an oven, I have spent much of the time shivering violently. When the servant girl came up to make my bed, I told her I had caught a bad chill and asked her to be good enough to fetch me up a mug of strong spiced ale. That was over three hours ago and still she has not returned.

Sept. 9th?
Hostel of St. Barnabas.

Days of nightmare. What is memory? What dream? GreyMorlock figures bending over me, prodding at my chest, thrusting me into my clothes, carrying me downstairs with a rag soaked in brandy stuffed into my mouth. A boat. Stars swirling round in the sky above me. Squeaking of oars. Voices whispering. Waking again to find the sun hammering nails into my naked eyes. My knapsack is lying on the sand beside me. Where am I? My fumbling fingers explore my body as though it is a stranger's. My joints are all on fire, and my head feels as though a red-hot gimlet is being screwed into my brain. Beneath my armpit the outline of an unfamiliar lump. Another in my groin. *Buboes!* Pain gives way to sheer, mindless terror. I am falling backward down the black well-shaft that has no bottom. Voices. Hands lifting me. Hands carrying me. Falling, falling without end. I open my eyes to see a stone vaulted roof arching above me. As I stare up at it, a cowled face swims into my field of vision. Its lips move. "Welcome, stranger." "Where am I?" (Is that really my own voice?) "The hostel of Saint Barnabas." "I have the plague?" the cowl nods. "Am I dying?" "We think not." Time passes. I sleep; I dream; I wake. Sleep; dream; wake. Strong, firm, gentle hands raise me and prop me back against straw-filled sacks. Soup is spooned into my mouth and a worried voice urges: "Drink, Robert," I swallow and choke. "Again." I swallow. "Again. Good i'faith. Most excellently done." "Who brought me here?" "Who knows, Robert? Friends to be sure. They could have drowned ye in the river like a puppy, for all ye could have stayed them." A pause, then: "Who is Weena?" "Weena?" "Aye. Ye called on her by the hour in your raving. Dost wish me to send word to her that ye lie here?" "She's dead." He rises from my bedside and sketches a token blessing over me. "My knapsack," I croak. "Fear not, Robert. 'Tis here." He lifts it onto my bed and then moves off down the ward. I fumble the buckle undone, extract my notebook and force myself to write a note to Tavener. Then I sleep again. When I wake next, I make this entry. It has taken me nearly three hours to complete it.

Sept. 11th.

Today Brother James trimmed my beard for me and has promised to see that my note is delivered to Tavener. He assures me too that "through God's infinite mercy" I have successfully weathered the worst of the storm. Twenty-four patients have died since I was brought in. The bell in the chapel never seems to stop its mournful tolling.

Sept. 12th.

The superstitious fear of infection is presumably what I have to thank for the fact that I still have all my possessions down to the last pencil—that and the fact that the innkeeper's livelihood was at stake. Had word got out that I had the plague, The Three Keys would now be a "sealed house."

Sept. 13th.

This afternoon I spent half an hour trying to persuade Brother Dominic, the physician, that the infection is transmitted primarily by rats and their fleas. I had hardly more success than I had with Secretary Robinson even though I thought to cite Harvey to illustrate how the bacillus was carried through the bloodstream. B.D. told me he thought it was an interesting theory but that proof was lacking. I told him that if he swabbed out his wards with a 250/1 solution of sulfuric acid, he'd soon have all the proof he needed. "And what is sulfuric acid, Robert?" On my telling him it was another name for oil of vitriol he nodded, but I suspect he was really no more convinced than Robinson had been.

Sept. 14th.

A message was brought in to me by a walking patient that a Master William Tavener was without and would speak with me but

was fearful of entry. He sent word to say that the work was finished
and that he had it now upon him. On hearing this I crawled off my
bed, staggered the length of the ward like a drunkard and so, by
painful degrees, proceeded to the hostel gate. "Tavener?" I croaked.
"Is that you, man?" He stood a little way off and stared in at me. "In
God's name, Doctor Pensley, ye are sadly changed!" "I'm recovered
now," I said, clutching at the iron rails of the gate for support. "It's
quite safe to come close." "That I durst not, Doctor," he called. "Go
ye back a way and I'll push them through to ye." I did as he said,
though how I contrived to remain standing is a miracle. Whereupon
he ran to the gate and quickly thrust a bundle wrapped in cloth
through onto the flagstones. I picked it up, unwrapped it with shaking
hands and found, lying inside, swaddled in lambswool, the two whole
prisms together with the two broken pieces. *And for the life of me I
could not tell the copy from the orignal!* My eyes filled with tears I
was quite powerless to prevent. "God bless you, William Tavener!" I
cried. "You are indeed a master among craftsmen!" and taking out
my watch and chain, I held them up so that he could see them
plainly, then laid them down upon the flagstones. He let the watch lie
there while I stepped back; then he darted forward and scooped it
into a leather bag he had ready for the purpose. "Farewell, Doctor,"
he called. "God be wi'ye!" and he was gone. Somehow I managed to
stagger back to the ward and there collapsed upon my cot.

Sept. 15.

Feel too weak to write much. Obviously overdid things yesterday.
The prism is a true marvel—a perfect replica. No doubt at all it will
fulfill its function.

16.

Vomiting all last night. Feel v. weak.

17.

Diarrhea and vomiting.

disgust

There it ends. The last entry is so faintly penciled that it is very
difficult to decipher. The word could possibly be read as "despair."
However, the Register itself leaves us in no doubt as to the final out-
come. One of the two entries for September 20th, 1665, reads:

Decd. at ye 5th hr, one Rbt. Penly (sic) *of med. yrs. of ye black flux.* It is matched by a previous entry for September 5th: *Admi. one Penly, sick nigh unto death.*

In the weeks which followed my initial perusal of the Hertford Manuscript I took certain steps to ascertain, for my own satisfaction, whether the journal was in fact nothing more than an elaborate and pointless forgery.

My first problem was to obtain a specimen of the true Doctor Pensley's handwriting. I wrote to Somerset House and inquired whether he had left a will, only to be informed that there was no one of that name in their probate records for the years 1894–1899. I then thought to try the civil records for Herne Hill and wrote to the Camberwell Town Clerk, but again drew a blank. I could find no Pensley in the London telephone directory, and a discreet advertisement placed in the personal column of *The Times* proved just as unrewarding. However, these initial disappointments served only to spur my determination. I contacted an old friend of mine in Cambridge and asked him to consult the university records on my behalf. Within a fortnight I learned that Robert James Pensley had been admitted to Emmanuel College as an Exhibitioner in the year 1868.

I traveled down to Cambridge and there in the college records I found at last what I had been seeking. It was not very much certainly —a mere signature—but when I laid it beside an entry in the Hertford text where the author had written out his own name, I was convinced that the writing was by the same hand. My instinctive conviction has since been confirmed by the opinion of a professional graphologist.

My next move was to consult the back files of local newspapers. The only one which still survives is *The Dulwich and District Observer,* and there in the yellowed print of the issue for the week of June 18th, 1894, tucked away among advertisements for safety bicycles and patent knife powder, I found: *Puzzling Disappearance of Well-Known Amateur Scientist.* The account, written in an excruciatingly "literary" style, described how Doctor Robert Pensley, the only surviving son of James and Martha Pensley, had vanished from his home in Herne Hill on the morning of June 7th and had not been seen or heard from since. There was a thinly veiled suggestion that the doctor had been suffering from severe mental strain brought on by overwork. His housekeeper, in an exclusive interview with "our

Reporter," described how her employer was in the habit of vanishing into his laboratory "for hours on end, bless him, and all night too sometimes." There the article ended, and since I could find no further references to the mystery in any later issue, I can only suppose that the matter had been purposely hushed up.

But I could not let the matter rest there. Some strange, haunting quality in that penciled manuscript beckoned to me like a forlorn will-o'-the-wisp, and I resolved to track down as many of the historical references as it was possible to do after an interval of over three hundred years. During the past eighteen months, whenever I have had the opportunity, I have consulted ancient documents in the Guildhall, the Stationers' Hall, the British Museum, and the London Records Office in an attempt to verify what I already *felt* to be true, namely that in some wholly inexplicable manner Robert Pensley *had* succeeded in transferring himself backward in time to the 17th Century and had there perished.

My first notable success was in establishing that one William Tavener, a member of the Guild of Spectacle Makers, had occupied premises next to the Church of St. Anne in Carter Lane. The date given was 1652. A further entry recorded that two apprentices had been bound to the aforesaid Master Tavener at premises in New Cheapside in 1668! So he, at least, seems to have escaped both the plague and the fire.

In a Victorian handbook entitled *The Inns of Elizabethan London* I came upon a reference to The Three Keys of Lower Wharf Street. Like most of the other establishments mentioned it was destroyed in the Great Fire of 1666.

The Hostel of Saint Barnabas—a Franciscan Charity Foundation —is reasonably well documented. It functioned until the early 19th Century when it was pulled down to make way for a new dockyard.

Last May, in the archives of the Mansion House, I unearthed the name of one Samuel Robinson, Esq., recorded as having been appointed to the post of *amanuensis privatus* to Sir Charles Doe, Sheriff, in the year 1663.

In 1665, Robert Hooke was certainly in London, working as "curator of Experiments" for the newly founded Royal Society, and I have no reason to doubt that he would have called upon the services of Master Tavener to supply him with his optical apparatus. Incidentally, it might not be inappropriate to point out that Robert Hooke, as well as formulating his famous Law, has also been credited with a multitude of other discoveries, among them the invention of the spring balance wheel without which the science of horology (not to mention navigation) would doubtless have languished for many years longer in the Dark Ages!

Yet, when all is said and done, such "facts" as I have been able to disinter seem to raise more questions than they answer. I feel I am forever condemned to pace the circumference of a circle which turns out to be not a circle at all but a spiral—my point of arrival is never the same as my point of departure. For to accept the Hertford Manuscript at its face value must surely mean accepting a concept in which Time is both predetermined and yet infinite, an endless snake with its tail in its own mouth, a cosmos in which the Past and the Future coexist and will continue to do so for all Eternity.

How then is it that I both *can* and *do* believe that Robert Pensley's journal, written in his own hand in the year 1665, was already lying there gathering dust on a shelf in the library of Hertford Castle for fifty years before its author had drawn his first infant breath in the year 1850? Or that he died, most horribly, on a straw pallet in a charity hospital in the district of Wapping, beside the silver Thames, clutching in his stiffening fingers a fragment of polished rock crystal which he had staked his life to obtain, only to lose the wager at the very moment when he must surely have believed that he had won?

From Competition 2:   Blurbs in Excess

The Muckers-about From Mid-future "M" (Exegesis on Eventuality "E")

by BRIAN ALDISS

Was it the lawn that stretched between the seemingly unexceptional gabled cottage and the toolshed set on a secant to the north northeast of it? Or was it something far more sinister—somehow slightly too green and *aware* in a manner both more and less than human? What was it that the voiceless Interloper from Intertemporality "I" had seen dimly reflected in the blade of a pair of pruning shears hanging on the wall of that same tiny shed where he stood motionlessly through the seasons, thinly disguised as a lawnmower? And what of the mysterious Onlooker from Otherwhen "O"? What was his game? Was it parchesi, or was it something infinitely more meaningless? And what creature from an unimaginable future passed on repassed behind the leaded panes of the cottage window on the sill of which the hellish avocado pit sent out its tender shoot . . . and waited? And, finally, what could possibly be the motives of the strange being buried up to its "neck" in the marigold plot? Only time could tell. And that, it seemed, it disdained to do.

—*Ralph C. Glisson*

Robert Bloch is, of course, best known as the author of *Psycho* and of the classic fantasy "The Hellbound Train," neither work being particularly light or cheery reading. In fact, Mr. Bloch is thought of as a writer of *scary* fiction, and while that impression is not inaccurate, he has also been known to have moments that are not entirely serious, as anyone who has heard him give a speech can testify. Here is such a moment.

A Case of the Stubborns

by ROBERT BLOCH

The morning after he died, Grandpa come downstairs for breakfast.

It kind of took us by surprise.

Ma looked at Pa, Pa looked at little Sister Susie, and Susie looked at me. Then we all just set there looking at Grandpa.

"What's the matter," he said. "Why you all staring at me like that?'

Nobody said, but I knowed the reason. Only been last night since all of us stood by his bedside when he was took by his attack and passed away right in front of our very eyes. But here he was, up and dressed and feisty as ever.

"What's for breakfast?" he said.

Ma sort of gulped. "Don't tell me you fixing to eat?"

"Course I am. I'm nigh starved."

Ma looked at Pa, but he just rolled his eyes. Then she went and hefted the skillet from the stove and dumped some eggs on a plate.

"That's more like," Grandpa told her. "But don't I smell sausages?" Ma got Grandpa some sausage. The way he dug into it, they sure was nothing wrong with his appetite.

After he started on seconds, Grandpa took heed of us staring at him again.

"How come nobody else is eating?" he asked.

"We ain't hungry," Pa said. And that was the gospel truth.

"Man's got to eat to keep up his strength," Grandpa told him. "Which reminds me—ain't you gonna be late at the mill?"

"Don't figure on working today," Pa said.

Grandpa squinted at him. "You all fancied-up this morning. Shave and a shirt, just like Sunday. You expecting company?"

Ma was looking out the kitchen window, and she give Grandpa a nod. "Yes, indeedy. Here he comes now."

Sure enough, we could see ol' Bixbee hotfooting up the walk.

Ma went through the parlor to the front door—meaning to head him off, I reckon—but he fooled her and come around the back way. Pa got to the kitchen door too late, on account of Bixbee already had it and his mouth open at the same time.

"Morning, Jethro," he said, in that treacle-and-molasses voice of his. "And a sad grievous morning it is, too! I purely hate disturbing you so early on this sorrowful occasion, but it looks like today's another scorcher." He pulled out a tape measure. "Best if I got the measurements so's to get on with the arrangements. Heat like this, the sooner we get everything boxed and squared away the better, if you take my meaning—"

"Sorry," said Pa, blocking the doorway so ol' Bixbee couldn't peek inside. "Needs be you come back later."

"How much later?"

"Can't say for sure. We ain't rightly made up our minds as yet."

"Well don't dilly-dally too long," Bixbee said. "I'm liable to run short of ice."

Then Pa shut the door on him and he took off. When Ma come back from the parlor, Pa made a sign for her to keep her gap shut, but of course that didn't stop Grandpa.

"What was that all about?" he asked.

"Purely a social call."

"Since when?" Grandpa looked suspicious. "Ol' Bixbee ain't nobody's friend—him with his high-toned airs! Calls hisself a Southern planter. Shucks, he ain't nothing but an undertaker."

"That's right, Grandpa," said sister Susie. "He come to fit you for your coffin."

"Coffin?" Grandpa reared up in his seat like a hog caught in a bobwire fence. "What in bo-did-dley blazes do I need with a coffin?"

"Because you're dead."

Just like that she come out with it. Ma and Pa was both ready to take after her but Grandpa laughed fit to bust.

"Holy hen-tracks, child—what on earth give you an idee like that?"

Pa moved in on Susie, taking off his belt, but Ma shook her head. Then she nodded to Grandpa.

"It's true. You passed on last night. Don't you recollect?"

"Ain't nothing wrong with my memory," Grandpa told her. "I had me one of my spells, is all."

Ma fetched a sigh. "Wasn't just no spell this time."

"A fit, mebbe?"

"More'n that. You was took so bad, Pa had to drag Doc Snodgrass out of his office—busted up the game right in the middle of a three-dollar pot. Didn't do no good, though. By the time he got here you was gone."

"But I ain't gone. I'm here!"

Pa spoke up. "Now don't git up on your high horse, Grandpa. We all saw you. We're witnesses."

"Witnesses?" Grandpa hiked his galluses like he always did when he got riled. "What kind talk is that? You aim to hold a jury trial to decide if I'm alive or dead?"

"But Grandpa—"

"Save your sass, sonny." Grandpa stood up. "Ain't nobody got a right to put me six feet under, 'thout my say-so."

"Where you off to?" Ma asked.

"Where I go evvy morning," Grandpa said. "Gonna set on the front porch and watch the sights."

Durned if he didn't do just that, leaving us behind in the kitchen.

"Wouldn't that frost you?" Ma said. She crooked a finger at the stove. "Here I went and pulled up half the greens in the garden, just planning my spread for after the funeral. I already told folks we'd be serving possum stew. What will the neighbors think?"

"Don't you go fret now," Pa said. "Mebee he ain't dead after all."

Ma made a face. "We know different. He's just being persnickety." She nudged at Pa. "Only one thing to do. You go fetch Doc Snodgrass. Tell him he'd best sashay over here right quick and settle this matter once and for all."

"Reckon so," Pa said and went out the back way. Ma looked at me and sister Susie.

"You kids go out on the porch and keep Grandpa company. See that he stays put till the Doc gets here."

"Yessum," said Susie, and we traipsed out of there.

Sure enough, Grandpa set in his rocker, big as life, squinting at cars over on the road and watching the drivers cuss when they tried to steer around our hogs.

"Lookee here!" he said, pointing. "See that fat feller in the Hup-mobile? He come barreling down the road like a bat outta hell— must of been doing thirty mile an hour. 'Fore he could stop, ol' Bes-sie poked out of the weeds right in front of him and run that car clean into the ditch. I swear I never seen anything so comical in all my life!"

Susie shook her head. "But you ain't alive, Grandpa."

"Now don't you start in on that again, hear!" Grandpa looked at her disgusted and Susie shut up.

Right then Doc Snodgrass come driving up front in his big Essex and parked alongside ol' Bessie's pork butt. Doc and Pa got out and moseyed up to the porch. They was jawing away something fierce, and I could see Doc shaking his head like he purely disbelieved what Pa was telling him.

Then Doc noticed Grandpa setting there, and he stopped cold in his tracks. His eyes bugged out.

"Jumping Jehosephat!" he said to Grandpa. "What you doing here?"

"What's it look like?" Grandpa told him. "Can't a man set on his own front porch and rockify in peace?"

"Rest in peace, that's what you should be doing," said Doc. "When I examined you last night you were deader'n a doornail!"

"And you were drunker'n a coot, I reckon," Grandpa said.

Pa give Doc a nod. "What'd I tell you?"

Doc paid him no heed. He come up to Grandpa. "Mebbe I was a wee bit mistaken," he said. "Mind if I examine you now?"

"Fire away," Grandpa grinned. "I got all the time in the world."

So Doc opened up his little black bag and set about his business. First off he plugged a stethyscope in his ears and tapped Grandpa's chest. He listened, and then his hands begun to shake.

"I don't hear nothing," he said.

"What you expect to hear—the Grand Ol' Opery?"

"This here's no time for funning," Doc told him. "Suppose I tell you your heart's stopped beating?"

"Suppose I tell you your stethyscope's busted?"

Doc begun to break out in a sweat. He fetched out a mirror and held it up to Grandpa's mouth. Then his hands got to shaking worse than ever.

"See this?" he said. "The mirror's clear. Means you got no breath left in your body."

Grandpa shook his head. "Try it on yourself. You got a breath on you would knock a mule over at twenty paces."

"Mebbe this'll change your tune." Doc reached in his pocket and pulled out a piece of paper. "See for yourself."

"What is it?"

"Your death certificate." Doc jabbed his finger down. "Just you read what it says on this line. 'Cause of death—card-yak arrest.' That's medical for heart attack. And this here's a legal paper. It'll stand up in court."

"So will I, if you want to drag the law into this," Grandpa told him. "Be a pretty sight, too—you standing on one side with your damnfool piece of paper and me standing on the other! Now which do you think the judge is going to believe?"

Doc's eyes bugged out again. He tried to stuff the paper into his pocket but his hands shook so bad he almost didn't make it.

"What's wrong with you?" Pa asked.

"I feel poorly," Doc said. "Got to get back to my office and lie down for a spell." He picked up his bag and headed for his car, not looking back.

"Don't lie down too long," Grandpa called. "Somebody's liable to write out a paper saying you died of a hangover."

When lunchtime come around, nobody was hungry. Nobody but Grandpa, that is.

He set down at the table and put away black-eyed peas, hominy grits, a double helping of chitlins, and two big slabs of rhubarb pie with gravy.

Ma was the kind who liked seeing folks enjoy her vittles, but she didn't look kindly on Grandpa's appetite. After he finished and went back on the porch, she stacked the plates on the drainboard and told us kids to clean up. Then she went into the bedroom and come out with her shawl and pocketbook.

"What you all dressed up about?" Pa said.

"I'm going to church."

"But this here's only Thursday."

"Can't wait no longer," Ma told him. "It's been hot all forenoon and looking to get hotter. I seen you wrinkle up your nose whilst Grandpa was in here for lunch."

Pa sort of shrugged. "Figgered the chitlins was mebbe a little bit spoiled, is all."

"Weren't nothing of the sort," Ma said. "If you take me meaning."

"What you fixing to do?"

"Only thing a body can do. I'm putting evvything in the hands of the Lord.

And off she skaddaddled, leaving sister Susie and me to scour the dishes whilst Pa went out back, looking powerful troubled. I spied him through the window, slopping the hogs, but you could tell his heart wasn't in it.

Susie and me, we went out to keep tabs on Grandpa.

Ma was right about the weather heating up. That porch was like a bake-oven in the devil's own kitchen. Grandpa didn't seem to pay it any heed, but I did. Couldn't help but notice Grandpa was getting ripe.

"Look at them flies buzzing round him," Susie said.

"Hush up, sister."

But sure enough, them old blueflies buzzed so loud we could hardly hear Grandpa speak. "Hi, young'uns," he said. "Come visit a spell."

"Sun's too hot for setting," Susie told him.

"Not so's I can notice." He weren't even working up a sweat.

"What about all them blueflies?"

"Don't bother me none." Big ol' fly landed right on Grandpa's nose and he didn't even twitch.

Susie begun to look scared. "He's dead for sure," she said.

"Speak up, child," Grandpa said. "Ain't polite to go mumbling your elder."

Just then he spotted Ma marching up the road. Hot as it was, she come along lickety-split, with the Reverend Peabody in tow. He was huffing and puffing, but she never slowed until they fetched up along-side the front porch.

"Howdy, Reverend," Grandpa sung out.

Reverend Peabody blinked and opened his mouth, but no words come out.

"What's the matter?" Grandpa said. "Cat got your tongue?"

The Reverend got a kind of sick grin on his face, like a skunk eating bumblebees.

"Reckon I know how you feel," Grandpa told him. "Sun makes a feller's throat parch up." He looked at Ma. "Addie, whyn't you go fetch the Reverend a little refreshment?"

Ma went in the house.

"Well, now, Rev," said Grandpa. "Rest your britches and be sociable."

The Reverend swallowed hard. "This here's not exactly a social call."

"Then what you come dragging all the way over here for?"

The Reverend swallowed again. "After what Addie and Doc told me, I just had to see for myself." He looked at the flies buzzing around Grandpa. "Now I wish I'd just took their word on it."

"Meaning what?"

"Meaning a man in your condition's got no right to be asking questions. When the good Lord calls, you're supposed to answer."

"I ain't heard nobody calling," Grandpa said. "Course my hearing's not what it use to be."

"So Doc says. That's why you don't notice your heart's not beating."

"Onny natural for it to slow down a piece. I'm pushing ninety you know."

"Did you ever stop to think that ninety might be pushing back? You lived a mighty long stretch, Grandpa. Don't you reckon mebbe it's time to lie down and call it quits? Remember what the Good Book says—the Lord giveth, and the Lord taketh away."

Grandpa got that feisty look on his face. "Well he ain't gonna taketh away me."

Reverend Peabody dug into his jeans for a bandanna and wiped his forehead. "You got no cause to fear. It's a mighty rewarding experience. No more sorrow, no more care, all your burdens laid to rest. Not to mention getting out of this hot sun."

"Can't hardly feel it." Grandpa touched his whiskers. "Can't hardly feel anything."

The Reverend give him a look. "Hands getting stiff?"

Grandpa nodded. "I'm stiff all over."

"Just like I thought. You know what that means? Rigor mortis is setting in."

"Ain't never heard tell of anybody named Rigger Morris," Grandpa said. "I got me a touch of the rheumatism, is all."

The Reverend wiped his forehead again. "You sure want a heap of convincing," he said. "Won't take the word of a medical doctor, won't take the word of the Lord. You're the contrariest old coot I ever did see."

"Reckon it's my nature," Grandpa told him. "But I ain't unreasonable. All I'm asking for is proof. Like the feller says, I'm from Missouri. You got to show me."

The Reverend tucked away his bandanna. It was sopping wet anyhow, wouldn't do him a lick of good. He heaved a big sigh and stared Grandpa right in the eye.

"Some things we just got to take on faith," he said. "Like you setting here when by rights you should be six feet under the daisies. If I can believe that, why can't you believe me? I'm telling you the mortal truth when I say you got no call to fuss. Mebbe the notion of lying in the grave don't rightly hold much appeal for you. Ashes to ashes, dust to dust—that's just a saying. You needn't trouble yourself about spending eternity in the grave. Whilst your remains rest peaceful in the boneyard, your soul is on the wing. Flying straight up, yesiree, straight into the arms of the Lord! And what a great day it's fixing to be—you free as a bird and scooting around with them heavenly hosts on high, singing the praises of the Almighty and twanging away like all git-out on your genuine 18-carrots solid golden harp—"

"I ain't never been much for music," Grandpa said. "And I get dizzy just standing on a ladder to shingle the privy." He shook his head. "Tell you what—you think heaven is such a hellfired good proposition, why don't you go there yourself?"

Just then Ma come back out. "We're fresh out of lemonade," she said. "All's I could find was a jug. I know your feeling about such things, Reverend, but—"

"Praise the Lord!" The Reverend snatched the jug out of her hand, hefted it up, and took a mighty swallow.

"You're a good woman," he told Ma. "And I'm much beholden to you." Then he started down the path for the road, moving fast.

"Here now!" Ma called after him. "What you aim to do about Grandpa?"

"Have no fear," the Reverend said. "We must put our trust now in the power of prayer."

He disappeared down the road, stirring dust.

"Danged if he didn't take the jug!" Grandpa mumbled. "You ask me, the onny power he trusts is in the corn likker."

Ma give him a look. Then she bust out crying and run into the house.

"Now what got into her?" Grandpa said.

"Never you mind," I told him. "Susie, you stay here and whisk those flies off Grandpa. I got things to attend to."

And I did.

Even before I went inside I had my mind set. I couldn't hold still to see Ma bawling that way. She was standing in the kitchen hanging onto Pa, saying, "What can we do? What can we do?"

Pa patted her shoulder. "There now, Addie, don't you go carrying on. It can't last forever."

"Nor can we," Ma said. "If Grandpa don't come to his senses, one of these mornings we'll go downstairs and serve up breakfast to a skeleton. And what do you think the neighbors will say when they see a bag of bones setting out there on my nice front porch? It's plumb embarrassing, that's what it is!"

"Never you mind, Ma," I said. "I got an idea."

Ma stopped crying. "What kind of idea?"

"I'm fixing to take me a hike over to Spooky Hollow."

"Spooky Hollow?" Ma turned so pale you couldn't even see her freckles. "Oh, no, boy—"

"Help is where you find it," I said. "And I reckon we got no choice."

Pa took a deep breath. "Ain't you afeard?"

"Not in daylight," I told him. "Now don't you fret. I'll be back afore dark."

Then I scooted out the back door.

I went over the fence and hightailed it along the back forty to the crick, stopping just long enough to dig up my piggy bank from where it was stashed in the weeds alongside the rocks. After that I waded across the water and headed for tall timber.

Once I got into the piney woods I slowed down a smidge to get my bearings. Weren't no path to follow, because nobody never made one. Folks tended to stay clear of there, even in daytimes—it was just too dark and too lonesome. Never saw no small critters in the brush, and even the birds kep' shut off this place.

But I knowed where to go. All's I had to do was top the ridge, then move straight on down. Right smack at the bottom, in the deepest, darkest, lonesomest spot of all, was Spooky Hollow.

In Spooky Hollow was the cave.

And in the cave was the Conjure Lady.

Leastwise I reckoned she was there. But when I come tippy-toeing down to the big black hole in the rocks, I didn't see a mortal soul, just the shadows bunching up on me from all around.

It sure was spooky, and no mistake. I tried not to pay any heed to the way my feet was itching. They wanted to turn and run, but wasn't about to be put off.

After a bit I started to sing out. "Anybody home? You got company."

"Who?"

"It's me—Jody Tolliver."

"Whoooo?"

I was wrong about the birds, because now when I looked up I could see the big screech-owl glaring at me from a branch over yonder near the cave.

And when I looked down again, there she was—the Conjure Lady, peeking out at me from the hole between the rocks.

It was the first time I ever laid eyes on her, but it couldn't be no one else. She was a teensy rail-thin chickabiddy in a linsey-woolsey dress, and the face under her poke bonnet was as black as a lump of coal.

Shucks, I says to myself, there ain't nothing to be afeared of— she's just a little ol' lady, is all.

Then she stared up at me and I saw her eyes. They was lots bigger than the screech-owl's, and twice as glarey.

My feet begun to itch something fierce, but I stared back. "Howdy, Conjure Lady," I said.

"Whoooo?" said the screech-owl.

"It's young Tolliver," the Conjure Lady told him. "What's the matter, you got wax in your ears? Now go on about your business you hear?"

The screech-owl give her a dirty look and took off. Then the Conjure Lady come out into the open.

"Pay no need to Ambrose," she said. "He ain't rightly used to company. All's he ever sees is me and the bats."

"What bats?"

"The bats in the cave." The Conjure Lady smoothed down her dress. "I beg pardon for not asking you in, but the place is purely a mess. Been meaning to tidy it up, but what with one thing and another—first that dadblamed World War and then this dadgummed Prohibition—I just ain't got round to it yet."

"Never you mind," I said, polite-like. "I come on business."

"Reckoned you did."

"Brought you a pretty, too." I give it to her.

"What is it?"

"My piggy bank."

"Thank you kindly," said the Conjure Lady.

"Go ahead, bust it open," I told her.

She whammed it down on a rock and the piggy bank broke, spilling out money all over the place. She scrabbled it up right quick.

"Been putting aside my cash earnings for nigh onto two years now," I said. "How much is they?"

"Eighty-seven cents, a Confederate two-bits piece and this here button." She kind of grinned. "Sure is a purty one, too! What's it say on there?"

"Keep Cool With Coolidge."

"Well ain't that a caution." The Conjure Lady slid the money into her pocket and pinned the button atop her dress. "Now, son—purty is as purty does. So what can I do for you?"

"It's about my Grandpa," I said. "Grandpa Titus Tolliver."

"Titus Tolliver? Why I reckon I know him! Use to run a still up in the toolies back of the crick. Fine figure of a man with a big black beard, he is."

"Is turns to was," I told her. "Now he's all dried-up with the rheumatiz. Can't rightly see too good and can't hear for sour apples."

"Sure is a crying shame!" the Conjure Lady said. "But sooner or later we all get to feeling poorly. And when you gotta go, you gotta go."

"That's the hitch of it. He won't go."

"Meaning he's bound-up?"

"Meaning he's dead."

The Conjure Lady give me a hard look. "Do tell," she said.

So I told. Told her the whole kit and kaboodle, right from the git-go.

She heard me out, not saying a word. And when I finished up, she just stared at me until I was fixing to jump out of my skin.

"I reckon you mightn't believe me," I said. "But it's the gospel truth."

The Conjure Lady shook her head. "I believe you, son. Like I say, I knowed your Grandpappy from the long-ago. He was plumb set in his ways then, and I take it he still is. Sounds to me like he's got a bad case of the stubborns."

"Could be," I said. "But they's nary a thing we can do about it, nor the Doc or the Reverend either."

The Conjure Lady wrinkled up her nose. "What you 'spect from them two? They don't know grit from granola."

"Mebbe so. But that leaves us betwixt a rock and a hard place—'less you can help."

"Let me think on it a piece."

The Conjure Lady pulled a corncob out of her pocket and fired up. I don't know what brand she smoked, but it smelled something fierce. I begun to get itchy again—not just in the feet but all over. The woods was darker now, and a kind of cold wind come wailing down between the trees, making the leaves whisper to themselves.

"Got to be some way," I said. "A charm, mebbe, or a spell."

She shook her head. "Them's ol' fashioned. Now this here's one of them newfangled mental things, so we got to use newfangled idees. Your Grandpa don't need hex nor hoodoo. Like he says, he's from Missouri. He got to be showed, is all."

"Showed what?"

The Conjure Lady let out a cackle "I got it!" She give me a wink. "Sure 'nough, the very thing! Now just you hold your water—I won't be a moment." And she scooted back into the cave.

I stood there, feeling the wind whooshing down the back of my neck and listening to the leaves that was like voices whispering things I didn't want to hear too good.

Then she come out again, holding something in her hand.

"Take this," she said.

"What is it?"

She told me what it was, and then she told me what to do with it.

"You really reckon this'll work?"

"It's the onny chance."

So I stuck it in my britches pocket and she give me a little poke. "Now, sonny, you best hurry and git home afore supper."

Nobody had to ask me twice—not with that chill wind moaning and groaning in the trees, and the dark creeping and crawling all around me.

I give her my much-obliged and lit out, leaving the Conjure Lady standing in front of the cave. Last I saw of her she was polishing her Coolidge button with a hunk of poison oak.

Then I was tearing through the woods, up the hill to the ridge and over. By the time I got to the clearing, it was pitch-dark, and when I waded the crick I could see the moonlight wiggling on the water. Hawks on the hover went flippy-flapping, but I didn't stop to heed. I made a beeline for the fence, up and over, then into the yard and through the back door.

Ma was standing at the stove holding a pot whilst Pa ladled up the soup. They looked downright pleasured to see me.

"Thank the Lord!" Ma said. "I was just fixing to send Pa after you."

"I come quick as I could."

"And none too soon," Pa told me. "We like to go clean out'n our heads, what with the ruckus and all."

"What kind of ruckus?"

"First off, Miz Francy. Folks in town told her about Grandpa passing on, so she done the neighborly thing—mixed up a mess of stew to ease our appeytite in time of sorrow. She come lollygagging up the walk, all rigged out in her Sunday go-to-meeting clothes, toting the bowl under her arm and looking like lard wouldn't melt in her mouth. Along about then she caught sight of Grandpa setting there on the porch, kind of smiling at her through the flies.

"Well, up went the bowl and down come the whole shebang. Looked like it was raining stew greens all over that fancy Sears and Roebuck dress. And then she turned and headed for kingdom come, letting out a whoop that'd peel the paint off a privy wall."

"That's sorrowful," I said.

"Save your grieving for worse," Pa told me. "Next thing you know, Bixbee showed up, honking his horn. Wouldn't come nigh Grandpa, nosiree—I had to traipse clear down to where he set in the hearse."

"What'd he want?"

"Said he'd come for the remains. And if we didn't cough them up

right fast, he was aiming to take a trip over to the county seat first
thing tomorrow morning to get hisself a injection."

"Injunction," Ma said, looking like she was ready to bust out with
the bawls again. "Said it was a scandal and a shame to let Grandpa
set around like this. What with the sun and the flies and all, he was
fixing to have the Board of Health put us under quar-and-tine."

"What did Grandpa say?" I asked.

"Nary a peep. Ol' Bixbee gunned his hearse out of here, and
Grandpa kep' right on rocking with Susie. She come in 'bout half
hour ago, when the sun went down—says he's getting stiff as a board
but won't pay it no heed. Just keeps asking what's to eat."

"That's good," I said. "On account of I got the very thing. The
Conjure Lady give it to me for his supper."

"What is it—pizen?" Pa looked worried. "You know I'm a God-
fearing man and I don't hold with such doings. How you 'spect to
pizen him if he's already dead?"

"Ain't nothing of the sort," I said. "This here's what she sent."

And I pulled it out of my britches pocket and showed it to them.

"Now what in the name of kingdom come is that?" Ma asked.

I told her what it was, and what to do with it.

"Ain't never heard tell of such foolishness in all my born days!"
Ma told me.

Pa looked troubled in his mind. "I knowed I shouldn't have let
you go down to Spooky Hollow. Conjure Lady must be short of her
marbles, putting you up to a thing like that."

"Reckon she knows what she's doing," I said. " 'Sides, I give all
my savings for this here—eighty-seven cents, a Confederate quarter
and my Coolidge button."

"Never you mind about no Coolidge button," Pa said. "I swiped it
off'n a Yankee, anyway—one of them revenooers." He scratched his
chin. "But hard money's something else. Mebbe we best give this notion a try."

"Now, Pa—" Ma said.

"You got any better plan?" Pa shook his head. "Way I see it, what
with the Board of Health set to come a-snapping at our heels tomorrow, we got to take a chance."

Ma fetched a sigh that come clean up from her shoes, or would of
if she'd been wearing any.

"All right, Jody," she told me. "You just put it out like the Conjure Lady said. Pa, you go fetch Susie and Grandpa. I'm about to dish up."

"You sure this'll do the trick?" Pa asked, looking at what I had in my hand.

"It'd better," I said. "It's all we got."

So Pa went out and I headed for the table, to do what the Conjure Lady had in mind.

Then Pa come back with sister Susie.

"Where's Grandpa?" Ma asked.

"Moving slow," Susie said. "Must be that Rigger Morris."

"No such thing." Grandpa come through the doorway, walking like a cockroach on a hot griddle. "I'm just a wee mite stiff."

"Stiff as a four-by-four board," Pa told him. "Upstairs in bed, that's where you ought to be, with a lily in your hand."

"Now don't start on that again," Grandpa said. "I told you I ain't dead so many times I'm blue in the face."

"You sure are," said sister Susie. "Ain't never seen nobody look any bluer."

And he was that—blue and bloated, kind of, but he paid it no heed. I recollected what Ma said about mebbe having to put up with a skeleton at mealtime, and I sure yearned for the Conjure Lady's notion to work. It plumb had to, because Grandpa was getting deader by the minute.

But you wouldn't think so when he caught sight of the vittles on the table. He just stirred his stumps right over to his chair and plunked down.

"Well, now," Grandpa said. "You done yourself proud tonight, Addie. This here's my favorite—collards and catfish heads!"

He was all set to take a swipe at the platter when he up and noticed what was setting next to his plate.

"Great day in the morning!" he hollered. "What in tarnation's this?"

"Ain't nothing but a napkin," I said.

"But it's black?" Grandpa blinked. "Who ever heard tell of a black napkin?"

Pa looked at Ma. "We figger this here's kind of a special occasion," he said. "If you take my meaning—"

Grandpa fetched a snort. "Consarn you and your meaning! A black napkin? Never you fear, I know what you're hinting around at, but it ain't a-gonna work—nosiree, bub!"

And he filled his plate and dug in.

The rest of us just set there staring, first at Grandpa, then at each other.

"What'd I tell you?" Pa said to me, disgusted-like.

I shook my head. "Wait a spell."

"Better grab whilst you can git," Grandpa said. "I aim to eat me up a storm."

And he did. His arms was stiff and his fingers scarce had enough curl left to hold a fork and his jaw muscles worked extra hard—but he went right on eating. And talking.

"Dead, am I? Ain't never seen the day a body'd say a thing like that to me before, let alone kinfolk! Now could be I'm tolerable stubborn, but that don't signify I'm mean. I ain't about to make trouble for anyone, least of all my own flesh and blood. If I was truly dead and knowed it for a fact—why, I'd the first one to go right upstairs to my room and lie down forever. But you got to show me proof 'fore I do. That's the pure and simple of it—let me see some proof!"

"Grandpa," I said.

"What's the matter, sonny?"

"Begging your pardon, but you got collards dribbling all over your chin."

Grandpa put down his fork. "So they is. I thank you kindly."

And before he rightly knowed what he was doing, Grandpa wiped his mouth on the napkin.

When he finished he looked down at it. He looked once and he looked twice. The he just set the napkin down gentle-like, stood up from the table, and headed straight for the stairs.

"Good-by all," he said.

We heard him go clumping up the steps and down the hall into his room, and we heard the mattress sag when he laid down on his bed.

Then everything was quiet.

After a while Pa pushed his chair back and went upstairs. Nobody said a word until he come down again.

"Well?" Ma looked at him.

"Ain't nothing more to worry about," Pa said. "He's laid down his burden at last. Gone to glory, amen."

"Praise be!" Ma said. Then she looked at me and crooked a finger at the napkin. "Best get rid of that."

I went round and picked it up. Sister Susie give me a funny look. "Ain't nobody fixing to tell me what happened?" she asked.

I didn't answer—just toted the napkin out and dropped it deep down in the crick. Weren't no sense telling anybody the how of it, but the Conjure Lady had the right notion, after all. She knowed Grandpa'd get his proof—just as soon as he wiped his mouth.

Ain't nothing like a black napkin to show up a little ol' white maggot.

Algis Budrys has long been one of sf's most knowledgeable and perceptive critics. The essay below will give you all the tools necessary to review this anthology for your local newspaper.

Books:
Where We Are and
Where We Came From

by ALGIS BUDRYS

I recommend the above books,* and had set out to tell you why in some detail. But there's a well-known series of critical dangers in dealing with "best" anthologies, and they caught up with me. "What do they mean by 'best,'?" I said to myself as so many others have, and "What they mean is, the 'best' novelettes and short stories they were able to find that someone else didn't have an option on," and so forth.

There's no lasting fun repeating someone else's lines, so I then cast about within my instinctive discontent, and found that I'd noticed a curious thing. All the stories are good—Wollheim and del Rey are excellent editors. But obviously "If This is Winnetka You Must be Judy," "The Bleeding Man," and "The Postponed Cure" cannot have derived from the same creative universe, or even from two. The Busby is as if from the mid-60s, the Strete is 1975 or maybe later,

* This article appeared under the heading "Books not reviewed this month: *The 1975 Annual World's Best SF*, Donald A. Wollheim, Ed. *Best Science Fiction Stories of the Year*, Lester del Rey, Ed."

and the Nodvik finds its creative roots straight in the cabinet of Dr. Gernsback. Yet all are science fiction and among the best of a recent year.

I thought more. I thought about where we are and where we came from. Attached is a brief, clumsy version of my thoughts. Its purpose here is to equip you in my best estimation with all the necessary tools for reviewing any such anthology yourself. Let's see what has historically been considered "best," and "most appropriate," and "typical."

There's a distinction between Theodore Sturgeon, author of "A Saucer of Loneliness," and Edward Bryant, author of "No. 2 Plain Tank Auxiliary Fill Structural Limit 17,605 Lbs. Fuel—PWA Spec. 522 Revised." It's not in the fact that the latter story isn't science fiction. Neither is the former. And there's a difference between Ray Bradbury and Harlan Ellison, despite the fact that each is the quintessential SF short story writer of his day. Other examples occur, but seem unnecessary at this time.

The short story played a vital, curious and complex role in midcentury "modern" science fiction, which can be said to have begun with the publication of John Campbell's "Twilight" in the late 1930s. In hindsight, this kind of SF can be seen to have lost its preeminence with the publication of Fritz Leiber's "Coming Attraction" in 1950, somewhat preceding such other portents as the magazine publication of Philip Jose Farmer's *The Lovers* and the simultaneous non-serialization of Asimov's *Pebble in the Sky*. There were signs of its coming before 1938, and many examples of it postdate 1950. So there were about 20 years of "modern" science fiction. But just as reveille was sounded by one short story, the appearance of another was the signal for the firing of the sunset gun.

"Modern" science fiction was so labeled for the public in 1947, when Raymond Healy and J. Francis "Mick" McComas, later one of this journal's founders, edited the definitive anthology *Adventures in Time and Space*. They codified and named a form that had been nothing but a pile of yellowing ephemera from garish periodicals. Groff Conklin reinforced them almost immediately with *The Best of Science Fiction, A Treasury of Science Fiction* and *Possible Worlds of Science Fiction*. Reginald Bretnor published *Modern Science Fiction,* a serious, weighty taxonomic study of the field, and that book signaled SF's availability as a fresh topic for serious academic study. It all happened nearly overnight, really, and "modern" science fiction was established as *the* science fiction, utterly different from monster movie or comic book writing.

Great and worthy consequences had followed from the master-stroke of (A) presenting evidence, in anthology form, that there *was* good reading, worthy of an educated person's time, to be found in the genre's past and thus to be expected in the future, and, (B), at least as important, giving it the distinctive "modern" label to set it apart from the "bad" reading undeniably to be found in the same place.

What it all was—"good" and "bad," "modern" and . . . what? It often shared space in the same issue—was "newsstand science fiction." (My label). It was post-1925 American-originated short-length SF as distinguished from, among many other things, European technological social allegories in novel form, popular cautionary novels by such sterile cuckoos as Franz Werfel and Pat Frank, phenomenological studies such as George Stewart's *Earth Abides,* and even the vigorous British Apocalyptic or George Allen England school which would shortly produce the novels of "John Wyndham" and John Christopher's *No Blade of Grass* as outstanding contrasts to the embarrassing latter American Technosophist works of Philip Wylie.

Magazines do not normally publish novels. They publish conden-sations, or expanded novelettes, as "complete novels," and they pub-lish "serials," which are three or four novelettes strung on a single plot, all but the ultimate episode reaching a partial and by definition incomplete climax. Now that there is a market for SF books, the SF magazines publish novels divided into parts by the wordlength cri-teria of magazine makeup. But there are *no* "modern science fiction" novels.

I'm pretty sure that the first real novel by a "modern science fiction" writer was *Stranger in A Strange Land,* which seems to me to represent the culminating point of a long and proud evolution on the part of the man who wrote *Beyond This Horizon,* the pioneering "modern science fiction" serial, as well as *Sixth Column,* which very nearly fulfills all the possibilities of the form except those attended to by Hal Clement. But *Stranger* dates from 1961 and is not "modern" science fiction although its first half set out to be. It has founded its own sub-genre—of which the *Dune* series and *Dhalgren* are prom-inent members—which might be called evangelical science fiction. Think of that what you will, it represents the making of the first good link between the traditions and practices of newsstand SF with those of all the other—or "bookstore"—kinds, and Heinlein is a pioneer several times over again.

But we digress.

It's been said, earliest by Professor J. Gunn, that the novelette is the natural form of science fiction. He means newsstand SF, and within that frame he's obviously right. And yet. . . .

And yet, agreeing as we must, nevertheless let's look at the short story a little while.

In a thousand or five thousand words it's possible to so skillfully present a situation that its preceding events and inevitable consequences are made not only clear to the reader but integral to the story. It's possible to deal with large matters in small compass, and this is pretty much what the "mainstream" short story as presently defined attempts, I think.

The method is not unknown to science fiction or fantasy. But it's a capacious burden on the writer who also has to create the universe in which the situation occurs. Accordingly, most SF "short stories" at the high noon of newsstand SF, when there was most demand for the length but least recompense on a word/idea ratio, were in fact short fictions of other kinds. They were 19th century rustic anecdotes— "Well, Lefty and me was sittin' round in our shelter with our spaceboots off when in walks this angel"—or verbal setpieces on a par of technique cliche with Restoration comedy—"For you see, Admiral, your navigator has been blind since the first rayblast"—or expressions of what is called mood—*"Ah, no, no,"* Dormi Fai seemed to whisper in effortful accents. *"I am not permitted to be one of you, but how can I now return to being one of us?"*

Not all the possibilities of the first two kinds are ludicrous, or unyielding to assimilation by the ingenuities of talent. Most of Sturgeon's most poignant stories begin anecdotally, for instance, as a device for making his presence nearer and hence more convincing with regard to the unusually outre circumstances he is about to deploy. For what can be done with setpieces, see Frederic Brown and need look no further. But it's "mood" that identifies the "modern" SF short story—the famous Campbellian high whine of "Twilight," the whispering footsteps of robots on ancient parquet in the "City" series, the acceptance of symbolically transfigured death as the only immortality in "Requiem" the bereft narrator of "Helen O'Loy," and finally what may have been the most "modern" science fiction story of them all—"A Saucer of Loneliness," based on a true incident reported in *The Reader's Digest,* all its SF merely dressing . . . not science, not technology, not speculation nor extrapolation nor fiction,

but full of melancholy. It appeared in *Galaxy* hot from Sturgeon's
typewriter; I don't know whether Campbell would have published it
in *Astounding,* given the chance, but he certainly published "I Am
Nothing," which is of highly similar creative origins and by a writer
marginally less gifted than Sturgeon at Sturgeon's own game.

Alienation—the brooding melancholies of solitude, of Paradise
glimpsed but barred, of arriving too late or too early, of foreign
tongues and ways inexpertly grasped, of meanings only sensed—
alienation is the great theme of "modern" science fiction. And well
it should be, considered that when it was written . . . when it was
written, not when it was anthologized, and not when it was imitated
for the market created by the anthologies . . . it was written by people whom no one with a shred of common sense would have anything
to do with, and published in magazines which obviously could not
be openly purchased by anyone with a concern for public moral
standing.

Obviously then, within the community of those in Coventry, alienation represented the bond of kinship, and empathy for the alien was
the most noble emotion. Nobility—the obligation of better-ex-
perienced, more competent individual toward younger, lesser spiritual kin—was of great concern to most "modern" SF writers. Now
contrast that to the sense of "Coming Attraction," in which pity and
sympathy are unsympathetic weaknesses in the fool whom God pro-
vides for the totally pragmatic survivor types. Leiber has always
found higher frets than anyone else can until he points them out; he
was also consciously out to tweak some aspects of "modern" SF at
the time, although perhaps not quite *that* consciously or inclusively.

Whatever that case may actually be, there were obviously a lot of
hitherto unsuspected possibilities in the good old instrument, and
these were swiftly attacked and possessed by all sorts of enterprising
persons who added them to their technical repertoires. This expanded SF to the point where "mood" writing—mood curiously
equated with melancholy, despite the fact that no dictionary compels
that interpretation—is far from the only serious kind, is a little old-
fashioned and is becoming identified with a delimitable sub-genre of
SF, with a beginning and end in time, and that end visibly in the
past.

But noble melancholy—usually labeled mood, but sometimes
"character insight" or "imagery," or any number of other things
reflecting its essentially conventionalized character—acquired one

deft and astonishingly likable spokesman just as the number of its days was about to be revealed. He was Theodore Sturgeon's apprentice, Ray Bradbury, and he found a home. He found in fact, two— *Planet Stories,* and the essentially identical *Startling Stories* and *Thrilling Wonder Stories* edited by non-fans Sam Merwin, Jr., and later Sam Mines.* Bradbury never sold to *Astounding,* hardly ever writes well at longer lengths—he's almost as poor a novelist as Stephen Vincent Benet was—and it doesn't matter. We are not sent born short story writers that often.

Up front, all those publications were obvious trash.

Planet Stories, for instance, always featured a "Complete Novel of Barbarian Worlds," usually by A. A. Craig burst from his disguise as Poul Anderson, and several "Novelets of Terror in the Stars," usually including *Empress of the Cyan Snake* or *Magenta Mistress of the Rim* by Emmett McDowell. *Startling Stories* always had a long science fantasy novelette, again of course a "novel," tending toward sword-and-sorcery, especially when by Leigh Brackett. After *Captain Future* fell victim to wartime paper shortages—and to the lowest sales figures in the stable—a Captain Future "novel" might lead *Thrilling Wonder Stories,* and if it didn't, then some other quick-fisted spacefarer took his place that month. All such publications always featured a metal-breasted valkyrie from the steno pool on the cover, subjected her to some sort of menace, and showed the hero charging on scene, blaster in hand.

These trappings were expressive of the publisher's opinion of his market, and thus of the magazine's ostensible editorial philosophy. It's a tribute to downright subversive shrewdness on the part of some authors, and to the actual good taste of several key editors, that this seemingly unredeemable junk gradually tended in the direction of, again, that treatment of alienation which we all knew was science fiction at its "best." This made that entire class of magazine particularly vulnerable just when TV began offering undiluted free junk to the audience for junk. Thus all those publications were wiped out swiftly in the early 1950s, but you can't make an omelette without getting egg on your face.

---

* *Whose assistant, Jerome Bixby, had been the best editor of* Planet Stories. *Bixby was instrumental in persuading Mines to publish* The Lovers, *and is the author of "It's a* Good Day," *an outstanding example of post-Modernist SF. He was Horace Gold's assistant at* Galaxy *and* Beyond *in a later incarnation. He also provided the central idea for the movie* Fantastic Voyage, *although Isaac Asimov novelized it. A generally unsung hero of our field. AJB*

Be *that* as it may, in all these publications* one can find a curious duality between the front-of-the-book stories and the altogether different short material nestled into the narrow columns alongside the boilerplate ad for High John the Conqueror Root. It was another World back there, with stories in the Thrilling magazines like Will Jenkins's "De Profundis," or Theodore Sturgeon's "The Sky Was Full of Ships." The one of those, first of all, makes an *ab initio* allusion that ought to be incomprehensible to customers for mail-order trusses; the latter is only one of dozens of excellently written cautionary stories produced by SF at a time when technocratic know-how was scheduled to make all men bestriders of the stars by next Tuesday. "De Profundis" is also, as you might suspect, one of the most melancholic SF stories of alienation ever written. That's particularly relevant since to the same magazines "Murray Leinster" also contributed a number of highly ingenious lead novelets about clever people who save the world with devices flanged up from tomato cans and belt buckles.

To these magazines, Bradbury contributed a number of stories, to rising reader approbation. A complete collection of *Planet Stories,* however, is the place to go for the best recapitulation of Bradbury's philogeny.

His career there begins more or less with "Lazarus Come Forth," a nearly conventional snap-ending story, going on through "Mars is Heaven" to what is thought of now as typically Bradburyesque writing in "Death-By-Rain" and "Zero Hour," to such obviously evocative and worthy tributes to Edgar Allan Poe or Thomas Wolfe as "Forever and The Earth," which is more of a eulogy and perhaps beyond the tastes of some of the readers.

That middle period—conventional pulp writing fully spurned, the merit of his new style heartily endorsed in the letter column and perhaps in the sales figures but more likely in the editor's personal approval, the interest in storytelling not yet intellectualized into a telling of anecdotes about storytelling—produced the stories later woven into *The Martian Chronicles.* Yes, folks, in this corner, lounging back against the ropes, *Magenta Mistress.* In the other corner, gritting gently, pink Mars.

* *I miss them. I miss Albert De Pina, Henry Hasse, Robertson Osborne, Gardner M. Fox, and Paul Payne. I miss the Vizigraph, I miss Wartears, I miss illustrations by Vestal and McWilliams and Donnel. Where are Sam Merwin's inept fanzine reviews today? Oh, God, just one more novelette from Vaseleos Garson! AJB*

It's interesting that up front A. A. Craig's Aresian thallasocrats were stormrunning their beak-prowed war galleys through the straits of Trivium Charontis while in the back, wan, solitary chaps from Waukegan were wincing at the clatter of beer cans down the crumbling banks of dry canals. It's almost like the role Leinster played at Thrilling, but not quite. A somewhat different yin calls forth a corresponding yang.

In *Astounding,* to copper the point, the intense emotionalism of Bradbury short fiction was not required, for the Murray Leinster of the lead novelettes was not quite the same Will Jenkins, and the Anderson was by no description A. A. Craig. ASF lead fiction did not as readily substitute lust and violence for love and mortality, so ASF short fiction had a somewhat more reserved balancing character. It was in *Astounding,* which kept trying to become *Science Fiction*— and had every right, in the popular eye, to call itself *Modern Science Fiction* but apparently never considered the attempt—that the melancholic tone sang its purest and noblest. In *Planet,* as represented by Bradbury, it was weepier. In the Thrilling books, it tended toward the bathetic.

But it was always there, whether in these named publications or in *Astonishing* or *Super Science* or *Future* or *Marvel* or *Dynamic*—I'd better stop; the heart can bear only so much. In essence, what was going on was that the fronts of all the magazines except *Astounding* derived from the great body of pulp smash-'em-up literature first exploited in the 19th century by E. Z. C. Judson as Ned Buntline, and so, too, did some of the backs of them; there was a lot of space to fill back there, and writers perfectly willing to find it. But it became true sometime around 1939, and it became increasingly and increasingly true, that "modern" science fiction—alienation science fiction —crept into even the outright pulps by the back door. As well it should; a fair number of individuals who could never be overt formula writers were finding science fiction. You couldn't sell them on the need to conform to the old pulp formulas, on the necessity of following rigidly marked paths, or on codified values; resistance to all that was what had brought them out of the respectable community and into this underground haven. They *could* write just about anything, when they chose, and they took pride in bringing a little something extra to it, whatever it was. But they felt best and most at home with themselves, I think, when they spoke of loneliness.

Those who gathered around John Campbell—a man whose childhood featured an identical-twin mother-and-aunt pair who delighted in swapping clothes and deliberately confusing the boy as to which was which—had a right to feel they'd made it into the company of the elect, and could reach out avuncularly toward their younger counterparts, the readers they saw in their minds. Those who stayed elsewhere were doubly confirmed in any feelings that isolation and melancholy were universals, and that their inclusion in a story would swiftly make an offworldly character and setting believable to the reader. Perhaps those writers who do not consciously analyze every creative choice they make were most likely to make that one.

Bradbury is an interesting case—he's a one-and-a-half generation writer of alienation. Sturgeon, please believe, was treated despicably as an adolescent. To survive, he became swift, charming and narrative, as a comfort to himself and then to his readers. Bradbury, who spent years preparing himself by minutely studying every nuance and aspect of every Sturgeon story he could get his hands on, came along some ten years behind him. So that although Bradbury was no doubt treated despicably as an adolescent—most people are, if they select for those memories; some do not accept it as a normal part of growing up—he always had Sturgeon's stories to comfort him . . . as did I, God knows, as did I, along with John's, and Will's, and Lester's and Cliff's, and so many others that (barely) got me through it.

Now, Sturgeon has always cut closer to the bone than most; few of his stories are laid particularly far away in time or space, and few of his aliens have funny outsides. It's not so much a faraway landscape washed by faerie seas as it is a sometimes unsmiling cartoon of the real world. Bradbury is the cartoonist *par excellence,* as Damon Knight pointed out long ago, and also, as in his Mexican cycle, exceeded even Sturgeon's unflagging attempts to use an accustomed SF style in "straight" stories. Unlike Sturgeon, he succeeded unreservedly and went on to establish two notions among the Publick General: (1) that Ray Bradbury is a hell of a writer, and (2) that although of course all those who stayed behind were less talented and perceptive, nevertheless there just might be *something* redeemable in the general body of sci-fi.

And now of course we are beyond the second and the two-and-one-halfth generation and solidly into the third since "Twilight," the third since "Bianca's Hands," for that matter. A post-Modern SFnist like Ed Bryant writes of alienation from the standpoint of a practitioner in the most chic, most contemporaneously relevant field of literature that is. He has it under control so well, is so much a part of his time that, like Sturgeon with *his* audience, he doesn't always even have to supply the ostensibly essential element of extrapolation; the flesh—the flesh, no bones at all—is sufficient to be recognized and welcomed.

But the big pulling of SF into its contemporary pattern—the concern for "relevance," the unrelenting familiarity with such sites of horror and maltreatment as contemporary Las Vegas and Los Angeles, the clinical detail of degradation and the alien *actions* (not so much as the fantastical thoughts) of which humans are capable—occurred in the half-generation. SF writers come in waves; there'll be very few new good ones for a while, and then Sheckley, Silverberg, Phil Dick, and a couple of other people will all arrive on the same day. Ten years will pass, and suddenly you've got Niven, Aldiss, Ballard, and Moorcock. A silence and then Disch, Russ, Malzberg; a few more years go by, and you've got McIntyre, Martin, and cetera. But in between you get these lone standouts, these people who run on their own clock. Stanley Weinbaum was one. Tom Sherred would have been one. Ray Bradbury is one. And Harlan Ellison, I think, learned not only from what had been written before him, but from the lives of writers before him, which was a new development.

I think he learned a lot from what happened to Bradbury. I think he combined that with all the strengths that spring from his inability to accept anyone else's view of the world at any given moment. And, like Bradbury, he's at his best when presenting his view in small and thus readily retainable formats; he's punchy, his thesis is always plain to see, and the remaining words in the story are freed for the purpose of building convincing atmosphere. His work isn't always good; it's nearly always memorable.

What's particularly his own invention, however, is his drive to multiply himself; to not merely write, but to attack the community at large with his own persona, and offer it the opportunity to take whatever benefits it can from the experience. He is a hard-voiced Bradbury, but more than that, he's a mobile archetype. In his assiduous campus proselytizing, first at Clarion and now everywhere, he is doing two things that were never fashionable before him but are firmly part of the tradition now. He has found and made popular the image of the radical SF writer, giving a number of succeeding writers a sense of their own special qualification. And he was and is at the forefront of the movement, reflected in the *Dangerous Visions* anthologies of short fiction, to bring to the public an entire body of literature as newly created by new people or by old people made new.

The field was ready for it. The central sense of what science fiction "is" had gone through enough generations to evolve toward it. Under the latest standards, what is best is not the alienation of the author allegorized within a fantastic story, but the alienation of the central character limned against a harshly "realistic" conventionalized picture either of the present or of a popularly recognized future such as an overpopulated world, or a politically stratified America, or even on occasion a world depopulated by war. The author is no longer a victim, not even in secret. The author is the expert. Having had the disease for a very long time, we must now beyond question possess the cure.

From Competition 4: Story Leads from the Year's Worst Fantasy and SF

Oh, it was a *wonderful* school, Joyce-Ann thought happily as she hurried down the gentle flower-dappled slope toward the one-room building. Just perfect for a new teacher's first school, and a delicious opportunity to light the lamp of learning in this remote and isolated mountain community. There had been, to be sure, something odd and disquieting about the appearance and behavior of the school board, but after all, children were children everywhere.

—Bob Leman

Lawrens taped his broken arm, watching his partner emerging from the wreck of the *Ares I*.

"Bad news," O'Brien reported crisply. "Only one oxygen tank survived the crash intact."

"That's not enough to last us until the rescue ship arrives!"

O'Brien nodded. "For *two* men, no."

"Oh my God! You aren't suggesting—"

"O'Brien's eyes gleamed as coldly as the Martian sky.

"I'm sure," said O'Brien, "we can settle this matter like rational, civilized human beings . . ."

—James E. Sutherland

Joanna Russ teaches at the University of Colorado and has contributed short fiction and criticism to *F&SF* for many years. She is also a novelist (most recently with the controversial *The Female Man*). This story concerns three teen-agers in a 1950s high school and a row in an old wooden boat. It moves from there to places less mundane, to Atlantis, to the stars, and along the way makes some penetrating observations about "fantasy" and "real life."

My Boat

by JOANNA RUSS

Milty, have I got a story for you!

No, sit down. Enjoy the cream cheese and bagel. I guarantee this one will make a first-class TV movie; I'm working on it already. Small cast, cheap production—it's a natural. See, we start with this crazy chick, maybe about seventeen, but she's a waif, she's withdrawn from the world, see? She's had some kind of terrible shock. And she's fixed up this old apartment in a slum really weird, like a fantasy world—long, blonde hair, maybe goes around barefoot in tie-dyed dresses she makes out of old sheets, and there's this account executive who meets her in Central Park and falls in love with her on account of she's like a dryad or a nature spirit—

All right. So it stinks. I'll pay for my lunch. We'll pretend you're not my agent, okay? And you don't have to tell me it's been done; I know it's been done. The truth is—

Milty, I have to talk to someone. No, it's a lousy idea, I know and I'm not working on it and I haven't been working on it, but what are you going to do Memorial Day weekend if you're alone and everybody's out of town?

I have to talk to someone.

Yes, I'll get off the Yiddische shtick. Hell, I don't think about it; I just fall into it sometimes when I get upset, you know how it is. You do it yourself. But I want to tell you a story and it's not a story for a script. It's something that happened to me in high school in 1952 and *I just want to tell someone.* I don't care if no station from here to Indonesia can use it; you just tell me whether I'm nuts or not, that's all.

Okay.

It was 1952, like I said. I was a senior in a high school out on the Island, a public high school but very fancy, a big drama program. They were just beginning to integrate, you know, the early fifties, very liberal neighborhood; everybody's patting everybody else on the back because they let five black kids into our school. Five out of eight hundred! You'd think they expected God to come down from Flatbush and give everybody a big fat golden halo.

Anyway, our drama class got integrated, too—one little black girl aged fifteen named Cissie Jackson, some kind of genius. All I remember the first day of the spring term, she was the only black I'd ever seen with a natural, only we didn't know what the hell it was, then; it made her look as weird as if she'd just come out of a hospital or something.

Which, by the way, she just had. You know Malcolm X saw his father killed by white men when he was four and that made him a militant for life? Well, Cissie's father had been shot down in front of her eyes when she was a little kid—we learned that later on—only it didn't make her militant; it just made her so scared of everybody and everything that she'd withdraw into herself and wouldn't speak to anybody for weeks on end. Sometimes she'd withdraw right out of this world and then they'd send her to the loony bin; believe me, it was all over school in two days. And she looked it; she'd sit up there in the school theater—oh, Milty, the Island high schools had *money,* you better believe it!—and try to disappear into the last seat like some little scared rabbit. She was only four eleven anyhow, and maybe eighty-five pounds sopping wet. So maybe that's why she didn't become a militant. Hell, that had nothing to do with it. She was scared of *everybody.* It wasn't just the white-black thing, either; I once saw her in a corner with one of the other black students: real uptight, respectable boy, you know, suit and white shirt and tie, hair straightened the way they did then with a lot of grease and carrying a new briefcase, too, and he was talking to her about something as if his life depended on it. He was actually crying and pleading with her. And all she did was shrink back into the corner as if she'd like to disappear and shake her head No No No. She always talked in a whisper unless she was on stage and sometimes then, too. The first week she forgot her cues four times—just stood there, glazed over, ready to fall through the floor—and a couple of times she just wandered off the set as if the play was over, right in the middle of a scene.

So Al Coppolino and I went to the principal. I'd always thought Alan was pretty much a fruitcake himself—remember, Milty this is 1952—because he used to read all that crazy stuff. The Cult of Chthulhu, Dagon Calls, The Horror Men of Leng—yeah, I remember that H. P. Lovecraft flick you got 10 per cent on for Hollywood *and* TV *and* reruns—but what did we know? Those days you went to parties, you got excited from dancing cheek to cheek, girls wore ankle socks and petticoats to stick their skirts out, and if you wore a sport shirt to school that was okay because Central High was liberal, but it better not have a pattern on it. Even so, I knew Al was a bright kid and I let him do most of the talking; I just nodded a lot. I was a big nothing in those days.

Al said, "Sir, Jim and I are all for integration and we think it's great that this is a really liberal place, but—uh—"

The principal got that look. Uh-oh.

"But?" he said, cold as ice.

"Well, sir," said Al, "it's Cissie Jackson. We think she's—um—sick. I mean wouldn't it be better if . . . I mean everybody says she just come out of the hospital and it's a strain for all of us and it must be a lot worse strain for her and maybe it's just a little soon for her to—"

"Sir," I said, "what Coppolino means is, we don't mind integrating blacks with whites, but this isn't racial integration, sir; this is integrating normal people with a filbert. I mean—"

He said, "Gentlemen, it might interest you to know that Miss Cecilia Jackson has higher scores on her IQ tests than the two of you put together. And I am told by the drama department that she has also more talent than the two of you put together. And considering the grades both of you have managed to achieve in the fall term, I'm not at all surprised."

Al said under his breath, "Yeah, and fifty times as many problems."

Well, the principal went on and told us about how we should welcome this chance to work with her because she was so brilliant she was positively a genius, and that as soon as we stopped spreading idiotic rumors, the better chance Miss Jackson would have to adjust to Central, and if he heard anything about our bothering her again or spreading stories about her, both of us were going to get it but good, and maybe we would even be expelled.

And then his voice lost the ice, and he told us about some white cop shooting her pa for no reason at all when she was five, right in front of her, and her pa bleeding into the gutter and dying in little Cissie's lap, and how poor her mother was, and a couple awful things that had happened to her, and if *that* wasn't enough to drive anybody crazy—though he said "cause problems," you know—anyhow, by the time he'd finished, I felt like a rat and Coppolino went outside the principal's office, put his face down against the tiles—they always had tiles up as high as you could reach, so they could wash off the "graffiti," though we didn't use the word "graffiti" in those days—and he blubbered like a baby.

So we started a Help Cecilia Jackson campaign.

And by God, Milty, could that girl *act!* She wasn't reliable, that was the trouble; one week she'd be in there, working like a dog, voice exercises, gym, fencing, reading Stanislavsky in the cafeteria, gorgeous performances, the next week: nothing. Oh, she was there in the flesh, all right, all eighty-five pounds of her, but she would walk through everything as if her mind was someplace else: technically perfect, emotionally nowhere. I heard later those were also the times she'd refuse to answer questions in history or geography classes, just fade out and not talk. But when she was concentrating, she could walk onto that stage and take it over as if she owned it. I never saw such a natural. At fifteen! And tiny. I mean not a particularly good voice—though I guess just getting older would've helped that—and a figure that, frankly, Milt, it was the old W. C. Fields joke, two aspirins on an ironing board. And tiny, no real good looks, but my God, you know and I know that doesn't matter if you've got the presence. And she had it to burn. She played the Queen of Sheba once, in a one-act play we put on before a live audience—all right, our parents and the other kids, who else?—and she *was* the role. And another time I saw her do things from Shakespeare. And once, of all things, a lioness in mime class. She had it all. Real, absolute, pure concentration. And she was smart, too; by then she and Al had become pretty good friends; I once heard her explain to him (that was in the green room the afternoon of the Queen of Sheba thing when she was taking off her make-up with cold cream) just how she'd figured out each bit of business for the character. Then she stuck her whole arm out at me, pointing straight at me as if her arm was a machine gun, and said:

"For you, Mister Jim, let me tell you: the main thing is *belief!*"

It was a funny thing, Milt. She got better and better friends with Al, and when they let me tag along, I felt privileged. He loaned her some of those crazy books of his and I overheard things about her life, bits and pieces. That girl had a mother who was so uptight and so God-fearing and so respectable it was a wonder Cissie could even breathe without asking permission. Her mother wouldn't even let her straighten her hair—not ideological reasons, you understand, not then, but because—get this—*Cissie was too young.* I think her mamma must've been crazier than she was. Course I was a damn stupid kid (who wasn't?) and I really thought all blacks were real loose; they went around snapping their fingers and hanging from chandeliers, you know, all that stuff, dancing and singing. But here was this genius from a family where they wouldn't let her out at night; she wasn't allowed to go to parties or dance or play cards; she couldn't wear make-up or even jewelry. Believe me, I think if anything drove her batty it was being socked over the head so often with a Bible. I guess her imagination just had to find some way out. Her mother, by the way, would've dragged her out of Central High by the hair if she'd found out about the drama classes; we all had to swear to keep that strictly on the q.t. The theater was even more sinful and wicked than dancing, I guess.

You know, I think it shocked me. It really did, Al's family was sort-of-nothing-really Catholic and mine was sort-of-nothing Jewish. I'd never met anybody with a mamma like that. I mean she would've beaten Cissie up if Cissie had ever come home with a gold circle pin on that white blouse she wore day in and day out; you remember the kind all the girls wore. And of course there were no horsehair petticoats for Miss Jackson; Miss Jackson wore pleated skirts that were much too short, even for her, and straight skirts that looked faded and all bunched up. For a while I had some vague idea that the short skirts meant she was daring, you know, sexy, but it wasn't that; they were from a much younger cousin, let down. She just couldn't afford her own clothes. I think it was the mamma and the Bible business that finally made me stop seeing Cissie as the Integration Prize Nut we had to be nice to because of the principal or the scared little rabbit who still, by the way, whispered everyplace but in drama class. I just saw Cecilia Jackson plain, I guess, not that it lasted for more than a few minutes, but I knew she was something special. So one day in the hall, going from one class to another, I met her and Al and I said, "Cissie, your name is going to be up there in lights someday. I think you're the best actress I ever met and I just want to say it's a privilege knowing you." And then I swept her a big corny bow, like Errol Flynn.

She looked at Al and Al looked at her, sort of sly. Then she let down her head over her books and giggled. She was so tiny you sometimes wondered how she could drag those books around all day; they hunched her over so.

Al said, "Aw, come on. Let's tell him."

So they told me their big secret. Cissie had a girl cousin named Gloriette, and Gloriette and Cissie together owned an honest-to-God slip for a boat in the marina out in Silverhampton. Each of them paid half the slip fee—which was about two bucks a month then, Milt—you have to remember that a marina then just meant a long wooden dock you could tie your rowboat up to.

"Gloriette's away," said Cissie, in that whisper. "She had to go visit auntie, in Carolina. And mamma's goin' to follow her next week on Sunday.

"So we're going to go out in the boat!" Al finished it for her. "You wanna come?"

"Sunday?"

"Sure, mamma will go to the bus station after church," said Cissie. "That's about one o'clock. Aunt Evelyn comes to take care of me at nine. So we have eight hours.

"And it takes two hours to get there," said Al. "First you take the subway; then you take a bus—"

"Unless we use your car, Jim!" said Cissie, laughing so hard she dropped her books.

"Well, thanks very much!" I said. She scooped them up again and smiled at me. "No, Jim," she said. "We want you to come, anyway. Al never saw the boat yet. Gloriette and me, we call it *My Boat*." Fifteen years old and she knew how to smile at you so's to twist your heart like a pretzel. Or maybe I just thought: what a wicked secret to have! A big sin, I guess, according to her family.

I said, "Sure, I'll drive you. May I ask what kind of boat it it, Miss Jackson?"

"Don't be so *damn* silly," she said daringly. "I'm Cissie or Cecilia. Silly Jim."

"And as for *My Boat,*" she added, "it's a big yacht. Enormous."

I was going to laugh at that, but then I saw she meant it. No, she was just playing. She was smiling wickedly at me again. She said we should meet at the bus stop near her house, and then she went down the tiled hall next to skinny little Al Coppolino, in her old, baggy, green skirt and her always-the-same white blouse. No beautiful, big, white, sloppy bobby socks for Miss Jackson; she just wore old loafers coming apart at the seams. She looked different, though: her head was up, her step springy, and she hadn't been whispering.

And then it occurred to me it was the first time I had even seen her smile or laugh—off stage. Mind you, she cried easily enough, like the time in class she realized from something the teacher had said that Anton Chekhov you know; the great Russian playwright—was dead. I heard her telling Alan later that she didn't believe it. There were lots of little crazy things like that.

Well, I picked her up Sunday in what was probably the oldest car in the world, even then—not a museum piece, Milty; it'd still be a mess—frankly I was lucky to get it started at all—and when I got to the bus station near Cissie's house in Brooklyn, there she was in her faded, hand-me-down, pleated skirt and that same blouse. I guess little elves named Cecilia Jackson came out of the woodwork every night and washed and ironed it. Funny, she and Al really did make a pair—you know, he was like the Woody Allen of Central High and I think he went in for his crazy books—sure, Milt, *very* crazy in 1952—because otherwise what could a little Italian plunk do who was five foot three and so brilliant no other kid could understand half the time what he was talking about? I don't know why I was friends with him; I think it made me feel big, you know, generous and good, like being friends with Cissie. They were almost the same size, waiting there by the bus stop, and I think their heads were in the same place. I know it now. I guess he was just a couple of decades ahead of himself, like his books. And maybe if the civil rights movement had started a few years earlier—

Anyway, we drove out to Silverhampton and it was a nice drive,

lots of country, though all flat—in those days there were still truck
farms on the Island—and found the marina, which was nothing more
than a big old quay, but sound enough; I parked the car and Al took
out a shopping bag Cissie'd been carrying. "Lunch," he said.

My Boat was there, all right, halfway down the dock. Somehow I
hadn't expected it would exist, even. It was an old leaky wooden
rowboat with only one oar, and there were three inches of bilge in
the bottom. On the bow somebody had painted the name, "My
Boat," shakily in orange paint. *My Boat* was tied to the mooring by a
rope about as sturdy as a piece of string. Still, it didn't look like it
would sink right away; after all, it'd been sitting there for months,
getting rained on, maybe even snowed on, and it was still floating. So
I stepped down into it, wishing I'd had the sense to take off my shoes
and started bailing with a tin can I'd brought from the car. Alan and
Cissie were taking things out of the bag in the middle of the boat. I
guess they were setting out lunch. It was pretty clear that *My Boat*
spent most of its time sitting at the dock while Cissie and Gloriette
ate lunch and maybe pretended they were on the *Queen Mary,* because neither Alan nor Cissie seemed to notice the missing oar. It
was a nice day but in-and-outish; you know, clouds one minute, sun
the next, but little fluffy clouds, no sign of rain. I bailed a lot of the
gunk out and then moved up into the bow, and as the sun came out I
saw that I'd been wrong about the orange paint. It was yellow.

Then I looked closer: it wasn't paint but something set into the
side of *My Boat* like the names on people's office doors; I guess I
must've not looked too closely the first time. It was a nice, flowing
script, a real professional job. Brass, I guess. Not a plate, Milt, kind
of—what do they call it, parquet? Intaglio? Each letter was put in
separately. Must've been Alan; he had a talent for stuff like that,
used to make weird illustrations for his crazy books. I turned around
to find Al and Cissie taking a big piece of cheesecloth out of the
shopping bag and draping it over high poles that were built into the
sides of the boat. They were making a kind of awning. I said:

"Hey, I bet you took that from the theater shop!"

She just smiled.

Al said, "Would you get us some fresh water, Jim?"

"Sure," I said. "Where, up the dock?"

"No, from the bucket. Back in the stern. Cissie says it's marked."

Oh, sure, I thought, sure. Out in the middle of the Pacific we set
out our bucket and pray for rain. There was a pail there all right,
and somebody had laboriously stenciled "Fresh Water" on it in green

paint, sort of smudgy, but that pail was never going to hold anything ever again. It was bone-dry, empty, and so badly rusted that when you held it up to the light, you could see through the bottom in a couple of places. I said, "Cissie, it's empty."

She said, "Look again, Jim."

I said, "But look, Cissie—" and turned the bucket upside-down.

Cold water drenched me from my knees to the soles of my shoes.

"See?" she said. "Never empty." I thought: Hell, I didn't look, that's all. Maybe it rained yesterday. Still a full pail of water is heavy and I had lifted that thing with one finger. I set it down—if it had been full before, it certainly wasn't now—and looked again.

It was full, right to the brim. I dipped my hand into the stuff and drank a little of it: cold and clear as spring water and it smelled—I don't know—of ferns warmed by the sun, of raspberries, of field flowers, of grass. I thought: my God, I'm becoming a filbert myself! And then I turned around and saw that Alan and Cissie had replaced the cheesecloth on the poles with a striped blue-and-white awning, the kind you see in movies about Cleopatra, you know? The stuff they put over her barge to keep the sun off. And Cissie had taken out of her shopping bag something patterned orange-and-green-and-blue and had wrapped it around her old clothes. She had on gold-colored earrings, big hoop things, and a black turban over that funny hair. And she must've put her loafers somewhere because she was barefoot. Then I saw that she had one shoulder bare, too, and I sat down on one of the marble benches of *My Boat* under the awning because I was probably having hallucinations. I mean she hadn't had *time*— and where were her old clothes? I thought to myself that they must've lifted a whole bagful of stuff from the theater shop, like that big old wicked-looking knife she had stuck into her amber-studded, leather belt, the hilt all covered with gold stones: red ones, green ones, and blue ones with little crosses of light winking in them that you couldn't really follow with your eyes. I didn't know what the blue ones were then, but I know now. You don't make star sapphires in a theater shop. Or a ten-inch, crescent-shaped steel blade so sharp the sun dazzles you coming off its edge.

I said, "Cissie, you look like the Queen of Sheba."

She smiled. She said to me, "Jim, iss not Shee-bah as in thee Bible, but Saba. Sah-bah. You mus' remember when we meet her."

I thought to myself: Yeah, this is where little old girl genius Cissie Jackson comes to freak out every Sunday. Lost weekend. I figured this was the perfect time to get away, make some excuse, you know, and call her mamma or her auntie, or maybe just the nearest hospital. I mean just for her own sake; Cissie wouldn't hurt anybody because she wasn't mean, not ever. And anyhow she was too little to hurt anyone. I stood up.

Her eyes were level with mine. And she was standing below me.

Al said, "Be careful, Jim. Look again. Always look again." I went back to the stern. There was the bucket that said "Fresh Water," but as I looked the sun came out and I saw I'd been mistaken; it wasn't old, rusty, galvanized iron with splotchy, green-painted letters.

It was silver, pure silver. It was sitting in a sort of marble well built into the stern, and the letters were jade inlay. It was still full. It would always be full. I looked back at Cissie standing under the blue-and-white-striped silk awning with her star sapphires and emeralds and rubies in her dagger and her funny talk—I know it now, Milt, it was West Indian, but I didn't then—and I knew as sure as if I'd seen it that if I looked at the letters "My Boat" in the sun, they wouldn't be brass but pure gold. And the wood would be ebony. I wasn't even surprised. Although everything had changed, you understand, I'd never seen it change; it was either that I hadn't looked carefully the first time, or I'd made a mistake, or I hadn't noticed something, or I'd just forgotten. Like what I thought had been an old crate in the middle of *My Boat,* which was really the roof of a cabin with little portholes in it, and looking in I saw three bunks below, a closet, and a beautiful little galley with a refrigerator and a stove, and off to one side in the sink, where I couldn't really see it clearly, a bottle with a napkin around its neck, sticking up from an ice bucket full of crushed ice, just like an old Fred Astaire-Ginger Rogers movie. And the whole inside of the cabin was paneled in teakwood.

Cissie said, "No Jim. Is not teak. Is cedar, from Lebanon. You see now why I cannot take seriously in this school this nonsense about places and where they are and what happen in them. Crude oil in Lebanon! It is cedar they have. And ivory. I have been there many, many time. I have talk' with the wise Solomon. I have been at court of Queen of Saba and have made eternal treaty with the Knossos women, the people of the double ax which is waxing and waning moon together. I have visit Akhnaton and Nofretari, and have seen great kings at Benin and at Dar. I even go to Atlantis, where the Royal Couple teach me many things. The priest and priestess, they show me how to make *My Boat* go anywhere I like, even under the sea. Oh, we have manhy improvin' chats upon roof of Pahlahss at dusk!"

It was real. It was all real. She was not fifteen, Milt. She sat in the bow at the controls of *My Boat,* and there were as many dials and toggles and buttons and switches and gauges on that thing as on a B-57. And she was at least ten years older. Al Coppolino, too, he looked like a picture I'd seen in a history book of Sir Francis Drake, and he had long hair and a little pointy beard. He was dressed like Drake, except for the ruff, with rubies in his ears and rings all over his fingers, and he, too, was no seventeen-year-old. He had a faint scar running from his left temple at the hairline down past his eye to his cheekbone. I could also see that under her turban Cissie's hair was braided in some very fancy way. I've seen it since. Oh, long before everybody was doing "corn rows." I saw it at the Metropolitan Museum, in silver face-mask sculptures from the city of Benin, in Africa. Old, Milt, centuries old.

Al said, "I know of other places, Princess. I can show them to you. Oh, let us go to Ooth-Nargai and Celephais the Fair, and Kadath in the Cold Waste—it's a fearful place, Jim, but *we* need not be afraid—and then we will go to the city of Ulthar, where is the very fortunate and lovely law that no man or woman may kill or annoy a cat."

"The Atlanteans," said Cissie in a deep sweet voice, "they promise' that next time they show me not jus' how to go undersea. They say if you think hard, if you fix much, if you believe, then can make *My Boat* go straight up. Into the stars, Jim!"

Al Coppolino was chanting names under his breath: Cathuria, Sona-Nyl, Thalarion, Zar, Baharna, Nir, Oriab. All out of those books of his.

Cissie said, "Before you come with us, you must do one last thing, Jim. Untie the rope."

So I climbed down *My Boat*'s ladder onto the quay and undid the braided gold rope that was fastened to the slip. Gold and silk intertwined, Milt; it rippled through my hand as if it were alive; I know the hard, slippery feel of silk. I was thinking of Atlantis and Celephais and going up into the stars, and all of it was mixed up in my head with the senior prom and college, because I had been lucky enough to be accepted by The-College-Of-My-Choice, and what a future I'd have as a lawyer, a corporation lawyer, after being a big gridiron star, of course. Those were my plans in the old days. Dead certainties every one, right? Versus a thirty-five-foot yacht that would've made John D. Rockefeller turn green with envy and places in the world where nobody'd ever been and nobody'd ever go again. Cissie and Al stood on deck above me, the both of them looking like something out of a movie—beautiful and dangerous and very strange—and suddenly I knew I didn't want to go. Part of it was the absolute certainty that if I ever offended Cissie in any way—I don't mean just a quarrel or disagreement or something you'd get the sulks about, but a real bone-deep kind of offense—I'd suddenly find myself in a leaky rowboat with only one oar in the middle of the Pacific Ocean. Or maybe just tied up at the dock at Silverhampton; Cissie wasn't mean. At least I hoped so. I just—I guess I didn't feel *good* enough to go. And there was something about their faces, too, as if over both of them, but especially over Cissie's, like clouds, like veils, there swam other faces, other expressions, other souls, other pasts and futures and other kinds of knowledge, all of them shifting like a heat mirage over an asphalt road on a hot day.

I didn't want that knowledge, Milt. I didn't want to go that deep. It was the kind of thing most seventeen-year-olds don't learn for years: Beauty. Despair. Mortality. Compassion. Pain.

And I was still looking up at them, watching the breeze fill out Al Coppolino's plum-colored velvet cloak and shine on his silver-and-black doublet, when a big, heavy, hard, fat hand clamped down on my shoulder and a big, fat, nasty, heavy, Southern voice said:

"Hey, boy, you got no permit for this slip! What's that rowboat doin' out there? And what's yo' name?"

So I turned and found myself looking into the face of the great-granddaddy of all Southern redneck sheriffs: face like a bulldog with jowls to match, and sunburned red, and fat as a pig, and mountain-mean. I said, "Sir?"—every high-school kid could say that in his sleep in those days—and then we turned toward the bay, me saying, "What boat sir?" and the cop saying just, "What the—"

Because there was nothing there. *My Boat* was gone. There was only a blue shimmering stretch of bay. They weren't out further and they weren't around the other side of the dock—the cop and I both ran around—and by the time I had presence of mind enough to look up at the sky—

Nothing. A seagull. A cloud. A plane out of Idlewild. Besides, hadn't Cissie said she didn't yet know how to go straight up into the stars?

No, nobody ever saw *My Boat* again. Or Miss Cecilia Jackson, complete nut and girl genius, either. Her mamma came to school and I was called into the principal's office. I told them a cooked-up story, the one I'd been going to tell the cop: that they'd said they were just going to row around the dock and come back, and I'd left to see if the car was okay in the parking lot, and when I came back, they were gone. For some crazy reason I *still* thought Cissie's mamma would look like Aunt Jemima, but she was a thin little woman, very like her daughter, and as nervous and uptight as I ever saw: a tiny lady in a much-pressed, but very clean, gray business suit, like a teacher's, you know, worn-out shoes, a blouse with a white frill at the neck, a straw hat with a white band, and proper white gloves. I think Cissie knew what I expected her mamma to be and what a damned fool I was, even considering your run-of-the-mill, seventeen-year-old, white, liberal racist, and that's why she didn't take me along.

The cop? He followed me to my car, and by the time I got there— I was sweating and crazy scared—

He was gone, too. Vanished.

I think Cissie created him. Just for a joke.

So Cissie never came back. And I couldn't convince Mrs. Jackson that Alan Coppolino, boy rapist, hadn't carried her daughter off to some lonely place and murdered her. I tried and tried, but Mrs. Jackson would never believe me.

It turned out there was no Cousin Gloriette.

Alan? Oh, he came back. But it took him awhile. I saw him yesterday, Milt, on the Brooklyn subway. A skinny, short guy with ears that stuck out, still wearing the sport shirt and pants he'd started out in, that Sunday more than twenty years ago, and with the real 1950's haircut nobody would wear today. Quite a few people were staring at him, in fact.

The thing is, Milt, *he was still seventeen.*

No, I know it wasn't some other kid. Because he was waving at me and smiling fit to beat the band. And when I got out with him at his old stop, he started asking after everybody in Central High just as if it had been a week later, or maybe only a day. Though when I asked him where the hell he'd been for twenty years, he wouldn't tell me. He only said he'd forgotten something. So we went up five flights to his old apartment, the way we used to after school for a couple of hours before his mom and dad came home from work. He had the old key in his pocket. And it was just the same, Milt: the gas refrig-

erator, the exposed pipes under the sink, the summer slipcovers
nobody uses any more, the winter drapes put away, the valance over
the window muffled in a sheet, the bare parquet floors, and the old li-
noleum in the kitchen. Every time I'd ask him a question, he'd only
smile. He knew me, though, because he called me by name a couple
of times. I said, "How'd you recognize me?" and he said, "Recognize? You haven't changed." Haven't changed, my God. Then I said,
"Look, Alan, what did you come back for?" and with a grin just like
Cissie's, he said, *"The Necronomicon* by the mad Arab, Abdul Al-
hazred, what else?" but I saw the book he took with him and it was
a different one. He was careful to get just the right one, looked
through every shelf in the bookcase in his bedroom. There were still
college banners all over the walls of his room. I know the book now,
by the way; it was the one you wanted to make into a quick script
last year for the guy who does the Poe movies, only I *told* you it
was all special effects and animation: exotic islands, strange worlds,
and the monsters' costumes alone—sure, H. P. Lovecraft. "The
Dream Quest of Unknown Kadath." He didn't say a word after that.
Just walked down the five flights with me behind him and then
along the old block to the nearest subway station, but of course by
the time I reached the bottom of the subway steps, he wasn't there.

His apartment? You'll never find it. When I raced back up, even
the house was gone. More than that, Milt, the street is gone; the address doesn't exist any more; it's all part of the new expressway now.

Which is why I called you. My God, I had to tell somebody! By
now those two psychiatric cases are voyaging around between the
stars to Ulthar and Ooth-Nargai and Dylath-Lenn—

But they're not psychiatric cases. *It really happened.*

So if they're not psychiatric cases, what does that make you and
me? Blind men?

I'll tell you something else, Milt: meeting Al reminded me of what
Cissie once said before the whole thing with *My Boat* but after we'd
become friends enough for me to ask her what had brought her out
of the hospital. I didn't ask it like that and she didn't answer it like
that, but what it boiled down to was that sooner or later, at every
place she visited, she'd meet a bleeding man with wounds in his
hands and feet who would tell her, "Cissie, go back, you're needed;
Cissie, go back, you're needed." I was fool enough to ask her if he
was a white man or a black man. She just glared at me and walked
away. Now wounds in the hands and feet, you don't have to look far

to tell what that means to a Christian, Bible-raised girl. What I wonder is: will she meet Him again, out there among the stars? If things get bad enough for black power or women's liberation, or even for people who write crazy books, I don't know what, will *My Boat* materialize over Times Square or Harlem or East New York with an Ethiopian warrior-queen in it and Sir Francis Drake Coppolino, and God-only-knows-what kind of weapons from the lost science of Atlantis? I tell you, I wouldn't be surprised. I really wouldn't. I only hope He—or Cissie's idea of him—decides that things are still okay, and they can go on visiting all those places in Al Coppolino's book. I tell you, I hope that book is a *long* book.

Still, if I could do it again. . . .

Milt, it is not a story. *It happened.* For instance, tell me one thing, how did she know the name Nofretari? That's the Egyptian Queen Nefertiti, that's how we all learned it, but how could she know the real name decades, literally decades, before anybody else? And Saba? That's real, too. And Benin? We didn't have any courses in African History in Central High, not in 1952! And what about the double-headed ax of the Cretans at Knossos? Sure, we read about Crete in high school, but nothing in our history books ever told us about the matriarchy or the labyris, that's the name of the ax. Milt, I tell you, there is even a women's lib bookstore in Manhattan *called—*

Have it your own way.

Oh, sure. She wasn't black; she was green. It'd make a great TV show. Green, blue, and rainbow-colored. I'm sorry, Milty, I know you're my agent and you've done a lot of work for me and I haven't sold much lately. I've been reading. No, nothing you'd like: existentialism, history, Marxism, some Eastern stuff—

Sorry, Milt, but we writers do read every once in a while. It's this little vice we have. I've been trying to dig deep, like Al Coppolino, though maybe in a different way.

Okay, so you want to have this Martian, who wants to invade Earth, so he turns himself into a beautiful, tanned girl with long, straight, blonde hair, right? And becomes a high-school student in a rich school in Westchester. And this beautiful blonde girl Martian has to get into all the local organizations like the women's consciousness-raising groups and the encounter therapy stuff and the cheerleaders and the kids who push dope, so he—she, rather—can learn about the Earth mentality. Yeah. And of course she has to seduce the principal and the coach and all the big men on campus, so we can make it into a series, even a sitcom maybe; each week this Martian falls in love with an Earth man or she tries to do something to destroy Earth or blow up something, using Central High for a base. Can I use it? Sure I can! It's beautiful. It's right in my line. I can work in everything I just told you. Cissie was right not to take me along; I've got spaghetti where my backbone should be.

Nothing. I didn't say anything. Sure. It's a great idea. Even if we only get a pilot out of it.

No, Milt, honestly, I really think it has this fantastic spark. A real touch of genius. It'll sell like crazy. Yeah, I can manage an idea sheet by Monday. Sure. "The Beautiful Menace from Mars?" Un-huh. Absolutely. It's got sex, it's got danger, comedy, everything; we could branch out into the lives of the teachers, the principal, the other kid's parents. Bring in contemporary problems like drug abuse. Sure. Another Peyton Place. I'll even move to the West Coast again. You are a genius.

Oh my God.

Nothing. Keep on talking. It's just—see that little skinny kid in the next booth down? The one with the stuck-out ears and the old-fashioned haircut? You don't? Well, I think you're just not looking properly, Milt. Actually I don't think I was, either; he must be one of the Met extras, you know, they come out sometimes during the intermission: all that Elizabethan stuff, the plum-colored cloak, the calf-high boots, the silver-and-black— As a matter of fact, I just remembered—the Met moved uptown a couple of years ago, so he couldn't be dressed like that, could he?

You still can't see him? I'm not surprised. The Light's very bad in here. Listen, he's an old friend—I mean he's the son of an old friend —I better go over and say hello, I won't be a minute.

Milt, this young man is important! I mean he's connected with somebody very important. Who? One of the biggest and best producers in the world, that's who! He—uh—they—wanted me to— you might call it do a script for them, yeah. I didn't want to at the time, but—

No, no, you stay right here. I'll just sort of lean over and say hello. You keep on talking about the Beautiful Menace from Mars; I can listen from there; I'll just tell him they can have me if they want me.

Your ten per cent? Of course you'll get your ten per cent. You're my agent, aren't you? Why, if it wasn't for you, I just possible might not have— Sure, you'll get your ten per cent. Spend it on anything you like: ivory, apes, peacocks, spices, and Lebanese cedarwood!

All you have to do is collect it.

But keep on talking, Milty, won't you? Somehow I want to go over to the next booth with the sound of your voice in my ears. Those beautiful ideas. So original. So creative. So true. Just what the public wants. Of course there's a difference in the way people perceive things, and you and I, I think we perceive them differently, you know? Which is why you are a respected, successful agent and I—well, let's skip it. It wouldn't be complimentary to either of us.

Huh? Oh, nothing. I didn't say anything. I'm listening. Over my shoulder. Just keep on talking while I say hello and my deepest and most abject apologies, Sir Alan Coppolino. Heard the name before, Milt? No? I'm not surprised.

You just keep on talking. . . .

John Varley began writing for *F&SF* in 1974 and in only a short time gained a reputation as one of sf's most exciting new storytellers. He is in his late twenties and writes: "I belong to the following minorities: whites, males, Texans, southpaws, Very Tall People. I am also that much rarer bird, a male feminist. I believe that people will all benefit when any group is allowed to break out of the limitations imposed on them by birth." Which has a lot to do with the inventive and entertaining story you are about to read . . .

In the Bowl

by JOHN VARLEY

Never buy anything at a secondhand organbank. And while I'm handing out good advice, don't outfit yourself for a trip to Venus until you *get* to Venus.

I wish I had waited. But while shopping around at Coprates a few weeks before my vacation, I happened on this little shop and was talked into an infraeye at a very good price. What I should have asked myself was what was an infraeye doing on Mars in the first place?

Think about it. No one wears them on Mars. If you want to see at night, it's much cheaper to buy a snooperscope. That way you can take the damn thing off when the sun comes up. So this eye must have come back with a tourist from Venus. And there's no telling how long it sat there in the vat until this sweet-talking old guy gave me his line about how it belonged to a nice little old schoolteacher who never . . . ah, well. You've probably heard it before.

If only the damn thing had gone on the blink before I left Venus-burg. You know Venusburg: town of steamy swamps and sleazy hotels where you can get mugged as you walk down the public streets, lose a fortune at the gaming tables, buy any pleasure in the known universe, hunt the prehistoric monsters that wallow in the fetid marshes that are just a swampbuggy ride out of town. You do? Then you should know that after hours—when they turn all the holos off and the place reverts to an ordinary cluster of silvery domes sitting in darkness and eight hundred degree temperature and pressure enough to give you a sinus headache just *thinking* about it, when they shut off all the tourist razzle-dazzle—it's no trouble to find your way to one of the rental agencies around the spaceport and get medicanical work done. They'll accept Martian money. Your Solar Express Card is honored. Just walk right in, no waiting.

However . . .

I had caught the daily blimp out of Venusburg just hours after I touched down, happy as a clam, my infraeye working beautifully. By the time I landed in Cui-Cui Town, I was having my first inklings of trouble. Barely enough to notice; just the faintest hazing in the right-side peripheral vision. I shrugged it off. I had only three hours in Cui-Cui before the blimp left for Last Chance. I wanted to look around. I had no intention of wasting my few hours in a bodyshop getting my eye fixed. If it was still acting up at Last Chance, then I'd see about it.

Cui-Cui was more to my liking than Venusburg. There was not such a cast-of-thousands feeling there. On the streets of Venusburg the chances are about ten to one against meeting a real human being; everyone else is a holo put there to spice up the image and help the streets look not quite so *empty*. I quickly tired of zoot-suited pimps that I could see right through trying to sell me boys and girls of all ages. What's the *point?* Just try to touch one of those beautiful people.

In Cui-Cui the ratio was closer to fifty-fifty. And the theme was not decadent corruption, but struggling frontier. The streets were very convincing mud, and the wooden storefronts were tastefully done. I didn't care for the eight-legged dragons with eyestalks that constantly lumbered through the place, but I understand they are a memorial to the fellow who named the town. That's all right, but I doubt if he would have liked to have one of the damn things walk through him like a twelve-ton tank made of pixie dust.

I barely had time to get my feet "wet" in the "puddles" before the blimp was ready to go again. And the eye trouble had cleared up. So I was off to Last Chance.

I should have taken a cue from the name of the town. And I had every opportunity to do so. While there, I made my last purchase of supplies for the bush. I was going out where there were no air stations on every corner, and so I decided I could use a tagalong.

Maybe you've never seen one. They're modern science's answer to the backpack. Or maybe to the mule train, though in operation you're sure to be reminded of the safari bearers in old movies, trudging stolidly along behind the White Hunter with bales of supplies on their heads. The thing is a pair of metal legs exactly as long as your legs, with equipment on the top and an umbilical cord attaching the contraption to your lower spine. What it does is provide you with the capability of living on the surface for four weeks instead of the five days you get from your Venus-lung.

The medico who sold me mine had me laying right there on his table with my back laid open so he could install the tubes that carry air from the tanks in the tagalong into my Venus lung. It was a golden opportunity to ask him to check the eye. He probably would have, because while he was hooking me up he inspected and tested my lung and charged me nothing. He wanted to know where I bought it, and I told him Mars. He clucked, and said it seemed all right. He warned me not to ever let the level of oxygen in the lung get too low, to always charge it up before I left a pressure dome, even if I was only going out for a few minutes. I assured him that I knew all that and would be careful. So he connected the nerves into a metal socket in the small of my back and plugged the tagalong into it. He tested it several ways and said the job was done.

And I didn't ask him to look at the eye. I just wasn't thinking about the eye then. I'd not even gone out on the surface yet. So I'd no real occasion to see it in action. Oh, things looked a little different, even in visible light. There were different colors and very few shadows, and the image I got out of the infraeye was fuzzier than the one from the other eye. I could close one eye, then the other, and see a real difference. But I wasn't thinking about it.

So I boarded the blimp the next day for the weekly scheduled flight to Lodestone, a company mining town close to the Fahrenheit Desert. Though how they were able to distinguish a desert from anything else on Venus was still a mystery to me. I was enraged to find that, though the blimp left half-loaded, I had to pay two fares: one for me, and one for my tagalong. I thought briefly of carrying the damn thing in my lap but gave it up after a ten-minute experiment in the depot. It was full of sharp edges and poking angles, and the trip was going to be a long one. So I paid. But the extra expense had knocked a large hole in my budget.

From Cui-Cui the steps got closer together and harder to reach. Cui-Cui is two thousand kilometers from Venusburg, and it's another thousand to Lodestone. After that the passenger service is spotty. I did find out how Venusians defined a desert, though. A desert is a place not yet inhabited by human beings. So long as I was still able to board a scheduled blimp, I wasn't there yet.

The blimps played out on me in a little place called Prosperity. Population seventy-five humans and one otter. I thought the otter was a holo playing in the pool in the town square. The place didn't look prosperous enough to afford a real pool like that with real water. But it was. It was a transient town catering to prospectors. I understand that a town like that can vanish overnight if the prospectors move on. The owners of the shops just pack up and haul the whole thing away. The ratio of the things you see in a frontier town to what really is there is something like a hundred to one.

I learned with considerable relief that the only blimps I could catch out of Prosperity were headed in the direction I had come from. There was nothing at all going the other way. I was happy to hear that and felt it was only a matter of chartering a ride into the desert. Then my eye faded out entirely.

I remember feeling annoyed; no, more than annoyed. I was really angry. But I was still viewing it as a nuisance rather than a disaster. It was going to be a matter of some lost time and some wasted money.

I quickly learned otherwise. I asked the ticket seller (this was in a saloon-drugstore-arcade; there was no depot in Prosperity) where I could find someone who'd sell and install an infraeye. He laughed at me.

"Not out here you won't, brother," he said. "Never have had anything like that out here. Used to be a medico in Ellsworth, three stops back on the local blimp, but she moved back to Venusburg a year ago. Nearest thing now is in Last Chance."

I was stunned. I knew I was heading out for the deadlands, but it had never occurred to me that any place would be lacking in something so basic as a medico. Why, you might as well not sell food or air as not sell medicanical services. People might actually *die* out here. I wondered if the planetary government knew about this disgusting situation.

Whether they did or not, I realized that an incensed letter to them would do me no good. I was in a bind. Adding quickly in my head, I soon discovered that the cost of flying back to Last Chance and buying a new eye would leave me without enough money to return to Prosperity and still make it back to Venusburg. My entire vacation was about to be ruined just because I tried to cut some corners buying a used eye.

"What's the matter with the eye?" the man asked me.

"Huh? Oh, I don't know. I mean, it's just stopped working. I'm blind in it, that's what's wrong." I grasped at a straw, seeing the way he was studying my eye.

"Say, you don't know anything about it, do you?"

He shook his head and smiled ruefully at me. "Naw. Just a little here and there. I was thinking if it was the muscles that was giving you trouble, bad tracking or something like that—"

"No. No vision at all."

"Too bad. Sounds like a shot nerve to me. I wouldn't try to fool around with that. I'm just a tinkerer." He clucked his tongue sympathetically. "You want that ticket back to Last Chance?"

I didn't know what I wanted just then. I had planned this trip for two years. I almost bought the ticket, then thought what the hell. I was here, and I should at least look around before deciding what to do. Maybe there was someone here who could help me. I turned back to ask the clerk if he knew anyone, but he answered before I got it out.

"I don't want to raise your hopes too much," he said, rubbing his chin with a broad hand. "Like I say, it's not for sure, but—"

"Yes, what is it?"

"Well, there's a kid lives around here who's pretty crazy about medico stuff. Always tinkering around, doing odd jobs for people, fixing herself up; you know the type. The trouble is she's pretty loose in her ways. You might end up worse when she's through with you than when you started."

"I don't see how," I said. "It's not working at all; what could she do to make it any worse?"

He shrugged. "It's your funeral. You can probably find her hanging around the square. If she's not there, check the bars. Her name's

Ember. She's got a pet otter that's always with her. But you'll know her when you see her."

Finding Ember was no problem. I simply backtracked to the square and there she was, sitting on the stone rim of the fountain. She was trailing her toes in the water. Her otter was playing on a small waterslide, looking immensely pleased to have found the only open body of water within a thousand kilometers.

"Are you Ember?" I asked, sitting down beside her.

She looked at me with that unsettling stare a Venusian can inflict on a foreigner. It comes of having one blue or brown eye and one that is all red, with no white. I looked that way myself, but I didn't have to look at it.

"What if I am?"

Her apparent age was about ten or eleven. Intuitively, I felt that it was probably very close to her actual age. Since she was supposed to be handy at medicanics, I could have been wrong. She had done some work on herself, but of course there was no way of telling how extensive it might have been. Mostly it seemed to be cosmetic. She had no hair on her head. She had replaced it with a peacock fan of feathers that kept falling into her eyes. Her scalp skin had been transplanted to her lower legs and forearms, and the hair there was long, blonde, and flowing. From the contours of her face I was sure that her skull was a mass of file marks and bone putty from where she'd fixed the understructure to reflect the face she wished to wear.

"I was told that you know a little medicanics. You see, this eye has—"

She snorted. "I don't know who would have told you *that*. I know a hell of a lot about medicine. I'm not just a back-yard tinkerer. Come on, Malibu."

She started to get up, and the otter looked back and forth between us. I don't think he was ready to leave the pool.

"Wait a minute. I'm sorry if I hurt your feelings. Without knowing anything about you I'll admit that you must know more about it than anyone else in town."

She sat back down, finally had to grin at me.

"So you're in a spot, right? It's me or no one. Let me guess: you're here on vacation, that's obvious. And either time or money is preventing you from going back to Last Chance for professional work." She looked me up and down. "I'd say it was money."

"You hit it. Will you help me?"

"That depends." She moved closer and squinted into my infraeye. She put her hands on my cheeks to hold my head steady. There was nowhere for me to look but her face. There were no scars visible on her; at least she was that good. Her upper canines were about five millimeters longer than the rest of her teeth.

"Hold still. Where'd you get this?"

"Mars."

"Thought so. It's a Gloom Piercer, made by Northern Bio. Cheap model; they peddle 'em mostly to tourists. Maybe ten, twelve years old."

"Is it the nerve? The guy I talked to—"

"Nope." She leaned back and resumed splashing her feet in the water. "Retina. The right side is detached, and it's flopped down over the fovea. Probably wasn't put on very tight in the first place. They don't make those things to last more than a year."

I sighed and slapped my knees with my palms. I stood up, held out my hand to her.

"Well, I guess that's that. Thanks for your help."

She was surprised. "Where you going?"

"Back to Last Chance, then to Mars to sue a certain organbank. There are laws for this sort of thing on Mars."

"Here, too. But why go back? I'll fix it for you."

We were in her workshop, which doubled as her bedroom and kitchen. It was just a simple dome without a single holo. It was refreshing after the ranch-style houses that seemed to be the rage in Prosperity. I don't wish to sound chauvinistic, and I realize that Venusians need some sort of visual stimulation, living as they do in a cloud-covered desert. Still, the emphasis on illusion there was never to my liking. Ember lived next door to a man who lived in a perfect replica of the Palace at Versailles. She told me that when he shut his holo generators off the residue of his *real* possessions would have fit in a knapsack. Including the holo generator.

"What brings you to Venus?"

"Tourism."

She looked at me out of the corner of her eye as she swabbed my face with nerve deadener. I was stretched out on the floor, since there was no furniture in the room except a few work tables.

"All right. But we don't get many tourists this far out. If it's none of my business, just say so."

"It's none of your business."

She sat up. "Fine. Fix your own eye." She waited with a half smile on her face. I eventually had to smile, too. She went back to work, selecting a spoon-shaped tool from a haphazard pile at her knees.

"I'm an amateur geologist. Rock hound, actually. I work in an office, and weekends I get out in the country and hike around. The rocks are an excuse to get me out there, I guess."

She popped the eye out of its socket and reached in with one finger to deftly unhook the metal connection along the optic nerve. She held the eyeball up to the light and peered into the lens.

"You can get up now. Pour some of this stuff into the socket and squint down on it." I did as she asked and followed her to the workbench.

She sat on a stool and examined the eye more closely. Then she stuck a syringe into it and drained out the aqueous humor, leaving the orb looking like a turtle egg that's dried in the sun. She sliced it open and started probing carefully. The long hairs on her forearms kept getting in the way. So she paused and tied them back with rubber bands.

"Rock hound," she mused. "You must be here to get a look at the blast jewels."

"Right. Like I said, I'm strictly a small-time geologist. But I read about them and saw one once in a jeweler's shop in Phobos. So I saved up and came to Venus to try and find one of my own."

"That should be no problem. Easiest gems to find in the known universe. Too bad. People out here were hoping they could get rich off them." She shrugged. "Not that there's not some money to be made off them. Just not the fortune everybody was hoping for. Funny; they're as rare as diamonds used to be, and to make it even better, they don't duplicate in the lab the way diamonds do. Oh, I guess they could make 'em, but it's way too much trouble." She was using a tiny device to staple the detached retina back onto the rear surface of the eye.

"Go on."

"Huh?"

"Why can't they make them in the lab?"

She laughed. "You *are* an amateur geologist. Like I said, they could, but it'd cost too much. They're a blend of a lot of different elements. A lot of aluminum, I think. That's what makes rubies red, right?"

"Yes."

"It's the other impurities that make them so pretty. And you have to make them in high pressure and heat, and they're so unstable that they usually blow before you've got the right mix. So it's cheaper to go out and pick 'em up."

"And the only place to pick them up is in the middle of the Fahrenheit Desert."

"Right." She seemed to be finished with her stapling. She straightened up to survey her work with a critical eye. She frowned, then sealed up the incision she had made and pumped the liquid back in. She mounted it in a caliper and aimed a laser at it, then shook her head when she read some figures on a readout by the laser.

"It's working," she said. "But you really got a lemon. The iris is out of true. It's an ellipse, about .24 eccentric. It's going to get worse. See that brown discoloration on the left side? That's progressive decay in the muscle tissue, poisons accumulating in it. And you're a dead cinch for cataracts in about four months."

I couldn't see what she was talking about, but I pursed my lips as if I did.

"But will it last that long?"

She smirked at me. "Are you looking for a six-month warranty? Sorry, I'm not a member of the VMA. But if it isn't legally binding, I guess I'd feel safe in saying it ought to last that long. Maybe."

"You sure go out on a limb, don't you?"

"It's good practice. We future medicos must always be on the alert for malpractice suits. Lean over here and I'll put it in."

"What I was wondering," I said, as she hooked it up and eased it back into the socket, "is whether I'd be safe going out in the desert for four weeks with this eye."

"No," she said promptly, and I felt a great weight of disappointment. "Nor with any eye," she quickly added. "Not if you're going alone."

"I see. But you think the eye would hold up?"

"Oh, sure. But you wouldn't. That's why you're going to take me up on my astounding offer and let me to be your guide through the desert."

I snorted. "You think so? Sorry, this is going to be a solo expedition. I planned it that way from the first. That's what I go out rock hunting for in the first place: to be alone." I dug my credit meter out of my pouch. "Now, how much do I owe you?"

She wasn't listening but was resting her chin on her palm and looking wistful.

"He goes out so he can be alone, did you hear that, Malibu?" The otter looked up at her from his place on the floor. "Now take me, for instance. Me, I know what being alone is all about. It's the crowds and big cities I crave. Right, old buddy?" The otter kept looking at her, obviously ready to agree to anything.

"I suppose so," I said. "Would a hundred be all right?" That was about half what a registered medico would have charged me, but like I said, I was running short.

"You're not going to let me be your guide? Final word?"

"No. Final. Listen, it's not you, it's just—"

"I know. You want to be alone. No charge. Come on, Malibu." She got up and headed for the door. Then she turned around.

"I'll be seeing you," she said, and winked at me.

It didn't take me too long to understand what the wink had been all about. I can see the obvious on the third or fourth go-around.

The fact was that Prosperity was considerably bemused to have a tourist in its midst. There wasn't a rental agency or hotel in the entire town. I had thought of that but hadn't figured it would be too hard to find someone willing to rent his private skycycle if the price was right. I'd been saving out a large chunk of cash for the purpose of meeting extortionate demands in that department. I felt sure the locals would be only too willing to soak a tourist.

But they weren't taking. Just about everyone had a skycycle, and absolutely everyone who had one was uninterested in renting it. They were a necessity to anyone who worked out of town, which everyone did, and they were hard to get. Freight schedules were as spotty as the passenger service. And every person who turned me down had a helpful suggestion to make. As I say, after the fourth or fifth such suggestion I found myself back in the town square. She was sitting just as she had been the first time, trailing her feet in the water. Malibu never seemed to tire of the waterslide.

"Yes," she said, without looking up. "It so happens that I *do* have a skycycle for rent."

I was exasperated, but I had to cover it up. She had me over the proverbial barrel.

"Do you always hang around here?" I asked. "People tell me to see you about a skycycle and tell me to look here, almost like you and this fountain are a hyphenated word. What else do you do?"

She fixed me with a haughty glare. "I repair eyes for dumb tourists. I also do body work for everyone in town at only twice what it would cost them in Last Chance. And I do it damn well, too, though those rubes'd be the last to admit it. No doubt Mr. Lamara at the ticket station told you scandalous lies about my skills. They resent it because I'm taking advantage of the cost and time it would take them to get to Last Chance and pay merely inflated prices, instead of the outrageous ones I charge them."

I had to smile, though I was sure I was about to become the object of some outrageous prices myself. She was a shrewd operator.

"How old are you?" I found myself asking, then almost bit my tongue. The last thing a proud and independent child likes to discuss is age. But she surprised me.

"In mere chronological time, eleven Earth years. That's just over six of your years. In real, internal time, of course, I'm ageless."

"Of course. Now about that cycle. . . ."

"Of course. But I evaded your earlier question. What I do besides sit here is irrelevant, because while sitting here I am engaged in contemplating eternity. I'm diving into my navel, hoping to learn the true depth of the womb. In short, I'm doing my yoga exercises." She looked thoughtfully out over the water to her pet. "Besides, it's the only pool in a thousand kilometers." She grinned at me and dived flat over the water. She cut it like a knife blade and torpedoed out to her otter, who set up a happy racket of barks.

When she surfaced near the middle of the pool, out by the jets and falls, I called to her.

"What about the cycle?"

She cupped her ear, though she was only about fifteen meters away.

"I said what about the cycle?"

"I can't hear you," she mouthed. "You'll have to come out here."

I stepped into the pool, grumbling to myself. I could see that her price included more than just money.

"I can't swim," I warned.

"Don't worry, it won't get much deeper than that." It was up to my chest. I sloshed out until I was on tiptoe, then grabbed at a jutting curlicue on the fountain. I hauled myself up and sat on the wet Venusian marble with water trickling down my legs.

Ember was sitting at the bottom of the waterslide, thrashing her feet in the water. She was leaning flat against the smooth rock. The water that sheeted over the rock made a bow wave at the crown of her head. Beads of water ran off her head feathers. Once again she made me smile. If charm could be sold, she could have been wealthy. What am I talking about? Nobody ever sells anything *but* charm, in one way or another. I got a grip on myself before she tried to sell me the north and south poles. In no time at all I was able to see her as an avaricious, cunning little guttersnipe again.

"One billion Solar Marks per hour, not a penny less," she said from that sweet little mouth.

There was no point in negotiating from an offer like that. "You brought me out here to hear *that?* I'm really disappointed in you. I didn't take you for a tease, I really didn't. I thought we could do business. I—"

"Well, if that offer isn't satisfactory, try this one. Free of charge, except for oxygen and food and water." She waited, threshing the water with her feet.

Of course there would be some teeth in that. In an intuitive leap of truly cosmic scale, a surmise worthy of an Einstein, I saw the string. She saw me make that leap, knew I didn't like where I had landed, and her teeth flashed at me. So once again, and not for the last time, I had to either strangle her or smile at her. I smiled. I don't know how, but she had this knack of making her opponents like her even as she screwed them.

"Are you a believer in love at first sight?" I asked her, hoping to throw her off guard. Not a chance.

"Maudlin wishful thinking, at best," she said. "You have *not* bowled me over, Mister—"

"Kiku."

"Nice. Martian name?"

"I suppose so. I never really thought of it. I'm not rich, Ember."

"Certainly not. You wouldn't have put yourself in my hands if you were."

"Then why are you so attracted to me? Why are you so determined to go with me, when all I want from you is to rent your cycle? If I was that charming, I would have noticed it by now."

"Oh, I don't know," she said, with one eyebrow climbing up her forehead. "There's *something* about you that I find absolutely fascinating. Irresistible, even." She pretended to swoon.

"Want to tell me what it is?"

She shook her head. "Let that be my little secret for now."

I was beginning to suspect she was attracted to me by the shape of my neck—so she could sink her teeth into it and drain my blood. I decided to let it lie. Hopefully she'd tell me more in the days ahead. Because it looked like there would be days together, many of them.

"When can you be ready to leave?"

"I packed right after I fixed your eye. Let's get going."

Venus is spooky. I thought and thought, and that's the best way I can describe it.

It's spooky partly because of the way you see it. Your right eye—the one that sees what's called visible light—shows you only a small circle of light that's illuminated by your hand torch. Occasionally there's a glowing spot of molten metal in the distance, but it's far too dim to see by. Your infraeye pierces those shadows and gives you a blurry picture of what lies outside the torchlight, but I would have almost rather been blind.

There's no good way to describe how this dichotomy affects your mind. One eye tells you that everything beyond a certain point is shadowy, while the other shows you what's in those shadows. Ember says that after a while your brain can blend the two pictures as easily as it does for binocular vision. I never reached that point. The whole time I was there I was trying to reconcile the two pictures.

I don't like standing in the bottom of a bowl a thousand kilometers wide. That's what you see. No matter how high you climb or how far you go, you're still standing in the bottom of that bowl. It has something to do with the bending of the light rays by the thick atmosphere, if I understand Ember correctly.

Then there's the sun. When I was there it was night time, which means that the sun was a squashed ellipse hanging just above the horizon is the east, where it had set weeks and weeks ago. Don't ask me to explain it. All I know is that the sun never sets on Venus. Never, no matter where you are. It just gets flatter and flatter and wider and wider until it oozes around to the north or south, depending on where you are, becoming a flat, bright line of light until it begins pulling itself back together in the west, where it's going to rise in a few weeks.

Ember says that at the equator it becomes a complete circle for a split second when it's actually directly underfoot. Like the lights of a terrific stadium. All this happens up at the rim of the bowl you're standing in, about ten degrees above the theoretical horizon. It's another refraction effect.

You don't see it in your left eye. Like I said, the clouds keep out virtually all of the visible light. It's in your right eye. The color is what I got to think of as infrablue.

It's quiet. You begin to miss the sound of your own breathing, and if you think about that too much, you begin to wonder why you *aren't* breathing. You know, of course, except the hindbrain, which never likes it at all. It doesn't matter to the autonomic nervous system that your Venus-lung is dribbling oxygen directly into your bloodstream; those circuits aren't made to understand things; they are primitive and very wary of improvements. So I was plagued by a feeling of suffocation, which was my medulla getting even with me, I guess.

I was also pretty nervous about the temperature and pressure. Silly, I know. Mars would kill me just as dead without a suit, and do it more slowly and painfully into the bargain. If my suit failed here, I doubt if I'd have felt anything. It was just the thought of that incredible pressure being held one millimeter away from my fragile skin by a force field that, physically speaking, isn't even there. Or so Ember told me. She might have been trying to get my goat. I mean, lines of magnetic force have no physical reality, but they're *there,* aren't they?

I kept my mind off it. Ember was there and she knew about such things.

What she couldn't adequately explain to me was why a skycycle didn't have a motor. I thought about that a lot, sitting on the saddle and pedaling my ass off with nothing to look at but Ember's silver-plated buttocks.

She had a tandem cycle, which meant four seats; two for us and two for our tagalongs. I sat behind Ember, and the tagalongs sat in two seats off to our right. Since they aped our leg movements with exactly the same force we applied, what we had was a four-human-power cycle.

"I can't figure out for the life of me," I said on our first day out, "what would have been so hard about mounting an engine on this thing and using some of the surplus power from our packs."

"Nothing hard about it, lazy," she said, without turning around. "Take my advice as a fledgling medico; this is much better for you. If you *use* the muscles you're wearing, they'll last you a lot longer. It makes you feel healthier and keeps you out of the clutches of money-grubbing medicos. I *know*. Half my work is excising fat from flabby behinds and digging varicose veins out of legs. Even out here, people don't get more than twenty years' use of their legs before they're ready for a trade-in. That's pure waste."

"I think I should have had a trade-in before we left. I'm about done in. Can't we call it a day?"

She tut-tutted, but touched a control and began spilling hot gas from the balloon over our heads. The steering vanes sticking out at our sides tilted, and we started a slow spiral to the ground.

We landed at the bottom of the bowl—my first experience with it, since all my other views of Venus had been from the air where it isn't so noticeable. I stood looking at it and scratching my head while Ember turned on the tent and turned off the balloon.

The Venusians use null fields for just about everything. Rather than try to cope with a technology that must stand up to the temperature and pressure extremes, they coat everything in a null field and let it go at that. The balloon on the cycle was nothing but a standard globular field with a discontinuity at the bottom for the air heater. The cycle body was protected with the same kind of field that Ember and I wore, the kind that follows the surface at a set distance. The tent was a hemispherical field with a flat floor.

It simplified a lot of things. Airlocks, for instance. What we did was to simply walk into the tent. Our suit fields vanished as they were absorbed into the tent field. To leave one need merely walk through the wall again, and the suit would form around you.

I plopped myself down on the floor and tried to turn my hand torch off. To my surprise, I found that it wasn't built to turn off. Ember turned on the campfire and noticed my puzzlement.

"Yes, it is wasteful," she conceded. "There's something in a Venusian that hates to turn out a light. You won't find a light switch on the entire planet. You may not believe this, but I was shocked silly a few years ago when I heard about light switches. The idea had never occurred to me. See what a provincial I am?"

That didn't sound like her. I searched her face for clues to what had brought on such a statement, but I could find nothing. She was sitting in front of the campfire with Malibu on her lap, preening her feathers.

I gestured at the fire, which was a beautifully executed holo of snapping, crackling logs with a heater concealed in the center of it.

"Isn't that an uncharacteristic touch? Why didn't you bring a fancy house, like the ones in town?"

"I like the fire. I don't like phony houses."

"Why not?"

She shrugged. She was thinking of other things. I tried another tack.

"Does your mother mind you going into the desert with strangers?"

She shot me a look I couldn't read.

"How should I know? I don't live with her. I'm emancipated. I think she's in Venusburg." I had obviously touched a tender area, so I went cautiously.

"Personality conflicts?"

She shrugged again, not wanting to get into it.

"No. Well, yes, in a way. She wouldn't emigrate from Venus. I wanted to leave and she wanted to stay. Our interests didn't coincide. So we went our own ways. I'm working my way toward passage off-planet."

"How close are you?"

"Closer than you might think." She seemed to be weighing something in her mind, sizing me up. I could hear the gears grind and the cash register bells cling as she studied my face. Then I felt the charm start up again, like the flicking of one of those nonexistent light switches.

"See, I'm as close as I've ever been to getting off Venus. In a few weeks, I'll be there. As soon as we get back with some blast jewels. Because you're going to adopt me."

I think I was getting used to her. I wasn't rocked by that, though it was nothing like what I had expected to hear. I had been thinking vaguely along the lines of blast jewels. She picks some up along with me, sells them, and buys a ticket off-planet, right?

That was silly, of course. She didn't need *me* to get blast jewels. She was the guide, not I, and it was her cycle. She could get as many jewels as she wanted, and probably already had. This scheme had to have something to do with me, personally, as I had known back in town and forgotten about. There was something she wanted from me.

"That's why you had to go with me? That's the fatal attraction? I don't understand."

"Your passport. I'm in love with your passport. On the blank labeled 'citizenship' it says 'Mars.' Under age it says, oh . . . about seventy-three." She was within a year, though I keep my appearance at about thirty.

"So?"

"So, my dear Kiku, you are visiting a planet which is groping its way into the stone age. A medieval planet, Mr. Kiku, that sets the age of majority at thirteen—a capricious and arbitrary figure, as I'm sure you'll agree. The laws of this planet state that certain rights of free citizens are withheld from minor citizens. Among these are liberty, the pursuit of happiness, and the ability *to get out of the goddam place!*" She startled me with her fury, coming so hard on the heels of her usual amusing glibness. Her fists were clenched. Malibu, sitting in her lap, looked sadly up at his friend, then over to me.

She quickly brightened and bounced up to prepare dinner. She would not respond to my questions. The subject was closed for the day.

I was ready to turn back the next day. Have you ever had stiff legs? Probably not; if you go in for that sort of thing—heavy physical labor—you are probably one of those health nuts and keep yourself in shape. I wasn't in shape, and I thought I'd die. For a panicky moment I thought I *was* dying.

Luckily, Ember had anticipated it. She knew I was a desk jockey, and she knew how pitifully under conditioned Martians tend to be. Added to the sedentary life styles of most modern people, we Martians come off even worse than the majority because Mars' gravity never gives us much of a challenge no matter how hard we try. My leg muscles were like soft noodles.

She gave me an old-fashioned massage and a new-fangled injection that killed off the accumulated poisons. In an hour I began to take a flickering interest in the trip. So she loaded me onto the cycle and we started off on another leg of the journey.

There's no way to measure the passage of time. The sun gets flatter and wider, but it's much too slow to see. Sometime that day we passed a tributary of the Reynoldswrap River. It showed up as a bright line in my right eye, as a crusted, sluggish semiglacier in my left. Molten aluminum, I was told. Malibu knew what it was, and barked plaintively for us to stop so he could go for a slide. Ember wouldn't let him.

You can't get lost on Venus, not if you can still see. The river had been visible since we left Prosperity, though I hadn't known what it was. We could still see the town behind us and the mountain range in front of us and even the desert. It was a little ways up the slope of the bowl. Ember said that meant it was still about three days journey away from us. It takes practice to judge distance. Ember kept trying to point out Venusburg, which was several thousand kilometers behind us. She said it was easily visible as a tiny point on a clear day. I never spotted it.

We talked a lot as we pedaled. There was nothing else to do and, besides, she was fun to talk to. She told me more of her plan for getting off Venus and filled my head with her naive ideas of what other planets were like.

It was a subtle selling campaign. We started off with her being the advocate for her crazy plan. At some point it evolved into an assumption. She took it as settled that I would adopt her and take her to Mars with me. I half believed it myself.

On the fourth day I began to notice that the bowl was getting higher in front of us. I didn't know what was causing it until Ember called a halt and we hung there in the air. We were facing a solid line of rock that sloped gradually upward to a point about fifty meters higher than we were.

"What's the matter?" I asked, glad of the rest.

"The mountains are higher," she said matter-of-factly. "Let's turn to the right and see if we can find a pass."

"Higher? What are you talking about?"

"Higher. You know, taller, sticking up more than they did the last time I was around, of slightly greater magnitude in elevation, bigger than—"

"I know the definition of higher," I said. "But why? Are you sure?"

"Of course I'm sure. The air heater for the balloon is going flat-out; we're as high as we can go. The last time I came through here, it was plenty to get me across. But not today."

"Why?"

"Condensation. The topography can vary quite a bit here. Certain metals and rocks are molten on Venus. They boil off on a hot day, and they can condense on the mountain tops where it's cooler. Then they melt when it warms up and flow back to the valleys."

"You mean you brought me here in the middle of winter?"

She threw me a withering glance.

"You're the one who booked passage for winter. Besides, it's night, and it's not even midnight yet. I hadn't thought the mountains would be this high for another week."

"Can't we get around?"

She surveyed the slope critically.

"There's a permanent pass about five hundred kilometers to the east. But that would take us another week. Do you want to?"

"What's the alternative?"

"Parking the cycle here and going on foot. The desert is just over this range. With any luck we'll see our first jewels today."

I was realizing that I knew far too little about Venus to make a good decision. I had finally admitted to myself that I was lucky to have Ember along to keep me out of trouble.

"We'll do what you think best."

"All right. Turn hard left and we'll park."

We tethered the cycle by a long tungsten-alloy rope. The reason for that, I learned, was to prevent it from being buried in case there was more condensation while we were gone. It floated at the end of the cable with its heaters going full blast. And we started up the mountain.

Fifty meters doesn't sound like much. And it's not, on level ground. Try it sometime on a seventy-five degree slope. Luckily for us, Ember had seen this possibility and come prepared with alpine equipment. She sank pitons here and there and kept us together with ropes and pulleys. I followed her lead, staying slightly behind her tagalong. It was uncanny how that thing followed her up, placing its feet in precisely the spots she had stepped. Behind me, my tagalong was doing the same thing. Then there was Malibu, almost running along, racing back to see how we were doing, going to the top and chattering about what was on the other side.

I don't suppose it would have been much for a mountain climber. Personally I'd have preferred to slide on down the mountainside and call it quits. I would have, but Ember just kept going up. I don't think I've ever been so tired as the moment when we reached the top and stood looking over the desert.

Ember pointed ahead of us.

"There's one of the jewels going off now," she said.

"Where?" I asked, barely interested. I could see nothing.

"You missed it. It's down lower. They don't form up this high. Don't worry, you'll see more by and by."

And down we went. This wasn't too hard. Ember set the example by sitting down in a smooth place and letting go. Malibu was close behind her, squealing happily as he bounced and rolled down the slippery rock face. I saw Ember hit a bump and go flying in the air to come down on her head. Her suit was already stiffened. She continued to bounce her way down, frozen in a sitting position.

I followed them down in the same way. I didn't much care for the idea of bouncing around like that, but I cared even less for a slow, painful descent. It wasn't too bad. You don't feel much after your suit freezes in impact mode. It expands slightly away from your skin and becomes harder than metal, cushioning you from anything but the most severe blows that could bounce your brain against your skull and give you internal injuries. We never got going nearly fast enough for that.

Ember helped me up at the bottom after my suit unfroze. She looked like she had enjoyed the ride. I hadn't. One bounce seemed to have impacted my back slightly. I didn't tell her about it but just started off after her, feeling a pain with each step.

"Where on Mars do you live?" she asked, brightly.

"Uh? Oh, at Coprates. That's on the northern slope of the Canyon."

"Yes, I know. Tell me more about it. Where will we live? Do you have a surface apartment, or are you stuck down in the underground? I can hardly wait to see the place."

She was getting on my nerves. Maybe it was just the lower-back pain.

"What makes you think you're going with me?"

"But of course you're taking me back. You said, just—"

"I said nothing of the sort. If I had a recorder I could prove it to you. No, our conversations over the last days have been a series of monologues. You tell me what fun you're going to have when we get to Mars, and I just grunt something. That's because I haven't the heart, or haven't *had* the heart, to tell you what a hare-brained scheme you're talking about."

I think I had finally managed to drive a barb into her. At any rate, she didn't say anything for a while. She was realizing that she had overextended herself and was counting the spoils before the battle was won.

"What's hare-brained about it?" she said at last.

"Just everything."

"No, come on, tell me."

"What makes you think I want a daughter?"

She seemed relieved. "Oh, don't worry about that. I won't be any trouble. As soon as we land, you can file dissolution papers. I won't contest it. In fact, I can sign a binding agreement not to contest anything before you even adopt me. This is strictly a business arrangement, Kiku. You don't have to worry about being a mother to me. I don't need one. I'll—"

"What makes you think it's just a business arrangement to *me?*" I exploded. "Maybe I'm old-fashioned. Maybe I've got funny ideas. But I won't enter into an adoption of convenience. I've already had my one child, and I was a good parent. I won't adopt you just to get you to Mars. That's my final word."

She was studying my face. I think she decided I meant it.

"I can offer you twenty thousand Marks."

I swallowed hard.

"Where did you get that kind of money?"

"I told you I've been soaking the good people of Prosperity. What the hell is there for me to spend it on out here? I've been putting it away for an emergency like this. Up against an unfeeling Neanderthal with funny ideas about right and wrong, who—"

"That's enough of that." I'm ashamed to say that I was tempted. It's unpleasant to find that what you had thought of as moral scruples suddenly seem not quite so important in the face of a stack of money. But I was helped along by my backache and the nasty mood it had given me.

"You think you can buy me. Well, I'm not for sale. I told you, I think it's wrong."

"Well *damn* you, Kiku, damn you to hell." She stomped her foot hard on the ground, and her tagalong redoubled the gesture. She was going to go on damning me, but we were blasted by an explosion as her foot hit the ground.

It had been quiet before, as I said. There's no wind, no animals, hardly anything to make a sound on Venus. But when a sound gets going, watch out. That thick atmosphere is murder. I thought my head was going to come off. The sound waves battered against our suits, partially stiffening them. The only thing that saved us from deafness was the millimeter of low-pressure air between the suit field and our eardrums. It cushioned the shock enough that we were left with just a ringing in our ears.

"What was that?" I asked.

Ember sat down on the ground. She hung her head, uninterested in anything but her own disappointment.

"Blast jewel," she said. "Over that way." She pointed, and I could see a dull glowing spot about a kilometer off. There were dozens of smaller points of light—infralight—scattered around the spot.

"You mean you set it off just by stomping the ground?"

She shrugged. "They're unstable. They're full of nitroglycerine, as near as anyone can figure."

"Well, let's go pick up the pieces."

"Go ahead." She was going limp on me. And she stayed that way, no matter how I cajoled her. By the time I finally got her on her feet, the glowing spots were gone, cooled off. We'd never find them now. She wouldn't talk to me as we continued down into the valley. All the rest of the day we were accompanied by distant gunshots.

We didn't talk much the next day. She tried several times to reopen the negotiations, but I made it clear that my mind was made up. I pointed out to her that I had rented her cycle and services according to the terms she had set. Absolutely free, she had said, except for consumables, which I had paid for. There had been no mention of adoption. If there had, I assured her, I would have turned her down just as I was doing now. Maybe I even believed it.

That was during the short time the morning after our argument when it seemed like she was having no more to do with the trip. She just sat there in the tent while I made breakfast. When it came time to go, she pouted and said she wasn't going looking for blast jewels, that she'd just as soon stay right there or turn around.

After I pointed out our verbal contract, she reluctantly got up. She didn't like it, but honored her word.

Hunting blast jewels proved to be a big anticlimax. I'd had visions of scouring the countryside for days. Then the exciting moment of finding one. Eureka! I'd have howled. The reality was nothing like that. Here's how you hunt blast jewels: you stomp down hard on the ground, wait a few seconds, then move on and stomp again. When you see and hear an explosion, you simply walk to where it occurred and pick them up. They're scattered all over, lit up in the infrared bands from the heat of the explosion. They might as well have had neon arrows flashing over them. Big adventure.

When we found one, we'd pick it up and pop it into a cooler mounted on our tagalongs. They are formed by the pressure of the explosion, but certain parts of them are volatile at Venus temperatures. These elements will boil out and leave you with a grayish powder in about three hours if you don't cool them down. I don't know why they lasted as long as they did. They were considerably hotter than the air when we picked them up. So I thought they should have melted right off.

Ember said it was the impaction of the crystalline lattice that gave the jewels the temporary strength to outlast the temperature. Things behave differently in the temperature and pressure extremes of Venus. As they cooled off, the lattice was weakened and a progressive decay set in. That's why it was important to get them as soon as possible after the explosion to get unflawed gems.

We spent the whole day at that.

Eventually we collected about ten kilos of gems, ranging from pea size up to a few the size of an apple.

I sat beside the campfire and examined them that night. Night by my watch, anyway. Another thing I was beginning to miss was the twenty-five-hour cycle of night and day. And while I was at it, moons. It would have cheered me up considerably to spot Diemos or Phobos that night. But the sun just squatted up there in the horizon, moving slowly to the north in preparation for its transition to the morning sky.

The jewels were beautiful, I'll say that much for them. They were a wine-red color, tinged with brown. But when the light caught them right, there was no predicting what I might see. Most of the raw gems were coated with a dull substance that hid their full glory. I experimented with chipping some of them. What was left behind when I flaked off the patina was a slippery surface that sparkled even in candlelight. Ember showed me how to suspend them from a string and strike them. Then they would ring like tiny bells, and every once in a while one would shed all its imperfections and emerge as a perfect eight-sided equilateral.

I was cooking for myself that day, Ember had cooked from the first, but she no longer seemed interested in buttering me up.

"I hired on as a guide," she pointed out, with considerable venom. "Webster's defines guide as—"

"I know what a guide is."

"—and it says nothing about cooking. Will you marry me?"

"No." I wasn't even surprised.

"Same reasons?"

"Yes. I won't enter into an agreement like that lightly. Besides, you're too young."

"Legal age is twelve. I'll be twelve in one week."

"That's too young. On Mars you must be fourteen."

"What a dogmatist. You're not kidding, are you? Is it really fourteen?"

That's typical of her lack of knowledge of the place she was trying so hard to get to. I don't know where she got her ideas about Mars. I finally concluded that she made them up whole in her daydreams.

We ate the meal I prepared in silence, toying with our collection of jewels. I estimated that I had about a thousand Marks worth of uncut stones. And I was getting tired of the Venusian bush. I figured on spending another day collecting, then heading back for the cycle. It would probably be a relief for both of us. Ember could start laying traps for the next stupid tourist to reach town, or even head for Venusburg and try in earnest.

When I thought of that, I wondered why she was still out here. If she had the money to pay the tremendous bribe she had offered me, why wasn't she in town where the tourists were as thick as flies? I was going to ask her that. But she came up to me and sat down very close.

"Would you like to make love?" she asked.

I'd had about enough inducements. I snorted, got up, and walked through the wall of the tent.

Once outside, I regretted it. My back was hurting something terrible, and I belatedly realized that my inflatable mattress would not go through the wall of the tent. If I got it through somehow, it would only burn up. But I couldn't back out after walking out like that. I felt committed. Maybe I couldn't think straight because of the back-

ache; I don't know. Anyway, I picked out a soft-looking spot of
ground and lay down.

I can't say it was all that soft.

I came awake in the haze of pain. I knew, without trying, that if I
moved I'd get a knife in my back. Naturally I wasn't anxious to try.

My arm was lying on something soft. I moved my head—
confirming my suspicions about the knife—and saw that it was
Ember. She was asleep, lying on her back. Malibu was curled up in
her arm.

She was a silver-plated doll, with her mouth open and a look of
relaxed vulnerability on her face. I felt a smile growing on my lips,
just like the ones she had coaxed out of me back in Prosperity. I
wondered why I'd been treating her so bad. At least it seemed to me
that morning that I'd been treating her bad. Sure, she'd used me and
tricked me and seemed to want to use me again. But what had she
hurt? Who was suffering for it? I couldn't think of anyone at the moment. I resolved to apologize to her when she woke up and try to
start over again. Maybe we could even reach some sort of accommo-
dation on this adoption business.

And while I was at it, maybe I could unbend enough to ask her to
take a look at my back. I hadn't even mentioned it to her, probably
for fear of getting deeper in her debt. I was sure she wouldn't have
taken payment for it in cash. She preferred flesh.

I was about to awaken her, but I happened to glance on my other
side. There was something there. I almost didn't recognize it for what
it was.

It was three meters away, growing from the cleft of two rocks. It
was globular, half a meter across, and glowing a dull-reddish color.
It looked like a soft gelatin.

It was a blast jewel, before the blast.

I was afraid to talk, then remembered that talking would not affect
the atmosphere around me and could not set off the explosion. I had
a radio transmitter in my throat and a receiver in my ear. That's how
you talk on Venus; you subvocalize and people can hear you.

Moving very carefully, I reached over and gently touched Ember
on the shoulder.

She came awake quietly, stretched, and started to get up.

"Don't move," I said, in what I hoped was a whisper. It's hard to do when you're subvocalizing, but I wanted to impress on her that something was wrong.

She came alert, but didn't move.

"Look over to your right. Move very slowly. Don't scrape against the ground or anything. I don't know what to do."

She looked, said nothing.

"You're not alone, Kiku," she finally whispered. "This is one I never heard of."

"How did it happen?"

"It must have formed during the night. No one knows much about how they form or how long it takes. No one's ever been closer than about five hundred meters to one. They always explode before you can get that close. Even the vibrations from the prop of a cycle will set them off before you get close enough to see them."

"So what do we do?"

She looked at me. It's hard to read expressions on a reflective face, but I think she was scared. I know I was.

"I'd say sit tight."

"How dangerous is this?"

"Brother. I don't know. There's going to be quite a bang when that monster goes off. Our suits will protect us from most of it. But it's going to lift us and accelerate us *very* fast. That kind of sharp acceleration can mess up your insides. I'd say a concussion at the very least."

I gulped. "Then—"

"Just sit tight. I'm thinking."

So was I. I was frozen there with a hot knife somewhere in my back. I knew I'd have to squirm sometime.

The damn thing was moving.

I blinked, afraid to rub my eyes and looked again. No, it wasn't. Not on the outside anyway. It was more like the movement you can see inside a living cell beneath a microscope. Internal flows, exchanges of fluids from here to there. I watched it and was hypnotized.

There were worlds in the jewel. There was ancient Barsoom of my childhood fairy tales; there was Middle Earth with brooding castles and sentient forests. The jewel was a window into something unimaginable, a place where there were no questions and no emotions but a vast awareness. It was dark and wet without menace. It was growing, and yet complete as it came into being. It was bigger than this ball of hot mud called Venus and had its roots down in the core of the planet. There was no corner of the universe that it did not reach.

It was aware of me. I felt it touch me and felt no surprise. It examined me in passing but was totally uninterested. I posed no questions for it, whatever it was. It already knew me and had always known me.

I felt an overpowering attraction. The thing was exerting no influence on me; the attraction was a yearning within me. I was reaching for a completion that the jewel possessed and I knew I could never have. Life would always be a series of mysteries for me. For the jewel, there was nothing but awareness. Awareness of everything.

I wrenched my eyes away at the last possible instant. I was covered in sweat, and I knew I'd look back in a moment. It was the most beautiful thing I will ever see.

"Kiku, listen to me."

"What?" I remembered Ember as from a huge distance.

"Listen. Wake up. Don't look at that thing."

"Ember, do you see anything? Do you feel something?"

"I see something. I . . . I don't want to talk about it. I can't talk about it. Wake up, Kiku, and don't look back."

I felt like I was already a pillar of salt; so why not look back? I knew that my life would never be quite like it had been. It was like some sort of involuntary religious conversion, like I knew what the universe was for all of a sudden. The universe was a beautiful silk-lined box for the display of the jewel I had just beheld.

"Kiku, that thing should have gone off. We shouldn't be here. I moved when I woke up. I tried to sneak up on one before and got five hundred meters away from it. I set my foot down soft enough to walk on water, and it blew. So this thing can't be here."

"That's nice," I said. "How do we cope with the fact that it is here?"

"All right, all right, it is here. But it must not be finished. It must not have enough nitro in it yet to blow up. Maybe we can get away."

I looked back at it, then away again. It was like my eyes were welded to it with elastic bands; they'd stretch enough to let me turn away, but they kept pulling me back.

"I'm not sure I want to."

"I know," she whispered. "I . . . hold on, don't look back. We have to get away."

"Listen," I said, looking at her with an act of will. "Maybe one of us can get away. Maybe both. But it's more important that you not be injured. If I'm hurt, you can maybe fix me up. If you're hurt, you'll probably die, and if we're both hurt, we're dead."

"Yeah. So?"

"So, I am the closest to the jewel. You can start backing away from it first, and I'll follow you. I'll shield you from the worst of the blast, if it goes off. How does that sound?"

"Not too good." But she thought it over and could see no flaws in my reasoning. I think she didn't relish being the protected instead of the heroine. Childish, but natural. She proved her maturity by bowing to the inevitable.

"All right. I'll try to get ten meters from it. I'll let you know when I'm there, and you can move back. I think we can survive it at ten meters."

"Twenty."

"But . . . oh, all right. Twenty. Good luck, Kiku. I think I love you." She paused. "Uh, Kiku?"

"What is it? You should get moving. We don't know how long it'll stay stable."

"All right. But I have to say this. My offer last night, the one that got you so angry?"

"Yeah?"

"Well, it wasn't meant as a bribe. I mean, like the twenty thousand Marks. I just . . . well, I don't know much about that yet. I guess it was the wrong time?"

"Yeah, but don't worry about it. Just get moving."

She did, a centimeter at a time. It was lucky that neither of us had to worry about holding our breath. I think the tension would have been unbearable.

And I looked back. I couldn't help it. I was in the sanctuary of a cosmic church when I heard her calling me. I don't know what sort of power she used to reach me where I was. She was crying.

"Kiku, please listen to me."

"Huh? Oh, what is it?"

She sobbed in relief. "I've been calling you for an hour. *Please* come on. Over here. I'm back far enough."

My head was foggy. "Oh, Ember, there's no hurry. I want to look at it just another minute. Hang on."

"*No!* If you don't start moving right this minute, I'm coming back and I'll drag you out."

"You can't do . . . Oh. All right, I'm coming." I looked over at her sitting on her knees. Malibu was beside her. The little otter was staring in my direction. I looked at her and took a sliding step, scuttling on my back. My back was not something to think about.

I got two meters back, then three. I had to stop to rest. I looked at the jewel, then back at Ember. It was hard to tell which drew me the strongest. I must have reached a balance point. I could have gone either way.

Then a small silver streak came at me, running as fast as it could go. It reached me and dived across.

"*Malibu!*" Ember screamed. I turned. The otter seemed happier than I ever saw him, even in the waterslide in town. He leaped, right at the jewel. . . .

Regaining consciousness was a very gradual business. There was no dividing line between different states of awareness for two reasons: I was deaf, and I was blind. So I cannot say when I went from dreams to reality; the blend was too uniform, there wasn't enough change to notice.

I don't remember learning that I was deaf or blind. I don't remember learning the hand-spelling language that Ember talked to me with. The first rational moment that I can recall as such was when Ember was telling me her plans to get back to Prosperity.

I told her to do whatever she felt best, that she was in complete control. I was desolated to realize that I was not where I had thought I was. My dreams had been of Barsoom. I thought I had become a blast jewel and had been waiting in a sort of detached ecstasy for the moment of explosion.

She operated on my left eye and managed to restore some vision. I could see things that were a meter from my face, hazily. Everything else was shadows. At least she was able to write things on sheets of paper and hold them up for me to see. It made things quicker. I learned that she was deaf, too. And Malibu was dead. Or might be. She had put him in the cooler and thought she might be able to patch him up when she got back. If not, she could always make another otter.

I told her about my back. She was shocked to hear that I had hurt it on the slide down the mountain, but she had sense enough not to scold me about it. It was short work to fix it up. Nothing but a bruised disc, she told me.

It would be tedious to describe all of our trip back. It was difficult, because neither of us knew much about blindness. But I was able to adjust pretty quickly. Being led by the hand was easy enough, and I stumbled only rarely after the first day. On the second day we scaled the mountains, and my tagalong malfunctioned. Ember discarded it and we traded off with hers. We could only do it when I was sitting still, as hers was made for a much shorter person. If I tried to walk with it, it quickly fell behind and jerked me off balance.

Then it was a matter of being set on the cycle and pedaling. There was nothing to do but pedal. I missed the talking we did on the way out. I missed the blast jewel. I wondered if I'd ever adjust to life without it.

But the memory had faded when we arrived back at Prosperity. I don't think the human mind can really contain something of that magnitude. It was slipping away from me by the hour, like a dream fades away in the morning. I found it hard to remember what it was that was so great about the experience. To this day, I can't really tell about it except in riddles. I'm left with shadows. I feel like an earthworm who has been shown a sunset and has no place to store the memory.

Back in town it was a simple matter for Ember to restore our hearing. She just didn't happen to be carrying any spare eardrums in her first-aid kit.

"It was an oversight," she told me. "Looking back, it seems obvious that the most likely injury from a blast jewel would be burst eardrums. I just didn't think."

"Don't worry about it. You did beautifully."

She grinned at me. "Yes, I did, didn't I?"

The vision was a larger problem. She didn't have any spare eyes and no one in town was willing to sell one of theirs at any price. She gave me one of hers as a temporary measure. She kept her infraeye and took to wearing an eye patch over the other. It made her look bloodthirsty. She told me to buy another at Venusburg, as our blood types weren't much of a match. My body would reject it in about three weeks.

The day came for the weekly departure of the blimp to Last

Chance. We were sitting in her workshop, facing each other with our legs crossed and the pile of blast jewels between us.

They looked awful. Oh, they hadn't changed. We had even polished them up until they sparkled three times as much as they had back in the firelight of our tent. But now we could see them for the rotten, yellowed, broken fragments of bone that they were. We had told no one what we had seen out in the Fahrenheit Desert. There was no way to check on it, and all our experience had been purely subjective. Nothing that would stand up in a laboratory. We were the only ones who knew their true nature. Probably we would always remain the only ones. What could we tell anyone?

"What do you think will happen?" I asked.

She looked at me keenly. "I think you already know that."

"Yeah." Whatever they were, however they survived and reproduced, the one fact we knew for sure was that they couldn't survive within a hundred kilometers of a city. Once there had been blast jewels in the very spot where we were sitting. And humans do expand. Once again, we would not know what we were destroying.

I couldn't keep the jewels. I felt like a ghoul. I tried to give them to Ember, but she wouldn't have them either.

"Shouldn't we tell someone?" Ember asked.

"Sure. Tell anyone you want. Don't expect people to start tiptoeing until you can prove something to them. Maybe not even then."

"Well, it looks like I'm going to spend a few more years tiptoeing. I find I just can't bring myself to stomp on the ground."

I was puzzled. "Why? You'll be on Mars. I don't think the vibrations will travel that far."

She stared at me. "What's this?"

There was a brief confusion; then I found myself apologizing profusely to her, and she was laughing and telling me what a dirty rat I was, then taking it back and saying I could play that kind of trick on her anytime I wanted.

It was a misunderstanding. I honestly thought I had told her about my change of heart while I was deaf and blind. It must have been a dream, because she hadn't gotten it and had assumed the answer was a permanent no. She had said nothing about adoption since the explosion.

"I couldn't bring myself to pester you about it anymore, after what you did for me," she said, breathless with excitement. "I owe you a lot, maybe my life. And I used you badly when you first got here."

I denied it, and told her I had thought she was not talking about it because she thought it was in the bag.

"When did you change your mind?" she asked.

I thought back. "At first I thought it was while you were caring for me when I was so helpless. Now I can recall when it was. It was shortly after I walked out of the tent for that last night on the ground."

She couldn't find anything to say about that. She just beamed at me. I began to wonder what sort of papers I'd be signing when we got to Venusburg: adoption, or marriage contract.

I didn't worry about it. It's uncertainties like that which make life interesting. We got up together, leaving the pile of jewels on the floor. Walking softly, we hurried out to catch the blimp.

From Competition 6:   Bawdy SF Limericks

Our robot detective, Daneel,
Has oft been mistaken for real,
  A lass on Aurora,
  Who offered her flora,
Learned all about case-hardened steel.
(*Apologies to the Good Doctor*)

—*Janice W. Leffingwell*

An ecdysiast on the Corso
Has a topological torso.
  Her Moebius strip
  Is well worth the trip
But her trefoil-like grinds are much more so.
(*C. M. Kornbluth's "The Unfortunate Topologist"*)

—*Margaret O. Ablitt*

Liz Hufford is in her mid-twenties and has worked as an artist-illus-trator and a speech professor. This was only her second story for *F&SF* (and, we believe, only her third published piece), but it is a perfect gem of an idea, cleanly and faultlessly executed.

This Offer Expires

by LIZ HUFFORD

The old store on Lesort Street had a sign in the window—TWELVE FOR ONE. It was remarkable that Welby Whaning noticed it. True, Welby passed the store every day, but it was characteristic of his life that he missed a few things. He walked with his head bowed, his shoulders hunched, and his coat held close around his neck. He took only hesitant glances at the world around him.

But even if Welby had been exceptionally alert, it would have been remarkable that he saw the sign. There were so many of them. Soft-drink advertisements, cigarette signs, and specials-of-the-week covered the two large windows of the store. Even the narrow glass door was placarded. The new sign was small and it sat in the left window. Still, one thing Welby tried never to overlook was a bargain.

What could one buy twelve for a dollar anymore? He pondered the sign as he passed. Only the appearance of the store prevented him from inquiring immediately. The store was grimy and dim. Though he had passed it every workday for twelve years, he had never once thought of entering. He was not at all sure he would want whatever was twelve for a dollar.

It was Friday when Welby Whaning decided to enter the store. The day was fair and still, and Welby's grip on the collar of his coat was relaxed. He had been paid and the check reflected the annual pay hike. It was a day when even Welby could be adventurous.

Twelve for a dollar. He pushed the door open. The uncovered plank floor creaked with his weight as the door closed behind him. He stood still a moment allowing his eyes to adjust to the darkness: the signs permitted only fragmented rays of sunlight. As soon as his vision cleared, he was mortified. The store was worse than he had imagined. To his left were stacks and racks of comics and lurid magazines; and some of the disgusting things were obviously secondhand. The middle counter displayed all manner of naked maidens, crocodiles, and little boys who protruded anatomically when the attached rubber ball was squeezed. There were playing cards both garish and vulgar and all manner of practical jokes. To the right of the store was a collection of clothing, appliances, and old furniture. In the back were shelves of groceries and a refrigerator. Whatever was twelve for a dollar, Welby was sure he wasn't interested. He turned to leave when a voice inquired, "May I help you?"

Welby was not prepared for the dark, voluptuous woman who faced him.

"No, thank you," he said. "I was just looking."

She smiled, her full lips curling provocatively.

"You seem like you're trying to avoid looking," she said.

"Oh," he said, laughing nervously and pulling his coat more closely around his neck, "actually I came to inquire about the sign— twelve for a dollar."

"TWELVE FOR ONE," the woman corrected him. Then she walked to the back of the store.

Welby waited for a moment or two. He expected the woman to return with whatever it was that was twelve for one. The woman did not come. He peered back into the store and saw her sitting by the cash register. She was reading and obviously had no intention of returning. He could have left the shop then, but he did not. Instead he reached for a pack of playing cards. Solitaire. He avoided even touching the nude decks. He walked back to the register and laid the box on the counter.

The woman turned to him. "Will that be all?"

Welby cleared his throat. "The sign—TWELVE FOR ONE?"

"Oh, yes," she said, "it's a special for our preferred customers."

"Oh, I see," he said, "a special for your regulars, eh?"

"I said preferred, not regular," she replied.

Welby was warm and uncomfortable again. He believed she was flirting with him.

The woman placed the cards in a bag, accepted his money, and returned his change.

"Shops down here," she said, "I mean in the center of town, we have to make some allowances." She nodded at the paraphernalia at the front of the store. "Sometimes we take merchandise if somebody can't pay his bill. We resell what we can, and the rest just sits around here."

"I see," Welby said, "but the twelve for one?"

"Simple," the woman said, "You bring us twelve items and we give you one."

"What?" Welby said.

"Twelve for one," the woman said.

"Why that's obnoxious," Welby said indignantly. "Someone should turn you in to the better business bureau."

The woman returned to her stool and book. Without lifting her eyes she passed Welby a slip of paper.

"It's the number of the better business bureau," she said.

"Huh," Welby said feeling more and more uncomfortable. "Wait a minute, is this some kind of joke?" He waved his arm at the counter of practical jokes. He looked for a hidden camera. He flashed an inane smile.

The woman looked up at him with her slow smile. Welby's warmth began to centralize. He must leave the store.

"See here," he said, pulling a pack of cigarettes from his pocket and counting out twelve. "Here are twelve cigarettes. Twelve for one."

The woman reached inside the low neckline of her dress and pulled out a cigarette.

"Twelve for one," she said.

Welby was sure he did not want to touch the thing. The woman had a certain attractiveness, but the cigarette, it would have been pressed against her body. Still, he found himself clutching it as he walked down the aisle of the shop.

"Twelve for one," the woman said as the door shut behind him.

What an experience he had had, Welby thought as he emerged from the store. He looked at the cigarette in his hand. What could this be—TWELVE FOR ONE?

He met the bus in front of the park and caught his breath on the ride out to his apartment. As he relaxed against the bus seat, he examined the cigarette. A thought occurred to him. Dope. He had read about this drug thing. Surely that was it. He had stumbled upon their code and gotten himself a marijuana cigarette. Or what was it they called it? A reefer. He thrust it into his pocket. If he was right, it wasn't wise to examine it on the bus. He would wait until he reached the apartment.

Welby slowly turned the cigarette. There was no trademark, but the tobacco and paper looked conventional. There was one way to find out. He had already locked and bolted the apartment door. He took the cigarette and a pack of matches into the bathroom. He sat on the closed toilet and pushed the door to. Then he locked it. With trembling hands he lighted the cigarette. He had some difficulty, as he was afraid to inhale. Once it was lit, he forced himself to take a substantial puff. It was marvelous. A well-defined but mild flavor, a wonderful aroma. He took another drag. He was very relaxed. The room became pastel; his vision came in swirls. He quickly put the cigarette out.

It was a narcotic: he had happened on the underground. The idea both terrified and delighted him. But why would they give him dope for twelve cigarettes? It became clear in an instant. They meant to addict him. Later they would charge him exorbitant prices to maintain his habit. He looked at the cigarette; he hoped no harm had been done. He waited to see if he was able to resist the cigarette. Though he felt no need to relight it, neither did he wish to part with it. He thought of the dark woman and her dark plan for him.

On Monday morning Welby regretfully passed the store. It could wait, he thought, it could wait until afternoon. Still, he was eager to confront the woman with his knowledge of her scheme.

The day was tedious. When the clock finally read 4:00, Welby sprinted from the office. When he reached the store, he walked boldly in. The woman was sitting on the stool by the register. The heels of her shoes were hooked on the spindles of the stool; her legs were wide apart.

Welby took a deep breath and moved toward her.

"I know what your game is," he confided masterfully.

The woman looked up. The black matt of her hair fell back to reveal her face. Her unnerving sullen smile flashed at him.

"Then you're the first," she said. She bent back to her reading.

Welby pulled out the cigarette, carefully wrapped in a white hanky.

"I know what this is. I know what you're doing here," he said.

"Another question I've never been able to answer myself," the woman replied. This time she didn't even look up.

"I have to tell the police," Welby said nervously. "There may be a reward."

The girl handed him a slip of paper.

It's the number," she said.

Welby stood with the paper in his hand, shifting his weight from one foot to the other.

"This is a narcotic," he said unwrapping the cigarette and waving it before her eyes. "I cannot fail to report this to the proper authorities."

"Let me save you the trouble, mister," she said. "That stuff won't test for anything."

"It's not narcotic?" he asked.

"You liked it, huh?" she said.

"It doesn't matter if I did or didn't. Anyway," he said, "if it's not illegal I'm keeping it."

He resolutely stuffed the cigarette back into his jacket. The woman was still looking at him.

"Well," he said, "as long as I'm here, what have you got today?"

"What have you got?" she said. She had an unsettling way of asking questions.

"What have I got?" he said to himself, patting his pockets.

"Twelve for one, eh?" Change. He dug into his pockets and produced twelve pennies. "Not that I'm a hoarder," he said. He had two coffee cans of pennies at home.

"Twelve for one," the woman smiled.

This time she reached into her shoe and pulled out a penny. She placed in his hand and returned to her reading.

"Oh, I see," Welby said. "I get one of whatever I give you."

"Looks like it," she said.

"Is it any good?" Welby asked, referring to her book.

"I don't get time to find out," she said.

Welby turned and walked toward the door.

"Twelve for one," a voice called from the back of the store. He nodded and pushed open the door.

Well, what have we here, thought Welby, turning the penny in his hand? He could scarcely imagine that it was a narcotic. He wiped it against his coat and tried to bend it in his hands. Maybe it's a new penny, he thought. But it was not. 1955.

Welby reached the park and caught his bus. Somewhow he felt no safer examining the penny on the bus than he had the cigarette. He pushed the coin deep in his pocket. It felt warm against his leg.

When he reached the apartment, he hung up his outer garments, fixed a cup of coffee, and retired to his reclining chair. He drew the cigarette from his jacket pocket. Tonight he would smoke the rest of it. It was as delightful and, therefore, as frightening as he remembered. But this time he smoked it all, surrendering himself to the experience. As the pastel, swirling world opened and closed around him, he dug out the penny from his pocket and wiped it off again. Then he held it to the light. It was a misprint; there was a double image of Lincoln. Welby looked around the room. There were double images of many things. It's the cigarette, he thought, as he dozed off.

Welby overslept the next morning. He hurried through his morning routine to catch the bus. Only then did he look at the penny again. It was still a double print. At lunchtime he looked in the yellow pages for the nearest coin dealer and took a taxi to the address. The man looked at the coin through a magnifying glass and offered him a hundred dollars. Welby declined the offer. He wished he hadn't smoked the cigarette.

Welby returned to work, but his mind was elsewhere. What was happening to him? He gave the woman twelve cigarettes and she gave him one marvelous one. He gave her twelve pennies and she gave him a valuable coin. Welby saw a pattern; he was that kind of incisive thinker.

But then Welby was thirty-eight years old. He had spent his life waiting for his big break. It had never come, or, more likely, he had failed to notice it. Welby was determined to profit from this experience.

Immediately after work he hurried to the store. The door was locked. He knocked loudly, but to no avail. The store was closed.

That night he sat in his apartment deliberating his next action. He could continue taking coins, of course. That would supplement his income handsomely. But Welby wanted to maximize the opportunity. He thought of taking cheap abstract paintings and receiving a

Picasso. He thought of taking costume jewelry and receiving a glittering diamond. He thought of buying some junked cars and returning with a Rolls.

He took the early bus the next day, but the store was not yet open. All morning he sat at his desk realizing with disgust how odious his employment was. At lunchtime he tried the store again with no success. For the first time he feigned illness and left the office at two thirty. He sat on the store step until 7:00 but no one came. When he stood up to catch the last bus, he noticed that the sign was gone.

Lost opportunities were not uncommon to Welby. Though this one hit him hard, he came to accept it. He inquired as to the owners and the closing, but he found no answers. He passed the store twice each day, and after a while he didn't try the door anymore. But he refused to part with the twelve imitation diamonds which he carried in his coat pocket. When his coat wore thin around the collar, he ordered a new one. Into it he transferred the jewels. It was this coat that felt heavy on Welby's shoulders as he walked from the office one spring afternoon.

The store on Lesort Street looked different. For a moment Welby couldn't figure out why. Then his heart leaped to his throat; the sign was up. Welby felt for the jewels in his pocket. Trembling, he pushed open the door. He strained his eyes to see in the dim interior. It was just the same: dirty magazines, stupid gags, junk, and groceries. And in the back the woman sat on her stool. Welby moved toward her. When she saw him she smiled, rose, and disappeared out a door in the back. It was then Welby tripped over the other man.

He was a short fat man wearing a plaid jacket and plaid pants. Welby pushed him aside as he pursued the woman.

"Twelve for one," Welby called cheerily, "twelve for one."

The woman did not respond. When he reached the door, he tried it, but it held fast. He knocked, but there was no answer.

"I'm going to wait until she comes back," a shrill voice told Welby. Whaning turned, expecting to see the plaid man. Instead he faced a thin, white-faced man in a gray coat.

"See what I've brought," the man continued, pointing to a stack of books nearby. "I'm a book collector. Dear me, but I would love an original Dickens." He looked around hopefully, as if some unseen presence might hear his request.

Welby was at once uncomfortable. He turned and looked about the store. His eyes were now accustomed to the uncertain light. He saw the fat plaid man looking at him. A man in a bow tie bent over the counter of practical jokes. Welby counted the men in the store. There were eleven of them and himself.

He swallowed hard and drew his coat close around his neck. He took long, determined strides until he reached the front door. He gave it a firm push, but the door held fast. The man by the appliances began laughing. Welby placed his shoulder against the door and pushed with all his weight. It did not weaken. Then he noticed the window: the sign was gone.

He went to the window. Looking out between the signs he saw some passers-by. He pounded on the window to attract their attention. They did not notice him. He was hollering now, and the other men clustered near him. They stood silently holding their books and coins and paintings.

"It doesn't seem to help," the man in the gray coat whispered pathetically.

Welby ignored him. His eye to the glass, he saw a young woman standing by the curb. He screamed at the top of his lungs and flailed his fists against the glass. Finally she saw him. She walked to the window.

"Call the police," he implored. "We'RE LOCKED IN." It was then he recognized her: the woman from the store. She pressed her hand to her lips and then placed it against the windowpane.

It was then that the chauffeured Silvercloud pulled up at the curb. The young man who emerged from it was incredibly handsome. His tailored clothes accentuated a superb physique. In his left hand he carried a brief case and a bouquet of flowers.

"There you are, love," he said in his deep, well-modulated voice. He took the woman's hand and led her smiling to the car.

F&SF ran a films column briefly in the late 1950s and then dropped it somewhere between *Curucu, Beast of the Amazon* and *Abbott and Costello Meet the Sky Marshal of the Universe.* In the late 1960s Stanley Kubrick's production of *2001: A Space Odyssey* seemed to mark the beginning of a better era for the sf movie, and we reinstated the films column. It has been in the capable hands of Baird Searles since then. Many of our readers think Mr. Searles is too tough on most movies, but here he's in a fine mood as he picks the ten best fantasy and sf films ever!

The Fantastic Ten

BAIRD SEARLES

I've been writing for this magazine for nearly a decade now, and it's been almost always edifying. But I must admit that there's been one frustration, one thing I haven't been able to do. It's the action which my colleagues on more general media take once a year—making a ten best list—and it's the only thing I really envy them for (except the ease with which the better known ones get invited to screenings). Good Lord, there have been years when I've had barely ten movies in this field to talk about at all, much less the ten best!

Since this particular column is perforce less immediate than most of those I do, I am going to indulge myself with a ten best list. And to really stretch it, it will be a ten best films in the field ever. Presumptuous, you say? Certainly, but on the other hand, you're at perfect liberty to do the same thing. I've emphasized before, and will continue to do so, that a critic is but a single voice—an educated one, hopefully—which the educated aficionado will use as a guide instead of an arbiter.

First the ground rules. I have included only films made since the advent of sound. I feel that silent movies were almost a separate art form, one which I, frankly, find trouble in dealing with. So this eliminates at least two great works: *Metropolis* and the original *Thief of Bagdad*.

As for the bounds of subject matter, luckily this magazine is eclectic enough to allow me to include the three major divisions of fantasy (or speculative fiction, if you will); that is, science fiction, the supernatural, and pure fantasy (which can all overlap, particularly in film, where the science fiction horror story is much closer to the supernatural horror story than to "real" science fiction, hence the linking of Dracula and Frankenstein, two very different kettles of fish).

As for that indefinable matter called style and the almost as indefinable thing of technique, there's not much that can be said without going into an endless essay on aesthetics. Let's leave it at the suggestion that I look for films that are successful cinematically *and* as sf or fantasy; some are more successful on one side or the other, of course.

And finally, they are given here in no particular order; I *would* blench at picking *the* best or *the* greatest.

Brian Aldiss, in *Billion Year Spree,* suggests *Frankenstein* as the first major work of true science fiction. It is singularly appropriate that *Frankenstein* (1931) should also be the first great science fiction film. Some consider *The Bride of Frankenstein* (1935) an even greater film; let's start out by cheating a bit and considering them one superb achievement. It's not the films' fault that they immediately instilled in the public a confusion between science fiction and horror (or to be more sociologically accurate, between *science* and horror) and gave us a never-ending succession of mad scientists. A nod also to the visually beautiful *Frankenstein: The True Story,* coscripted by Christopher Isherwood, that was made for TV a few years back.

H. G. Wells's *Things to Come* (1935) was perhaps the first film to evoke an awesome sense of wonder, with its spectacular sets and generally intelligent script (by Wells), which gave us themes that would be used again and again: the destruction of civilization, the reign of anarchy, and a genuine superculture based on science and sanity.

Anyone who knew John W. Campbell's *Who Goes There?* would be hard put to find much of it left in *The Thing (from Another World)* (1951), but producer (and probably director) Howard

Hawks made a splendid film, whose verisimilitude of acting, direction, and dialogue made the speculative element (an unfriendly—to say the least—alien) all the more real and hair raising. Again, not the film's fault that it opened the floodgates on another cycle of horror/science fiction films that all featured awful thingies usually thawed from an icecap or animated by atomic fall-out.

Part of that flood was a low-budget, modest little film called *The Incredible Shrinking Man* (1957) on a script by Richard Matheson. This one was different in all sorts of ways; the atomic fall-out was a catalyst, but the awful thingie was a common basement spider (natural size, no less). The combination here of artful effects and simple but original concept is nearly perfect. And the film's final five minutes is one of the most abstractly poetic in all cinema.

Going against the 1950s grain of scientific horrors was the large-budgeted *Forbidden Planet* (1956). It was pure space opera, beautifully produced and with a plot that could thrill the noninitiates but did not insult the intelligence or taste of the genre fan. The "monster from the id," made manifest by the superior technology of a vanished alien race, was truly intriguing; for once, film concepts had almost caught up with literary sf (usually, they're about twenty years behind).

A restrictive, scientifically controlled future has been a (maybe *the*) sf-movie staple since *1984*. It has now, in fact, become a cliché. But George Lucas (later to achieve fame for *American Graffiti*), in *THX-1138* (1971), used the theme to create an extraordinary future ambience of a closed city of endless, incoherent announcements and irrational spaces, in which the contemporary viewer is as lost as a Neanderthal in Disney World. Particularly striking visually, it uses white-on-white as a constant reminder of sterility.

There is no real point in adding any wordage to the amount already devoted to Stanley Kubrick's *2001: A Space Odyssey* (1968), particularly for those of us who saw it before the innumerable imitations and downright rip-offs in the way of other films, TV commercials, and bad pop arangements of *Zarathustra*, which have probably spoiled it for anyone who was unlucky enough or young enough to have to have seen it after the fact. I would like to add one personal note: During the forties and fifties, Clarke, Heinlein et al. had, through words, created for me the beauty and terror of traveling in space. Kubrick and Clarke, in this transcendental film, *showed* it to me.

The area of pure fantasy has been the most ill served by the cinema; rightly or wrongly, movie makers think that a fantasy that is *not* science fiction or supernatural must be for children, and therefore must be made cute and adorned with darling little songs, or if for "adults," be simply cute, as witness a spate of awfuls from the forties concerning meddlesome angels, dancing caterpillars, and lackwit leprechauns. Jean Cocteau took an epitomal pure fantasy, a fairy tale, and made it for adults without a trace of cuteness. *La Belle et a Bête* (1946) was greeted as a masterpiece of surrealism by the American intelligentsia of the time. It is anything but. It is a perfectly consistent fantasy of a world where magic works; here again are beauty and terror—a half human beast who rends animals whose blood turns to smoke on his hands, a castle of statues whose living eyes watch the events from every baroque chimney corner and where living arms come from the wall bearing candles that flame by themselves, a bower for Beauty that is half boudoir, half forest glade— brought before our believing eyes.

Walt Disney is usually neglected in accounts of the fantastic film, but I would venture to say that for nine out of ten, the first fantasy movie in our experience was *Snow White* or *Bambi* or *Cinderella*. Disney did not totally succumb to cuteness for a while, and his greatest masterpiece as a visual fantasist must be *Fantasia* (1940). Without going into the aesthetic factors that make this one of the great choreographic experiences of all time, I can but note that here we are served (with amazingly little that is precious or cute): a witch's Sabbath, unicorns in decorator colors, ahuman elves, a family of Pegasi, a noble Satan, battling dinosaurs, a trip through space, Apollo and Diana, and dancing hippopotami. Need I say more?

There has never been a big (artistically and commercially) supernatural film, in the sense that *2001* was *the* big sf film. But lurking about on your TV screens is a very small one that, for my taste, comes close to a work of genius. Herk Harvey obviously made *Carnival of Souls* (1962) on the slimmest of shoestrings, but this tale of a girl pursued by *something* amidst the most mundane surroundings shows what an original idea, a resourceful director, and a cameraman with an extraordinary eye for atmosphere can bring together on a shoestring. I have never seen this film in a theater; the first time I saw it on TV it scared the hell out of me and it's a measure of its worth that even though that initial shock value is gone, I will watch it again and again because it's so splendidly done. There aren't many horror films that stand *that* test.

Frankenstein, Things to Come, The Thing, The Incredible Shrinking Man, Forbidden Planet, THX-1138, 2001: A Space Odyssey, La Belle et a Bête, Fantasia, and *Carnival of Souls.* These are the fantastic films I respect most. I also love them.

I might also mention those films that I considered for that list, but that didn't quite measure up for one reason or another (the most common being too specialized a quality):

The Innocents, with the most terrifying slow build of suspense in cinema, but as ambiguous as its source, James's *The Turn of the Screw; The Time Machine,* George Pal's sweet and mostly effective variation on H. G. Wells's classic; *King Kong,* with its brilliant effects and the inspired idea to give the monstrous ape a touch of humanity, but still basically a pulp adventure; the Lugosi *Dracula* nearly as skillful as the *Frankenstein,* but because of Stoker's involved source novel, less coherent in plot.

Dr. Phibes Rises Again, a rarity three times over—a sequel better than the original, and a horror film that is continuously funny and totally stylish; *Jason and the Argonauts,* in which Ray Harryhausen's special effects genius was used for a plot (an innocently adventurous retelling of the Argosy) instead of the usual vice versa; *Blood on Satan's Claw,* the best example of British genius in historical atmosphere, in which a Satanic artifact creates chaos in a seventeenth-century village; *Village of the Damned,* maybe the best ever translation of a genre novel (Wyndham's *The Midwich Cuckoos*) into film.

Zardoz, for the richness and profusion of its science-fictional concepts and arresting images and the fact that it made no concession to a mass audience; the Czech puppet feature *The Emperor's Nightingale,* in which Jiri Trnka made of the Hans Christian Andersen story a film of whimsy and innocence, but no treacle whatever (Death is a major character). Also his *A Midsummer Night's Dream,* with its inhumanly elegant elfin characters; and *The Tales of Hoffman,* though a filmed opera, also served a profusion of fantastic images— human dragonflies, a courtesan's bed of a huge oyster shell, a duet sung with a reflection in the water.

There is the temptation to make a list of the ten worst, too, but for one thing there are a lot more than ten. I'll cite a few, though, as representative: *Alphaville,* in which Godard was so determined to Tell

Us Something that the whole thing became boring nonsense; *The Giant Claw,* as the perfect example of the cheapo, stupid film that's so bad it's not even funny; *Planet of the Apes,* another bit of errant nonsense passing itself off as sf and commercially successful enough to spawn sequel after sequel; heretically enough, *Invasion of the Body Snatchers,* as an example of how one bit of inconsistent plotting can ruin a beautifully built concept; and *The Jungle Book*, to exemplify what the Disney treatment can do to a great classic fantasy.

Well, that was fun. Practically cathartic, in fact, getting all that out of my system. Trouble is, now I want to do it *every* year!

James Tiptree calls himself "an amateur—I don't write to eat." Exactly what Mr. Tiptree does to eat remains unknown; however, he tells us: "I do not, repeat it, work for the CIA, the FBI, NSA, the Treasury, the narcs, or the Metropolitan Park Police." Well, sf people are a nosy bunch, and we won't give up, but meanwhile there is more than enough to consider in Mr. Tiptree's fiction. It includes perhaps thirty stories published during the last five years, a consistently high quality and inventive body of work which has earned him a reputation as one of the major voices in science fiction.

The Women
Men Don't See

by JAMES TIPTREE, JR.

I see her first while the Mexicana 727 is barreling down to Cozumel Island. I come out of the can and lurch into her seat, saying "Sorry," at a double female blur. The near blur nods quietly. The younger one in the window seat goes on looking out. I continue down the aisle, registering nothing. Zero. I never would have looked at them or thought of them again.

Cozumel airport is the usual mix of panicky Yanks dressed for the sand pile and calm Mexicans dressed for lunch at the Presidente. I am a used-up Yank dressed for serious fishing; I extract my rods and duffel from the riot and hike across the field to find my charter pilot. One Captain Estéban has contracted to deliver me to the bonefish flats of Bélise three hundred kilometers down the coast.

Captain Estéban turns out to four feet nine of mahogany Maya *puro*. He is also in a somber Maya snit. He tells me my Cessna is grounded somewhere and his Bonanza is booked to take a party to Chetumal.

Well, Chetumal is south; can he take me along and go on to Bélise after he drops them? Gloomily he concedes the possibility—*if* the other party permits, and *if* there are not too many *equipajes*.

The Chetumal party approaches. It's the woman and her young companion—daughter?—neatly picking their way across the gravel and yucca apron. Their Ventura two-suiters, like themselves, are small, plain and neutral-colored. No problem. When the captain asks if I may ride along, the mother says mildly "Of course," without looking at me.

I think that's when my inner tilt-detector sends up it first faint click. How come this woman has already looked me over carefully enough to accept on her plane? I disregard it. Paranoia hasn't been useful in my business for years, but the habit is hard to break.

As we clamber into the Bonanza, I see the girl has what could be an attractive body if there was any spark at all. There isn't. Captain Estéban folds a serape to sit on so he can see over the cowling and runs a meticulous check-down. And then we're up and trundling over the turquoise Jello of the Caribbean into a stiff south wind.

The coast on our right is the territory of Quintana Roo. If you haven't seen Yucatan, imagine the world's biggest absolutely flat green-gray rug. An empty-looking land. We pass the white ruin of Tulum and the gash of the road to Chichen Itza, a half-dozen coconut plantations, and then nothing but reef and low scrub jungle all the way to the horizon, just about the way the conquistadores saw it four centuries back.

Long strings of cumulus are racing at us, shadowing the coast. I have gathered that part of our pilot's gloom concerns the weather. A cold front is dying on the henequen fields of Mérida to west, and the south wind has piled up a string of coastal storms: what they call *llovisnas*. Estéban detours methodically around a couple of small thunderheads. The Bonanza jinks, and I look back with a vague notion of reassuring the women. They are calmly intent on what can be seen of Yucatan. Well, they were offered the copilot's view, but they turned it down. Too shy?

Another *llovisna* puffs up ahead. Estéban takes the Bonanza upstairs, rising in his seat to sight his course. I relax for the first time in too long, savoring the latitudes between me and my desk, the week of fishing ahead. Our captain's classic Maya profile attracts my gaze: forehead sloping back from his predatory nose, lips and jaw stepping back below it. If his slant eyes had been any more crossed, he couldn't have made his license. That's a handsome combination, believe it or not. On the little Maya chicks in their minishifts with iridescent gloop on those cockeyes, it's also highly erotic. Nothing like the oriental doll thing; these people have stone bones. Captain Estéban's old grandmother could probably tow the Bonanza . . .

I'm snapped awake by the cabin hitting my ear. Estéban is barking into his headset over a drumming racket of hail; the windows are dark gray.

One important noise is missing—the motor. I realize Estéban is fighting a dead plane. Thirty-six hundred; we've lost two thousand feet!

He slaps tank switches as the storm throws us around; I catch something about *gasolina* in a snarl that shows his big teeth. The Bonanza reels down. As he reaches for an overhead toggle, I see the fuel gauges are high. Maybe a clogged gravity feed line; I've heard of dirty gas down here. He drops the set. It's a million to one nobody can read us through the storm at this range anyway. Twenty-five hundred—going down.

His electric feed pump seems to have cut in: the motor explodes—quits—explodes—and quits again for good. We are suddenly out of the bottom of the clouds. Below us is a long white line almost hidden by rain: The reef. But there isn't any beach behind it, only a big meandering bay with a few mangrove flats—and it's coming up at us fast.

This is going to be bad, I tell myself with great unoriginality. The women behind me haven't made a sound. I look back and see they're braced down with their coats by their heads. With a stalling speed around eighty, all this isn't much use, but I wedge myself in.

Estéban yells some more into his set, flying a falling plane. He is doing one jesus job, too—as the water rushes up at us he dives into a hair-raising turn and hangs us into the wind—with a long pale ridge of sandbar in front of our nose.

Where in hell he found it I never know. The Bonanza mushes down, and we belly-hit with a tremendous tearing crash—bounce—hit again—and everything slews wildly as we flat-spin into the mangroves at end of the bar. Crash! Clang! The plane is wrapping itself

into a mound of strangler fig with one wing up. The crashing quits
with us all in one piece. And no fire. Fantastic.

Captain Estéban prys open his door, which is now in the roof.
Behind me a woman is repeating quietly. "Mother. Mother." I climb
up the floor and find the girl trying to free herself from her mother's
embrace. The woman's eyes are closed. Then she opens them and
suddenly lets go, sane as soap. Estéban starts hauling them out. I grab
the Bonanza's aid kit and scramble out after them into brilliant sun
and wind. The storm that hit us is already vanishing up the coast.

"Great landing, Captain."

"Oh, *yes!* It was beautiful." The women are shaky, but no hysteria. Estéban is surveying the scenery with the expression his ances-
tors used on the Spaniards.

If you've been in one of these things, you know the slow-motion
inanity that goes on. Euphoria, first. We straggle down the fig tree
and out onto the sandbar in the roaring hot wind, noting without
alarm that there's nothing but miles of crystalline water on all sides.
It's only a foot or so deep, and the bottom is the olive color of silt.
The distant shore around us is all flat mangrove swamp, totally
uninhabitable.

"Bahia Espiritu Santo." Estéban confirms my guess that we're
down in that huge water wilderness. I always wanted to fish it.

"What's all that smoke?" The girl is pointing at the plumes blowing around the horizon.

"Alligator hunters," says Estéban. Maya poachers have left burn-
offs in the swamps. It occurs to me that any signal fires we make
aren't going to be too conspicuous. And I now note that our plane is
well-buried in the mound of fig. Hard to see it from the air.

Just as the question of how the hell we get out of here surfaces in
my mind, the older woman asks composedly, "If they didn't hear
you, Captain, when will they start looking for us? Tomorrow?"

"Correct," Estéban agrees dourly. I recall that air-sea rescue is
fairly informal here. Like, keep an eye open for Mario, his mother
says he hasn't been home all week.

It dawns on me we may be here quite some while.

Furthermore, the diesel-truck noise on our left is the Caribbean
piling back into the mouth of the bay. The wind is pushing it at us,
and the bare bottoms on the mangroves show that our bar is covered
at high tide. I recall seeing a full moon this morning—believe it, St.

Louis—which means maximal tides. Well, we can climb up in the plane. But what about drinking water?

There's a small splat! behind me. The older woman has sampled the bay. She shakes her head, smiling ruefully. It's the first real expression on either of them; I take it as the signal for introductions. When I say I'm Don Fenton from St. Louis, she tells me their name is Parsons, from Bethesda, Maryland. She says it so nicely I don't at first notice we aren't being given first names. We all compliment Captain Estéban again.

His left eye is swelled shut, an inconvenience beneath his attention as a Maya, but Mrs. Parsons spots the way he's bracing his elbow in his ribs.

"You're hurt, Captain."

"*Roto*—I think is broken." He's embarrassed at being in pain. We get him to peel off his Jaime shirt, revealing a nasty bruise in his superb dark-bay torso.

"Is there tape in that kit, Mr. Fenton? I've had a little first-aid training."

She begins to deal competently and very impersonally with the tape. Miss Parsons and I wander to the end of the bar and have a conversation which I am later to recall acutely.

"Roseate spoonbills," I tell her as three pink birds flap away.

"They're beautiful," she says in her tiny voice. They both have tiny voices. "He's a Mayan Indian, isn't he? The pilot, I mean."

"Right. The real thing, straight out of the Bonampak murals. Have you seen Chichén and Uxmal?"

"Yes. We were in Mérida. We're going to Tikal in Guatemala . . . I mean, we were."

"You'll get there." It occurs to me the girl needs cheering up. "Have they told you that Maya mothers used to tie a board on the infant's forehead to get that slant? They also hung a ball of tallow over its nose to make its eyes cross. It was considered aristocratic."

She smiles and takes another peek at Estéban. "People seem different in Yucatan," she says thoughtfully. "Not like the Indians around Mexico City. More, I don't know, independent."

"Comes from never having been conquered. Mayas got massacred and chased a lot, but nobody ever really flattened them. I bet you didn't know that the last Mexican-Maya war ended with a negotiated truce in nineteen thirty-five?"

"No!" Then she says seriously, "I like that."

"So do I."

"The water is really rising very fast," says Mrs. Parsons gently from behind us.

It is, and so is another *llovisna*. We climb back into the Bonanza. I try to rig my parka for a rain catcher, which blows loose as the storm hits fast and furious. We sort a couple of malt bars and my bottle of Jack Daniels out of the jumble in the cabin and make ourselves reasonably comfortable. The Parsons take a sip of whiskey each, Estéban and I considerably more. The Bonanza begins to bump soggily. Estéban makes an ancient one-eyed Maya face at the water seeping into his cabin and goes to sleep. We all nap.

When the water goes down, the euphoria has gone with it, and we're very, very thirsty. It's also damn near sunset. I get to work with a bait-casting rod and some treble hooks and manage to foul-hook four small mullets. Estéban and the women tie the Bonanza's midget life raft out in the mangroves to catch rain. The wind is parching hot. No planes go by.

Finally another shower comes over and yields us six ounces of water apiece. When the sunset envelops the world in golden smoke, we squat on the sandbar to eat wet raw mullet and Instant Breakfast crumbs. The women are now in shorts, neat but definitely not sexy.

"I never realized how refreshing raw fish is," Mrs. Parsons says pleasantly. Her daughter chuckles, also pleasantly. She's on Mamma's far side away from Estéban and me. I have Mrs. Parsons figured now: Mother Hen protecting only chick from male predators. That's all right with me. I came here to fish.

But something is irritating me. The damn women haven't complained once, you understand. Not a peep, not a quaver, no personal manifestations whatever. They're like something out of a manual.

"You really seem at home in the wilderness, Mrs. Parsons. You do much camping?"

"Oh goodness no." Diffident laugh. "Not since my girl scout days. Oh, look—are those man-of-war birds?"

Answer a question with a question. I wait while the frigate birds sail nobly into the sunset.

Bethesda . . . Would I be wrong in guessing you work for Uncle Sam?"

"Why, yes. You must be very familiar with Washington, Mr. Fenton. Does your work bring you there often?"

Anywhere but on our sandbar the little ploy would have worked. My hunter's gene twitches.

"Which agency are you with?"

She gives up gracefully. "Oh, just GSA records. I'm a librarian."

Of course, I know her now, all the Mrs. Parsonses in records divisions, accounting sections, research branches, personnel and administration offices. Tell Mrs. Parsons we need a recap on the external service contracts for fiscal '73. So Yucatan is on the tours now? Pity . . . I offer her the tired little joke. "You know where the bodies are buried."

She smiles deprecatingly and stands up. "It does get dark quickly, doesn't it?"

Time to get back into the plane.

A flock of ibis are circling us, evidently accustomed to roosting in our fig tree. Estéban produces a machete and a Maya hammock. He proceeds to sling it between tree and plane, refusing help. His machete stroke is noticeably tentative.

The Parsons are taking a pee behind the tail vane. I hear one of them slip and squeal faintly. When they come back over the hull, Mrs. Parsons asks, "Might we sleep in the hammock, Captain?"

Estéban splits an unbelieving grin. I protest about rain and mosquitoes.

"Oh, we have insect repellent and we do enjoy fresh air."

The air is rushing by about force five and colder by the minute.

"We have our raincoats," the girl adds cheerfully.

Well, okay, ladies. We dangerous males retire inside the damp cabin. Through the wind I hear the women laugh softly now and then, apparently cosy in their chilly ibis roost. A private insanity, I decide. I know myself for the least threatening of men; my non-charisma has been in fact an asset jobwise, over the years. Are they having fantasies about Estéban? Or maybe they really are fresh-air nuts . . Sleep comes for me in invisible diesels roaring by on the reef outside.

We emerge dry-mouthed into a vast windy salmon sunrise. A diamond chip of sun breaks out of the sea and promptly submerges in cloud. I go to work with the rod and some mullet bait while two showers detour around us. Breakfast is a strip of wet barracuda apiece.

The Parsons continue stoic and helpful. Under Estéban's direction they set up a section of cowling for a gasoline flare in case we hear a plane, but nothing goes over except one unseen jet droning toward Panama. The wind howls, hot and dry and full of coral dust. So are we.

"They look first in the sea," Estéban remarks. His aristocratic frontal slope is beaded with sweat; Mrs. Parsons watches him concernedly. I watch the cloud blanket tearing by above, getting higher and dryer and thicker. While that lasts nobody is going to find us, and the water business in now unfunny.

Finally I borrow Estéban's machete and hack a long light pole. "There's stream coming in there, I saw it from the plane. Can't be more than two, three miles."

"I'm afraid the raft's torn." Mrs. Parsons shows me the cracks in the orange plastic; irritatingly, it's a Delaware label.

"All right," I hear myself announce. "The tide's going down. If we cut the good end of that air tube, I can haul water back in it. I've waded flats before."

Even to me it sounds crazy.

"Stay by plane," Estéban says. He's right, of course. He's also clearly running a fever. I look at the overcast and taste grit and old barracuda. The hell with the manual.

When I start cutting up the raft, Estéban tells me to take the serape. "You stay one night." He's right about that, too; I'll have to wait out the tide.

"I'll come with you," says Mrs. Parsons calmly.

I simply stare at her. What new madness has got into Mother Hen? Does she imagine Estéban is too battered to be functional? While I'm being astounded, my eyes take in the fact that Mrs. Parsons is now quite rosy around the knees, with her hair loose and a sunburn starting on her nose. A trim, in fact a very neat shading-forty.

"Look, that stuff is horrible going. Mud up to your ears and water over your head."

"I'm really quite fit and I swim a great deal. I'll try to keep up. Two would be much safer, Mr. Fenton, and we can bring more water."

She's serious. Well, I'm about as fit as a marshmallow at this time of winter, and I can't pretend I'm depressed by the idea of company. So be it.

"Let me show Miss Parsons how to work this rod."

Miss Parsons is even rosier and more windblown, and she's not clumsy with my tackle. A good girl, Miss Parsons, in her nothing way. We cut another staff and get some gear together. At the last minute Estéban shows how sick he feels: he offers me the machete. I thank him, but, no; I'm used to my Wirkkala knife. We tie some air into the plastic tube for a float and set out along the sandiest looking line.

Estéban raises one dark palm. *"Buen viaje."* Miss Parsons has hugged her mother and gone to cast from the mangrove. She waves. We wave.

An hour later we're barely out of waving distance. The going is purely god-awful. The sand keeps dissolving into silt you can't walk on or swim through, and the bottom is spiked with dead mangrove spears. We flounder from one pothole to the next, scaring up rays and turtles and hoping to god we don't kick a moray eel. Where we're not soaked in slime, we're desiccated, and we smell like the Old Cretaceous.

Mrs. Parsons keeps up doggedly. I only have to pull her out once. When I do so, I notice the sandbar is now out of sight.

Finally we reach the gap in the mangrove line I thought was the creek. It turns out to open into another arm of the bay, with more mangroves ahead. And the tide is coming in.

"I've had the world's lousiest idea."

Mrs. Parsons only says mildly, "It's so different from the view from the plane."

I revise my opinion of the girl scouts, and we plow on past the mangroves toward the smoky haze that has to be shore. The sun is setting in our faces, making it hard to see. Ibises and herons fly up around us, and once a big hermit spooks ahead, his fin cutting a rooster tail. We fall into more potholes. The flashlights get soaked. I am having fantasies of the mangrove as universal obstacle; it's hard to recall I ever walked down a street, for instance, without stumbling over or under or through mangrove roots. And the sun is dropping, down, down.

Suddenly we hit a ledge and fall over it into a cold flow.

"The stream! It's fresh water!"

We guzzle and gargle and douse our heads; it's the best drink I remember. "Oh my, oh my—!" Mrs. Parsons is laughing right out loud.

"That dark place over to the right looks like real land."

We flounder across the flow and follow a hard shelf, which turns into solid bank and rises over our heads. Shortly there's a break beside a clump of spiny bromels, and we scramble up and flop down at the top, dripping and stinking. Out of sheer reflex my arms goes around my companion's shoulder—but Mrs. Parsons isn't there; she's up on her knees peering at the burnt-over plain around us.

"Its so good to see land one can walk on!" The tone is too innocent. *Noli me tangere.*

"Don't try it." I'm exasperated; the muddy little woman, what does she think? "That ground out there is a crust of ashes over muck, and it's full of stubs. You can go in over your knees."

"It seems firm here."

"We're in an alligator nursery. That was the slide we came up. Don't worry, by now the old lady's doubtless on her way to be made into handbags."

"What a shame."

"I better set a line down in the stream while I can still see."

I slide down and rig a string of hooks that may get us breakfast. When I get back Mrs. Parsons is wringing muck out of the serape.

"I'm glad you warned me, Mr. Fenton. It *is* treacherous."

"Yeah." I'm over my irritation; god knows I don't want to *tangere* Mrs. Parsons, even if I weren't beat down to mush. "In its quiet way, Yucatan is a tough place to get around in. You can see why the Mayas built roads. Speaking of which—look!"

The last of the sunset is silhouetting a small square shape a couple of kilometers inland: a Maya *ruina* with a fig tree growing out of it.

"Lot of those around. People think they were guard towers."

"What a deserted-feeling land."

"Let's hope it's deserted by mosquitoes."

We slump down in the 'gator nursery and share the last malt bar, watching the stars slide in and out of the blowing clouds. The bugs aren't too bad; maybe the burn did them in. And it isn't hot any more, either—in fact, it's not even warm, wet as we are. Mrs. Parsons continues tranquilly interested in Yucatan and unmistakably uninterested in togetherness.

Just as I'm beginning to get aggressive notions about how we're going to spend the night if she expects me to give her the serape, she stands up, scuffs at a couple of hummocks and says, "I expect this is as good a place as any, isn't it, Mr. Fenton?"

With which she spreads out the raft bag for a pillow and lies down on her side in the dirt with exactly half the serape over her and the other corner folded neatly open. Her small back is toward me.

The demonstration is so convincing that I'm halfway under my share of serape before the preposterousness of it stops me.

"By the way. My name is Don."

"Oh, of course." Her voice is graciousness itself. "I'm Ruth."

I get in not quite touching her, and we lie there like two fish on a plate, exposed to the stars and smelling the smoke in the wind and feeling things underneath us. It is absolutely the most intimately awkward moment I've had in years.

The woman doesn't mean one thing to me, but the obtrusive recessiveness of her, the defiance of her little rump eight inches from my fly—for two pesos I'd have those shorts down and introduce myself. If I were twenty years younger. If I wasn't so bushed . . . But the twenty years and the exhaustion are there, and it comes to me wryly that Mrs. Ruth Parsons has judged things to a nicety. If I *were* twenty years younger, she wouldn't be here. Like the butterfish that float around a sated barracuda, only to vanish away the instant his intent changes, Mrs. Parsons knows her little shorts are safe. Those firmly filled little shorts, so close . . .

A warm nerve stirs in my groin—and just as it does I become aware of a silent emptiness beside me. Mrs. Parsons is imperceptibly inching away. Did my breathing change? Whatever, I'm perfectly sure that if my hand reached, she'd be elsewhere—probably announcing her intention to take a dip. The twenty years bring a chuckle to my throat, and I relax.

"Good night, Ruth."

"Good night, Don."

And believe it or not, we sleep, while the armadas of the wind roar overhead.

Light wakes me—a cold white glare.

My first thought is 'gator hunters. Best to manifest ourselves as *turistas* as fast as possible. I scramble up, noting that Ruth has dived under the bromel clump.

"Quien estas? A secorro! Help, *senores!"*

No answer except the light goes out, leaving me blind.

I yell some more in a couple of languages. It stays dark. There's a vague scrabbling, whistling sound somewhere in the burn-off. Liking everything less by the minute, I try a speech about our plane having crashed and we need help.

A very narrow pencil of light flicks over us and snaps off.

"Eh-ep," says a blurry voice and something metallic twitters. They for sure aren't locals. I'm getting unpleasant ideas.

"Yes, help!"

Something goes crackle-crackle whish-whish, and all sounds fade away.

"What the holy hell!" I stumble toward where they were.

"Look," Ruth whispers behind me. "Over by the ruin."

I look and catch a multiple flicker which winks out fast.

"A camp?"

And I take two more blind strides; my leg goes down through the crust, and a spike spears me just where you stick the knife in to unjoint a drumstick. By the pain that goes through my bladder I recognize that my trick kneecap has caught it.

For instant basket case you can't beat kneecaps. First you discover your knee doesn't bend any more, and so you try putting some weight on it, and a bayonet goes up your spine and unhinges your jaw. Little grains of gristle have got into the sensitive bearing surface. The knee tries to buckle and can't, and mercifully you fall down.

Ruth helps me back to the serape.

"What a fool, what a god-forgotten imbecile—"

"Not at all, Don. It was perfectly natural." We strike matches; her fingers push mine aside, exploring. "I think it's in place, but it's swelling fast. I'll lay a wet handkerchief on it. We'll have to wait for morning to check the cut. Were they poachers, do you think?"

"Probably," I lie. What I think they were is smugglers.

She comes back with a soaked bandanna and drapes it on. "We must have frightened them. That light . . . it seemed so bright."

"Some hunting party. People do crazy things around here."

"Perhaps they'll come back in the morning."

"Could be."

Ruth pulls up the wet serape, and we say goodnight again. Neither of us are mentioning how we're going to get back to the plane without help.

I lie staring south where Alpha Centauri is blinking in and out of the overcast and cursing myself for the sweet mess I've made. My first idea is giving way to an even less pleasing one.

Smuggling, around here, is a couple of guys in an outboard meeting a shrimp boat by the reef. They don't light up the sky or have some kind of swamp buggy that goes whoosh. Plus a big camp . . . paramilitary-type equipment?

I've seen a report of Guévarista infiltrators operating on the British Honduran border, which is about a hundred kilometers—sixty miles—south of here. Right under those clouds. If that's what looked us over, I'll be more than happy if they don't come back . . .

I wake up in pelting rain, alone. My first move confirms that my leg is as expected—a giant misplaced erection bulging out of my shorts. I raise up painfully to see Ruth standing by the bromels, looking over the bay. Solid wet nimubs is pouring out of the south.

"No planes today."

"Oh, good morning, Don. Should we look at that cut now?"

"It's minimal." In fact the skin is hardly broken, and no deep puncture. Totally out of proportion to the havoc inside.

"Well, they have water to drink," Ruth says tranquilly. "Maybe those hunters will come back. I'll go see if we have a fish—that is, can I help you in any way, Don?"

Very tactful. I emit an ungracious negative, and she goes off about her private concerns.

They certainly are private, too; when I recover from my own sanitary efforts, she's still away. Finally I hear splashing.

"It's a big fish!" More splashing. Then she climbs up the bank with a three-pound mangrove snapper—and something else.

It isn't until after the messy work of filleting the fish that I begin to notice.

She's making a smudge of chaff and twigs to singe the fillets, small hands very quick, tension in that female upper lip. The rain has eased off for the moment; we're sluicing wet but warm enough. Ruth brings me my fish on a mangrove skewer and sits back on her heels with an odd breathy sigh.

"Aren't you joining me?"

"Oh, of course." She gets a strip and picks at it, saying quickly, "We either have too much salt or too little, don't we? I should fetch some brine." Her eyes are roving from nothing to noplace.

"Good thought." I hear another sigh and decide the girl scouts need an assist. "Your daughter mentioned you've come from Mérida. Seen much of Mexico?"

"Not really. Last year we went to Mazatlan and Cuernavaca . . ." She puts the fish down, frowning.

"And you're going to see Tikál. Going to Bonampak too?"

"No." Suddenly she jumps up brushing rain off her face. "I'll bring you some water, Don."

She ducks down the slide, and after a fair while comes back with a full bromel stalk.

"Thanks." She's standing above me, staring restlessly round the horizon."

"Ruth, I hate to say it, but those guys are not coming back and it's probably just as well. Whatever they were up to, we looked like trouble. The most they'll do is tell someone we're here. That'll take a day or two to get around, we'll be back at the plane by then."

"I'm sure you're right, Don." She wanders over to the smudge fire.

"And quit fretting about your daughter. She's a big girl."

"Oh, I'm sure Althea's all right . . . They have plenty of water now." Her fingers drum on her thigh. It's raining again.

"Come on, Ruth. Sit down. Tell me about Althea. Is she still in college?"

She gives that sighing little laugh and sits. "Althea got her degree last year. She's in computer programming."

"I'm in Foreign Procurement Archives." She smiles mechanically, but her breathing is shallow. "It's very interesting."

"I know a Jack Wittig in Contracts, maybe you know him?"

It sounds pretty absurd, there in the 'gator slide.

"Oh, I've met Mr. Wittig. I'm sure he wouldn't remember me."

"Why not?"

"I'm not very memorable."

Her voice is purely factual. She's perfectly right, of course. Who was that woman, Mrs. Jannings, Janny, who coped with my per diem for years? Competent, agreeable, impersonal. She had a sick father or something. But dammit, Ruth is a lot younger and better-looking. Comparatively speaking.

"Maybe Mrs. Parsons doesn't want to be memorable."

She makes a vague sound, and I suddenly realize Ruth isn't listening to me at all. Her hands are clenched around her knees, she's staring inland at the ruin.

"Ruth, I tell you our friends with the light are in the next county by now. Forget it, we don't need them."

Her eyes come back to me as if she'd forgotten I was there, and she nods slowly. It seems to be too much effort to speak. Suddenly she cocks her head and jumps up again.

"I'll go look at the line, Don. I thought I heard something—"
She's gone like a rabbit.

While she's away I try getting up onto my good leg and the staff.
The pain is sickening; knees seem to have some kind of hot line to
the stomach. I take a couple of hops to test whether the Demerol I
have in my belt would get me walking. As I do so, Ruth comes up
the bank with a fish flapping in her hands.

"Oh, no, Don! *No!*" She actually clasps the snapper to her breast.

"The water will take some of my weight. I'd like to give it a try."

"You mustn't!" Ruth says quite violently and instantly modulates
down. "Look at the bay, Don. One can't see a thing."

I teeter there, tasting bile and looking at the mingled curtains of
sun and rain driving across the water. She's right, thank god. Even
with two good legs we could get into trouble out there.

"I guess one more night won't kill us."

I let her collapse me back onto the gritty plastic, and she positively
bustles around, finding me a chunk to lean on, stretching the serape
on both staffs to keep rain off me, bringing another drink, grubbing
for dry tinder.

"I'll make us a real bonfire as soon as it lets up, Don. They'll see
our smoke, they'll know we're all right. We just have to wait."
Cheery smile. "Is there any way we can make you more comfortable?"

Holy Saint Sterculius: playing house in a mud puddle. For a fatu-
ous moment I wonder if Mrs. Parsons has designs on me. And then
she lets out another sigh and sinks back onto her heels with that listening look. Unconsciously her rump wiggles a little. My ear picks up
the operative word: *wait.*

Ruth Parsons is waiting. In fact, she acts as if she's waiting so hard
it's killing her. For what? For someone to get us out of here, what
else? . . . But why was she so horrified when I got up to try to leave?
Why all this tension?

My paranoia stirs. I grab it by the collar and start idly checking
back. Up to when whoever it was showed up last night, Mrs. Parson
was, I guess, normal. Calm and sensible, anyway. Now's she's humming like a high wire. And she seems to want to stay here and wait.
Just as an intellectual pastime, why?

Could she have intended to come here? No way. Where she
planned to be was Chetumal, which is on the border. Come to think,
Chetumal is an odd way round to Tikál. Let's say the scenario was

that she's meeting somebody in Chetumal. Somebody who's part of an organization. So now her contact in Chetumal knows she's overdue. And when those types appeared last night, something suggests to her that they're part of the same organization. And she hopes they'll put one and one together and come back for her?

"May I have the knife, Don? I'll clean the fish."

Rather slowly I pass the knife, kicking my subconscious. Such a decent ordinary little woman, a good girl scout. My trouble is that I've bumped into too many professional agilities under the careful stereotypes. *I'm not very memorable . . .*

What's in Foreign Procurement Archieves? Wittig handles classified contracts. Lots of money stuff; foreign currency negotiations, commodity price schedules, some industrial technology. Or—just as a hypothesis—it could be as simple as a wad of bills back in that modest beige Ventura, to be exchanged for a packet from say, Costa Rica. If she were a courier, they'd want to get at the plane. And then what about me and maybe Estéban? Even hypothetically, not good.

I watch her hacking at the fish, forehead knotted with effort, teeth in her lip. Mrs. Ruth Parsons of Bethesda, this thrumming, private woman. How crazy can I get? *They'll see our smoke . . .*

"Here's your knife, Don. I washed it. Does the leg hurt very badly?"

I blink away the fantasies and see a scared little woman in a mangrove swamp.

"Sit down, rest. You've been going all out."

She sits obediently, like a kid in a dentist chair.

"You're stewing about Althea. And she's probably worried about you. We'll get back tomorrow under our own steam, Ruth."

"Honestly I'm not worried at all, Don." The smile fades; she nibbles her lip, frowning out at the bay.

"Ruth, you know you surprised me when you offered to come along. Not that I don't appreciate it. But I rather thought you'd be concerned about leaving Althea. Alone with our good pilot, I mean. Or was it only me?"

This gets her attention at last.

"I believe Captain Estéban is a very fine type of man."

The words surprise me a little. Isn't the correct line more like "I trust Althea," or even, indignantly, "Althea is a good girl"?

"He's a man. Althea seemed to think he was interesting."

She goes on staring at the bay. And then I notice her tongue flick out and lick that prehensile upper lip. There's a flush that isn't sunburn around her ears and throat too, and one hand is gently rubbing her thigh. What's she seeing, out there in the flats?

Captain Estéban's mahogany arms clasping Miss Althea Parsons' pearly body. Captain Estéban's archaic nostrils snuffling in Miss Parsons' tender neck. Captain Estéban's copper buttocks pumping into Althea's creamy upturned bottom . . . The hammock, very bouncy. Mayas know all about it.

Well, Well. So Mother Hen has her little quirks.

I feel fairly silly and more than a little irritated. Now I find out . . . But even vicarious lust has much to recommend it, here in the mud and rain. I settle back, recalling that Miss Althea the computer programmer had waved good-bye very composedly. Was she sending her mother to flounder across the bay with me so she can get programmed in Maya? The memory of Honduran mahogany logs drifting in and out of the opalescent sand comes to me. Just as I am about to suggest that Mrs. Parsons might care to share my rain shelter, she remarks serenely, "The Mayas seem to be a very fine type of people. I believe you said so to Althea."

The implications fall on me with the rain. *Type.* As in breeding, bloodline, sire. Am I supposed to have certified Estéban not only as a stud but as a genetic donor?

"Ruth, are you telling me you're prepared to accept a half-Indian grandchild?"

"Why, Don, that's up to Althea, you know."

Looking at the mother, I guess it is. Oh, for mahogany gonads.

Ruth has gone back to listening to the wind, but I'm not about to let her off that easy. Not after all that *noli me tangere* jazz.

"What will Althea's father think?"

Her face snaps around at me, genuinely startled.

"Althea's father?" Complicated semismile. "He won't mind."

"He'll accept it too, eh?" I see her shake her head as if a fly were bothering her, and add with a cripple's malice: "Your husband must be a very fine type of a man."

Ruth looks at me, pushing her wet hair back abruptly. I have the impression that mousy Mrs. Parsons is roaring out of control, but her voice is quiet.

"There isn't any Mr. Parsons, Don. There never was. Althea's father was a Danish medical student . . . I believe he has gained considerable prominence."

"Oh." Something warns me not to say I'm sorry. "You mean he doesn't know about Althea?"

"No." She smiles, her eyes bright and cuckoo.

"Seems like rather a rough deal for her."

"I grew up quite happily under the same circumstances."

Bang, I'm dead. Well, well, well. A mad image blooms in my mind: generations of solitary. Parsons women selecting sires, making impregnation trips. Well, I hear the world is moving their way.

"I better look at the fish line."

She leaves. The glow fades. *No.* Just no, no contact. Good-bye, Captain Estéban. My leg is very uncomfortable. The hell with Mrs. Parsons' long-distance orgasm.

We don't talk much after that, which seems to suit Ruth. The odd day drags by. Squall after squall blows over us. Ruth singes up some more fillets, but the rain drowns her smudge; it seems to pour hardest just as the sun's about to show.

Finally she comes to sit under my sagging serape, but there's no warmth there. I doze, aware of her getting up now and then to look around. My subconscious notes that she's still twitchy. I tell my subconscious to knock it off.

Presently I wake up to find her penciling on the water-soaked pages of a little notepad.

"What's that, a shopping list for alligators?"

Automatic polite laugh. "Oh, just an address. In case we—I'm being silly, Don."

"Hey," I sit up, wincing. "Ruth, quit fretting. I mean it. We'll all be out of this soon. You'll have a great story to tell."

She doesn't look up. "Yes . . . I guess we will."

"Come on, we're doing fine. There isn't any real danger here, you know. Unless you're allergic to fish?"

Another good-little-girl laugh, but there's a shiver in it.

"Sometimes I think I'd like to go . . . really far away."

To keep her talking I say the first thing in my head.

"Tell me, Ruth. I'm curious why you would settle for that kind of lonely life, there in Washington? I mean, a woman like you—"

"Should get married?" She gives a shaky sign, pushing the notebook back in her wet pocket.

"Why not? It's the normal source of companionship. Don't tell me you're trying to be some kind of professional man-hater."

"Lesbian, you mean?" Her laugh sounds better. "With my security rating? No, I'm not."

"Well, then. Whatever trauma you went through, these things don't last forever. You can't hate all men."

The smile is back. "Oh, there wasn't any trauma, Don, and I *don't* hate men. That would be as silly as—as hating the weather." She glances wryly at the blowing rain.

"I think you have a grudge. You're even spooky of me."

Smooth as a mouse bite she says, "I'd love to hear about your family, Don?"

Touché. I give her the edited version of how I don't have one any more, and she says she's sorry, how sad. And we chat about what a good life a single person really has, and how she and her friends enjoy plays and concerts and travel, and one of them is head cashier for Ringling Brothers, how about that?

But it's coming out jerkier and jerkier like a bad tape, with her eyes going round the horizon in the pauses and her face listening for something that isn't my voice. What's wrong with her? Well, what's wrong with any furtively unconventional middle-aged woman with an empty bed. And a security clearance. An old habit of mind remarks unkindly that Mrs. Parsons represents what is known as the classic penetration target.

"—so much more opportunity now." Her voice trails off.

"Hurrah for women's lib, eh?"

"The lib?" Impatiently she leans forward and tugs the serape straight. "Oh, that's doomed."

The word apocalyptic jars my attention.

"What do you mean, doomed?"

She glances at me as if I weren't hanging straight either and says vaguely, "Oh . . ."

"Come on, why doomed? Didn't they get that equal rights bill?"

Long hesitation. When she speaks again her voice is different.

"Women have no rights, Don, except what men allow us. Men are more aggressive and powerful, and they run the world. When the next real crisis upsets them, our so-called rights will vanish like—like that smoke. We'll be back where we always were: property. And whatever has gone wrong will be blamed on our freedom, like the fall of Rome was. You'll see."

Now all this is delivered in a gray tone of total conviction. The last time I heard that tone, the speaker was explaining why he had to keep his file drawers full of dead pigeons.

"Oh, come on. You and your friends are the backbone of the system; if you quit, the country would come to a screeching halt before lunch."

No answering smile.

"That's fantasy." Her voice is still quiet. "Women don't work that way. We're a—a toothless world." She looks around as if she wanted to stop talking. "What women do is survive. We live by ones and twos in the chinks of your world-machine."

"Sounds like a guerrilla operation." I'm not really joking, here in the 'gator den. In fact, I'm wondering if I spent too much thought on mahogany logs.

"Guerrillas have something to hope for." Suddenly she switches on the jolly smile. "Think of opossums, Don. Did you know there are opossums living all over? Even in New York City."

I smile back with my neck prickling. I thought I was the paranoid one.

"Men and women aren't different species, Ruth. Women do everything men do."

"Do they?" Our eyes meet, but she seems to be seeing ghosts between us in the rain. She mutters something that could be "My Lai" and looks away. "All the endless wars . . ." Her voice is a whisper. "All the huge authoritarian organizations for doing unreal things. Men live to struggle against each other; we're just part of the battlefields. It'll never change unless you change the whole world. I dream sometimes of—of going away—" She checks and abruptly changes voice. "Forgive me, Don, it's so stupid saying all this."

"Men hate wars too, Ruth," I say as gently as I can.

"I know." She shrugs and climbs to her feet. "But that's your problem, isn't it?"

End of communication. Mrs. Ruth Parsons isn't even living in the same world with me.

I watch her move around restlessly, head turning toward the ruins. Alienation like that can add up to dead pigeons, which would be GSA's problem. It could also lead to believing some joker who's promising to change the world. Which could just probably be my problem if one of them was over in that camp last night, where she keeps looking. *Guerrillas have something to hope for . . . ?*

Nonsense. I try another position and see that the sky seems to be clearing as the sun sets. The wind is quieting down at last too. Insane to think this little woman is acting out some fantasy in this swamp. But that equipment last night was no fantasy; if those lads have some connection with her, I'll be in the way. You couldn't find a handier spot to dispose of a body . . . Maybe some Guévarista is a fine type of man?

Absurd. Sure . . . The only thing more absurd would be to come through the wars and get myself terminated by a mad librarian's boyfriend on a fishing trip.

A fish flops in the stream below us. Ruth spins around so fast she hits the serape. "I better start the fire," she says, her eyes still on the plain and her head cocked, listening.

All right, let's test.

"Expecting company?"

It rocks her. She freezes, and her eyes come swiveling around at me like a film take captioned Fright. I can see her decide to smile.

"Oh, one never can tell!" She laughs weirdly, the eyes not changed. "I'll get the—the kindling." She fairly scuttles into the brush.

Nobody, paranoid or not, could call *that* a normal reaction.

Ruth Parsons is either psycho or she's expecting something to happen—and it has nothing to do with me; I scared her pissless.

Well, she could be nuts. And I could be wrong, but there are some mistakes you only make once. Reluctantly I unzip my body belt, telling myself that if I think what I think, my only course is to take something for my leg and get as far as possible from Mrs. Ruth Parsons before whoever she's waiting for arrives.

In my belt also is a .32 caliber asset Ruth doesn't know about— and it's going to stay there. My longevity program leaves the shootouts to TV and stresses being somewhere else when the roof falls in. I can spend a perfectly safe and also perfectly horrible night out in one of those mangrove flats . . . am I insane?

At this moment Ruth stands up and stares blatantly inland with her hand shading her eyes. Then she tucks something into her pocket, buttons up and tightens her belt.

That does it.

I dry-swallow two 100 mg tabs, which should get me ambulatory and still leave me wits to hide. Give it a few minutes. I make sure my compass and some hooks are in my own pocket and sit waiting while

Ruth fusses with her smudge fire, sneaking looks away when she thinks I'm not watching.

The flat world around us is turning into an unearthly amber and violet light show as the first numbness seeps into my leg. Ruth has crawled under the bromels for more dry stuff; I can see her foot. Okay. I reach for my staff.

Suddenly the foot jerks, and Ruth yells—or rather, her throat makes that *Uh-uh-uhhh* that means pure horror. The foot disappears in a rattle of bromel stalks.

I lunge upright on the crutch and look over the bank at a frozen scene.

Ruth is crouching sideways on the ledge, clutching her stomach. They are about a yard below, floating on the river in a skiff. While I was making up my stupid mind, her friends have glided right under my ass. There are three of them.

They are tall and white. I try to see them as men in some kind of white jumpsuits. The one nearest the bank is stretching out a long white arm toward Ruth. She jerks and scuttles further away.

The arm stretches after her. It stretches and stretches. It stretches two yards and stays hanging in air. Small black things are wiggling from its tip.

I look where their faces should be and see black hollow dishes with vertical stripes. The stripes move slowly . . .

There is no more possibility of their being human—or anything else I've ever seen. What has Ruth conjured up?

The scene is totally silent. I blink, blink—this cannot be real. The two in the far end of the skiff are writhing those arms around an apparatus on a tripod. A weapon? Suddenly I hear the same blurry voice I heard in the night.

"Guh-give," it groans. "G-give . . ."

Dear god, it's real, whatever it is. I'm terrified. My mind is trying not to form a word.

And Ruth—Jesus, of course—Ruth is terrified too; she's edging along the bank away from them, gaping at the monsters in the skiff, who are obviously nobody's friends. She's hugging something to her body. Why doesn't she get over the bank and circle back behind me?

"G-g-give." That wheeze is coming from the tripod. "Pee-eeze give." The skiff is moving upstream below Ruth, following her. The arm undulates out at her again, its black digits looping. Ruth scrambles to the top of the bank.

"Ruth!" My voice cracks. "Ruth, get over here behind me!"

She doesn't look at me, only keeps sidling farther away. My terror detonates into anger.

"Come back here!" With my free hand I'm working the .32 out of my belt. The sun has gone down.

She doesn't turn but straightens up warily, still hugging the thing. I see her mouth working. Is she actually trying to *talk* to them?

"Please . . ." She swallows "Please speak to me. I need your help."

"RUTH!!"

At this moment the nearest white monster whips into a great S-curve and sails right onto the bank at her, eight feet of snowy rippling horror.

And I shoot Ruth.

I don't know that for a minute—I've yanked the gun up so fast that my staff slips and dumps me as I fire. I stagger up, hearing Ruth scream "No! No! No!"

The creature is back down by his boat, and Ruth is still farther away, clutching herself. Blood is running down her elbow.

"Stop it, Don! They aren't attacking you!"

"For god's sake! Don't be a fool, I can't help you if you won't get away from them!"

No reply. Nobody moves. No sound except the drone of a jet passing far above. In the darkening stream below me the three white figures shift uneasily; I get the impression of radar dishes focusing. The word spells itself in my head: *Aliens.*

Extraterrestrials.

What do I do, call the President? Capture them singlehanded with my peashooter? . . . I'm alone in the arse end of nowhere with one leg and my brain cuddled in meperidine hydrocholoride.

"Prrr-eese," their machine blurs again. "Wa-wat hep . . ."

"Our plane fell down," Ruth says in a very distinct, eerie voice. She points up at the jet, out towards the bay. "My—my child is there. Please take us *there* in your boat."

Dear god. While she's gesturing, I get a look at the thing she's hugging in her wounded arm. It's metallic, like a big glimmering distributor head. What—?

Wait a minute. This morning: when she was gone so long, she could have found that thing. Something they left behind. Or dropped. And she hid it, not telling me. That's why she kept going under that bromel clump—she was peeking at it. Waiting. And the owners came back and caught her. They want it. She's trying to bargain, by god.

"—Water," Ruth is pointing again. "Take us. Me. And him."

The black faces turn toward me, blind and horrible. Later on I may be grateful for that "us." Not now.

"Throw your gun away, Don. They'll take us back." Her voice is weak.

"Like hell I will. You—who are you? What are you doing here?"

"Oh god, does it matter? He's frightened," she cries to them. "Can you understand?"

She's as alien as they, there in the twilight. The beings in the skiff are twittering among themselves. Their box starts to moan.

"Ss-stu-dens," I make out. "S-stu-ding . . . no—huh-arm-ing . . . w-we . . . buh . . ." It fades into garble and then says "G-give . . . we . . . g-go . ."

Peace-loving cultural-exchange students—on the interstellar level now. Oh, no.

"Bring that thing here, Ruth—right now!"

But she's starting down the bank toward them saying, "Take me."

"Wait! You need a tourniquet on that arm."

"I know. Please put the gun down, Don."

She's actually at the skiff, right by them. They aren't moving.

"Jesus Christ." Slowly, reluctantly I drop the .32. When I start down the slide, I find I'm floating; adrenaline and Demerol are a bad mix.

The skiff comes gliding toward me, Ruth in the bow clutching the thing and her arm. The aliens stay in the stern behind their tripod, away from me. I note the skiff is camouflaged tan and green. The world around us is deep shadowy blue.

"Don, bring the water bag!"

As I'm dragging down the plastic bag, it occurs to me that Ruth really is cracking up, the water isn't needed now. But my own brain seems to have gone into overload. All I can focus on is a long white rubbery arm with black worms clutching the far end of the orange tube, helping me fill it. This isn't happening.

"Can you get in, Don?" As I hoist my numb legs up, two long white pipes reach for me. *No you don't.* I kick and tumble in beside Ruth. She moves away.

A creaky hum starts up, it's coming from a wedge in the center of the skiff. And we're in motion, sliding toward dark mangrove files.

I stare mindlessly at the wedge. Alien technological secrets? I can't see any, the power source is under that triangular cover, about two feet long. The gadgets on the tripod are equally cryptic, except that one has a big lens. Their light?

As we hit the open bay, the hum rises and we start planing faster and faster still. Thirty knots? Hard to judge in the dark. Their hull seems to be a modified trihedral much like ours, with a remarkable absence of slap. Say twenty-two feet. Schemes of capturing it swirl in my mind: I'll need Estéban.

Suddenly a huge flood of white light fans out over us from the tripod, blotting out the aliens in the stern. I see Ruth pulling at a belt around her arm, which is still hugging the gizmo.

"I'll tie that for you."

"It's all right."

The alien device is twinkling or phosphorescing slightly. I lean over to look, whispering, "Give that to me, I'll pass it to Estéban."

"No!" She scoots away, almost over the side. "It's theirs, they need it!"

"What? Are you crazy?" I'm so taken aback by this idiocy I literally stammer. "We have to, we—"

"They haven't hurt us. I'm sure they could." Her eyes are watching me with feral intensity; in the light her face has a lunatic look. Numb as I am, I realize that the wretched woman is poised to throw herself over the side if I move. With the gizmo.

"I think they're gentle," she mutters.

"For Christ's sake, Ruth, they're *aliens!*"

"I'm used to it," she says absently. "There's the island! Stop! Stop here!"

The skiff slows, turning. A mound of foliage is tiny in the light. Metal glints—the plane.

"Althea! Althea! Are you all right?"

Yells, movement on the plane. The water is high, we're floating over the bar. The aliens are keeping us in the lead with the light hiding them. I see one pale figure splashing toward us and a dark one behind, coming more slowly. Estéban must be puzzled by that light.

"Mr. Fenton is hurt, Althea. These people brought us back with the water. Are you all right?"

"A-okay," Althea flounders up, peering excitedly. "You all right? Whew, that light!" Automatically I start handing her the idiotic water bag.

"Leave that for the captain," Ruth says sharply. "Althea, can you climb in the boat? Quickly, it's important."

"Coming!"

"No, no!" I protest, but the skiff tilts as Althea swarms in. The aliens twitter, and their voice box starts groaning. "Gu-give . . . now . . . give . . ."

"Que llega?" Estéban's face appears beside me, squinting fiercely into the light.

"Grab it, get it from her—that thing she has—" but Ruth's voice rides over mine. "Captain, lift Mr. Fenton out of the boat. He's hurt his leg. Hurry, please."

"Goddamn it, wait!" I shout, but an arm has grabbed my middle. When a Maya boosts you, you go. I hear Althea saying, "Mother, your arm!" and fall onto Estéban. We stagger around in water up to my waist; I can't feel my feet at all.

When I get steady, the boat is yards away, the two women, head-to-head, murmuring.

"Get them!" I tug loose from Estéban and flounder forward. Ruth stands up in the boat facing the invisible aliens.

"Take us with you. Please. We want to go with you, away from here."

"Ruth! Estéban, get that boat!" I lunge and lose my feet again. The aliens are chirruping madly behind their light.

"Please take us. We don't mind what your planet is like; we'll learn—we'll do anything! We won't cause any trouble. Please. Oh *please.*" The skiff is drifting farther away.

"Ruth! Althea! You're crazy, wait—" But I can only shuffle nightmarelike in the ooze, hearing that damn voice box wheeze, "N-not come . . . more . . . not come . . ." Althea's face turns to it, open-mouthed grin.

"Yes, we understand," Ruth cries. "We don't want to come back. Please let us go with you!"

I shout and Estéban splashes past me shouting too, something about radio.

"Yes-s-s" groans the voice.

Ruth sits down suddenly, clutching Althea. At that moment Estéban grabs the edge of the skiff beside her.

"Hold them, Estéban! Don't let her go."

He gives me one slit-eyed glance over his shoulder, and I recognize his total uninvolvement. He's had a good look at that camouflage paint and the absence of fishing gear. I make a desperate rush and slip again. When I come up Ruth is saying, "We're going with these people, Captain. Please take your money out of my purse, it's in the plane. And give this to Mr. Fenton."

She passes him something small; the notebook. He takes it slowly.

"Estéban! Don't!"

He has released the skiff.

"Thank you so much," Ruth says as they float apart. Her voice is shaky; she raises it. "There won't be any trouble, Don. Please send this cable. It's to a friend of mine, she'll take care of everything." Then she adds the craziest touch of the entire night. "She's a grand person; she's director of nursing training at N.I.H."

As the skiff drifts, I hear Althea add something that sounds like "Right on."

Sweet Jesus . . . Next minute the humming has started; the light is receding fast. The last I see of Mrs. Ruth Parsons and Miss Althea Parsons is two small shadows against that light, like two opossums. The lights snaps off, the hum deepens—and they're going, going, gone away.

In the dark water beside me Estéban is instructing everybody in general to *chingarse* themselves.

"Friends, or something," I tell him lamely. "She seemed to want to go with them."

He pointedly silent, hauling me back to the plane. He knows what could be around here better than I do, and Mayas have their own longevity program. His condition seems improved. As we get in I notice the hammock has been repositioned.

In the night—of which I remember little—the wind changes. And at seven thirty next morning a Cessna buzzes the sandbar under cloudless skies.

By noon we're back in Cozumel. Captain Estéban accepts his fees and departs laconically for his insurance wars. I leave the Parsons' bags with the Caribe agent, who couldn't care less. The cable goes to a Mrs. Priscilla Hayes Smith also of Bethesda. I take myself to a medico and by three PM I'm sitting on the Cabañas terrace with a fat leg and a double margharita, trying to believe the whole thing.

The cable said, *Althea and I taking extraordinary opportunity for travel. Gone several years. Please take charge our affairs. Love, Ruth.*

She'd written it that afternoon, you understand.

I order another double, wishing to hell I'd gotten a good look at that gizmo. Did it have a label, Made by Betelgeusians? No matter how weird it was, *how* could a person be crazy enough to imagine—?

Not only that but to hope, to plan? *If I could only go away . . .* That's what she was doing, all day. Waiting, hoping, figuring how to get Althea. To go sight unseen to an alien world . . .

With the third margharita I try a joke about alienated women, but my heart's not in it. And I'm certain there won't be any bother, any trouble at all. Two human women, one of them possibly pregnant, have departed for, I guess, the stars; and the fabric of society will never show a ripple. I brood; do all Mrs. Parsons' friends hold themselves in readiness for any eventuality, including leaving Earth? And will Mrs. Parsons somehow one day contrive to send for Mrs. Priscilla Hayes Smith, that grand person?

I can only send for another cold one, musing on Althea. What suns will Captain Estéban's sloe-eyed offspring, if any, look upon? "Get in, Althea, we're taking off for Orion." "A-okay, Mother." Is that some system of upbringing? *We survive by ones and twos in the chinks of your world-machine . . . I'm used to aliens . . .* She'd meant every word. Insane. How could a woman choose to live among unknown monsters, to say good-bye to her home, her world?

As the margharitas take hold, the whole mad scenario melts down to the image of those two small shapes sitting side by side in the receding alien glare.

Two of our opossums are missing.

Manly Wade Wellman is one of the genre's finest fantasy writers, the author of more than fifty books and hundreds of stories and articles. He writes: "Some twenty-five years ago, I began wandering the Southern Appalachians, looking for old songs and old tales, making friends with the mountain people, finally building a cabin among them where I spend what time I can spare." From these people grew a group of tales Mr. Wellman has contributed to *F&SF* over the years, including this story about some witch business in Sawback Mountain country.

The Ghastly Priest
Doth Reign

by MANLY WADE WELLMAN

The jury found Jack Bowdry not guilty of murder. All anybody could testify was that he'd cursed and damned Kib Wordin for a witch-man and gave him twenty-four hours to leave the Sawback Mountain country, and twenty-five hours later Kib Wordin lay dead under the creepy tree in his cabin yard with a homemade silver bullet in his head. Come to think, a witch-man had died at that red-painted cabin thirty years back, and another witch-man years before that.

Anyway, Jack's neighbors helped him fetch his stuff from the county jail and rejoiced him up Walnut Creek to his home place next to Hosea's Hollow. They'd shucked his corn for him, handed and hung his tobacco in the curing barn. All vowed he'd done a good thing about Kib Wordin, whatever the jury couldn't decide, and at sundown that pretty fall day they good-byed him at his door.

Tolly Paradine, the schoolmaster's daughter, waited with him, making him feel almighty big because she was so little, with her pale-gold hair and rosy-gold cheeks. He stood a foot over her and near about a foot broader, with his brickbat jaw and big hands dangling from his blue shirtsleeves, with gray-threaded black hair, with thirty-four years to Tolly's twenty.

"I redded your place up for you," she said. "Jack, I'm proud you'll neighbor us again. And glad Kib Wordin won't pester me no more to come live with him."

He stared up slope to the ridge. "Better haste to catch up you daddy yonder," he said. "I'll come visit tomorrow if you say I can."

"Well you know you can, Jack." She upped to kiss his rough cheek, then ran after her folks. Jack looked again at what he'd seen to make him hurry her off from there.

Against the soft, evening sky at ridge top stood a squatty man, with a long, ashy-pale coat down to his ankles. As Jack looked, the fellow slid away into some brushy trees.

"Huh," said Jack Bowdry, deep in his deep chest, and faced toward his notch-logged cabin with its lime-painted clay chinking. He pushed the door open and set foot on the sill. Then he scowled down at what he'd near about stepped on. A gold coin, big as a half dollar, a double eagle such as was still round when Roosevelt started being President. It looked put there for him to pick up.

He glowered back to where that long-coated somebody had been. Then he toed the coin down into the yard and kicked it away in a twinkle of light into the bushes and went inside.

His cabin was just the one long room. The plank floor was swept. On the fireplace crane hung a kettle of stewed chicken, dumplings, carrots, the things Tolly knew he relished most. Jack built a fire under the kettle and put the match to the wick of his lamp. It let him see his bed at the far end, made up with a brown blanket and a white pillow, more of Tolly's doing. A smile creased the corners of Jack's wide mouth as he set the lamp on the fireboard, under his rifle and shotgun on the deer horns up there, and next to the row of books he'd read over and over.

Grandma Cutshaw's Bible; *Amateur Builder's Handbook;* Macaulay's poems that Jack almost knew by heart; *Guide to Rocks and Minerals; Jack Ranger's School Days; Robinson Crusoe;* Hill's *Manual of Social and Business Forms,* how to make a will, figure interest, all like that; and—

But he had only seven books. What was this one with the white paper cover at the end of the row?

He took it down. *Albertus Magnus, or White and Black Magic for Man and Beast*. Jack had heard tell of it, that you couldn't throw or give it away or burn it, you must bury it and say a funeral over it like for a dead man. Tolly had never left that here for him, nor either that gold eagle on the door log. The book flopped open in his hand:

> . . . in the red forest there is a red church, and in the red church stands a red altar, and upon the red altar there lies a red knife; take the red knife and cut red bread.

Jack slammed it shut and put it back on the shelf. Tomorrow he'd show it to Tolly's educated father. He took down the Macaulay and opened it to wash away the taste of the other book. Here was *The Battle of Lake Regillus:*

> Those trees in whose dim shadow
> The ghastly priest doth reign,
> The priest who slew the slayer,
> And shall himself be slain.

Now, what in hell might that mean? He shoved the Macaulay back, too, and spooned out a plateful of chicken stew and carried it to his table. Tasty, the stew was. He was glad to find himself enjoying to eat, proving to himself that he wasn't pestered by all these funny happenings. Even after two big helps, enough was left in the kettle to hot up for noon dinner tomorrow. Jack lighted his corncob pipe and went yet again for a book. Better be the Bible this time. He carried it and the lamp to the table.

Grandma used to cast signs, open the Bible anywhere and put a finger on whatever text is there. Do that three times and figure out the meaning. Jack opened the Bible midway and stabbed down his big finger.

> . . . preparest a table for me in the presence of mine enemies.

The Twenty-third Psalm. Tolly had prepared Jack a mighty good table. But the presence of enemies, now. He opened farther along, pointed again.

> . . . cried out, Great is Diana of the Ephesians.

Book of Acts that time, and Saint Paul getting hollered at, scolded. One more time, the very last page, a verse at the end of Revelation.

> . . . Without are dogs, and sorcerers . . .

Just then, a scrabbling at the door.

Jack sailed out of his chair, dropping the Bible and snatching his double-bitted ax from beside the fireplace. He ran and grabbed the latch string and yanked the door inward. "What's going on out here?" he roared.

A half-cowering shape backed off down the path toward the road.

"Where did you come from?" Jack yelled at it.

It stood up then, in a drench of moonlight, in its long pale coat, lifting its hands toward him. Not a dog, after all. Jack charged, ax lifted, and the shape scuttled away among the trees. Jack stood alone in the moon-bright road. Something else hurried at him from down slope. Again he whirled up the ax.

"Jack!" cried Tolly Paradine's voice.

He caught her wrist. "I thought you were that other one yonder."

"No, I came to tell you—"

"Inside, quick." He whirled her along the path and into the cabin and slammed the door behind them. Tolly looked at him with big scared eyes, and her golden skin was as pale as her hair.

"How come you to be out?" Jack demanded.

"Daddy was reading in a book he's got," she quavered. "It's *The Golden Bough,* somebody named Frazer wrote it."

"Ain't never heard tell of it." He cracked the door open, peered out, then shut them in again. "What's a book got to do with it?"

"Daddy says there's some kind of old worship." She dropped into his chair. "Long time ago, over the sea, somewhere near Rome. But longer ago than Rome." She trembled her lips. "Folks worshiped Diana."

"Just so happens I was reading in the Bible about Diana," Jack told her. "Wasn't she the hunting goddess, goddess of the moon? I recollect that from a book in school."

"Daddy say she was all kinds of goddess. They worshiped her with fire; sometimes they killed people for a sacrifice. Why, Daddy says some scholars think the whole witch business comes down from old worship of Diana. Like Kib Wordin's witch stuff."

"There's another tale about Diana," remembered Jack, leaning against the fireboard. "A man was out hunting and he seen her in swimming, naked as a jaybird. It was just a happen-so, but she flung water on him and turned him into a buck deer for his own dogs to pull down and kill. Ain't what sounds like a good goddess to worship."

"In those old days, the chief priest lived under a sacred tree," Tolly pattered on. "And when somebody killed him, that fellow got be the priest, till another killed *him,* and—"

She felt quiet. Jack frowned.

"What sort of tree is it got to be?" he asked her.

"Daddy never said that." Her eyes got wider. "You're thinking on that tree at Kib Wordin's place. Maybe one like that. No telling what a tree can get to be, over thousands of years, no more than what worship can get to be."

"And before Kib Wordin, a witch-man died up there," Jack reminded. "And before him, another one."

"And now—" she began, but again she stopped.

"And now, you aim to say, it's me," he finished for her. He shook his head, and his black hair stirred. "All right, what if old Jack Bowdry just ain't accepting the nomination? What if I just ain't having it, no way?"

"Daddy explained me about it," she stammered. "A branch from that old witch tree could be planted and grow to a witch tree itself, and be their worship place." She looked near about ready to cry. "You don't believe it's so," she half accused.

"Yes, I do. Stuff tonight makes me to believe."

He told her about the man in the long gray coat, the gold coin, the messages from the books.

"What man was it?" asked Tolly. "I don't call to mind anybody with a coat like that."

"I doubt if he wore it to be known," said Jack. "Anyway, it's like he was here to threaten me, and the money to buy me, and this here book to teach me."

He took down *Albertus Magnus*. "No, Tolly don't touch it. Anyway, I've seen that tree at Wordin's place, far off. Maybe it's what's grown up to cause this witch business."

"Kib Wordin read to me out of that book one time," she said. "Told me he'd put a spell on me so I couldn't refuse him."

"But you refused him."

"It was just about then when you—" She broke off. "You know."

"Sure enough I know. I put that silver bullet right back of his ear."

"You killed the priest, and that makes you the new one," said Tolly. "It's in Daddy's books. If you say no, they'll kill you, whoever they are."

"Ain't I a sitting duck to be killed?" he cried out. "Whoever wants that priest job next, won't he kill me if he can?"

"But when you see what's happening—"

"Stop rooting against me, Tolly!" he yelled, and she shrank down in the chair. "Whatever happens, I still ain't their man."

He glared at the book in his hand and walked to the door.

"What are you going to do?" Tolly squeaked behind him.

"A couple things needing to be done. The first of them won't take but two-three minutes."

He dragged the door open and stepped out into the night. Scraps of moonlight flitted among the trees as he walked to the road. He knelt and groped with his free hand until he found soft earth. Powerfully he scooped out great clods. He pushed *Albertus Magnus* into the hole, dragged the loosened earth back over it and rammed it down hard.

Still kneeling, he tried to think of the burial service. "Ashes to ashes, dust to dust," he said aloud, and the night around him was as still as stone. "Until the day break and the shadows flee away," he recollected a few more words to say. Then he got up. There was Tolly, standing beside him.

"Get back inside," he grumbled.

"Not with you out here."

He took her arm and pulled her to the door and inside. "Sit," he ordered her, pointing to the chair. "Don't you leave out of here till I get back."

"What you aiming to do, Jack?"

"I've kindly got it in mind that that witch tree up yonder's been growing long enough."

"If you don't come back—"

"Just start pestering about that when I don't."

He rolled his shirt sleeves back from his corded arms and took the double-bitted ax again. Out he tramped, slamming the door behind him.

Out to the road, past the grave where he'd buried *Albertus Magnus,* up slope. He moved between bunches of big trees he'd once reckoned he knew as friends, oaks and walnuts and tall watching pines, with sooty shadows among them. They stared at him from both sides; they seemed to hold their breath. He heard only his own dull footsteps until, before he knew it, he was where the path turned off to the red-painted cabin where once he'd sneaked up on Kib Wordin.

There was light through the trees there; not the moon glow on the road, but a dull red light. Jack stole along the path. Now he saw the slumpy-roofed cabin where three witch-men had lived and died, with its sneaky look like a hungry beast waiting, waiting. The red light soaked out through curtains at the windows. Who was inside there now? Doing what?

He decided not to knock and find out. He took careful steps into the yard, and he was right under the tree he'd come to find.

Never had he relished the look of that tree, even from far off, and he didn't relish its look now. It seemed to move or shiver in the dull red light. Its coaly black trunk might could be a foot and a half thick above roots that clutched deep down among rocks. Just above Jack's head the branches kinked this way and that way, like nothing so much as snakes. They wiggled, or maybe it was just the stir of lean, ugly leaves.

He walked all the way round, bending his head under the snaky branches, studying the trunk. Finally he set his booted feet just so on the damp-feeling earth. He shifted his grip on the ax helve and hiked it high. If whoever or whatever was in yonder with the red light heard him chop and came out, he'd be ready, ax in hand. Hard and deep he drove down the blade just above the roots.

Sound rose round him, soft to hear but scary to feel. It was like an echoed cry of pain, as if the wood he chopped was living flesh. He ripped the ax loose and raised it, and knew without looking up that those branches sure enough squirmed. A whisper sneaked in the air, like an angry voice. Again he swung the ax. A big chip sailed loose, showing white wood that glowed with its own pale, sick light.

Jack recollected the old Cherokee who'd said that trees felt when they were chopped, and it hadn't made him like to cut timber any right much. But this tree was different, it was an enemy tree. He looked toward the cabin. Not a stir from there. He slashed and slashed at the blackness of the trunk, every blow flinging white chips away. Sweat popped out on him. The murmur kept murmuring, but it didn't slow him up a hooter. Another six or seven chops at the right place, and that tree would fall. It would slap down right on the pulpy shingles of that red-lighted cabin. Once more he heaved up his ax.

And something grabbed onto it and held it on high.

At once he was fighting to get the ax back, but he couldn't. They crawled and struggled above him, those snaky branches, winding the ax helve, sliding twigs round his right arm like a basket weaving itself there. He let go the ax to fight that grip on him. His feet came clear of the ground with the effort, and the branches bent with his weight. Powerfully he fought his way round the trunk, the twigs still netting his arm. His hand and wrist tingled as if they were being bitten, sucked.

His free left hand hustled his great big clasp knife out of his pants pocket. He yanked the longest blade open with his teeth and slashed at those snaring twigs.

They parted under the edge that was as sharp as a whetrock could make it. As his right hand came free, more twigs scrambled down to spiral his left arm. His whipped the knife over to his right hand to hack and chop those new tethers. Free for a second, he tried to flounder away, but he slipped on soggy earth and fell to his knee. The branches grabbed and tied him again.

He started to curse, but saved his breath. He slashed with the knife, passing it from hand to hand. He cleared the twigs from wrists and arms, but a thicker branch wound him, tying his right arm to his side. It squeezed tighter than the strongest wrestler he'd ever tried holds with; he sawed at it, and it was hard to cut through. He got it whittled free of him, just as a bigger branch snapped a loop on his ankle and flung him full length.

"If I knew where your heart was," he panted as if the tree could hear, and maybe it did. Twenty twigs scraped and felt for new holds on him, wove and twisted round him, made it harder for him to cut at them. The cut ends kept crawling back, thicker, harder to slice away. He wished he had his ax, flung down yonder out of reach.

He turned himself over, and over again, He was as strong as any man in the Sawback Mountain country, and the surge of his turning broke some twigs, not all of them. Hacking at the ones still at him, he saw the cabin door open and somebody stepping out in the red light.

Hunched, wearing a long pale coat, it must be the one who'd spied at his homecoming. Close it came. A hand lifted a dark-shining blade, a big corn knife, just over him.

"Stay right there," said the quiet, cold voice of Tolly, from just beyond them.

The fellow froze, the corn knife drooped.

"Put that thing to Jack and I'll shoot you," Tolly said, as quiet as if she was saying the time of day. "I've got Jack's shotgun here, and a bunch of silver dimes wadded down both barrels on top of the buckshot."

The corn knife sank and pointed to the ground.

"You want to kill Jack and be the priest," Tolly said. "Then what if I killed you and got to be priestess? What if I used that witch book to witch your soul right down to the floor of hell?"

The fellow spun round and scurried off. Jack heard the long coat whip, heard a crash among dark trees. Tolly ran close.

"Look out," Jack wheezed.

But she stood right over him, laid the shotgun muzzles to that pallid wound he'd cut in the trunk, and slammed loose with both barrels. Flame flashed, the two shots howled like two claps of thunder, and something screamed a death scream. All those holds on Jack turned weak and fell away. With one floundering, scrambling try he ripped free of them and came to his feet beside Tolly.

The tree blazed up like fat meat where the blasts had driven into it. Jack pulled Tolly clear as the whole thing fell away from them, fell right on the roof of the cabin. The flames ran up into the branches and caught the shingles, burning blood red and sick white. Still holding to Tolly, Jack started her away at a run to the road and down the mountain.

Once they looked back. Flames jumped high and bright into the high darkness against the stars, gobbling that tree and that cabin, putting an end to both of them.

Tolly and Jack got married Thanksgiving week. Before that, the neighbor folks built a bedroom to Jack's cabin at the left, a lean-to kitchen at the right. Before that, too, half a dozen sorry men and women left out of the Sawback Mountain country. Nobody knew where they went, or even for dead sure which was the one who wore the long coat. All anybody was certain sure of was that you could live another sight better there without that half dozen people and whatever they'd been up to.

From Competition 7:   A Lexicon from an Alien Language

FARN - v.i., to argue politics, esp. with a medicine man.

GARFT - n., a form of chastisement, consisting in removing the skin or other integument by means of heated pincers.

NASIFURM - n., the unbearable ennui that afflicts the wheen player during the lentil season.

OGFARKN - v.i., to best a medicine man in an argument.

OGFARN GARFT - p.c., to be admonished by a medicine man.

ORFITIVE - adj., both decorative and nourishing; used only of life-forms with even numbers of limbs.

RHULF - n., a term of opprobrium, properly used only in castigating gravid bark peelers. *Literally,* the egg of the crested greal.

SNOAF - v.i., to lean upon a deciduous plant less than two meters high.

TUNDIFY - v.t., to chew upon the liver of one who has offended you, after the manner of gravid bark peelers.

—*Bob Leman*

Harvey Jacobs was born in 1930 in New York City and still lives there. He is a magazine writer (with stories in many publications, from *Midstream* to *Playboy*), a novelist (*Summer on a Mountain of Spice*), and has worked for ABC-TV for some time. This very short piece is one of our favorite Jacob stories. Another was "The Egg of the Glak," which appeared in *The Best from F&SF:* 18th Series.

Dress Rehearsal

by HARVEY JACOBS

Sam Derby felt old, even up there where time was an ice cube. He tried a knee bend and gave it up when his knees cracked like dice. Xarix appeared on the wall screen just as Sam Derby recovered his posture and let out a grunt.

"Are you stable?" Xarix said.

"I'm fine," Sam said. "How are you."

"It's time for the dress rehearsal," Xarix said. "Will you transport to the Green Theater?"

"You mean the Blue Theater, don't you?"

"The Green Theater. The children are performing in the Blue Theater."

"Ah, the kiddies, yes."

Some kiddies, Sam Derby thought to himself. He once knew a man named Louie who carried pictures of two apes in his wallet. When somebody asked him about his family, he showed the pictures of the young apes and beamed when the somebody told him what a lovely family he had. Up there the apes would look like gods. What they called kiddies wouldn't serve for bait back home. Sam Derby often wondered about the kind of sex that produced such results. *Yuch.*

Still, they loved their offspring. Chip off the old block, like that. To each his own.

The capsule came to Sam Derby's door. He got in and pressed the circular button marked The Green Theater. The capsule hummed and moved. It was a nice feeling to be inside, warm, vibrated, moving, and no meter ticking off a dime every few seconds to remind you of time and your own heartbeat.

Sam Derby, a senior citizen, with a First Indulgence classification, had the right to be gently lifted from the capsule and aimed at the door of the Green Theater. Xarix waited for him. As the doors of the Green Theater slid apart, Xarix appeared like a developing photograph.

"So, Professor," Xarix said, "how do you feel about the approach of Minus Hour."

"Not Minus Hour," Sam Derby said. "Zero Hour. You're the one who should set an example."

"God, yes," Xarix said. "If one of my students said that, I would have him boiled in . . . oil?"

"Oil is correct," Sam Derby said. "Where is everybody?"

"Supply," Xarix said. "They'll be here at the drop of a hat."

"Good. Well said," Sam Derby said.

"Thank you. I like that expression, at the drop of a hat. I have this vision of hats dropping. It amuses me."

"You have a nice sense of humor."

"I think so. Yes. I could have been a schpritzer."

"Not exactly a hundred percent," Sam Derby said. "A man who gives a schpritz is a comic. A comic is a schpritzer. Say, 'I could have been a comic.' It's a lot better."

"Thank you."

"Don't mention it."

Xarix and Sam Derby went to the podium at the front of the Green Theater.

"What do you want from me today?" Sam Derby said. "I can't tell them much more."

"I thought a kind of pep talk was in order. Good luck, go get 'em, half time in the locker room. Do it for the old Prof. You know what I'm after."

"I'll do that. When does the next class start?"

"Not for a week. You have yourself a vacation, a well-deserved holiday, Sam."

"Sam? What happened to Professor?"

"Under the circumstances I felt justified in using the familiar. We've worked together twelve solstices."

"Use what you want," Sam Derby said. "I wasn't complaining. In fact, I'm flattered. I was just surprised. I began to feel disposable."

"Disposable?"

"Like a tissue. I finished my work. The class is graduating, in a manner of speaking. How do I know there's another class? How do I know you won't dispose of me?"

"But that's ridiculous. You're one of us."

"Its nice of you to say so."

"Tell me," Xarix said, "are you sorry you came?"

"No," Sam Derby said. "I must admit, when you first came to get me, I wasn't so happy."

"You had a clear choice."

"Choice? You said I had a choice. But when one of us sees one of you for the first time coming from noplace, not the most beautiful thing in the universe, no insult intended, choice isn't choice. I was scared out of my rectum."

"Surprise is our schtik. The startle effect."

"You startled. Now that I'm here, now that I've had time to think things over, I'm really glad I flew up here. I like it here."

"Good."

"Besides, what did I have down there? Did I have respect? Honors? Medals? I had Social Security. I had a pension from the guild. The people who saw my work were dropping like flies. One day before you came I went to three funerals one after the other, bang, bang, bang."

"Alevai, Rest in peace."

"Wait. No alevai. Alevai is *it should happen*."

"Whoops."

"Whoops. If one of them said whoops, you would give him such a knock with the ray his kishkas would burn."

"There's an advantage to executive status," Xarix said. "Sam, do you think they'll be successful?"

"Why not? You send one here, one there, they have papers, they have skills, and they know how to behave. It's amazing how they look, exactly like people. Who should find out what they're up to? You got no problem with the spies. Your problem might be that Earth is already taken over by meshuganas. Maybe from another

planet. I never met a producer, an agent, a successful man who
couldn't be from Mars."

"Why Mars?"

"A figure of speech."

"Ah."

"I keep asking myself, Xarix, why you want Earth?"

"Because it's there."

"So all this trouble, spies, saboteurs, chazzerai, because it's there?"

"Sufficient reason."

"Sufficient reason. Be gazoont."

"Amen."

"You could say that. In all my years on stage I never would believe such a plot. Never. Too fantastic. So who knew?"

"We knew. Our computers knew. When we asked them the name
of the man for the job, Sam, your card came out with two others.
Stanislavski and Lee Strasberg. One was dead, and the other is too
much with the guttural noises, the schlepping and yutzing. Out of all
the actors past or present, your card came out, Sam Derby."

"It's nice to know. Nobody on Earth even remembers there was a
theater on Second Avenue."

"Let me say that for an alien you've dedicated yourself wonderfully well to our purposes. We had the human forms down pat. We
had the technicalities worked out. But nuances of manner, subtleties
of speech, are all important. Only you could impart such wisdom."

"Wisdom. There is a word. Xarix, I'll tell you, don't worry yourself. Your people, whatever you call it, will blend like a snowflake on
white bread. Down there, anybody will swear they're just like everybody else. They have the tools."

"Thanks to you, Sam. Professor."

"So."

When the students came, there was much excitement. Take off was
only hours away. The combination of youth, travel and purpose produced a familiar tension. Sam Derby stood on the podium delivering
his pep talk and feeling some of the excitement himself.

"Remember, you're going to take over a planet, not to play pi-
nochle. Do what I told you, be discreet, and the magic word is to
blend in the soup. Now, let me hear all together in unison, what you
say when you meet a person of rank and power."

"Oy vay, vots new, hello, howdy doo?"

"Good. Now, in sexual encounter, what is the correct approach?"

"Hey, dollink, let's schtup, don't futz, hurry up."

"Wonderful. And for you in the diplomatic corps, very important, when you run into a prince, a king, a president, let's hear it."

"Honorable Ganef, it's a real Watergate to make the acquaintance of so illustrious a nebbish schlemiel nudnik putz as thyself. May you fornicate with a horse before the night falls."

"Georgeous," Sam Derby said. "I'm proud of you. Go, and give my regards to Broadway."

"You think they're ready?" Xarix said.

"Ready for Freddy," Sam Derby said. "If they learned my lessons and wave the arms you gave them, they'll be accepted anyplace. Like brothers."

Tom Reamy worked in the aerospace industry most of his adult life until the bottom fell out during the 1974 recession and he got laid off. He then began writing sf seriously, and this, his second story for *F&SF*, won the Science Fiction Writers of America Nebula Award for best novelet, 1976. Awards are no guarantee of quality, but this beautiful story deserves every accolade it receives.

San Diego Lightfoot Sue

by TOM REAMY

This all began about ten years ago in a house at the top of a flight of rickety wooden stairs in Laurel Canyon. It might be said there were two beginnings, though the casual sorcery in Laurel Canyon may have been the cause and the other merely the effect—if you believe in that sort of thing.

The woman sat cross-legged on the floor reading the book. The windows were open to the warm California night, and the only sounds that came through them was the distant, muffled, eternal roar of Los Angeles traffic. The brittle pages of the book crackled as she turned them carefully. She read slowly because her Latin wasn't what it used to be. She lit a cigarette and left it to burn unnoticed in the ashtray on the floor beside her.

"Here's a good one," she said to the big orange tom curled in the chair she leaned against. "You don't know where I can find a hazel-nut bush with a nest of thirteen white adders under it, do you, Punkin?" The cat didn't answer; he only opened one eye slightly and twitched the tip of his tail.

She turned a page, and several two-inch rectangles of white paper fell into her lap. She picked them up and examined them, but they were blank. She stuck them back in the book and kept reading.

She found it a while later. It was a simple spell. All she had to do was write the word-square on a piece of white parchment with black ink and then burn it while thinking of the person she wished to summon.

"I wonder if Paul Newman is doing anything tonight," she chuckled.

She stood up and went to the drafting table, opened a drawer and removed a pen and a bottle of india ink. She put a masking tape dispenser on the edge of the book to hold it open and carefully lettered the word-square on one of the pieces of paper stuck between the pages. She supposed that's why her mother, or whoever, had put them there—they looked like parchment, anyway.

The word-square was eight letters wide and eight letters high; eight, eight-letter words stacked on top of one another. She imagined they were words, though they were in no language she knew. The peculiar thing about the square was that it read the same sideways or upside down—even in a mirror image, it was the same.

She put the cap back on the ink and went to the ashtray, kneeling beside it. She lay the parchment on the dead cigarette butts. "Well, here goes," she said to the cat. "I wonder if it's all right to burn it with a cigarette lighter? Maybe I need a black taper made of the wax of dead bees or something."

She composed herself, trying to take it seriously, and thought of a man, not a specific man, just *the* man. "I feel like Snow White singing 'Someday My Prince Will Come,'" she muttered. She flicked the cigarette lighter and touched the flame to the corner of the piece of paper.

It flamed up so quickly and so brightly that she gasped and drew back. "God!" she grunted and hurried to a window to escape the billows of black smoke that smelled of rotten eggs. The cat was already out, sitting on the farthest point of the deck railing, looking at her with round startled eyes.

The woman glanced back at the black smoke spreading like a carpet on the ceiling and then at the wide-eyed cat. She suddenly collapsed against the window sill in a fit of uncontrollable laughter. "Come on back in, Punkin," she gasped. "It's all over." The cat gave

her an incredulous look and hopped off the railing into the shrub-
bery.

This also began about ten years ago in Kansas, the summer he was
fifteen, when the air smelled like hot metal and rang with the cries of
cicadas. It ended a month later when he was still fifteen, when the
house in Laurel Canyon burned with a strange green fire that made
no heat.

His name was John Lee Peacock, a good, old, undistinguished
name in Southern Kansas. His mother and his aunts and his aunts'
husbands called him John Lee. The kids in school called him
Johnny, which he preferred. His father never called him anything.

His father had been by-passed by the world, but he wouldn't have
cared, even if he had been aware of it. Wash Peacock was a dirt
farmer who refused to abandon the land. The land repaid his taci-
turn loyalty with annual betrayal. Wash had only four desires to life:
to work the land, three hot meals each day, sleep, and copulation
when the pressures built high enough. The children were strangers
who appeared suddenly, disturbed his sleep for a while, then faded
into the gray house or the County Line Cemetery.

John Lee's mother had been a Willet. The aunts were her sisters:
Rose and Lilah. Wash had a younger brother somewhere in Pennsyl-
vania—or, had had one the last time he heard. That was in 1927, the
year Wash's mother died. Grace Elizabeth Willet married Delbert
Washburn Peacock in the fall of 1930. She did it because her father,
old Judge Willet, thought it was a good idea. Grace Elizabeth was a
plain, timid girl who, he felt, was destined to be the family's maiden
aunt. He was right, but she would have been much happier if he
hadn't interfered.

The Peacocks had owned the land for nearly a hundred years and
were moderately prosperous. They had survived the Civil War, Re-
construction, and statehood, but wouldn't survive the Depression.
Judge Willet felt that Wash was the best he could do for Grace
Elizabeth. He was a nice-looking man, and what he lacked in imagination, he made up in hard work.

But the Peacocks had a thin, unfortunate blood line. Only a few of
the many children lived. It was the same with Wash and Grace
Elizabeth. She had given birth eight times, but there were only three
of them left. Wash, Jr., her first born, had married one of the trashy
O'Dell girls and had gone to Oklahoma to work in the oilfields. She

hadn't heard from him in thirteen years. Dwayne Edward, the third born, had stayed in Los Angeles after his separation from the army. He sent a card every Christmas and she had kept them all. She wished some of the girls had lived. She would have liked to have a girl, to make pretty things for her, to have someone to talk to. But she had lost the three girls and two of the boys. She had trouble remembering their names sometimes, but it was all written in the big Bible where she could remind herself when the names began to slip away.

John Lee was the youngest. He had arrived late in her life, a comfort for her weary years. She wanted him to be different from the others. Wash, Jr. and Dwayne had both been disappointments; too much like their father: unimaginative plodding boys who had done badly in school and got into trouble with the law. She still loved them because they were her children, but she sometimes forgot why she was supposed to. She wanted John Lee to read books (God! How long since she'd read a book; she used to read all the time when she was a girl), to know about art and faraway places. She knew she hoped for too much, and so she was content when she got a part of it.

Wash didn't pay any more attention to John Lee than he had the others. He neither asked nor seemed to want the boy's help in the field. So Grace Elizabeth kept him around the house, helping with her chores, talking to him, having him share with her what he had learned in school. She gave him as much as she could. There wasn't money for much, but she managed to hold back a few dollars now and then.

She loved John Lee very much; he was probably the only thing she did love. So, on that shimmering summer day about ten years ago, when he was fifteen, she died for him.

She was cleaning up the kitchen after supper. Wash had gone back to the fields where he would stay until dark. John Lee was at the kitchen table, reading, passing on bits of information he knew she would like to hear. She leaned against the sink with the cup towel clutched in her hand and felt her supper turn over in her stomach. She had known it was coming for months. Now it was here.

He's too young, she thought. If he could only have a couple more years. She watched him bent over the book, the evening sun glinting on his brown hair. He's even better looking than his father, she thought. So like his father. But only on the outside. Only on the outside.

She spread the cup towel on the rack to dry and walked through the big old house. She hadn't really noticed the house in a long time. It had grown old and gray slowly, as she had, and so she had hardly noticed it happening. Then she looked at it again and it wasn't the house she remembered moving into all those years ago. Wash's father had built it in 1913 when the old one had been unroofed by a twister. He had built it like they did in those days: big, so generations could live in it. It had been freshly painted when she moved in, a big white box eight miles from Hawley, a mile from Miller's Corners.

Then the hard times began. But Wash had clung to the land during the Depression and the dust. He hadn't panicked like most of the others. He hadn't sold the land at give-away prices or lost it because he couldn't pay the taxes. Things had gotten a little better when the war began, but never as good as before the Depression. Now they were bad again. At the end of each weary year there was only enough money to do it all over again.

She supposed that being the oldest, Wash, Jr., would get it. She was glad John Lee wouldn't. She went upstairs to his room and packed his things in a pasteboard box. She left it where he would find it and went to her own room. She opened a drawer in the old highboy that had belonged to her grandmother and removed an envelope from beneath her cotton slips. She took it to the kitchen and handed it to John Lee.

He took it and looked at her. "What is it, Mama?"

"Open it in the morning, John Lee. You'd better go to bed now."

"But it's not even dark yet." There's something wrong, there's something wrong.

"Soon, then. I want to sit on the porch awhile and rest." She kissed him and patted his shoulder and left the room. He watched the empty doorway and felt the blood singing in his ears. After a while, he got a drink of water from the cooler and went to his room. He lay on the bed, looking at the water spots on the ceiling paper, and clutched the envelope in his hands. Tears formed in his eyes and he tried to blink them away.

Grace Elizabeth sat on the porch in her rocker, moving gently, mending Wash's clothes until it got too dark to see. Then she folded them neatly in her lap, leaned back in the chair, and closed her eyes.

Wash found her the next morning only because he wondered why his breakfast wasn't waiting for him. She was buried in the County Line Cemetery with five of her children after a brief service at the First Baptist Church in Hawley. Aunt Rose and Aunt Lilah had a fine time weeping into black lace handkerchiefs and clucking over Poor John Lee.

On the way back from the funeral John Lee rode in the front seat of the '53 Chevrolet beside his father. Neither of them spoke until they had turned off the highway at Miller's Corners.

"Write a letter to Wash, Jr. Tell him to come home." John Lee didn't answer. He could smell the dust rising up behind the car. Wash parked it in the old carriage house and hurried to change clothes, hurried to make up the half day he had lost. John Lee went to the closet in the front hall and took down a shoe box, in which his mother kept such things, and looked for an address. He found it after a bit, worked to the bottom, unused for thirteen years. He wrote the letter anyway.

He had left the envelope unopened under his pillow. Now he opened it, although he had guessed what it was. He counted the carefully hoarded bills: a hundred and twenty-seven dollars. He sat on the edge of the bed, on the crazy quilt his mother had made for him, in the quiet room, in the silent weary house. He wiped his eyes with his knuckles, picked up the pasteboard box, and walked the mile to Miller's Corners.

His Sunday suit, worn to the funeral that morning, once belonging to Dwayne, and before that, Wash, Jr., was white at the cuffs from the dusty road. His shoes, his alone, were even worse. It was a scorcher. "It's gonna be another scorcher," she always used to say, looking out the kitchen window after putting away the breakfast dishes. He sat on the bench at the Gulf station, cleaning the dust off the best he could.

The cicadas screeched from the mesquite bushes, filling the hot still air with their insistent calls for a mate. John Lee rather liked the sound, but it had bothered his mother. "Enough to drive a body ravin' mad," she used to say. She always called them locusts, but he had learned in school their real name was cicada. And when they talked about a plague of locusts in the Bible, they really meant grasshoppers. "Well, I'll declare," she had said. "Always wondered why locusts would be considered a plague. Far's I know, they don't do anything but sit in the bushes and make noise. Now, grasshoppers I can understand." And she would smile at him in her pleased and proud way that caused a pleasant hurting in the back of his throat.

"Hello, John Lee."

He looked up quickly. "Hello, Mr. Cuttsanger. How are you today?" He liked Mr. Cuttsanger, a string-thin man the same age as his mother, who had seemingly permanent grease stains on his hands. He wiped at them now with a dull red rag, but it didn't help.

"I'm awfully sorry about your mother, boy. Wish I coulda gone to the funeral but I couldn't get away. We were in the same grade together all through school, you know."

"Yes, I know. She told me."

"What're you doin' here still dressed up?" he asked, sticking the rag in his hip pocket and looking at the box.

"I reckon I have to catch a bus, Mr. Cuttsanger." His heart did a little flip-flop. Not the old school bus either, but a real bus.

"Where you off to, John Lee?"

"Where do your buses go, Mr. Cuttsanger?"

Mr. Cuttsanger sat on the bench beside John Lee. "The westbound will be through here in about an hour goin' to Los Angeles. The eastbound comes through in the mornin' headed for St. Louie. You already missed it."

"Los Angeles. My brother, Dwayne, lives in California." But he didn't know where. He had seen the Christmas cards in the shoe box, but he hadn't paid any attention to the return address.

Mr. Cuttsanger nodded. "Good idea, goin' to stay with Dwayne. Nothin' for you here on this played-out old farm. Heard Grace Elizabeth say the same thing. Your father ought to sell it and go with you. But I guess I know Wash better'n that." He arose from the bench with a little sigh. He went into the station and returned with a small red flag. He stuck it in a pipe welded at an angle to the pole supporting the Gulf sign. "There. He'll stop when he sees that. You buy your ticket from the driver."

"Thank you, Mr. Cuttsanger. I need to mail a letter also." He took the letter he had carefully addressed in block printing to Delbert Washburn Peacock, Jr., Gen. Del., Norman, Okla., from his pocket and handed it to Mr. Cuttsanger. "I don't have a stamp."

Mr. Cuttsanger looked at the letter. "Is Wash, Jr., still in Norman?" He said it as if he doubted it.

"I don't know. That's the only address I could find."

Mr. Cuttsanger tapped the letter against the knuckle of his thumb.

"You leave a nickel with me and I'll get a stamp from Clayton in the mornin'. Sure was a lot simpler before they closed the post office." He sat back on the bench in the shade of the car shed. John Lee followed his eyes as he looked at Miller's Corners evaporating under the cloudless sky. An out-of-state car blasted through doing seventy. Mr. Cuttsanger sighed and accepted a nickel from John Lee. "They don't even have to slow down any more. Used to be thirty-five-mile speed-limit signs at each end of town. Guess they don't need 'em now. Ain't nothin' here but me and the cafe. Myrtle's been saying for nearly a year she was gonna move to Hawley or maybe even Liberal. Closed the post office in fifty-five, I think it was. That foundation across the highway is where the grocery store used to be. Don't reckon you remember the grocery store?"

"No, sir, but I remember the feed store."

"Imagine that. You musta been about four, five years old."

"I was born in forty-eight."

"Closed the feed store in fifty-two. Imagine you rememberin' that far back." He continued to ramble on in his pleasant friendly voice. John Lee asked questions and made comments to keep him going, to make the time pass faster. A whole hour before the bus would come.

But it finally did, cutting off the highway in a cloud of dust and a dragon hiss of air brakes. John Lee looked at the magic name in the little window over the windshield: LOS ANGELES. He swallowed and solemnly shook hands with Mr. Cuttsanger.

"Good-by, Mr. Cuttsanger."

"Good-by, John Lee. You take care now."

John Lee nodded and picked up the box and walked to the bus, his legs trembling. The door sighed open and the driver got out. He opened a big door on the side of the bus under *Continental Trailways*. He took the pasteboard box.

"Where you goin'?"

"I'd like a ticket to Los Angeles, please." He couldn't keep from smiling when he said the name. The driver put a tag on the box, put it in with the suitcases, and closed the door. John Lee followed him into the bus. Inside it was cool like some of the stores in Liberal.

He bought his ticket and sat down in the front seat, scooting to the window as the bus lurched back onto the highway. He looked back at Miller's Corners and waved to Mr. Cuttsanger, but he was taking down the red flag and didn't see.

John Lee leaned back in the seat and hugged himself. Once more he couldn't keep from smiling. After a bit, he looked around at the other people. There weren't many and some weren't wearing Sunday clothes; so he decided it would be all right to take off his jacket. He settled back in the seat, watching the baked Kansas countryside rush past the window. Strange, he thought, it looks the same way it does from the school bus. Even though he tried to prevent it, the smile returned unbidden every once in a while.

The bus went through Hawley without stopping, past the white rococo courthouse with its high clock tower; past the school, closed for the summer; over the hump in the highway by the old depot where the railroad tracks had been taken out; across the bridge over Crooked Creek.

It stopped in Liberal and the driver called out, "Rest stop!" John Lee didn't know what a rest stop was, and so he stayed on the bus. He noticed that some of the other passengers didn't get off either. He decided there was nothing to worry about.

He tried to see everything when the bus left Liberal, to look on both sides at once, because it was the farthest he had ever been. But Oklahoma looked just like Kansas, Texas looked just like Oklahoma, and New Mexico looked like Texas, only each seemed a little bleaker than the one before. The bus stopped in Tucumcari for supper. John Lee had forgotten to eat dinner, and his bladder felt like it would burst.

He was nervous but he managed all right. He'd eaten in a cafe before, and, by watching the others, he found out where the toilet was and how to pay for his meal. It was dark when the bus left Tucumcari. He tried to go to sleep, to make the time pass faster, the way he always did when the next day was bringing wondrous things. But, as usual, the harder he tried, the wider awake he was.

He awoke when the bus stopped for breakfast and quickly put his coat over his lap, hoping no one had noticed. He waited until everyone else had gotten off, then headed for the toilet keeping his coat in front of him. He didn't know for sure where he was, but all the cars had Arizona license plates.

It was after dark when the bus pulled into the Los Angeles terminal, though it seemed to John Lee as if they had been driving through town for hours. He had never dreamed it was so big. He watched the other passengers collect their luggage and got his pasteboard box.

Then he went out into: Los Angeles.

He walked around the street with the box clutched in his arms in total bedazzlement. Buildings, lights, cars, people, so many different kinds of people. It was the first time he had ever seen a Chinese, except in the movies, although he wasn't absolutely sure that it wasn't a Japanese. There were dozens of picture shows, lined up in rows. He liked movies and used to go nearly every Saturday afternoon, a long time ago before the picture show in Hawley closed.

And buses, with more magic names in the little windows: SUNSET BLVD; HOLLYWOOD BLVD; PASADENA; and lots of names he didn't recognize; but they were no less magic, he was sure, because of that.

He was standing on the curb, just looking, when a bus with HOLLYWOOD BLVD in the little window pulled over and opened its door right in front of him. The driver looked at him impatiently. It was amazing how the bus had stopped especially for him. He got on. There didn't seem to be anything else he could do.

"Vine!" the driver bawled sometime later. John Lee got off and stood at the corner of Hollywood and Vine grinning at the night. He walked down Hollywood Boulevard, gawking at everything, reading the names in stars on the sidewalk. He never imagined there would be so many cars or so many people at night. There were more than you would see in Liberal, even on Saturday afternoon. And the strange clothes the people wore. And men with long hair like the Beatles. Mary Ellen Walker had a colored picture of them pasted on her notebook.

He didn't know how far he had walked—the street never seemed to end—but the box was heavy. He was hungry and his Sunday shoes had rubbed a blister on his heel. He went into a cafe and sat in a booth, glad to get rid of the weight of the box. Most of the people looked at him as he came in. Several of them smiled He smiled back. A couple of people had said hello on the street too. Hollywood was certainly a friendly place.

He told the waitress what he wanted. He looked around the cafe and met the eyes of a man at the counter who had smiled when he came in. The man smiled again. John Lee smiled back, feeling good. The man got off the stool and came to the booth carrying a cup of coffee.

"May I join you?" He seemed a little nervous.

"Sure." The man sat down and took a quick sip of the coffee. "My name is John Lee Peacock." He held out his hand. The man looked startled, then took it, giving it a quick shake and hurriedly breaking contact. "I'd rather be called Johnny, though."

The man's skin was moist. John Lee guessed he was about forty and a little bit fat. He nodded, quickly, like a turkey. "Warren."

"Pleased to meet you, Mr. Warren. You live in Hollywood?"

"Yes."

The waitress brought the food and put it on the table. Warren was flustered. "Oh . . . ah . . . put that on my ticket."

The waitress looked at John Lee. Her mouth turned down a little at the corners. "Sure, honey," she said to Mr. Warren.

John Lee discarded the straw from his ice tea and put sugar in it. "Aren't you eating?"

"Ah . . . no. No, I've already eaten." He took another nervous sip of the coffee, and John Lee heard a smothered snicker from the booth behind him. "You didn't have to pay for my supper. I've got money."

"My pleasure."

"Thank you, Mr. Warren."

"You're welcome. Uh . . . how long you been in town?"

"Just got here a little while ago. On a Continental Trailways bus, all the way from Miller's Corners, Kansas." John Lee still couldn't believe where he was. He had to say it out loud. "I sure do like bein' in Los Angeles, Mr. Warren."

"You have a place to stay yet?"

He hadn't really thought about that. "No, sir. I guess I haven't."

Warren smiled and seemed to relax a little. It was working out okay, but the kid was putting on the hick routine a little thick. "Don't worry about it tonight. You can stay at my place and look for something tomorrow."

"Thank you, Mr. Warren. That's very nice of you."

"My pleasure. Uh . . . what made you come to Los Angeles?"

John Lee swallowed a mouth full of food. "My mamma died the other day. Before she died, she gave me the money to get away."

"I want to sit on the porch a while and rest," she had said.

"It was either Los Angeles or St. Louis, and the Los Angeles bus came by first." He pushed the gray memories back out of the way. "And here I am!"

Warren looked at him, no longer smiling. "How old are you?"

"I was fifteen last January." He wondered if he was expected to ask Mr. Warren's age.

"God!" Warren breathed. He slumped in the seat for a moment, then seemed to come to a decision. "Look, uh . . . Johnny. I just remembered something. I won't be able to put you up for the night after all. As a matter of fact, I have to dash. I'm sorry."

"That's all right, Mr. Warren. It was kind of you to make the offer."

"My pleasure. So long." He hurried away. John Lee watched him stop at the cash register. When he left, the cashier looked at John Lee and nodded.

"Nice goin' there, John Lee Peacock, sugah." The voice whispered in his ear with a honeyed Southern accent. He turned and looked nose to nose into a grinning black face. "Got yoself a free dinnah and didn't have to put out."

"What," he said, completely befuddled.

A second face, a white one, appeared over the back of the seat. It said, "May we join you?" doing a good imitation of Mr. Warren.

"Yeah, I guess so." They came around and sat opposite him, both of them as skinny as Mr. Cuttsanger. He thought they walked a little funny.

The black one said, "I'm Pearl and this is Daisy Mae."

"How ja do," Daisy Mae said, chewing imaginary gum.

"Really?" John Lee asked, grinning.

"Really, what, sugah?" Pearl asked.

"Are those really your names?"

"Isn't he *cute?*" shrieked Daisy Mae.

Pearl patted his hand. "Just keep your eyes and ears open and your pants shut, sugah. You'll get the hang of it." He lit a pale blue cigarette and offered one to John Lee. John Lee shook his head. Pearl saw John Lee's bemused expression and wiggled the cigarette. "Nieman-Marcus," he said matter-of-factly.

"Well, if it isn't the Queen of Spades and Cotton Tail." They all three looked up at a chubby young man, standing with his hand delicately on his hip. His fleshy lips coiled into a smirk at John Lee. He wore light eye make-up with a tiny diamond in one pierced ear. He was with a muscular young man who looked at John Lee coldly. "You girls stage another commando raid on Romper Room?"

"Why, lawdy, Miss Scawlett, how you do talk!" Pearl did his best Butterfly McQueen imitation, and his hands were like escaping blackbirds.

"This is a cub scout meeting and we're den mothers," Daisy Mae said in a flat voice. The muscular young man grabbed Miss Scarlett's arm and pulled him away.

"It's a den of something!" he shot back over his shoulder

"Did you see how Miss Scarlett looked at our John Lee?" Daisy Mae rolled his eyes.

"The bitch is in heat."

"Who was that gorgeous butch number she was with?"

"Never laid eyes on him before."

"Your eyes aren't what you'd like to lay on him," Daisy Mae said dryly.

Pearl quickly put his hands over John Lee's ears. "Don't talk like that afore this sweet child! You *know* I don't like rough trade!"

John Lee laughed and they laughed with him He didn't know what they were talking about most of the time, but he decided he liked these two strange people. "Doesn't . . . uh . . . Miss Scarlett like you?"

"Sugah," Pearl said seriously, taking his hands away, "Miss Scawlett doesn't like anybody."

"Stay away from her, John Lee," Daisy Mae said, meaning it.

"She has a problem," Pearl pronounced.

"A *big* problem," Daisy Mae agreed.

"What?" John Lee asked, imagining all sorts of things.

"She's hung like a horse." Pearl nodded sagely.

"A *big* horse." Daisy Mae nodded also.

John Lee could feel his ears getting red. Damnation, he thought. He laughed in embarrassment. "What's wrong with that?" He remembered Leo Whittaker in his room at school who bragged that he had the biggest one in Kansas and would show it to you if you would go out under the bleachers.

"Sugah," Pearl said, patting his hand again, "Miss Scawlett is a *lady*."

"It's a wonder it doesn't turn green and fall off the way she keeps it tied down. Makes her walk bowlegged."

"Don't be catty, Daisy Mae. Just count your blessin's." Daisy Mae put his chin on the heel of his hand and stared morosely at nothing, like Garbo in *Anna Christie*. "John Lee, sugah," Pearl continued, "was all that malarkey you gave that score the truth?"

"Huh?" John Lee asked, completely confused.

"It was," Daisy Mae said in his incredible but true voice.

"You really don't have a place to stay tonight?"

"Huh-uh." He wondered why Pearl doubted him.

"And he's also really fif-*teen*." Daisy Mae said, cocking his eyes at Pearl.

"Daisy Mae, sugah," Pearl said with utmost patience, "I'm only bein' a Sistuh of Mercy, tryin' to put a roof ovuh this sweet child's head, tryin' to keep him from bein' picked up by the po-leece fah vay-gran-cee."

Daisy Mae shrugged fatalistically.

"Why does it matter that I'm fifteen?" John Lee really wanted to know what they were talking about.

"You *are* from the boonies," Daisy Mae said in wonder.

"Sugah, you come stay with us. There's a lot you've got to learn. If we leave you runnin' around loose, you gonna get in seer-ee-us trouble. Sugah, this town is full of tiguhs and . . . you . . . are . . . a . . . juicy . . . lamb."

"Your fangs are showing," Daisy Mae said tonelessly.

Pearl turned to him, about to cut him dead, but instead threw up his arms and did Butterfly McQueen again. "Lawzy, Miss Daisy Mae, you done got a spot on yo' pretty shirt!" He turned back to John Lee with a martyred expression. "I wash and clean and iron and scrub and work my fanguhs to the bone, and this slob can get covered in spaghetti sauce eatin' *jelly beans!*"

John Lee dissolved in a fit of giggles. Pearl couldn't hold his outraged expression any longer and began to grin. Daisy Mae chuckled and said, "Don't pay any attention to her, John Lee. She's got an Aunt Jemimah complex."

Pearl got up. "Let's get out of this meat market. There are too many eyes on our little rump roast."

Daisy Mae put his hand on John Lee's. "John Lee, if we run into a cop, *try* to look twenty-one."

He wiped the laugh tears from his eyes. "I'll do my best." He got the pasteboard box and followed them out of the cafe. They cut hurriedly around the corner past a large sidewalk newsstand, then jaywalked to a parking lot. Pearl and Daisy Mae acted like a couple of cat burglars, and John Lee had to hurry to keep up.

They got into a '63 Corvair and drove west on Hollywood Boulevard until it became a residential street, then turned right on Laurel Canyon. They wound up into the Hollywood Hills, Pearl and Daisy Mae chattering constantly, making John Lee laugh a lot. He felt very good and very lucky.

Pearl pulled into a garage sitting on the edge of the pavement with no driveway. They went up a long flight of rickety wooden steps to a small two-bedroom house with a porch that went all the way around. Pearl flipped on the lights. "It ain't Twelve Oaks, sugah, but we like it."

John Lee stared goggle-eyed. He'd been in Aunt Rose's and Aunt Lilah's fancy houses lots of times, but they ran to beige, desert rose, and old gold. These colors were absolutely electric. The wild patterns made him dizzy, and there were pictures and statues and things hanging from the ceiling.

"Golly," he said.

"Take a load off," Daisy Mae said, pointing to a big reclining chair covered in what looked like purple fur. John Lee put the box on the floor and gingerly sat down. He leaned back and was surprised at how comfortable it was. Pearl put a record on the record player, but John Lee didn't recognize the music. He yawned. Daisy Mae stood over the box. "What's in this carton you keep clutching to your bosom?"

"My things."

"Pardon my nose," Daisy Mae said and opened it. He pulled out some of John Lee's everyday clothes. "You auditioning for the six-teenth road company of *Tobacco Road?*"

"Don't pay any attention," Pearl said, sitting beside John Lee. "She's a costumer at Paramount. Thinks she knows *every*-thing about clothes."

"Don't knock it. I had to dress thirty bitchy starlets to buy that chair you got your black ass on. I'll hang these up for you, John Lee."

John Lee yawned again. "Thank you."

Peal threw up his hands. "Land o' Goshen, this child is ex-*haus*ted!"

Daisy Mae carried the box into a bedroom. "Two days on a Continental Trailways bus would give Captain Marvel the drearies."

Pearl took John Lee's arm and pulled him out of the chair. "Come on, sugah. We gotta give you a nice bath and put you to *bed,* afore you co-lapse." He led him to the bathroom, showed him where everything was, and turned on the shower for him. "Give a holler if you need anything."

"Thank you." Pearl left. John Lee had never taken a shower before, although he had seen them at Aunt Rose's and Aunt Lilah's. He took off his clothes and got in.

The door opened and Pearl came in, pushing back the shower curtain. "You all right, sugah? Oh, sugah, you are *all right!*" He leered at John Lee, but in such a way that made him laugh. His ears turned red anyway. Pearl winked and closed the curtain. "You don't mind if I brush my teeth?"

"No. Go ahead." He could hear Pearl sloshing and brushing. After a bit there was silence. He pulled back the shower curtain a little and peeped out. Pearl was leaning against the wash basin, a toothbrush in his hand, his head down, and his eyes closed. John Lee watched him, wondering if he should say anything.

"John Lee," Pearl said without looking up, his voice serious and the accent totally absent.

"Yes, Pearl?" He spoke quietly and cautiously.

"John Lee, don't pay any attention when we tease you about how cute you are, or when we ogle your body. It's just the way we are. It's just the way the lousy world is."

"I won't, Pearl." He felt the hurting in the back of his throat, but he didn't know why.

Pearl suddenly stood up, the big grin back on his face. "Well. Look at me. Poor Pitiful Pearl. Now. What do you sleep in? Underwear? Pee-jays? Nightshirt? Your little bare skin?"

"My pajamas are in the box, I think."

"Good enough." Pearl left the bathroom and returned when John Lee was drying on a big plush towel printed like the American flag. Pearl reached in and hung the pajamas on the doorknob without looking in. "There you go, sugah."

"Thank you, Pearl."

He left the bathroom in his pajamas with his Sunday suit over his arm. Daisy Mae took the suit. "I'll clean and press that for you."

"You don't have to, Daisy Mae." The names were beginning to sound normal to him.

Daisy Mae grinned. "It won't hurt me."

"Thank you."

Pearl took his arm. "Time for you to go to bed." He led John Lee into the bedroom. There was an old, polished brass bed. John Lee stared at it, then ran his hand over the turned-back sheets. Even Aunt Rose hadn't thought about red silk sheets. He never imagined such luxury.

"Golly," he said.

Pearl laughed and grabbed him in a big hug and kissed him on the forehead. "Sugah, you are just not to be be-*lieved!*" John Lee grinned uncomfortably and turned red. Pearl pulled the sheet up around his neck and patted his cheek. "Sleep tight."

"Good night, Pearl."

Daisy Mae stuck his head in to say good night. Pearl turned at the door and smiled fondly at him, then went out, closing it. John Lee wiggled around on the silk sheets. Golly, he thought, golly, golly, golly!

Pearl walked dreamily into the living room and collapsed becomingly onto the big purple fur chair. He sighed hugely. "Daisy Mae. Now I know what it must feel like to be a mother."

The next morning John Lee woke slowly and stretched until his muscles popped. He looked at the ceiling, but there was no faded water-stained paper, only neat white tiles with an embossed flower in the center of each. He slid to the side of the bed and felt the silk sheets flow like water across his skin. He went to the bathroom and relieved himself, splashing cold water on his face and combing the tangles out of his hair. He sure needed a haircut. He wondered if he ought to let it grow long now that he was in Hollywood.

Hollywood.

He'd almost forgotten. He bet Miss Mahan was worried about him. He sure liked Miss Mahan and a pang of guilt struck him. He should have told her he wouldn't be back in school this fall, especially after she was nice enough to come to mamma's funeral and all. Well, there was nothing he could do now. Mr. Cuttsanger would tell her—and everybody else—where he was.

He went back to his room and put on his best pair of blue jeans, a white tee-shirt and his gray sneakers. He wondered where everyone was. The house was very quiet. He guessed they had both gone to work. He went out on the back porch—only Pearl called it a deck—and saw Daisy Mae lying there on a blanket stark naked. He started to go back in, but Daisy Mae looked up. "Good morning, slugabed, you sleep well?"

John Lee fidgeted, trying not to look at Daisy Mae. "Yeah. Real good. Where's Pearl?"

"She's at work. Does windows for May Company."

"Didn't you have to work today at Paramount?"

"Got a few days off. Just finished something called *Wives and*

Lovers. Gonna be a dog. You want some breakfast, or you wanta join me?"

"Uh . . . what're you doin'?" He sure didn't seem to care if anybody saw him naked.

"Gettin' some sun, tryin' to get rid of his fish-belly white."

"You always do it with . . . uh . . . no clothes on?" You're acting like a hick again, John Lee Peacock. Damnation, he thought.

Daisy Mae chuckled. "Sure. Otherwise, I'd look like a two-tone Ford. If it embarrasses you, I'll put some clothes on."

"No," he protested quickly. "No, of course it doesn't embarrass me. I think I *will* join you."

"Okay." He pointed back over his head without looking. "There's another blanket there on the chaise."

John Lee spread the blanket on the porch and pulled his tee-shirt over his head. He pulled off his shoes and socks. Daisy Mae wasn't paying any attention to him. He looked around. The next house up the hill overlooked them, but that was the only one. He didn't see anybody up there. He took a deep breath, slipped off his pants and his shorts, and quickly lay down on his stomach. He might as well get some sun on his back first.

Daisy Mae spoke without looking at him. "Don't stay in one position more than five minutes, or you'll blister."

"Okay." He estimated five minutes had passed, swallowed, and turned over on his back. He looked straight into the eyes of a woman leaning on the railing of the next house up, watching him. He froze. The bottom dropped out of his stomach. Then he jumped up and grabbed his pants. He knew he was acting like an idiot, but he couldn't stop himself. He hopped on one foot, trying to get the pants on, but his toes kept getting in the way. They caught on the crotch and he fell flat on his butt. He managed to wiggle into them, sitting on the floor.

Daisy Mae looked up. "You sit on a bee or something?"

"No." He motioned with his head at the woman, afraid to look at her because he knew he was beet red all over.

Daisy Mae looked up, grinned, and waved. "Hi, Sue." He didn't do anything to cover himself, didn't seem to care that she saw him.

"Hello, Daisy Mae." Her voice was husky and amused. "Who's your bashful friend?"

"John Lee Peacock from Kansas. This is Sue. San Diego Lightfoot Sue."

Damnation, John Lee thought, I'm acting like a fool, sitting here hunkered up against this shez, as Daisy Mae calls it. Doesn't anyone in Hollywood have a normal name? He forced himself to look up. She was still leaning on the railing, looking at him. Only now she was smiling. She was wearing a paint-stained sweat shirt and blue jeans. Her hair was tied up in a scarf but auburn strands dangled out. She wasn't wearing any make-up that he could see. She was kinda old, he thought, but really very stunning. Her smile was nice. He felt himself smiling back.

"Nothing to be bashful about, John Lee Peacock. I've seen more male privates than you could load in a boxcar." Her voice was still amused but she wasn't putting him down.

"Maybe so," he answered, "but I haven't had any ladies see mine." His boldness made him start getting red again.

She laughed and he felt goose bumps pop out on his arms. "You could have a point there, John Lee. How would you like to make a little money?"

"Huh?"

"It's okay," Daisy Mae said, getting up and wrapping a towel around his waist. "Sue's an artist. She wants you to pose for her."

John Lee looked back up at her. "That's right," she said. "I'm as safe as mother's milk."

"Well, okay, I guess. But you don't need to pay me for something like that." He got up and kicked his underwear under the chaise.

"Of course I'll pay you. It's very hard work. Come on up."

"Uh . . . how do I get up there?"

"Go down to the street and come up my steps. Front door's open, come on in. You'll find me." She smiled again and went out of sight.

He looked at Daisy Mae. "Will it be all right with Pearl?"

"Sure. We've both posed for her. She's good. Scoot." Daisy Mae went into the house. John Lee put on his tee-shirt and shoes. He wondered if he should take off his pants and put on his underwear, but decided against it.

He opened her front door and went in as she had told him. She was right about him finding her. The whole house was one big room. A small kitchen was in one corner behind a folding screen. A day bed was against one wall between two bureaus that had been painted yellow. There was a door to a closet and another to a bathroom. There were a couple of tired but comfortable-looking easy chairs, a drafting table with a stool pushed under it, and an easel under a skylight. Pictures were everywhere; some in color, mostly black and white sketches; thumbtacked all over the walls, leaning in stacks against the bureaus, chairs, walls. A big orange cat lay curled in a chair. It opened one eye, gave John Lee the once over, and went back to sleep.

Sue was standing at the easel, frowning at the painting he couldn't see. She had a brush stuck behind one ear and was holding another like a club. "I'm glad you showed up, John Lee. This thing is going nowhere." She flipped a cloth over it and leaned it against the wall.

John Lee stared at the pictures. Nearly all of them were of people, most of them naked, though there were a couple of the cat. Some of the people were women but most of them seemed to be men. He spotted a sketch of Pearl and Daisy Mae, leaning against each other naked, looking like a butterfly with one black and one white wing.

She watched him look for a while. "This is just the garbage. I sell the good stuff. That one of Pearl and Daisy Mae turned out rather well. It's hanging in a gay bar in the Valley. Got eleven hundred for it."

"Golly."

"You're right. It was a swindle."

"Do you . . . ah . . . want me to . . . do you want to paint my picture with my . . . clothes off?" He waved his hand vaguely at some of the nude sketches. Damn his ears!

She didn't seem to notice. "If you don't mind. Don't worry about it. It'll be a few days yet. Give you a chance to get used to the idea. I want to make some sketches and work on your face for a while." She came to him and put her hand on his cheek. "You've got something in your face, John Lee. I don't know . . . what it is. More than simple innocence. I just hope I can capture it. Hold still, I want to feel your bones." He grinned and it made her smile. "Makes you feel like a horse up for sale, doesn't it?" She ran her cool fingers over his face, and he didn't want her to ever stop. He closed his eyes.

Suddenly, she caught her fingers in his hair and shook him. She laughed and hugged him against her warm soft breasts. His stomach did a flip-flop. She released him quickly and crossed her arms with her hands under her armpits. She laughed a little nervously. "You're just like Punkin. Scratch his ears and he'll go to sleep on you."

"Punkin?"

She pointed at the cat. "Don't you think he looks remarkably like a pumpkin when he's curled up asleep like that?"

"Yeah." He laughed.

"Do you want to start now?"

"I guess."

"Okay. Just sit in that chair and relax." She pulled the stool from beneath the drafting table and put it in front of the chair. She sat on the stool with her legs crossed, a sketch pad propped on one knee. She lit a cigarette and held it in her left hand while she worked rapidly with a stick of charcoal. "You can talk if you want to. Tell me about yourself."

So he did. He told her about Miller's Corners, Hawley, the farm, school, Miss Mahan who also painted but only flowers, Mr. Cuttsanger, his mother, a lot about his mother, not much about his father because he didn't really know very much when you got right down to it. He made her chuckle about Aunt Rose and Aunt Lilah. She kept turning the pages of the sketch pad and starting over. He wanted to see what she was drawing, but he was afraid to move.

She seemed to read his mind. "You don't have to sit so still, John Lee. Move when you want to." He changed positions but he still couldn't see. Punkin suddenly leaped in his lap, making him jump. The cat walked up his chest and looked into his eyes. Then he began to purr and curled up with his head under John Lee's chin.

Sue chuckled. "You are a charmer, John Lee. He treats most people with majestic indifference." John Lee grinned and stroked the cat. Punkin squirmed in delicious ecstasy. Then John Lee's stomach rumbled.

Sue put the pad down and laughed. "You poor lamb. I'm starving you to death." She looked at her watch. "Good grief, it's two thirty. What do you want to eat?"

"Anything."

"Anything it is."

He stood with Punkin curled in his arms, watching her do wonderful things with eggs, ham, green peppers, onions, and buttered toast. He said he loved scrambled eggs; and she laughed and said scrambled eggs indeed, you taste my omelets and you'll be my slave forever. She pulled down a table that folded against the wall, set out the two steaming plates with two glasses of cold milk. He was quite willing to be her slave forever, even without the omelet.

Punkin sat on the floor with his tail curled around his feet, watching them, making short, soft clarinet sounds. She laughed.

"Isn't that pitiful? The cat food's under the sink if you'd like to feed him."

"Sure." He tried to pour the cat food into the bowl, but Punkin kept grabbing the box with his claws and sticking his head in it. John Lee sat on the floor having a fit of giggles. God o' mighty, he thought, everything is so wonderfully, marvelously, absolutely perfectly good.

She continued sketching after they did the dishes. He sat in the chair feeling luxuriously content. He smiled.

"May I share it?" Sue asked, almost smiling herself.

"Huh? Oh, nothin'. I was just . . . feeling good." Then he felt embarrassed. "You . . . ah . . . been painting pictures very long?"

"Oh, I've dabbled at it quite a while, but I've only been doing it seriously for a couple of years." She smiled in a funny, wry way. "I'm just an aging roundheel who decided she'd better find another line of work while she could."

He didn't know what she was talking about. "You're not old."

"I stood on the shore and chunked rocks at the Mayflower." She sighed. "I'm forty-five."

"Golly. I thought you were about thirty."

She laughed her throaty laugh that made him tingle. "Honey, at your age everyone between twenty-five and fifty looks alike."

"I think you're beautiful," he said and wished he hadn't, but she smiled and he was glad he had.

"Thank you, little lamb. You should have seen me when I was your age." She stopped drawing and sat with her head to one side, remembering. "You should have seen me when I was fifteen." Then she shifted her position on the stool and laughed. "I was quite a dish —if I do say so myself. We were practically neighbors, you know that?" she said, changing the subject. "I'm an old Okie from way back. Still can't bear to watch *The Grapes of Wrath.* We came to California in '33 and settled in San Diego. Practically starved to death. My father died in '35, and my mother went back to telling fortunes and having seances—among other things. My father wouldn't let her do it while he was alive."

"Golly," he said bug-eyed. "A real fortune teller?"

"Well," she said wryly, "I never thought of it as being very real, but I don't know anymore." She looked at him speculatively for a moment, then shrugged. "Whether she was real or not, I don't know but I guess she was pretty good, 'cause there seemed to be plenty of money after that. Then the war started. And if you're twenty-three, in San Diego, during a war, you can make lots of money if you keep your wits about you." She shifted again on the stool. "Well, we won't go into that."

"Where's your mother now?"

"Oh, she's dead . . . I imagine. It was in '45, I think. Yeah, right after V-J Day, I went over for a visit and she wasn't there. Never heard from her again. You know, her house is still there in San Diego. I get a tax bill every year. I don't know why I keep paying it. Guess I'd rather do that than go through all that junk she had accumulated. I was down there a few years ago and went by the place. Everything was still there just as it was; two feet deep in dust, of course. I'm surprised vandals haven't stripped the place, considering what the neighborhood's become. I took a few things as keepsakes, but I didn't hang around long. It's worse than it was when she was there."

She worked a while in silence, then stopped drawing again and looked at him in a way that made his stomach feel funny. "If I were twenty and you were twenty . . . you're gonna be a ring-tailed boomer when you're twenty, John Lee." She suddenly laughed and began drawing. "If I'm gonna make people older and younger, I might as well make myself fifteen—no point in wasting five years."

He didn't know what a ring-tailed boomer was, but the way she said it made his ears turn red. Her mentioning San Diego reminded him. "Why do they call you San Diego Lightfoot Sue?"

"Daisy Mae has a big mouth," she said wryly. "I'll tell you about it someday."

"I sure like Pearl and Daisy Mae," he said and smiled.

"So do I."

"Pearl is awfully nice to me."

"Some people have a cat and some people have a dog."

He sure wished he knew what people were talking about, at least some of the time.

It seemed to him hardly any time had passed when Pearl sashayed in with a May Co. carton under his arm. "It is I, Lady Bountiful, come to free the slaves," he brayed and presented the box to John Lee with a flourish. "It's a Welcome To California present."

"Golly." He took the box gingerly.

"Well, *open* it." John Lee fumbled at the string while Pearl planted a kiss on Sue's cheek. "Sugah, you look more like Lauren Bacall every *day!*"

Sue grinned. "Hello, Pearl. How are you?"

He sighed an elaborate sigh. "I am *worn* to a frazzle. I've been slaving over a tacky May Company window all day. If they would *only* let me be *cre-a-tive!*"

"Wilshire Boulevard would never survive it."

John Lee stared at the contents of the box. "How did you know what size I wore?"

"Daisy Mae has tape measures in her eyeballs." He made fluttering motions with his hands. "Well, try them *on.*"

John Lee grinned and hurried to the bathroom with the box. He put it on the side of the tub and went through it. There were pants, a shirt, socks, shoes, and, he was glad to see, underwear and it looked kinda skimpy. He quickly shucked off his clothes and slipped on the gold shorts. Golly, he thought. They fit like his hide, and he kept wanting to pull them up, but that's all there was to them.

The shirt was yellow and soft. He rubbed it on his face, then slipped it over his head. It fit tight around his waist, and the neck was open halfway to his navel. He looked for buttons but there weren't any. The sleeves were long and floppy and had little pearl snaps on the cuffs.

He slipped on the pants, which had alternating dark-brown and light-brown vertical stripes. He was surprised to find that they didn't come any higher than the shorts. He gave them an experimental tug and decided they wouldn't fall off. They were tight almost to the knees and got loose and floppy at the bottom.

He sat on the commode to put on the shoes but stood again to hitch the pants up in back. He slipped on the soft, fuzzy gold socks. The shoes were brown and incredibly shiny. And they didn't even have shoestrings. He stood up, gave the pants a hitch, and looked at himself in the mirror. He couldn't make himself stop grinning.

He opened the bathroom door and walked out, still grinning. Pearl made his eyes go big and round, and Sue leaned against one of the yellow bureaus with her mouth puckered up. John Lee walked nervously to them, the shoes making a thump at every step. "The pants are a little bit too tight," he said and didn't know what to do with his hands.

"Oh, sugah, you are *wrong* about that!"

"If he had his hair slicked down with pomade, he'd look like an adagio dancer . . . or something," Sue said in a flat voice.

Pearl lowered his eyebrows at her, then twirled his finger at John Lee. "Turn around."

He turned nervously, worried because Sue didn't seemed pleased.

"John Lee, sugah," Pearl said in awe, "you have *got* the *Power!*"

"Pearl. Don't you think you went a little overboard?" Sue put her hand on the back of John Lee's neck. "If he walked down Hollywood Boulevard in that, he'd have to carry a machine gun."

"Well!" Pearl swelled up in mock outrage. "At least they're not *lavender!*"

Sue laughed. John Lee laughed too, but he wasn't exactly sure why. They were saying things he didn't understand again. But he felt an overwhelming fondness for Pearl at that moment. He reached out and shook Pearl's hand. "Thank you, Pearl. I think the clothes are beautiful." Then, because he felt Pearl would be pleased, he kissed him on the cheek.

The effect was startling. Pearl's face seemed to turn to putty and went through seven distinct expression changes. His mouth worked like a goldfish and he kept blinking his eyes. Then he pulled himself together and said too loudly, "Listen, you all. Dinner will be ready in exactly seventy-two minutes. We're having my world-famous sowbelly and chittlin lasagne." He hurried out, walking too fast.

John Lee was up very early the next morning. Sue opened the door still in her bathrobe. "I didn't know what time you wanted me to come over," he said apologetically. "Did I wake you up?"

Sue smiled and motioned him in. "Ordinarily, I'm not coordinated enough to tie my shoes before noon, but I woke up about two hours ago ready to go to work. I didn't even take time to dress." She indicated one wall of the room. "Check out the gallery while I put the wreck together."

All the old sketches had been cleared away from the wall. John Lee saw himself thumbtacked in neat rows. "Golly," he said, walking slowly down the rows. The sketches were all of his face: some sheets were covered with eyes, laughing, sleepy, dreamy, contemplative; others with mouths, smiling, grinning, pouting, pensive. There were noses and ears and combinations. He recognized some of the full-face sketches: this one was when he was talking about his mother; that one when he was petting Punkin; that one when he was telling of

Aunt Rose and Aunt Lilah; another when he sat in rapt attention, listening to Sue.

She emerged from the bathroom dressed much as she had been the day before except that she wore a little make-up and her hair fell through the scarf, hanging long and fluffy down her back. John Lee thought she was absolutely gorgeous. "What do you think," she asked tentatively, not quite smiling.

He couldn't think of anything to say that wasn't obvious to the eye, and so he just grinned in extreme pleasure.

She smiled happily. "I think I've caught you, John Lee. I really feel good about it. You're just what I've been needing."

"What're you gonna draw today?"

She indicated a large canvas in position on the easel. "I'm ready to start, if you are."

Oh, Lord, he thought, just don't turn red. "Yeah. I guess so."

"You can keep your pants on for a while, if it'll make you more comfortable. I'll work on your head and torso." She was businesslike, not seeming to notice his nervousness. It made him feel a little better.

He took a deep breath. "No . . . I might as well get it over with." She nodded and began puttering around with paints and turpentine, not looking at him, without seeming to be deliberately not looking at him. He pulled the tee-shirt over his head and wondered what to do with it. Quit stalling, he admonished, and slipped off his sneakers and socks. He looked at her but she was still ignoring him. He quickly pulled off his pants and shorts. He stood there feeling as if there were a cyclone in his stomach. "Well," he said, "I'm ready."

She turned and looked at him as if she had seen him naked every day of his life. "You have absolutely nothing to be embarrassed about, John Lee."

"Well," he said, "well . . ."

"What's the matter?"

"I don't know what to do with my *hands!*" Then he couldn't keep from laughing and she laughed with him. "What do you want me to do?"

"Let's see . . ." She moved one of the chairs under the light. "Lean against the chair. I want you relaxed . . ."

"I'll try," he chuckled.

She smiled. "I want you relaxed and completely innocent of your nudity. Sort of the *September Morn* effect."

"You're asking a lot." He leaned against the chair, trying to look innocent.

She gave a throaty laugh and shook her head. "You look more like a chicken thief. Don't try too hard. Just relax and be comfortable, like you were yesterday."

"I had my clothes on yesterday."

"I know. You'll do okay as soon as you get used to it."

"I still don't know what to do with my hands."

"Don't do anything with them. Just forget 'em; let them find their own position. I know it's not easy. Just forget I'm here. Pretend you're in the woods completely alone. You've just been swimming in a little lake, and now you're relaxing in the sun, leaning against a warm rock. Try to picture it."

"Okay, I'll try."

"You're not thinking about anything, just resting, feeling the sun on your body." She watched him. A pucker of concentration appeared over his nose. He shifted his hips slightly to get more comfortable, and his fidgety hands finally came to rest at his sides. His diaphragm moved slowly as his breathing became softer. The frown gradually disappeared from his face, and the quality she couldn't put a name to took its place. God, she thought, it brought back memories she had thought were put away forever. She felt like a giddy young girl.

"That's it, John Lee," she said very softly, trying not to disturb him. She picked up a stick of charcoal and began to work rapidly. A pleased smile flickered across his lips and then disappeared. "Beautiful, John Lee, beautiful. Don't close your eyes; watch the sun reflecting on the water."

She got the basic form the way she wanted it in charcoal, then began squeezing paint from tubes onto a palette. She applied the base colors quickly, almost offhandedly. After about fifteen minutes she said, "When you get tired, let me know and we'll take a break."

"No. I'm fine."

After another half hour she saw his thumb twitch. "If you're not tired," she said, putting the palette down, "I am. Would you like some coffee?"

"Yeah," he said without moving. "Are you sure I can get back in the same position again?"

"I'm sure." She tossed him her bathrobe and he put it on. "Do a few knee bends and get the kinks out." She poured two cups of coffee from the electric percolator. "I told you it was hard work."

He grinned and stretched his arms forward, rolling the muscles in his shoulders. "I'm not tired."

She handed him a cup. "You've been warned." She opened the back door when she heard a plaintive cry from outside. Punkin strolled in and looked up at her, demanding attention. She picked him up and he started purring loudly.

John Lee found it easy to keep the same position the rest of the morning. Sue had made him as comfortable as she could because of his inexperience. She worked steadily with concentration. He missed the easy chatter of the day before, but he didn't want to disturb her. They took periodic breaks, though she sometimes became so engrossed she forgot. Then she would admonish him gently for not reminding her. When they broke for lunch, she made him do knee bends and push-ups and then massaged his back and shoulders with green rubbing alcohol.

Daisy Mae strolled in with a foil-covered Pyrex dish. "You didn't do that when Pearl and I posed for you," he said with feigned huffiness and slipped the dish into the oven.

"Hello, Daisy Mae," John Lee grinned, putting on the robe. "Look at the sketches."

"Hello, John Lee. I knew Sue would get so absorbed she'd forget to feed you. So I brought the leftover lasagne." He looked over the sketches, critically, with his fingers theatrically stroking his chin. "I think the girl shows some promise, though I see years of study ahead."

Sue kissed him on the cheek and began setting the table for three. Daisy Mae sprawled in a chair like a wilting lily. "God!" he grunted. "I got a call from Paramount this morning. I start back to work Thursday. We're doing a *west*-ern. On lo-*ca*-tion. My *God*. In *Arizona!* Centipedes! Tarantulas! Scorpions! Rattlesnakes! Sweaty starlets! If I'm not back in five weeks, send the Ma-*rines!*"

Sue laughed. "You can console yourself with thoughts of all those butch cowboys."

"Darling," he said, arching his wrist at her, "some of those cowboys are about as butch as Pamela Tiffin. I could tell you stories . . ."

"Don't bother. I've heard most of them."

"I haven't," John Lee piped in brightly.

Sue started to say something, but Daisy Mae beat her to it. "Someday, John Lee. You're much too young to lose *all* your illusions."

When they had eaten, Sue thanked him for bringing the lasagne and shooed him out. He started to peek under the cloth covering the painting, but she slapped his hand. "You know better than that."

"Can John Lee bunk over here tomorrow night? I'm giving myself a going-away party before I'm exiled to the burning deserts, and it's liable to last all night."

She stood very still for a moment. Then she nodded with a jerk of her head. "Of course." Daisy Mae waltzed out with his Pyrex dish. Sue looked after him for a moment, then at John Lee sitting bewildered on the day bed. She gave him a quick nervous smile. "You ready?"

He took off the bathrobe, hardly feeling embarrassed at all, and took his place, bringing back the woods, the lake, and the warm rock, but needing them only for a moment to get started.

At four thirty she covered the painting and began washing the brushes. She had said hardly anything at all since Daisy Mae left, giving him only an occasional soft-voiced direction. He put his clothes on and went to her. "Is it turning out the way you'd hoped?"

Her eyes met his. He saw sadness in them and something that had gotten lost. "Yes," she said almost unaudibly. Then she smiled. "You're a joy to paint, John Lee. Now, run along before Pearl comes traipsing in. I'd rather not have company this evening. Be over bright and early, and I think we'll finish it tomorrow."

Punkin stopped him on the steps, wanting to be petted. He picked up the cat and glanced back to see Sue watching him through the window. She turned away quickly.

The painting was completed at three P.M. the next afternoon. Sue stood back from it and looked at John Lee, smiling. He went to her hesitantly, almost fearfully, still naked, and looked at it. "Golly," he breathed. When she painted a nude, she really painted everything. He felt the heat starting at his ears and flowing downward. He was almost used to being naked in front of her, but it was an astonishing shock to *see* himself being naked.

She laughed fondly. "John Lee, you're a regular traffic light."

"No, I'm not," he muttered and got even redder.

Suddenly, her arms were around him, hugging him tightly to her. He felt electricity bouncing in the bottom of his stomach. He threw his arms around her and wanted to be enveloped by her. "John Lee, my little lamb," she whispered in his ear, bending her head because she was an inch taller, "do you like it?"

"Yes" he breathed, with that peculiar pain in the back of his throat again. "Oh, yes."

He shifted his head slightly so he could see. The painting was done in pale sun-washed colors. He leaned against a suggestion of something white which might have been a large rock. It was everything she had said she wanted, and more. He seemed totally innocent of clothing, so completely comfortable was he in his nudity. His body was relaxed, but there was no lethargy in it. There was something slightly supernatural about the John Lee in the painting, as if perhaps he were a fawn or a wood sprite, definitely an impression of a forest creature. The various shades of pale green in the background implied a forest, and there was a dappling of leaf shadows on his shoulder and chest—but only a suggestion. However, these were unimportant. The figure dominated the painting, executed in fine detail, like a Raphael. The face was innocent, totally uncorrupted by worldly knowledge. But there was a quality in it even purer than simple innocence. The eyes were lost in a reverie.

"Do I look like that?" he asked, slightly overwhelmed.

"Well . . ." she said with a husky chuckle, "yes, you do. Although I will have to admit I idealized you somewhat."

"Is it okay if I bring Pearl and Daisy Mae over to see it?" he asked with growing excitement. "Pearl was supposed to come home at noon today to help with the party. Only she . . . I mean he, calls it a Druid ritual."

She laughed and released him. "All right."

He raced happily to the door then skidded to a halt. He hurried back, grinning sheepishly, and picked up his pants. He put them on, hopping on one foot, then out the door, clattering down the steps. She looked at the empty doorway for a moment, then rubbed at her eyes but was unable to stop the tears.

"Hell!" she said out loud. "Oh, hell!"

John Lee came over from the party about ten o'clock dressed in his new clothes and carrying a Lufthansa flight bag Pearl had packed for him. He flopped into one of the chairs, grinning. Sue was in the other, reading. She looked at him speculatively. Punkin leaped lightly from her lap and stretched mightily, his rear end high in the air, his chin against the floor, and his toes splayed. Then he hopped into

John Lee's lap. Stroking the cat and still grinning, he met her eyes. They both burst into a fit of giggles.

"John Lee, you have *no* staying power," she choked out between gasps of laughter.

He got himself under control, gulping air. "I'd much rather be over here with you."

"I hope Pearl gave you a whip and a chair to go with those clothes."

"No, but he warned me to stay out of corners and, above all, bedrooms."

There was a light tap on the door. "I've been expecting this," she muttered. "Come on in!"

The door opened, and a pale, slim, good-looking young man wafted in like the queen of Rumania inspecting the hog pens. "Hello," he sighed, not quite holding out his hand to be kissed. "Pearl was telling us about the painting you did of John Lee. May I see it?" He looked at John Lee and smiled anemically.

"Of course." Sue got up and turned the light on over the easel. A shriek of laughter drifted over from next door. The young man strolled to the painting and stood motionless for a full two minutes staring at it.

Then he sighed. "Pearl is so lucky. My last one ran off with my stereo, my Polaroid, and knocked out three fillings."

"That's . . . ah . . . too bad," she said, valiantly not smiling.

"Yes," he said and sighed again. "I'd like to buy it."

"It's not for sale."

"I'll give you a thousand."

She shook her head.

"Two thousand."

"Sorry."

He sighed again as if he expected nothing from life but an endless series of defeats. "Oh, well. Thank you for letting me see it."

"You're extremely welcome."

He drifted to the door like a wisp of fog, turned, gave John Lee a wan smile, and departed. They both stared at the closed door.

"I feel as if I just played the last act of *La Traviata*," Sue said in a stunned voice.

"If I remember correctly," John Lee said, "that was Cow-Cow."

She lifted the painting from the easel. "There's only one thing to do if we don't want a parade through here all night. Be back shortly." She left, taking the painting with her.

When she returned half an hour later, he was dozing. "The showing was an unqualified success. I was offered se-ven thou-sand dollars for it. You never saw so many erotic fantasies hanging out. It was like waving a haunch of beef at a bunch of half-starved tigers." She put the painting back on the easel and stood looking at it. "It *is* good though, isn't it, John Lee?" She sounded only partially convinced. "It really is good." She looked at him, sprawled in the chair, half asleep, smiling happily at her. "Well," she laughed, "neither the artist nor the model are qualified judges. And that crowd at Pearl's could only see a beautiful child with his privates exposed."

She sat on the arm of the chair, putting her hand on the side of his face. He closed his eyes and moved his face against her hand the way Punkin would do. "You're such a child, John Lee," she said softly, feeling her eyes getting damp. "Your body may fool people for a while, but up here," she caught her fingers in his hair, "up here, you're an innocent, trusting, guileless child. And I think you may break my heart." She closed her eyes, trying to hold back the tears, afraid she was making a fool of herself.

He looked up at her, feeling things he had never felt before, wanting things he had never wanted before. Perhaps if he hadn't been floating in the dreamlike area between wakefulness and sleep, his natural shyness might have prevented him. He slipped his arms slowly around her neck and pulled her gently to him. He felt her tense as if about to pull away, then her lips were like butterfly wings against his. She lay across him with her face buried in his neck. He stroked her hair and brushed his lips against her cheek.

"Is this what you want, John Lee?" she asked, her voice unsteady. "Is this what you really want?"

"Yes," he answered. "You're all I want."

"You're sure you're not just feeling sorry for an old lady?" she said shakily, trying to sound if she were making a joke, but not succeeding completely.

He held her tighter. "I love you, San Diego Lightfoot Sue."

She stood up, wiping at her eyes with trembling fingers. "Daisy Mae and his big mouth," she said, half laughing and half crying. John Lee stood up also, giving the striped pants a hitch in the back. "Oh, John Lee," she said, hugging him to her, "take off those awful clothes."

He stood on tiptoe to kiss her because his mouth came only to her chin. He removed the clothes, feeling no embarrassment at all. She turned out the light and locked the door before undressing, feeling embarrassment herself for the first time in nearly thirty years. She turned back the cover on the day bed, and they lay in the warm night, listening to the shrieks of strained laughter from Pearl's, feeling, exploring, each trying to touch every part of the other's body with every part of his own. Then, she showed him what to do and kissed him when he was clumsy.

They lay together, drowsily. Flamenco music drifted over from the party next door. Sue had her arms around John Lee, her breasts pressed against his back, her face against his neck. "John Lee?"

"Mmmm?"

"John Lee, when you're twenty . . . have you thought, I'll be fifty?"

"I love you, Sue. It doesn't matter to me."

She was silent for a moment. "Perhaps it doesn't now. You're too young to know the difference, and I still have a few vestiges of my looks left. But in a few years you'll want a girl your own age, and in a few years I'll be an old woman." He started to protest, but she put her fingers on his lips, brushing them with feathery touches. "Your lips are like velvet, John Lee," she whispered. He opened his mouth slightly and touched her fingers with his tongue. Then she clamped her arms around him and began weeping on his shoulder. "My God, John Lee! I don't want to be like your favorite aunt, or even your mother! I don't want to see you married to some empty-headed girl, some pretty *young* girl, having your babies like a brood sow, living in a tract house in Orange County. I want to be the one to have your babies, but I'm too old . . ."

He twisted in her arms to face her and stopped her words with his mouth. The second time, she showed him how to make it last longer, how to make it better, and he was very adept. He fell asleep in her arms where she held him like a teddy bear, but she lay awake for many hours, making a decision.

The next morning, he moved his things from Pearl's to Sue's.

When he had gone, Pearl began to sob, large tears rolling down his face. His hands clutched at each other like graceful black spiders. Daisy Mae put down the glass of tomato juice with the raw egg and Tabasco he had made for his hangover and took Pearl in his arms.

"Oh, Pearl, you knew it would happen. Just like it always happens," he soothed.

"But John Lee was different from the others," he forced out between heaving sobs.

"Yes, he was. But he's just next-door. He's still our friend. We can see him anytime."

"But it's not the same. Sue will be taking care of him, not me! Oh, Daisy Mae," he wailed, "if this is what it's like to lose a child, I don't want to be a mother any more!"

Sue began a new painting that morning. "I want you like you were last night," she told John Lee, "sitting all asprawl in the chair, half asleep, with Punkin in your lap, but *not* in those same clothes." They went through his meager wardrobe. She selected a pair of khaki-colored jeans and gave him one of her short-sleeve sweat shirts. She showed him how to sit. "Leave your shoes off. I have a foot fetish." She ran her fingernails quickly across the bottom of his foot. His leg jerked and he grabbed her, giggling, and pulling her in his lap. She submitted happily to his kisses for a moment, then pulled away.

"Okay," she laughed, "calm yourself. We've got work to do."

"Yes, ma'am," he said primly, striking a pose and beaming at her.

Thank God, she thought, he doesn't seem to have any regrets.

"My *Gawd!*" Pearl shrieked, seeing the new painting for the first time. He bulged his eyes and hugged himself. *"Sue!* That's the most erotic thing I've seen in my *life!* It's practically porno-*graphic!* If I look at it any longer, I'm gonna embarrass myself." He turned away dramatically and saw John Lee grinning and blushing.

"I embarrass myself a little with that one," Sue admitted. "Talk about erotic fantasies."

The painting was in dark brooding colors, but a light from somewhere fell across John Lee, sitting deep in the chair, one bare foot tucked under him and the other dangling. One hand lay on his thigh and the other negligently stroked the orange cat in his lap. His face was sleepy and sensual. His eyes looked directly at you. They were the eyes of an innocent fawn, but they were also the eyes of a stag in rut.

"You're not . . . ah . . . gonna show it to a bunch of people, are you?" John Lee asked tentatively.

When he woke the next morning, the bed beside him was empty. He rubbed the sleep from his eyes and unfolded the note lying on her pillow. "John Lee, my love," it read in her masculine scrawl, "I had to go to San Diego for the day and didn't want to wake you. I'll be back tonight late. Sue."

He was asleep when she came in. She sat on the edge of the bed and moved her hand lightly across his chest. "John Lee. Wake up, honey."

He squirmed on the bed. "Sue?" he mumbled without opening his eyes. He turned over on his stomach, burying his head, fighting wakefulness.

She pulled back the covers and slapped him lightly on his bare bottom. "Wake up. I want to do another painting. Get dressed."

"I'm too sleepy. Leave your number and I'll call you."

"Okay, smarty," she laughed, "you've got thirty seconds before I get out the ice cubes."

"White slaver," he grinned, sitting up and kissing her.

"Where did you hear that?"

"I spent the day with Pearl and Daisy Mae."

She kissed him and stood up. "Come on, get a move on." She put a new canvas on the easel. "Why wasn't Pearl at work? And I thought Daisy Mae had left for, my God, Arizona."

"Today is Saturday," he said and went into the bathroom.

"So it is. I sorta lose track." She began squeezing black and white paint from tubes.

John Lee washed his face and ran a comb through his hair. He came out of the bathroom and put on the same clothes he had worn for the last painting. "These okay?" She nodded. "Shoes or foot fetish?" he grinned.

She wrinkled her nose at him. "Shoes."

He put on his Sunday shoes rather than the sneakers. "Daisy Mae doesn't leave for a couple of weeks yet. They're having fittings and things. Wardrobe gave her . . . him an 1865 lady's riding skirt with a *zipper* on the side. And *welder* in *Duluth* would know better than that. What do you want me to do?"

"Just stand there." Her voice was tense and hurried.

"Stand?" he groaned. "Don't you want to do another one of me sitting down?" He snapped his fingers. "Do one of me asleep in bed!" She didn't laugh at his joke, and so he stood where she indicated. She began, using only black and white. "Don't artists need the northern light, or something?" he asked hopefully, pointing to the dark skylight.

She smiled. "That's just an excuse artists have been using for the last few thousand years when they didn't feel like working. Be patient with me, John Lee. You can sleep all day tomorrow. I have to go back to San Diego."

"Can't I go with you?"

"No, John Lee." Her voice was so serious that he didn't say anything else.

She finished just before dawn. He was about to fall asleep standing, and so she undressed him and put him to bed. He put his arms around her and kissed her, wanting her to stay a little while. "No," she said, running her fingers through his hair, "you're too sleepy. I'll be back in a few days and we can stay in bed for a week."

He smiled and his eyelids began to droop. "That'll be nice."

"Yes, my little lamb, very nice." She kissed him gently on the mouth. He was asleep before she got out the door.

He woke up late Sunday afternoon and immediately looked at the painting. It wasn't as well done as the other two, he thought. It had a hurried look. It was also in black and white. The John Lee in the painting was just standing there, his arms hanging at his sides, looking at you from beneath lowered brows. John Lee looked at the floor where he had been standing when he posed, but nothing was there. Yet, in the painting, there were lines on the floor. He was standing within a pentagram. And he looked different; he looked older, at least five years older, at least twenty.

Tuesday night Pearl and Daisy Mae took him to Graumann's Chinese where he thought the movie was great and had a wonderful time standing in the footprints, though he had never heard of most of the people who had made them. After the movie they went to a Chinese restaurant where he ate Chinese food for the first time. He didn't really like it, but he told Pearl he did because it made him happy. It was nearly midnight when he got back to Laurel Canyon. Pearl wanted him to stay in his old room, but he said he'd better not because Sue might come home during the night and he wanted to be there.

He went up the wooden steps feeling incredibly content. If Sue were only there. Punkin came down the banister like a tightrope walker, making little soft sounds of greeting. John Lee picked him up and made crooning noises. The cat butted his head against John Lee's chin, making him chuckle. He carried Punkin into the house and turned on the light.

His head exploded. His legs wouldn't hold him up any longer, and he fell to his knees, dropping the cat. There was something white beside him, but he couldn't make his eyes focus. He thought he heard a voice, but he wasn't sure because of the wind screaming through his head. The white thing grabbed him and pulled him to his feet. It shouted more words at him, but he couldn't understand what they were. Something crashed into his face. The fog cleared a little. There was a man dressed in white, holding the front of his shirt. He could smell the sour whiskey on his breath. He slapped John Lee again and shoved him against the wall, but he managed to stay on his feet.

The wind was dying in his head. He heard the man's angry words. "Jesus Christ!" he said, looking at the picture of John Lee sitting in the chair. He took a knife from his pocket and slashed through the canvas.

"Stop it!" John Lee croaked and took an unsteady step in the man's direction.

He whirled, pointing the knife at John Lee. "Jesus Christ!" he said again, in amazement. "You're just a little kid! She threw me over for a little kid!" The man's face seemed to collapse as he lunged at John Lee with the knife. John Lee grabbed his arm, but the man was far too strong. The the man stepped on Punkin's tail. The cat screeched and sank his claws into the man's leg. He bawled and fell against John Lee. They both went to the floor, the man on top, his face beside John Lee's.

"Jesus God," the man whispered in bewilderment. Then his breath crept out in an adenoidal whine and didn't go back in again. John Lee squirmed from beneath him. The man rolled onto his back. The knife handle stuck straight up in his chest, blood already clinging to it. John Lee tried to get to his feet but could only make it to his knees. He saw Pearl and Daisy Mae run in, but there was something very wrong with them. They floated slowly through the air, running toward him but getting farther away. Their mouths moved but only honking sounds came out. Then the floor hit him in the face.

The first thing John Lee felt was someone clutching his hand. He opened his eyes and they felt sticky. Pearl's tense and worried face leaned over him, smiling tentatively. "Pearl?" His face hurt and his mouth wouldn't work properly. He sounded as if he were talking with a mouth full of cotton.

"Don't try to talk, John Lee, sugah," Pearl said anxiously. "You're in the hospital. They said you had a mild concussion. I was scared to death. You've been unconscious for ages. This is *Thursday*."

John Lee put his hand to his face and felt bandages on his mouth and a compress under his lip. "What happened," he had to swallow to get the words out, "happened to my mouth?" It hurt to talk.

"You got a split lip. It's all purple and swelled up. But don't sweat it, sugah. It makes you ve-ry sex-y."

John Lee grinned but stopped when it hurt too much. "Is Sue back?"

"She sat with you all night. I made her go home and sleep. They put you in a tacky ward, but Sue had you moved to this nice private room."

"The man . . ." He tried hard to remember what happened. "The man. . . ."

"He's dead, sugah. You never saw so many police cars and ambulances and red lights. I don't know what they're gonna do, John Lee." Pearl was distraught.

Sue came in. "Don't upset him, Pearl. Everything will be all right." She smiled brightly, and John Lee felt everything would be. "How are you feeling, little lamb?"

"Awful," he groaned and tried to laugh, but it hurt too much.

Pearl gave his arm a pat and said. "I'd better get back to work before May Company fires my little black fanny. Bye, sugah."

"Bye, Pearl." Pearl left with a big grin. Sue sat in the chair he had vacated. She took John Lee's hand and held it to her face.

"I'm so sorry," she said as if in pain.

He wanted to bring back her bright smile. "You're looking particularly beautiful today." He had never seen her dressed up before. She wore a silk suit in soft green, her auburn hair loose and long.

She did smile. "Thank you—and thank Playtex, Maidenform, and Miss Clairol. You look . . . pretty awful." But she said it as if she didn't mean it.

"Pearl said I looked ve-ry sex-y."

She grinned and then her face was serious. "John Lee, are you lucid enough to listen and understand what I have to say?" He nodded. "All right. There'll be a . . . hearing . . . or something in a few days, when you're feeling better, with the juvenile authorities. You won't be in any trouble, because they know Jocko attacked you. They know it was an accident . . ."

"Who was he?" he interrupted.

She looked at him for a moment. "Someone I used to know," she said softly.

"Did you love him? Was he your lover?" He didn't know if he was saying it right. He wanted to know, but he also wanted her to know that he didn't care.

"They're not exactly the same thing, but, yes, to both." She didn't look at him.

"You gave him up for me," he said in wonder, loving her so much it hurt.

She looked at him then and smiled, but there was a funny look in her eyes. "I'd give up most anything for you, John Lee."

The next couple of weeks were a blur. A bunch of people talked to him: men in blue suits and tight-faced women in gray. He told them everything that happened, and they went away to be replaced by others, but none of them would let him see Sue again. There was one lady he liked, who said she was a judge. He told her that his grandfather was a judge but he died a long time ago. She asked him about everything and he told her. She had a kind voice and made the others behave the way Miss Mahan would.

"But, Your Honor," one of the men said, "this child has killed a drunken sailor in a knife fight over a prostitute!"

The judge laughed pleasantly. "Really, Mr. Maley, there's no need for exaggeration. You're not addressing a jury. John was merely protecting himself when attacked. The man's death resulted when he fell on his own knife."

"You can't deny he's been living with a known prostitute. I wouldn't be surprised if she hasn't seduced him."

"Please, Mr. Maley," the judge frowned, displeased, "don't speak that way in front of the child."

"You saw those paintings! Disgusting!"

The judge stood up and began putting on her coat. "Artists have been painting nudes for several thousand years, Mr. Maley. You should see the collection in the Vatican. And these are very good paintings. I made an artist an offer for the nude myself. Come along, John. I'll take you to dinner. Good evening, gentlemen."

Dwayne came to see him one day, but John Lee would never have recognized him. He hadn't seen him since he went away to the army seven years before. Dwayne was twenty-nine, big and good-looking like all the Peacock men. He shook hands with John Lee, saying little, and went away after talking to the judge.

Aunt Rose and her husband flew out from Hawley. She touched him a lot and clucked a lot. Of course, she'd *like* to take care of him,

him being the youngest son of her late sister and all, but the way things were, the economy and the cost of living and all, she just didn't see how she could.

It was a terrible thing, her sister marrying into the Peacock family, such an unfortunate family. Poor Grace Elizabeth's husband had died the same day she was buried, the very day John Lee had left on the bus. He had fallen off the tractor and been run over by his own plow. He had crawled almost all the way to the house before he bled to death. Such a tragic family the Peacocks. Her sister had lost six of her children, five of them in infancy and poor Wash Jr.

They had tracked him down in Oklahoma because the farm was his now; or, she should say, they had tracked down his wife; or she should say, his ex-wife. Wash, Jr., had been killed six years ago when a pipe fell off a rig and crushed his skull. His wife hadn't even notified the family. Then she married a Mexican driller from Texas and was living in Tulsa, but what could you expect from one of them trashy O'Dell girls. It was a good thing she had had none of Wash Jr.'s children, just three stillbirths, because she had no claim on the family at all now. Of course, she had two fat brown babies by her new husband, but you know how Mexicans are: like rabbits.

Dwayne hadn't wanted the farm. He just told them to sell it and send him the money. Dwayne was the logical person to take John Lee, being his closest kin. Her sister, Lilah, was in no shape to take care of him. If Dwayne couldn't, then she didn't know what would happen to the poor thing, him living with a prostitute and all.

Aunt Rose and her husband flew back to Hawley.

The judge told him how sorry she was, but if one of his relatives didn't assume custody, as a minor he would have to be declared a ward of the state. But it wouldn't be too bad. He'd have a nice place to live, could finish school, and would have lots of other boys his own age. He asked her why he couldn't live with Sue, but she said it was out of the question and wouldn't discuss it further.

But Dwayne did assume custody, and John Lee moved into his brother's small apartment on Beachwood near Melrose. "Half the money from the sale of the farm is rightfully yours," Dwayne said, dressing for work. "You'll have to go to school this fall. The judge said so. Other than that, your time is your own. But you're not supposed to see that woman again." He showed John Lee how to turn the couch into a bed and then left for work. He was a bartender at a place on Highland and worked from six until it closed at two in the morning.

John Lee caught the bus to Melrose and Vine and rode to Hollywood and Highland. He took a taxi to the house in Laurel Canyon. Sue wasn't at home and he couldn't find Punkin. The three paintings had been framed and were hanging. She had repaired the damaged one. No other paintings were in sight. Everything had been pushed against the walls, leaving most of the floor bare. There were blue chalk marks on the bare board that had been hastily and inadequately rubbed out. The room smelled oddly.

He found an envelope on the kitchen table with his name on it. He removed the folded piece of notepaper. "John Lee, my little lamb," it read, "I knew you would come, although they told us we mustn't see each other again. You must stay away for a while, John Lee. Only a little while, then it won't matter what they say. There'll be nothing they can do. I love you. Sue."

Pearl wasn't at home either, and so he went back to Dwayne's apartment, watched television for a while, took a bath, and went to bed on the convertible sofa. He didn't know when Dwayne came in about two thirty.

Dwayne always slept until nearly noon. John Lee found little to talk to him about, and Dwayne seemed to prefer no conversation at all. John Lee watched television a lot, went to many movies, and waited for Sue.

He fell asleep in front of the television a few days later and was awakened by Dwayne and the man who was with him. Dwayne frowned at him and the man smiled nervously. The man said something to Dwayne, but he shook his head and led the man into the bedroom, closing the door. John Lee went to bed and didn't know when the man left.

The next morning he looked into the bedroom. Dwayne was sprawled on the bed, naked, asleep. A twenty dollar bill lay beside, him partially under his hip. John Lee closed the door and fixed breakfast.

Dwayne came in while he was washing the dishes. He didn't say anything for a while, fixing a cup of instant coffee. He sat at the table in his underwear, sipping the coffee. John Lee continued with the dishes, not looking at him. Then he felt Dwayne's eyes on him and he turned. "I don't want you to think I'm queer," Dwayne said flatly.

"I don't do anything, just lay there. If those guys want to pay me good money, it's no skin off my nose." He turned back to his coffee.

John Lee hung up the dishtowel to dry. "I understand," he said, but he wasn't sure that he did. "It's all right with me."

Dwayne didn't answer but went on sipping coffee as if John Lee weren't there. He made sure, from then on, he was asleep before Dwayne came home.

Sue called a few nights later. He had never heard her voice over the phone, but it sounded different: brighter, less throaty, younger. "Come over, John Lee, my little lamb," she laughed gleefully. "I'm ready. Come over for the showing."

The taxi had to stop a block away because of the police cars and fire trucks. John Lee ran terrified through the milling crowd, but when he reached Sue's house there was nothing to see. The rickety wooden steps went up the hill for about twenty feet and ended in midair. There was nothing beyond them, only a rectangle of bare earth where the house had been. But nothing else, not even the concrete foundation.

He felt a touch on his arm. He whirled to stare wide-eyed at Pearl. He couldn't speak, his throat was frozen. His heart was pounding too hard and he couldn't breathe. Pearl took his arm and led him into the house where he had spent his first night in Hollywood.

Pearl gave him a sip of brandy which burned his throat and released the muscles. "What happened? Where's Sue?" he asked, afraid to get an answer.

"I don't know," Pearl said without any trace of corn pone accent. He seemed on the verge of hysteria himself. "There was a fire . . ."

"A fire?" he asked, uncomprehending.

"I think it was a fire . . ." Pearl nervously dropped the brandy bottle. He picked it up, ignoring the stain on the carpet.

"Where's Sue?"

"She . . . she was in the house. I heard her scream," he said rapidly, not looking at John Lee.

John Lee didn't feel anything. His body was frozen and numb. Then, he couldn't help himself. He began to bawl like a baby. It was all slipping away. He could feel the good things escaping his fingers.

Pearl sat beside him on the purple fur chair and tried to comfort him. "She was over there all evening, singing to herself. I could hear her, she was very happy. I went over but she wouldn't let me in. She said I knew better than to look at an artist's work before it was finished. She said anyway it was a private showing for you. I didn't hear her singing after that, and then, a little while ago, I heard a noise like thunder or an explosion. I looked over, and there was a bright green light in the house, like it was burning on the inside, but not like fire either. I heard her scream. It was an awful, terrible scream. There was another voice, a horrible gloating voice, I couldn't understand. Then the whole house began to glow with that same green light. It got brighter and brighter, but there was no heat from it. Then it went away and the house wasn't there anymore."

Pearl got up and handed John Lee an envelope. "I found this on the deck. She must have tossed it down earlier." John Lee took the envelope with his name on it. He recognized her handwriting, but it was more hurried and scrawled than usual. He opened it and read the short note.

He went back to school that fall and lived with Dwayne. He said his name was Johnny, because John Lee was home and Sue. He met a lot of girls who wanted him, but they were pallid and dull after Sue. He went with them and slept with them but was unable to feel anything for them. He never turned down any man who propositioned him either, and there were many. He didn't care about the money, he only needed someone to relieve the pressures that built up in him. It didn't make any difference, man or woman. He let lonely middle-aged women keep him, but he never found what he was looking for.

By the time he was eighteen he had grown a couple of inches and had filled out. He moved from the apartment on Beachwood and got a place of his own. He never saw Dwayne again.

The envelope with his name on it was soiled and frayed from much handling. He read it every night. "John Lee, my little lamb," it read. "I tried very hard, so very hard. I thought I had succeeded but something is going wrong. I can feel it. I wish you could have seen me when I was fifteen, John Lee. I wish you could have seen me when when I was fifteen. I'm afraid." It was unsigned.

Out of Dickinson By Poe
or
The Only Begotten Son of
Edgar & Emily

Strange tryst was that from which stillborn
I still knew life midsummer morn,
And son of Emily/Edgar both
Did such dry teat and swill sour broth,
And midnight know when noon was there,
And every summer breeze foreswear.
Gone blind from stars and dark of moon
This boychild grew from wry cocoon;
For I was spun from spider hands
And misconceived in Usher Lands,
And all of Edgar's nightmares mine
And Em's dust-heart my valentine.
Thus mute old maid and maniac.
Then birthed me forth to cataract -
That whirlpool sucked to darkest star
Where all the unborn children are.
So I was torn from maelstrom flesh
And saw in x-ray warp and mesh
A sigh of polar-region breath
That whispered skull-and socket death.
Em could not stop for Death, so Poe
Meandered graveyards to and fro
And laid his tombstone marble bride
as Jekyll copulated Hyde
And birthed a panic-terror son.
And thus was I, mid-night, begun.
                              —*Ray Bradbury*

Edward Wellen is a full-time professional writer who lives in New Rochelle, New York. He has been contributing to *F&SF* since 1963 but is probably even better known in the crime fiction field. His work is notable for its consistent high quality and the fact that it contains hardly a wasted word, whether in a 30,000-word novella or a short chiller like "Sanity Clause."

Sanity Clause

by EDWARD WELLEN

Ho ho ho.

They said he used to come down the chimney. But of course these days there were no more chimneys. They said he used to travel in an eight-reindeer-power sleigh. But of course these days there were no more reindeer.

The fact was that he traveled in an ordinary aircar and came in through an ordinary iris door.

But he did have on a red suit with white furry trim, and he did carry a bundle of toys, the way they said he did in the old old days. And here he came.

His aircar parked itself on the roof of the Winterdream condom, and he worked his way down through the housing complex. The Winterdream condom's 400 extended families, according to his list, had an allotment of nine children under seven.

The first eight were all sanes and did not take up more than two minutes of his time apiece. The ninth would be Cathy Lesser, three.

Like the others, the Clements and the Lessers had been awaiting his yearly visit in fearful hope. The door of the Clement-Lesser apartment irised open before he had a chance to establish his presence. He bounced in.

He read in its eyes how the family huddle saw him. His eyes how they twinkled! His dimples how merry! His cheeks were like roses, his nose like a cherry! His droll little mouth was drawn up like a bow, and the beard of his chin was as white as the snow. The stump of a pipe he held tight in his teeth, and the smoke it encircled his head like a wreath. He had a broad face and a little round belly that shook when he laughed, like a bowlful of jelly.

"Ho ho ho."

He looked around for Cathy. The child was hanging back, hiding behind her mother's slacks.

"And where is Cathy?"

Her mother twisted around and pushed Cathy forward. Slowly Cathy looked up. She laughed when she saw him, in spite of herself. A wink of his eye and a twist of his head soon gave her to know she had nothing to dread.

"Ho ho ho. And how is Cathy?"

He knew as soon as he saw her eyes. He vaguely remembered them from last year, but in the meanwhile something in them had deepened.

Cathy stuck her thumb in her mouth, but her gaze locked wonderingly and hopefully on the bulging sack over his shoulder.

"Cat got Cathy's tongue?"

"She's just shy," her mother said.

"Cathy doesn't have to be shy with me." He looked at the mother and spoke softly. "Have you noticed anything . . . special about the child?"

The child's mother paled and clamped her mouth tight. But a grandmother quickly said, "No, nothing. As normal a little girl as you'd want to see."

"Yes, well, we'll see." It never paid to waste time with the relatives; he had a lot of homes to visit yet. Kindly but firmly he eased the Lessers and the Clements out of the room and into the corridor, where other irises were peeping.

Now that she was alone with him Cathy looked longingly at the closed door. Quickly he unslung his bundle of toys and set it down. Cathy's eyes fixed on the bulging sack.

"Have you been a good little girl, Cathy?"

Cathy stared at him and her lower lip trembled.

"It's all right, Cathy. I know you've been as good as any normal little girl can be, and I've brought you a nice present. Can you guess what it is?"

He visualized the beautiful doll in the lower left corner of the bag. He watched the little girl's eyes. She did not glance at the lower left corner of the bag. He visualized the swirly huge lollipop in the upper right corner of the bag. She did not glance at the upper right corner of the bag. So far so good. Cathy could not read his mind.

"No? Well, here it is."

He opened the bag and took out the doll. A realistic likeness of a girl with Cathy's coloring, it might have been the child's sibling.

"Ooo," with mouth and eyes to match.

"Yes, isn't she pretty, Cathy? Almost as pretty as you. Would you like to hold her?"

Cathy nodded.

"Well, let's see first what she can do. What do you think she can do? Any idea?"

Cathy shook her head.

Still all right. Cathy could not see ahead.

He cleared a space on the table and stood the doll facing him on the far edge. It began walking as soon as he set it down. He lifted Cathy up so she could watch. The doll walked toward them and stopped on the brink of the near edge. It looked at the girl and held out its arms and said, "Take me."

He lowered Cathy to the floor, and the doll's eyes followed her pleadingly. Cathy gazed up at the doll. It stood within her sight but out of her reach. The girl's eyes lit up. The doll trembled back to pseudo life and jerkily stepped over the edge of the table.

He caught it before it hit the floor, though his eyes had been on Cathy. He had got to Cathy too in the nick of time. Strong telekinesis for a three-year-old.

"Here, Cathy, hold the doll."

While she cradled the doll, he reached into a pocket and palmed his microchip injector.

"Oh, what lovely curls. Just like the dolly's." He raised the curls at the nape of Cathy's neck, baring the skin. "Do you mind if I touch them?" For some reason he always steeled himself when he planted the metallic seed under the skin, though he knew the insertion didn't hurt. At most, a slight pulling sensation, no more than if he had tugged playfully at her curls. Then a quick forgetting of the sensation. He patted the curls back in place and pocketed the injector.

"Let's play that game again, shall we, sugar plum?"

Gently he pried the doll from her and once more put it on the far edge of the table. This time it did not walk when he set it down. With one arm he lifted Cathy up and held her so she could see the doll. The fingers of his free hand hovered over studs on his broad black belt. The doll looked at the girl and held out its arms and said, "Take me."

The girl's eyes yearned across the vastness of the table. The doll suddenly trembled into pseudo life and began to walk toward them, jerkily at first, then more and more smoothly. He fingered a stud. The doll slowed. It moved sluggishly, as if bucking a high wind, but it kept coming. He fingered another stud. The doll slowed even more. In smiling agony it lifted one foot and swung it forward and set it down, tore the other free of enormous g's and swung it forward, and so kept coming. He fingered a third stud.

He sweated. He had never had to use this highest setting before. If this failed, it meant the child was incurably insane. Earth had room only for the sane. The doll had stopped. It fought to move, shuddered and stood still.

The girl stared at the doll. It remained where it was, out of reach. A tear fattened and glistened, then rolled down each cheek. It seemed to him a little something washed out of the child's eyes with the tears.

He reached out and picked up the doll and handed it to Cathy.

"She's yours to keep, Cathy, for always and always."

Automatically cradling the doll, Cathy smiled at him. He wiped away her tears and set her down. He irised the door open. "It's all right now. You can come in."

The Lessers and Clements timidly flooded back into the room.

"Is she—?"

"Cathy's as normal as any little girl around."

The worried faces regained permanent-press smoothness.

"Thank you, thank you. Say thank you, Cathy."

Cathy shook her head.

"Cathy!"

"That's quite all right. I'll settle for a kiss."

He brought his face close to Cathy's. Cathy hesitated, then gave his rosy cheek a peck.

"Thank *you*, Cathy." He shouldered his toys and straightened up. "And to all a good night."

And laying a finger aside of his nose, and giving a nod, through the iris he bounded. The Clement-Lesser apartment was on the ground floor, and the corridor let him out onto a patch of lawn. He gave his aircar a whistle. It zoomed from the roof to his feet.

As he rode through the night to his next stop, an image flashed into his mind. For an instant he saw, real as real, a weeping doll. It was just this side of subliminal. For a moment he knew fear. Had he failed after all with Cathy? Had she put that weeping doll in his mind?

Impossible. It came from within. Such aberrations were the aftermath of letdown. Sometimes, as now after a trying case, he got these weird flashes, these near-experiences of a wild frighteningly free vision, but always something in his mind mercifully cut them short.

As if on cue, to take him out of himself, the horn of his aircar sounded its *Ho ho ho* as it neared the Summerdaze condom. He looked down upon the chimneyless roofs. Most likely the chimney in the Sanity Clause legend grew out of folk etymology, the word *chimney* in this context coming from a misunderstanding of an ancient chant of peace on Earth: *Ho . . . Ho . . . Ho Chi Minh*. His eyes twinkled, his dimples deepened. There was always the comfort of logic to explain the mysteries of life.

The aircar parked itself on the roof of the Summerdaze condom, and he shouldered his bundle of toys and worked his way down through the housing complex.

Ho ho ho

Isaac Asimov began writing a monthly science column for *F&SF* in November 1958. He has not missed an issue since, and the column is by far the most popular feature of *F&SF* (with Dr. Asimov receiving almost as much mail as our subscription department). Dr. Asimov's usual subjects range from astronomy and mathematics through earth science and physics, but he also regularly drops in a general/contro-versial article (which gets even more mail!). Here is one such, on the nature of intelligence.

Science: Thinking About Thinking

by ISAAC ASIMOV

I have just returned from a visit to Great Britain. In view of my an-tipathy to travelling (which has not changed) I never thought I would walk the streets of London or stand under the stones of Stonehenge, but I did. Of course, I went by ocean liner both ways, since I don't fly.

The trip was an unqualified success. The weather during the ocean crossings was calm; the ships fed me (alas) all I could eat; the Brit-ish were impeccably kind to me, even though they did stare a bit at my vari-colored clothes, and frequently asked me what my bolo ties were.

Particularly pleasant to me was Steve Odell, who was publicity di-rector of Mensa, the organization of high-IQ people which more or less sponsored my visit. Steve squired me about, showed me the sights, kept me from falling into ditches and under cars, and throughout maintained what he called his "traditional British reserve."

For the most part, I managed to grasp what was said to me despite the funny way the British have of talking. One girl was occasionally incomprehensible, however, and I had to ask her to speak more slowly. She seemed amused by my failure to understand her, although I, of course, attributed it to her imperfect command of the language. "You," I pointed out, "understand *me.*"

"Of course I understand you," she said. "You speak slowly in a Yankee drool."

I had surreptitiously wiped my chin before I realized that the poor thing was trying to say "drawl."

But I suppose the most unusual part of the trip (which included three speeches, three receptions, innumerable interviews by the various media, and five hours of book-signing at five book stores in London and Birmingham) was being made a vice-president of International Mensa.

I took it for granted that the honor was bestowed upon me for the sake of my well-known intelligence, but I thought of it during my five-day return on the *Queen Elizabeth Two,* and it dawned on me that I didn't really know much about intelligence. I *assume* I am intelligent, but how can I *know?*

So I think I had better think about it—and where better than here among all my Gentle Friends and Readers?

One common belief connects intelligence with : 1) the ready accumulation of items of knowledge, 2) the retention of such items, and 3) the quick recall, on demand, of such items.

The average person, faced with someone like myself (for instance) who displays all these characteristics in abundant degree is quite ready to place the label of "intelligent" upon the displayer and to do so in greater degree the more dramatic the display.

Yet surely this is wrong. One may possess all three characteristics and yet give evidence of being quite stupid; and, on the other hand, one may be quite unremarkable in these respects and yet show unmistakable signs of what would surely be considered intelligence.

During the 1950s, the nation was infested with television programs in which large sums were paid out to those who could come up with obscure items of information on demand (and under pressure). It turned out that some of the shows weren't entirely honest, but that is irrelevant.

Millions of people who watched thought mental calisthenics indicated intelligence.* The most remarkable contestant was a postal employee from St. Louis who, instead of applying his expertise to one category as did others, took the whole world of factual items for his province. He amply displayed his prowess and struck the nation with awe. Indeed, just before the quiz-program fad collapsed, there were plans to pit this man against all comers in a program to be entitled, "Beat the Genius."

Genius? Poor man! He had barely competence enough to make a poor living, and his knack of total recall was of less use to him than the ability to walk a tight-rope would have been.

But not everyone equates the accumulation and ready regurgitation of names, dates, and events with intelligence. Very often, in fact, it is the lack of this very quality that is associated with intelligence. Have you never heard of the absent-minded professor?

According to one kind of popular stereotype, all professors and all intelligent people generally, are absent-minded and couldn't remember their own names without a supreme effort. But then what makes them intelligent?

I suppose the explanation would be that a very knowledgeable person bends so much of his intellect to his own sector of knowledge that he has little brain to spare for anything else. The absent-minded professor is therefore forgiven all his failings for the sake of his prowess in his chosen field.

Yet that cannot be the whole story either, for we divide categories of knowledge into a hierarchy and reserve our admiration for some only, labelling successful jugglery in those and those only as "intelligent."

We might imagine a young man, for instance, who has an encyclopedic knowledge of the rules of baseball, its procedures, its records, its players and its current events. He may concentrate so thoroughly on such matters that he is extremely absent-minded with respect to mathematics, English grammar, geography and history. He is not then forgiven his failure in some respects for the sake of his success in

---

* I was asked to be on one of these shows and refused, feeling that I would gain nothing by a successful display of trivial mental pyrotechnics and would suffer needless humiliation if I were human enough to muff a question.

others; he is *stupid!* On the other hand, the mathematical wizard who cannot, even after explanation, tell a bat boy from a home run, is nonetheless *intelligent.*

Mathematics is somehow associated with intelligence in our judgments, and baseball is not, and even moderate success in grasping the former is enough for the label of intelligent, while supreme knowledge of the latter gains you nothing in that direction (though much, perhaps in others).

So the absent-minded professor, as long as it is only his name he doesn't remember, or what day it is, or whether he has eaten lunch, or has an appointment to keep (and you should hear the stories about Norbert Wiener) is still intelligent as long as he learns, remembers, and recalls a great deal about some category *associated* with intelligence.

And what categories are these?

We can eliminate every category in which excellence involves merely muscular effort or coordination. However admirable a great baseball player may be, or a great swimmer, painter, sculptor, flautist or cellist may be, however successful, famous and beloved, excellence in these fields is, in itself, no indication of intelligence.

Rather it is in the category of theory that we find an association with intelligence. To study the technique of carpentry, and write a book on the various fashions of carpentry through the ages is a sure way of demonstrating intelligence, even though one could not, on any single occasion, drive a nail into a beam without smashing one's thumb.

And if we confine ourselves to the realm of thought, it is clear that we are readier to associate intelligence with some fields than with others. We are almost sure to show more respect for a historian than for a sports writer; for a philosopher than for a cartoonist, and so on.

It seems an unavoidable conclusion to me that our notions of intelligence are a direct inheritance from the days of ancient Greece when the mechanical arts were despised as fit only for artisans and slaves, while only the "liberal arts" (from the Latin word for "free men") were respectable, because they had no practical use and were therefore fit for free men.

So non-objective is our judgment of intelligence, that we can see

its measure change before our eyes. Until fairly recently, the proper
education for young gentlemen consisted very largely in the brute
inculcation (through beatings, if necessary) of the great Latin writers.
To know no Latin seriously disqualified anyone for enlistment in
the ranks of the intelligent.

We might, of course, point out that there is a difference between
"educated" and "intelligent" and that the foolish spouting of Latin
marked only a fool after all—but that's just theory. In actual fact,
the uneducated intelligent man is invariably down-graded and underestimated and, at best, is given credit for "native wit" or "shrewd
common sense." And women, who were not educated, were shown
to be unintelligent by their lack of Latin, and that was the excuse for
not educating them. (Of course that's circular reasoning, but circular
reasoning has been used to support all the great injustices of history.)

Yet see how things change. It used to be Latin that was the mark
of intelligence, and now it is science, and I am the beneficiary. I
know no Latin except for what my fly-paper mind has managed to
pick up accidentally, but I know a great deal of science—so without
changing a single brain-cell, I would be dumb in 1775 and terribly
smart in 1975.

You might say that it isn't knowledge itself, not even the properly
fashionable category of knowledge, that counts, but the *use* that is
made of it. It is, you might argue, the fashion in which the knowledge is displayed and handled, the wit, originality and creativity with
which it is put to use, that counts. Surely, *there* is the measure of intelligence.

And to be sure, though teaching, writing, scientific research, are
examples of professions often associated with intelligence, we all
know there can be pretty dumb teachers, writers and researchers.
The creativity or, if you like, the intelligence can be missing and still
leave behind a kind of mechanical competence.

But if creativity is what counts, that, too, only counts in approved
and fashionable areas. A musician, unlearned, uneducated, unable to
read music perhaps, may be able to put together notes and tempos in
such a way as to create, brilliantly, a whole new school of music. Yet
that in itself will not earn him the accolade of "intelligent." He is
merely one of those unaccountable "creative geniuses" with a "gift

from God." Since he doesn't know how he does it, and cannot explain it after he's done it,* how can he be considered intelligent?

The critic who, after the fact, studies the music, and finally, with an effort, decides it is not merely an unpleasant noise by the old rules, but is a great accomplishment by certain new rules—why *he* is intelligent. (But how many critics would you exchange for one Louis Armstrong?)

But in that case, why is the brilliant scientific genius considered intelligent? Do you suppose he knows how his theories come to him or can explain to you how it all happened? Can the great writer explain how he writes so that you can do as he does?

I am not, myself, a great writer by any standard I respect, but I have my points and I have this value for the present occasion—that I am one person, generally accepted as intelligent, whom I can view from within.

Well, my clearest and most visible claim to intelligence is the nature of my writing—the fact that I write a great many books in a great many fields in complex yet clear prose, displaying great mastery of much knowledge in doing so.

So what?

No one ever taught me to write. I had worked out the basic art of writing when I was eleven. And I can certainly never explain what that basic art is to anyone else.

I dare say that some critic, who knows far more of literary theory than I do (or than I would ever care to) might, if he chose, analyze my work and explain what I do and why, far better than I ever could. Would that make him more intelligent than I am? I suspect it might, to many people.

In short, I don't know of any way of defining intelligence that does not depend on the subjective and the fashionable.

Now, then, we come to the matter of intelligence-testing, the determination of "intelligence quotient" of "IQ."

If, as I maintain and firmly believe, there is no objective definition of intelligence, and what we call intelligence is only a creation of cul-

---

* *The great trumpeter, Louis Armstrong, on being asked to explain something about jazz, is reported to have said (translated into conventional English), "If you've got to ask, you aren't ever going to know." —These are words fit to be inscribed on jade in letters of gold.*

tural fashion and subjective prejudice, what the devil is it we test when we make use of an intelligence test?

I hate to knock the intelligence test, because I am a beneficiary of it. I routinely end up on the far side of 160 when I am tested, and even then I am invariably underestimated because it almost always takes me less time to do a test than the time allotted.

In fact, out of curiosity, I got a paperback book containing a sizable number of different tests designed to measure one's IQ. Each test had a half-hour time limit. I worked on each one as honestly as I could, answering some questions instantly, some after a bit of thought, some by guesswork, and some not at all. —And naturally, I got some answers wrong.

When I was done, I worked out the results according to directions and it turned out I had an IQ of 135. —But wait! I had not accepted the half-hour limit offered me, but broke off each section of the test at the 15-minute mark and went on to the rest. I therefore doubled the score and decided I have an IQ of 270. (I'm sure that the doubling is unjustified, but the figure of 270 pleases my sense of cheerful self-appreciation, and so I intend to insist on it.)

But however much all this soothes my vanity, and however much I appreciate being Vice-President of Mensa, an organization which bases admission to its membership on IQ, I must, in all honesty, maintain that it means nothing.

What, after all, does such an intelligence test measure but those skills that are associated with intelligence by the individuals designing the test. And those individuals are subject to the cultural pressures and prejudices that force a subjective definition of intelligence.

Thus, important parts of any intelligence test measure the size of one's vocabulary, but the words one must define are just those words one is apt to find in reading approved works of literature. No one asks for the definition of "two-bagger" or "snake-eyes" or "jive," for the simple reason that those who designed the tests don't know these terms or are rather ashamed of themselves if they do.

This is similarly true of tests of mathematical knowledge, of logic, of shape-visualization, and of all the rest. You are tested in what is culturally fashionable—in what educated men consider to be the criteria of intelligence—i.e. of minds like their own.

The whole thing is a self-perpetuating device. Men in intellectual control of a dominating section of society define themselves intelligent, then design tests that are a series of clever little doors that can let through only minds like their own, thus giving them more evidence of "intelligence" and more examples of "intelligent people" and therefore more reason to devise additional tests of the same kind. More circular reasoning!

And once someone is stamped with the label "Intelligent" on the basis of such tests and such criteria, any demonstration of stupidity no longer counts. It is the label that matters, not the fact. I don't like to label others, so I will merely give you two examples of clear stupidity which I myself perpetrated (though I can give you two hundred, if you like)—

1) On a certain Sunday, something went wrong with my car and I was helpless. Fortunately, my younger brother, Stan, lived nearby, and since he is notoriously good-hearted, I called him. He came out at once, absorbed the situation and began to use the yellow pages and the telephone to try to reach a service station while I stood by with my lower jaw hanging loose. Finally, after a period of strenuous futility, Stan said to me with just a touch of annoyance, "With all your intelligence, Isaac, how is it you lack the brains to join the AAA?" Whereupon, I said, "Oh, I belong to the AAA," and produced the card. He gave me a long, strange look and called the AAA. I was on my wheels in half an hour.

2) Sitting in Ben Bova's room (he's editor of *Analog*) at a recent science fiction convention, I was waiting, rather impatiently, for my wife to join us. Finally, there was a ring at the door. I sprang to my feet with an excited "Here's Janet!" flung open a door and dashed into the closet—when Ben opened the room-door and let her in.

Stan and Ben love to tell these stories about me, and they're harmless. Because I have the label "intelligent," what would surely be evidence of stupidity is converted into lovable eccentricity.

This brings us to a serious point. There has been talk in recent years of racial differences in IQ. Men like William B. Shockley, who has a Nobel Prize (in physics), point out that measurements show the average IQ of Blacks to be substantially lower than that of Whites, and this has created quite a stir.

Many people who, for one reason or another, have already concluded that Blacks are "inferior," are delighted to have "scientific" reason to suppose that the undesirable position in which Blacks find themselves is their own fault after all.

Shockley, of course, denies racial prejudice (sincerely, I'm sure) and points out that we can't deal intelligently with racial problems if, out of political motives, we ignore an undoubted scientific finding; that we ought to investigate the matter carefully, and study the intellectual inequality of man. Nor is it just a matter of Blacks versus Whites; apparently some groups of Whites score less well than do other groups of Whites, and so on.

Yet to my mind, the whole hip-hurrah is a colossal fraud. Since intelligence is (as I believe) a matter of subjective definition and since the dominant intellectuals of the dominant sector of society have naturally defined it in a self-serving manner, what is it we say when we say that Blacks have a lower average *IQ* than Whites have? What we are saying is that the Black sub-culture is substantially different from the dominant White sub-culture and that the Black values are sufficiently different from dominant White values to make Blacks do less well on the carefully-designed intelligence tests produced by the Whites.

In order for Blacks, on the whole, to do as well as Whites, they must abandon their own sub-culture for the White and produce a closer fit to the IQ-testing situation. This they may not want to do; and even if they want to, conditions are such that it is not made easy for them to fulfill that desire.

To put it as succinctly as possible—Blacks in America have had a sub-culture created for them, chiefly by White action, and have been kept in it chiefly by White action. The values of that sub-culture are defined as inferior to those of the dominant culture so that the Black IQ is arranged to be lower; and the lower IQ is then used as an excuse for the continuation of the very conditions that produced it. Circular reasoning? Of course.

But then, I don't want to be an intellectual tyrant, and insist that what I speak must be the truth.

Let us say that I am wrong; that there *is* an objective definition of intelligence, that it *can* be measured accurately, and that Blacks *do* have lower IQ ratings than Whites do, on the average, not because of any cultural differences but because of some innate biologically-based intellectual inferiority. Now what? How should Whites treat Blacks?

That's a hard question to answer, but perhaps we can get some good out of supposing the reverse. What if we test Blacks and find out, more or less to our astonishment, that they end up showing a *higher* IQ than do Whites, on the average.

How should we then treat them? Should we give them a double vote? Give them preferential treatment in jobs, particularly in the government? Let them have the best seats in the bus and theater? Give them cleaner rest-rooms than Whites have, and a higher average pay-scale?

I am *quite* certain that the answer would be a decided, forceful, and profane negative for each of the propositions and any like them. I suspect that if it were reported that Blacks had higher IQ ratings than Whites do, most Whites would at once maintain, with considerable heat, that IQ could not be measured accurately and that it was of no significance if it could be, that a person was a person regardless of book-learning, fancy education, big words, and fol-de-rol, that plain ordinary horse sense was all anyone needed, that all men were equal in the good old United States and those damned pinko professors and their IQ tests could just shove it—

Well, if we're going to ignore IQ when *we* are on the low end of the scale, why should we pay such pious attention to it when *they* are?

But hold on. I may be wrong again. How do I know how the dominants would react to a high-IQ minority? After all, we *do* respect intellectuals and professors to a certain extent, don't we? Then, too, we're talking about oppressed minorities and a high-IQ minority wouldn't be oppressed in the first place, so the artificial situation I set up by pretending the Blacks scored high is just a straw-man, and knocking it down has no value.

Really? Let's consider the Jews, who, for some two millennia, have been kicked around whenever Gentiles found life growing dull. Was this because Jews, as a group, are low-IQ? You know, I *never* heard that maintained by anyone, however anti-Semitic.

I do not, myself, consider Jews, as a group, to be markedly high-IQ. The number of stupid Jews I have met in the course of a lifetime is enormous. That, however, is not the opinion of the anti-Semite, whose stereotype of the Jews gives them a gigantic and dangerous intelligence. Although they may make up less than half a per cent of a nation's population, they are forever on the point of "taking over."

But then, shouldn't they, if they are high-IQ? Oh, no, for that intelligence is merely "shrewdness," or "low cunning," or "devious slyness," and what really counts is that they lack the Christian, or the Nordic, or the Teutonic, or the what-have-you virtues of other sorts.

In short, if you are on the rotten end of the game-of-power, any excuse will do to keep you there. If you are seen as low-IQ, you are despised and kept there because of that. If you are seen as high-IQ, you are feared and kept there because of that.

Whatever significance IQ may have, then, it is, at present, being made a game for bigots.

Let me end, then, by giving you my own view. Each of us is part of any number of groups corresponding to any number of ways of subdividing mankind. In each of these ways, a given individual may be superior to others in the group, or inferior, or either, or both, depending on definition and on circumstance.

Because of this, "superior" and "inferior" have no useful meaning. What *does* exist, objectively, is "different." Each of us is different. I am different, and you are different, and you, and you, and you—

It is this difference that is the glory of Homo sapiens and the best possible salvation, because what some cannot do, others can, and where some cannot flourish, others can, through a wide range of conditions. I think we should value these differences as mankind's chief asset, as a species, and try never to use them to make our lives miserable, as individuals.

From Competition 8:   Near-Miss SF Titles

Brunner's *The Sheep Look Wooly*
Dick's *The Three Stigmata of Roger Elwood*
   The Man in the High Collar
Silverberg's *Itching Inside*
Zelazny's *Creatures of Light and Heavy*
> —*F. M. Busby*

Heinlein's *Time for Enough Love*
Blish's *A Six-Pack of Conscience*
Gerrold's *With A Finger In My Nose*
Campbell's *Who Is It, Please*
Ellison's *The Beast Who Shouted Love At the Heart of the Artichoke*
> —*Joe Haldeman*

Gerrold's *With A Finger In My Knows*
Ellison's *The Dead Bird*
> —*Mark Robert Kelly*

Gerrold's *The Man Who Fondled Himself*
Bradbury's *Something Wasted This Way Comes*
> —*R. Tyler Sperry II*

Asimov's *The Streaking Sun*
> —*Terry Naylor*

Bradbury's *Bayonne Is Heaven!*
> —*Reid Powell*

238

Asimov's *Foundation*
Foundation^2
Foundation^3
—*David A. Wilson*

Vonnegut's *Slaughterhouse 5*
Cattle 0
—*Carolyn Appleman*

Sheckley's *Can You Do Anything When I Feel This?*
—*Ken Scott*

C. M. Kornbluth was seventeen years old and Frederik Pohl was not yet twenty when the two began writing stories together. Their collaboration spanned a period of about twenty years and produced roughly thirty-five short stories and seven novels (including the classic *The Space Merchants*). Cyril Kornbluth died in 1958, still a young man. This unusual story came to us from Fred Pohl with the following note: "I've been wanting for years to write a story about a science-fiction writer who couldn't be a science-fiction writer because he happened to be born in a time when that art was not possible, and the other day I realized that that story could fit nicely into the framework of an incomplete fragment of Cyril's. . . ."

Mute Inglorious Tam

by FREDERIK POHL and C. M. KORNBLUTH

On a late Saturday afternoon in summer, just before the ringing of Angelus, Tam of the Wealdway straightened from the furrows in his plowed strip of Oldfield and stretched his cracking joints.

He was a small and dark man, of almost pure Saxon blood. Properly speaking, his name was only Tam. There was no need for further identification. He would never go a mile from a neighbor who had known him from birth. But sometimes he called himself by a surname—it was one of many small conceits that complicated his proper and straightforward life—and he would be soundly whipped for it if his Norman masters ever caught him at it.

He had been breaking clods in the field for fifteen hours, interrupted only by the ringing of the canonical hours from the squat, tiny church, and a mouthful of bread and soft cheese at noon. It was not easy for him to stand straight. It was also not particularly wise. A man could lose his strip for poor tilth, and Tam had come close enough, often enough. But there were times when the thoughts that chased themselves around his head made him forget the steady chop of the wooden hoe, and he would stand entranced, staring toward Lymeford Castle, or the river, or toward nothing at all, while he invented fanciful encounters and impossible prosperings. It was another of Tam's conceits, and a most dangerous one, if it were known. The least it might get him was a cuff from a man-at-arms. The most was a particularly unpleasing death.

Since Salisbury, in Sussex, was flat ground, its great houses were not perched dramatically on crags, like the keeps of robber barons along the Rhine or the grim fortresses of the Scottish lairds. They were the least they could be to do the job they had to do, in an age which had not yet imagined the palace or the cathedral.

In the year 1303 Lymeford Castle was a dingy pile of stone. It housed Sir and Lady Robert Bowen (sometimes they spelled it Bohun, or Beauhun, or Beauhaunt) and their household servants and men-at-arms in very great discomfort. It did not seem so to them particularly. They had before them the housing of their Saxon subjects to show what misery could be. The castle was intended to guard a bridge across the Lyme River: a key point on the high road from Portsmouth to London. It did this most effectively. William of Normandy, who had taken England by storm a couple of centuries earlier, did not mean for himself or his descendants to be taken in the same way on another day. So Lymeford Castle had been awarded to Sir Robert's great-great-great-grandfather on the condition that he defend it and thereby defend London as well against invasion on that particular route from the sea.

That first Bowen had owned more than stones. A castle must be fed. The castellan and his lady, their household servants and their armed men could not be expected to till the field and milk the cows. The founder of Sir Robert's line had solved the problem of feeding the castle by rounding up a hundred of the defeated Saxon soldiers, clamping iron rings around their necks and setting them to work at the great task of clearing the untidy woods which surrounded the castle. After cleaning and plowing from sunup to sunset the slaves were free to gather twigs and mud, with which they made themselves kennels to sleep in. And in that first year, to celebrate the harvest and to insure a continuing supply of slaves, the castellan led his men-at-arms on a raid into Salisbury town itself. They drove back to Lymeford, with whips, about a hundred Saxon girls and women.

After taking their pick, they gave the rest to the slaves, and the chaplain read a single perfunctory marriage service over the filthy, ring-necked slaves and the weeping Salisbury women. Since the male slaves happened to be from Northumbria, while the women were Sussex bred, they could not understand each other's dialects. It did not matter. The huts were enlarged, and next midsummer there was another crop, this time of babies.

The passage of two centuries had changed things remarkably little. A Bowen (or Beauhaunt) still guarded the Portsmouth-London high road. He still took pride in his Norman blood. Saxons still tilled the soil for him and if they no longer had the iron collar, or the name of slaves, they still would dangle from the gallows in the castle courtyard for any of a very large number of possible offenses against his authority. At Runnymede, many years before, King John had signed the Great Charter conferring some sort of rule of law to protect his barons against arbitrary acts, but no one had thought of extending those rights to the serfs. They could die for almost anything or for nothing at all: for trying to quit their master's soil for greener fields; for failing to deliver to the castle their bushels of grain, as well as their choicest lambs, calves and girl-children; for daring in any way to flout the divine law that made one kind of man ruler and another kind ruled. It was this offense to which Tam was prone, and one day, as his father had told him the day before he died, it would cost him the price that no man can afford to pay, though all do.

Though Tam had never even heard of the Magna Carta, he sometimes thought that a world might sometime come to be in which a man like himself might own the things he owned as a matter of right and not because a man with a sword had not decided to take them from him. Take Alys his wife. He did not mind in any real sense that the men-at-arms had bedded her before he had. She was none the worse for it in any way that Tam could measure; but he had slept badly that night, pondering why it was that no one needed to consult him about the woman the priest had sworn to him that day, and whether it might not be more—more—he grappled for a word ("fair" did not occur to him) and caught at "right"—more right that he should say whose pleasures his property served.

Mostly he thought of sweeter and more fanciful things. When the falconers were by, he sometimes stole a look at the hawk stooping on a pigeon and thought that a man might fly if only he had the wings and the wit to move them. Pressed into driving the castellan's crops into the granary, he swore at the dumb oxen and imagined a cart that could turn its wheels by itself. If the Lyme in flood could carry a tree bigger than a house faster than a man could run, why could that power not pull a plow? Why did a man have to plant five kernels of corn to see one come up? Why could not all five come up and make him five times as fat?

He even looked at the village that was his home, and wondered why it had to be so poor, so filthy and so small; and that thought had hardly occurred even to Sir Robert himself.

In the year 1303 Lymeford looked like this:

The Lyme River, crossed by the new stone structure that was the fourth Lymeford Bridge, ran south to the English Channel. Its west bank was overgrown with the old English oak forest. Its right bank was the edge of the great clearing. Lymeford Castle, hard by the bridge, covered the road that curved northeast to London. For the length of the clearing, the road was not only the king's high-way, it was also the Lymeford village street. At a discreet distance from the castle it began to be edged with huts, larger or smaller as their tenants were rich or fecund. The road widened a bit halfway to the edge of the clearing, and there on its right side sat the village church.

The church was made of stone, but that was about all you could say for it. All the wealth it owned it had to draw from the village, and there was not much wealth there to draw. Still, silver pennies had to be sent regularly to the bishop, who in turn would send them on to Rome. The parish priest of Lymeford was an Italian who had never seen the bishop, to whom it had never occurred to try to speak the language and who had been awarded the living of Lymeford by a cardinal who was likewise Italian and likewise could not have described its location within fifty miles. There was nothing unusual in that, and the Italian collected the silver pennies while his largely Norman, but Saxon speaking, locum tenens scraped along on donations of beer, dried fish and the old occasional calf. He was a dour man who would have been a dreadful one if he had had a field of action that was larger than Lymeford.

Across the street from the church was The Green, a cheerless trampled field where the compulsory archery practice and pike drill were undergone by every physically able male of Lymeford, each four weeks, except in the worst of winter and when plowing or harvest was larger in Sir Robert's mind than the defense of his castle.

His serfs would fight when he told them to, and he would squander their lives with the joy a man feels in exercising the one extravagance he permits himself on occasion. But that was only at need, and the fields and the crops were forever. He saw to the crops with some considerable skill. A three-field system prevailed in Lymeford. There was Oldfield, east of the road, and the first land brought under cultivation by the slaves two hundred years ago. There was Newfield, straddling the road and marked off from Oldfield by a path into the woods called the Wealdway, running southeast from The Green into the oak forest at the edge of the clearing. There was Fallowfield, last to be cleared and planted, which for the most part lay south of the road and the castle. From the left side of the road to the river, The Mead spread its green acres. The Mead was held in common by all the villagers. Any man might turn his cows or sheep to graze on it anywhere. The farmed fields, however, were divided into long, narrow strips, each held by a villager who would defend it with his fists or his sickle against the encroachment of a single inch. In the year 1303 Oldfield and Newfield were under cultivation, and Fallowfield was being rested. Next year it would be Newfield and Fallowfield farmed, and Oldfield would rest.

While Angelus clanged on the cracked church bell, Tam stood with his head downcast. He was supposed to be praying. In a way he was, the impenetrable rote-learned Latin slipping through his brain like the reiteration of a mantra, but he was also pleasantly occupied in speculating how plump his daughter might become if they could farm all three fields each year without destroying the soil, and at the same time thinking of the pot of fennel-spiced beer that should be waiting in his hut.

As the Angelus ceased to ring, his neighbor's hail dispelled both dreams.

Irritated, Tam shouldered his wooden-bladed hoe and trudged along the Wealdway, worn deep by two hundred years of bare peasant feet.

His neighbor, Hud, fell in with him. In the bastard MidlandSussex hybrid that was the Lymeford dialect, Hud said, "Man, that was a long day."

"All the days are long in the summer."

"You were dreaming again, man. Saw you."

Tam did not reply. He was careful of Hud. Hud was as small and dark as himself, but thin and nervous rather than blocky. Tam knew he got that from his father Robin, who had got it from his mother Joan—who had got it from some man-at-arms on her wedding night spent in the castle. Hud was always asking, always talking, always seeking new things. But when Tam, years younger, had dared to try to open his untamable thoughts to him, Hud had run straight to the priest.

"Won't the players be coming by this time of year, man?" he pestered.

"They might."

"Ah, wouldn't it be a great thing if they came by tomorrow? And then after Mass they'd make their pitch in The Green, and out would come the King of England and Captain Slasher and the Turkish Champion in their clothes colored like the sunset, and St. George in his silver armor!"

Tam grunted. " 'Tisn't silver. Couldn't be. If it was silver the robbers in the Weald would never let them get this far."

The nervous little man said, "I didn't mean it *was* silver. I meant it *looked* like silver."

Tam could feel anger welling up in him, drowning the good aftertaste of his reverie and the foretaste of his fennel beer. He said angrily, "You talk like a fool."

"Like a fool, is it? And who is always dreaming the sun away, man?"

"God's guts, leave off!" shouted Tam, and clamped his teeth on his words too late. He seldom swore. He could have bitten his tongue out after he uttered the words. Now there would be confession of blasphemy to make, and Father Bloughram, who had been looking lean and starved of late, would demand a penance in grain instead of any beggarly saying of prayers. Hud cowered back, staring. Tam snarled something at him, he could not himself have said what, and turned off the deep-trodden path into his own hut.

The hut was cramped and murky with wood smoke from its open hearth. There was a smoke hole in the roof that let some of it out. Tam leaned his hoe against the wattled wall, flopped down onto the bundle of rags in the corner that was the bed for all three of the members of his family and growled at Alys his wife: "Beer." His mind was full of Hud and anger, but slowly the rage cooled and the good thoughts crept back in: Why not a softer bed, a larger hut?

Why not a fire that did not smoke, as his returning grandfather, who wore a scar from the Holy Land to his grave, had told him the Saracens had? And with the thought of a different kind of life came the thought of beer; he could taste the stuff now, sluicing the dust from his throat; the bitterness of the roasted barley, the sweetness of the fennel. "Beer," he called again, and became aware that his wife had been tiptoeing about the hut.

"Tam," she said apprehensively, "Joanie Brewer's got the flux."

His brows drew together like thunderclouds. "No beer?" he asked.

"She's got the flux, and not for all the barley in Oldfield could she brew beer. I tried to borrow from Hud's wife, and she had only enough for him, she showed me—"

Tam got up and knocked her spinning into a corner with one backhanded blow. "Was there no beer yesterday?" he shouted. "God forgive you for being the useless slut you are! May the Horned Man and all his brood fly away with a miserable wretch that won't brew beer for the husband that sweats his guts out from sunup to sunset!"

She got up cringing, and he knocked her into the corner again.

The next moment there was a solid crack across his back, and he crashed to the dirt floor. Another blow took him on the legs as he rolled over, and he looked up and saw the raging face of his daughter Kate and the wooden-bladed hoe upraised in her hands.

She did not strike him a third time, but stood there menacingly. "Will you leave her alone?" she demanded.

"Yes, you devil's get!" Tam shouted from the floor, and then, "You'd like me to say no, wouldn't you? And then you'd beat in the brains of the old fool that gave you a name and a home."

Weeping, Alys protested, "Don't say that, husband. She's your child, I'm a good woman, I have nothing black on my soul."

Tam got to his feet and brushed dirt from his leather breeches and shirt. "We'll say no more about it," he said. "But it's hard when a man can't have his beer."

"You wild boar," said Kate, not lowering the hoe. "If I hadn't come back from the Mead with the cow, you might have killed her."

"No, child," Tam said uneasily. He knew his temper. "Let's talk of other things." Contemptuously she put down the hoe, while Alys got up, sniffling, and began to stir the peaseporridge on the hearth. Suddenly the smoke and heat inside the hut was more than Tam could bear, and muttering something, he stumbled outside and breathed in the cool air of the night.

It was full dark now and, for a wonder, stars were out. Tam's Crusader grandfather had told him of the great bright nights in the mountains beyond Acre, with such stars that a man could spy friend's face from foe's at a bowshot. England had nothing like that, but Tam could make out the Plow, fading toward the sunset, and Cassiopeia pursuing it from the east. His grandfather had tried to teach him the Arabic names for some of the brighter stars, but the man had died when Tam was ten and the memories were gone. What were those two, now, so bright and so close together? Something about twin peacocks? Twins at least, thought Tam, staring at Gemini, but a thought of peacocks lingered. He wished he had paid closer attention to the old man, who had been a Saracen's slave for nine years until a lucky raid had captured his caravan and set him free.

A distant sound of yelping caught his ear. Tam read the sound easily enough; a vixen and her half-grown young, by the shrillness. The birds came into the plowed fields at night to steal the seed, and the foxes came to catch the birds, and this night they had found something big enough to try to catch them—wolf, perhaps, Tam thought, though it was not like them to come so near to men's huts in good weather. There were a plenty of them in Sir Robert's forest, with fat deer and birds and fish beyond counting in the streams; but it was what a man's life was worth to take them. He stood there, musing on the curious chance that put venison on Sir Robert's table and peaseporridge on his, and on the lights in the sky, until he realized Alys had progressed from abject to angry and must by now be eating without him.

After the evening meal Alys scurried over to Hud's wife with her tale of beastly husbands, and Kate sat on a billet of wood, picking knots out of her hair.

Tam squatted on the rags and studied her. At fifteen years, or whatever she was, she was a wild one. How had it happened that the babe who cooed and grasped at the grass whistle her father made her had turned into this stranger? She was not biddable. Edwy's strip adjoined Tam's in Fallowfield, and Edwy had a marriageable son. What was more reasonable than that Kate should marry him? But she had talked about his looks. True, the boy was no beauty. What did that matter? When, as a father should, he had brushed that aside, she had threatened plainly to run away, bringing ruin and the rope on all of them. Nor would she let herself be beaten into good sense, but instead kicked—with painful accuracy—and bit and scratched like a fiend from hell's pit.

He felt a pang at that thought. Oh, Alys was an honest woman. But there were other ways the child of another could be fobbed off on you. A moment of carelessness when you didn't watch the cradle —it was too awful to think of, but sometimes you had to think of it. Everybody knew that Old People liked nothing better than to steal somebody's baby and slip one of their own into the cradle. He and Alys had duly left bowls of milk out during the child's infancy, and on feast days bowls of beer. They had always kept a bit of iron by Kate, because the Old People hated iron. But still. . . .

Tam lighted a rushlight soaked in mutton fat at what was left of the fire. Alys would have something to say about his extravagance, but a mood for talking was on him, and he wanted to see Kate's face. "Child," he said, "one Sunday now the players will come by and pitch on The Green. And we'll all go after Mass and see them play. Why, St. George looks as if he wears armor all of silver!"

She tugged at her hair and would not speak or look at him.

He squirmed uncomfortably on the ragged bed. "I'll tell you a story, child," he offered.

Contemptuously, "Tell your drunken friend. I've heard the two of you, Hud and yourself, lying away at each other with the beer working in you."

"Not that sort of story, Kate. A story no one has ever told."

No answer, but at least her face was turned toward him. Emboldened, he began:

" 'Tis a story of a man who owned a great strong wain that could move without oxen, and in it he—"

"What pulled it, then? Goats?"

"Nothing pulled it, child. It moved by itself. It"—he fumbled, and found inspiration—"it was a gift from the Old People, and the man put on it meal and dried fish and casks of water, and he rode in it to one of those bright stars you see just over church. Many days he traveled, child. When he got there—"

"What road goes to a star, man?"

"No road, Kate. This wain rode in the air, like a cloud. And then—"

"Clouds can't carry casks of water," she announced. "You talk like Edwy's mad son that thinks he saw the Devil in a turnip."

"Listen now, Kate!" he snapped. "It is only a story. When the man came to—"

"Story! It's a great silly lie."

"Neither lie nor truth," he roared. "It is a story I am telling you."

"Stories should be sense," she said positively. "Leave off your dreaming, father. All Lymeford talks of it, man. Even in the castle they speak of mad Tam the dreamer."

"Mad, I am?" he shouted, reaching for the hoe. But she was too quick for him. She had it in her hands; he tried to take it from her, and they wrestled, rock against flame, until he heard his wife's cater-wauling from the entrance, where she'd come running, called by the noise; and when he looked round, Kate had the hoe from him and space to use it and this time she got him firmly atop the skull—and he knew no more that night.

In the morning he was well enough, and Kate was wisely nowhere in sight. By the time the long day was through he had lost the anger.

Alys made sure there was beer that night, and the nights that followed. The dreams that came from the brew were not the same as the dreams he had tried so hard to put into words. For the rest of his life, sometimes he dreamed those dreams again, immense dreams, dreams that—had he had the words, and the skill, and above all the audience—a hundred generations might have remembered. But he didn't have any of those things. Only the beer.

R. Bretnor and *F&SF* go back a ways. His memorable story about Papa Schimmelhorn, "The Gnurrs Come from the Voodvork Out," appeared in our second issue, Winter 1950. Over the years his contributions to the magazine have been notable for their variety and high quality, for example, this delightful story about an old English ballad that sends two professors traveling in time in an attempt to trace its origins.

Old Uncle Tom Cobleigh and All

R. BRETNOR

It is indeed fortunate that the police cannot solve all mysterious disappearances, for if they had solved Professor Davey's—and if anyone had believed them—it would have upset Murrain University more than any number of student riots, and my own situation would have been far less comfortable than it is.

The quarrel between Professor Davey and Professor Addleweed was, I am sure, due not so much to intellectual conviction as to the difference in their social origins. Lucius Addleweed was a Boston Brahmin, with Harvard in his blood and bones. Davey, the son of an often drunken and habitually unemployed West Virginia coal miner, had scraped through to his Ph.D. in English by grace of native cunning, the G.I. Bill, and a number of grants scrounged for him by Left-oriented members of various faculties. Addleweed, holding the prestigious Sarah Grimsby Murrain Chair of Polite Letters, was the foremost authority on certain minor Nineteenth Century Irish essayists. Davey, on the other hand, had made his reputation largely by discovering and heralding an allegedly black poet named Gooey-duck, who had invented what he called "positional poetry," a technique in which one four-letter Anglo-Saxon word, interminably repeated, conveyed its subtleties of meaning by its many placements on the bare page, as though Mr. Mondrian and the Museum of Modern Art had claimed it for their own. Unhappily, the two men had written their doctoral dissertations on the same subject: the ability of the lowly and unlettered to transmit information from one generation to another, Addleweed contending that their stupidity and lack of adequate frames of reference distorted anything they might latch onto, Davey asserting that their simplicity and purity of spirit guaranteed the essential accuracy of legend, folk song, and many-times-retold country tales over any number of generations.

I myself, as Natural Philosopher in Residence under the Hober Murrain Twitchett Memorial Endowment for the Investigation of the Arcane Sciences, would of course have been completely out of it had I not, quite by accident, managed to bring back to life Roger Bacon's endochronic speculum—that "mirror to reveal the past" which our great predecessor had so wisely veiled behind double meanings and the most recondite allusions. On my appointment I had been summoned before the Chairman of the Chemistry Department, under whom for some reason I was supposed to function, and had been told my status in no uncertain terms.

"Grumpole," he had started impolitely, "get this through your mushy little skull. Twitchett was a nut—but he left us forty million dollars on condition we hire some other nut like you to mess around with alchemy and all that other crap he had a thing about. All right, you mess around with it. Keep your graduate students messing around with it—you can have a couple if you can round 'em up. But don't get in our hair. And stay out of the goddamn papers, understand?"

I followed his instructions to the letter, messing around, as he put it, with my two graduate students and, once or twice a year, publishing an adequately obfuscated paper in an adequately obscure journal—or at least lending my name as co-author to those written by the young men working under me. While I was completely uninterested in alchemy, the situation was ideal; my own major area of research—sorcery. It is a great pity, really, that Mr. Shagreen did not see eye to eye with me. We could have done great things together.

Mr. Shagreen became my third graduate student. He was from

somewhere near the Persian Gulf, and very smooth and plump. His wealthy parents had sent him to an excellent English public school and then to Trinity College, Dublin, where he had been graduated with honors. When he spoke, he sometimes sounded disconcertingly like one of the more lucid characters in *Finnegans Wake,* but there was much more to him than that. He had taken his M.S. in physics at a major Indian university, where the head of his department—how different from my own!—had doubled in brass as his spiritual mentor, or *guru.** I accepted him as what he seemed to be: an ambitious doctoral candidate sensibly taking advantage of a fat grant. I did not guess that alchemy was really his true love, or that he had enough Greek and Latin and even Arabic to dig far deeper than I into its occult literature. I didn't realize it until he—or perhaps I should say he and I—remade the speculum.

Prior to his arrival our work had all been on an abstract level: the discussion and comparison of theories, the elaboration of historical fact and legendary fancy. Mr. Shagree's project, however, required all the trimmings—retorts and alembics, furnaces and bellows, elixirs and reagents. I did my utmost to discourage him, pointing out that no funds had been allocated for such purposes. He countered with the statement that, as his family was very rich, this did not matter; he himself would pay all expenses. But actually it was because of his birthday present to me that finally I relented. Having learned what my true interest was, he wrote to an uncle of his in Iran, skilled craftsmen were set instantly to work, and six months later I was the astonished owner of a splendid carpet, rich in reds, deep blues, and glowing greens and yellows, woven especially for me in the design of a perfect pentacle surrounded by all the proper cabalistic signs and symbols. Three men were needed to bear it to my office and spread it out before my eyes, and Mr. Shagreen managed it all with an almost childish delight, animated solely by the desire to please me, his mentor, and (as I found out later) to impress Miss Willa Kornmulder, my secretary, one of those opulently rounded blondes with a lovely complexion and no features worth mentioning.

"Look there, will you, old Grumps, my dear!" he cried affectionately as it was displayed before me. "I've had a magic carpet made for

---

* *The dubious reader is referred to* Explorations in Tibet, *by Swami Pranavananda, F.R.G.S., the frontispiece of which shows the author's guru, head of the physics department at a major Indian university.*

you, indeed! And it's the truth that you can fly upon it from here to Araby the Blest, if you've a mind to."

I was touched. I completely ignored Willa's giggling comment about the possibility of my being sky-jacked, and next day I bestirred myself in his behalf and secured him laboratory space—a dark cellar of a room in an ancient brick warehouse now devoted mainly to smelly experiments with small rodents, California pocket gophers and the like. He was perfectly happy there and in no time had converted it into a scene which I'm sure Paracelsus would have found congenial, with its hubblings and bubblings and decoctings, stinks, reeks, and stenches—and with Miss Kornmulder helping him in her spare time, at least when they weren't love-making.

How little one really knows even of one's close associates! When Mr. Shagreen asked me to contrive a simple love spell for him, I did notice that his lecherous eye was on her, but no one told me that she had already had affairs, not only with several students in a number of departments, but also, unsatisfactorily, with Professor Davey, and perhaps more pleasantly because they still were friends, with Professor Addleweed.

Nobody warned me, and consequently I was completely unprepared when it happened—and it happened very suddenly. I had paid little attention to Mr. Shagreen's work, countersigning his strange requisitions mechanically, for after all he *was* paying for them—so much gray quicksilver, so much purple laudanum, so many pecks of most peculiar charcoal from Sinkiang, one ounce troy of the finest platinum, forty of fine silver, eight gills of urine from a female camelopard taken by a Nubian virgin during the vernal equinox— that last was rather hard to come by—and I know not what. Also, I had listened to him patiently enough when he explained to me that the speculum, completed, would resemble in its functioning nothing so much as a programmed computer. "It is science, that's what it is, old Grumps," he'd say, "not any magic mish-mash, not at all. There's no magic when one knows what causes what and what one's doing. Why, I shall manipulate the metal's body spiritual, as you might say, so that it'll be attuned not only to the celestial configurations, but to my voice indeed, and what we wish, and every heart's desire. And this in turn will dominate its body physical, its atoms and its molecules, in their innumerable dimensions and permutations. Oh, it's all down in black and white, my dear fellow, if you just happen to know a little of the Arabic and whatever. Friar Bacon set it down, taking care to hide a bit here and a dribbling there against the curiosity of the unthinking, but I have riddled it all out now, indeed—"

He said a great deal more in the same vein, and I paid no heed—not even when he invited me to watch the final casting of the speculum. I turned him down, on one pretext or another, and he went off muttering petulantly, "You should, you really should, old Grumpole! For it's going to make us famous, you and me. Famous, I dare say!"

Fame, of course, was one thing I did *not* want; I was completely satisfied with matters as they stood.

It was next morning that he came to me, Willa Kornmulder helping him, both of them panting from the weight of a large object hidden under a paisley shawl. Dramatically, he pulled the shawl away. "There you have it, Grumps!" he laughed triumphantly. "We've made a magic mirror for your magic carpet. Here it is!"

I beheld a bronze frame, nearly four feet in diameter, on an ornate bronze standard. Within it was a disk—a disk obviously made of metal, silver-gray perhaps, or perhaps the disturbing green of a cloud-shaded sea, sea-metal tense in its uneasiness, straining against its own tremendous tides. I saw that Mr. Shagreen had indeed produced something rich and strange, and cleared my throat to cover my abrupt chill of apprehension. I sat back in my chair, forcing myself to be elaborately calm. "And does it work?" I asked.

At once, his face fell. "I—I'm sure it will," he said uncertainly. "There's but one thing lacking, Dr. Grumpole, indeed there is, and that is—well, the Word of Power."

It was my turn to laugh triumphantly—and with relief. "In other words, my boy," I said, "you need a bit of magic, don't you? Well, well, you've come to the right shop for that. I've no doubt that given a few months we can pop up with just the old one Roger had in mind. Now let me think—there really were so many of 'em I don't know where to start—"

And, certain that we'd never find the right one, I—God help me! —uttered three of four at random, well known ones with which even amateur practitioners are conversant. And with the last—no, I shall not repeat it here!—the face of that strange mirror blanched suddenly, and stilled within itself, and vanished. Where it had been there was a window into an unformed world, shadowy, vague as a drifting fog at nightfall. And a deep voice from nowhere, from somewhere in the air surrounding us, said, *"Time Was!"*

Even I knew, then, that it was the voice of Friar Bacon's terrible brazen head.

"It *works!*" breathed Mr. Shagreen. "Grumps! Grumps! That is the *past* we're gazing at, indeed! Now all we have to do is think of any certain moment, and order it!"

"The Custer Massacre!" exclaimed Miss Kornmulder excitedly. "I was watching it last night on Channel Twel—"

Before she could so much as finish, the shadows disappeared. Bright sunlight took their place—sunlight and shots and screams of dying men. And, in the portal, the horribly painted, savage, howling face of a Sioux brave confronted us. For an instant only—then a war arrow, with a whistling scream, missed my left ear by a scant two inches and buried itself in the far wall, quivering beside the portrait of Hober Murrain Twitchett that hung there.

"Time *Is!*" Shagreen screamed desperately; and I, in the nick of time, shouted out the Word of Power. Instantly, the speculum confronted us again, once more its restless, solid self.

"For God's sake!" complained Willa Kornmulder. "That was lots better than Channel Twelve. Why did you guys have to go and turn it off?"

I pointed to the arrow with a trembling hand. Mr. Shagreen and I were thunderstruck by what had happened, and by its implications, he by the wonder and the fear of it, I—an older and, I think, wiser man—by the desperate need to keep it absolutely secret lest the vulgar press get wind of it or, even worse, the head of my department and his hirelings. With admirable presence of mind, I started marshalling my arguments. He listened, offering only a feeble and ill-considered opposition. Miss Kornmulder, ignored by both of us, sulked and pouted for a few minutes, then disappeared. Mr. Shagreen declared that *his* discovery was of earth-shaking importance and should be made public. I countered with the statement that, without the pentacle and my Word of Power, there'd have been no discovery, and that, as *magic,* it should be kept from the uninitiated and uncomprehending—certainly until we ourselves had had a chance to explore all its possibilities and perils. Back and forth we argued for perhaps fifteen minutes, and I know that he was about to bow before my logic—to say nothing of the arrow's—for finally he had admitted the crucial role magic had played in it, when sud-

denly the decision was rudely taken from us. Miss Kornmulder came
back into the room, accompanied by Professor Addleweed, who
seemed tremendously excited.

Addleweed's quarrel with Davey had, I knew, been going badly for
him. Three weeks before, Davey had announced a sensational artistic
breakthrough by Gooeyduck who, by adding the word *mother* to his
monosyllabic repertoire, had "immeasurably expanded the emotional
and cultural scope of positional poetry." Addleweed promptly had
denounced the whole thing as hogwash and a prime example of how
the semiliterate, the pushing, the unscrupulous, and the unwashed
could—especially when mistakenly sanctified by being granted Doc-
torates of Philosophy—take advantage of a gullible academic community. Thereupon Davey had delivered an impassioned lecture trac-
ing positional poetry back, by way of voodoo, hot jazz, and soul
food, to the folk art of Dahomey and Basutoland. A group of
Davey's more excited students had set fire to Addleweed's office and
had (rather to his relief) destroyed all his examination records for
the past seven years. Finally, though I didn't know it then, Davey
had challenged Addleweed to a contest of theories, through their simultaneous application to a specific problem—the results to be published in the student paper, and the entire student body to decide the
winner by voice vote. Foolishly, Addleweed had accepted, not knowing that Davey had proposed a problem to which he already had an
answer, and Davey had neatly pulled the rug from under him.

The problem had appeared a straightforward one: to take a rural
English ballad (which Addleweed was sure was of doubtful authen-
ticity) and, each employing his own methods, trace it to its origins
and determine the degree of accuracy with which the local yokels
had passed it to posterity. Its first verse and chorus went:

Tom Pearce, Tom Pearce, lend me your gray mare.
All along, down along, out along lee.
For I want to go to Widdecombe Fair,
Wi' Bill Brewer, Jan Stewer, Peter Gurney, Peter Davy, Dan'l
Whiddon, Harry Hawk, Old Uncle Tom Cobleigh and all—Old
Uncle Tom Cobleigh and all.

The "All along, down along," and the roster of names were
repeated in each of the half dozen or more succeeding verses, which
told a vaguely gruesome tale of the loss of the entire company and
the subsequent haunting of "the moor of a night." Davey had first
been attracted to it because of the fact that one of them had borne

his own name (even if spelled a little differently), and on impulse he had consulted the vast genealogical archives of the Mormon Church, which contain every parish record in Western Europe, and which of course had already been computerized. Listing several variant spellings for each name, he had asked the computer to scan for the simultaneous death or disappearance, during the 18th or early 19th Centuries, of such a group of Englishmen—and, much to his astonishment, the computer had replied that, yes indeed, on Midsummer's Eve, 1769, near Marlow in Buckinghamshire, had died "William Brewer, John Stewart, Peter Garney, Daniel Whidden, Mr. Henry Hawke, Thomas Joseph Pierce, and Thomas Cobleigh, Esq., aged 77." The only one not mentioned was his namesake, but Davey, after a momentary flicker of annoyance, told himself that probably the man had simply been shrewd enough to escape their common fate, or—even more likely—that here was a splendid example of oral tradition being more accurate than recorded history. He promptly announced his discovery to the world via the underground press and one or two impressionable TV commentators; the tabloids and straight media at once took it up; and instantly poor Addleweed became the laughingstock, not only of our English Department, but of campuses from coast to coast. The Chancellor's Office even sent him a formal note requesting him to list his publications during the preceding several years "together with any other information which he thought might justify his retention on the Faculty." He had, of course, taken the precaution of checking with the Mormons, and they had corroborated the information Davey had been given, adding that each name had at least been followed by the designation *Gentleman,* while Sir John Stewart had actually been a baronet—matters which Davey had not seen fit to mention. Still, there was scant consolation in this for Addleweed. Indeed, after Gooeyduck had published a positional ode entitled "White Fascist Pig Addleweed, How You Like *That,* Man?" which was a howling success, nobody would so much as listen to him; and he had lost all hope even of defending himself against his adversary when Willa Kornmulder (recollecting, I imagine tender moments they had spent together) betrayed us to him.

Addleweed was a very tall, lean, long-jawed man with a great many teeth and some untidy butter-colored hair. Now, as he came in behind Miss Kornmulder, his pale eyes opened wide at the sight of that uneasy speculum, and he exclaimed without preamble, "What's this, Thaddeus Grumpole? I hear you've made yourself a *time machine?*"

"Oh, but it isn't a *machine,* no, not a bit of it!" Mr. Shagreen protested. "Never a cog does it have; nor gear, nor noisy moving part will you find in it. It is an *instrument,* a device indeed, derived by marriage of modern physics and art alchemical to open, as it were, windows to the past, to what's long gone—and that discreetly too, without discomfiture to anyone—"

"Dr. Grumpole didn't invent it," Miss Kornmulder broke in, making calf eyes at him. *"Tuffy* did. And I just know he won't mind your using it, Lucius honey, to prove that bastard Davey doesn't know his hind end from a hot rock."

At that point, I decided to intervene. "We have decided," I declared firmly, "that for the moment no disclosure can be made. The device is still untried, and certainly much scientific enquiry must precede any actual use of it. As a scholar, Dr. Addleweed, I'm sure you'll understand."

Addleweed stared coldly at me, and his grin, despite the number of its teeth, was a most unpleasant one. *"Untried,* you say?" He pointed at the arrow in the wall. "Someone, it seems to me, has tried it to rather good effect. A two-way window to the past—it's fabulous! Grumpole, how can you keep so great a wonder bottled up? Our friend Tuffy here deserves full and immediate recognition—and so of course do you, and so does Murrain. We must inform the President and Chancellor, the Academic Senate, and for reasons of security, I would imagine, the F.B.I. and the Department of Defense. Willa, my dear, why don't you start phoning people right away?"

One of the precious lessons of maturity is how to give in with good grace. Shagreen and I glanced at each other. We both sat down. "Professor Addleweed," I said, returning the grin as cheerfully as I could, "naturally what I said does not preclude the sound suggestions of reputable scholars—yourself, for instance—regarding the direction our initial experiments will take. However, we must ask both you and Miss Kornmulder here to say not a word to *anyone.*"

"I wouldn't dream of it," he answered, now toothier than ever. "Shall we start at once?"

"Why not? Suppose we start with just a simple demonstration? We'll look in on my office here, yesterday after hours."

He nodded, and I walked over to the speculum. I pointed at it, and rapidly, in a low voice, repeated several Words of Power, some false, some genuine; and in their midst I sandwiched in the true one, the actuator—it never would have done to let him know it—and, as the mirror came to life, I saw Mr. Shagreen beam his approval at me. Around us, suddenly, the deep voice said, *"Time Was!"*

"This office at eight o'clock last night!" I ordered—and we were looking through into the night before.

Momentarily, Addleweed lost his insouciance. He paled. *"Wh-who said that?"* he demanded.

"With good reason—oh, I assure you, with good, sufficient reason," Mr. Shagreen told him, "we believe it to have been that very head, that same fine brazen head, of which, you will recall, Friar Bacon told us."

"Well, it's a good trick, Tuffy." Addleweed made a remarkable recovery. "Now shall we see if you can cross over there into *Time Was?"*

"I assure you that I can and will, indeed," Shagreen declared. "That's the beauty of it, do you see?—that we can shuttle ourselves back and forth at will, for the alchemical instructions I have found are complete astoundingly." Then, literally, he stepped into the speculum and through it and stood before us in the yesterday. He smiled, took from my desk a ball-point pen, walked back toward us, whispered, *"Enfold me!"* and was back abruptly in our midst.

"Time is!" he ordered, and again the speculum took form. I remembered that I had been unable to find my pen all day.

Addleweed made no effort now to hide his excitement and his eagerness. "Could you see us?" he asked. "Or could you see the speculum?"

"Not a bit of it, indeed," Shagreen replied. "Neither a jot nor tittle, but I could feel it there behind my back directly, for in the past it follows you, you understand? And never leaves you, so you can always pop back safely to here and now—very pretty programming, though perhaps in perfect modesty I shouldn't say so, and a great convenience."

"A great *in*convenience for Professor Peter Davey," gloated Addleweed. "Let's waste no time. We know the date. Send me back into the Eighteenth Century, give me an hour or two or three to find the facts, and we'll demolish him, I promise you!"

"Oh, we will, will we?" brayed a new voice from the door. It was a coarse voice with a thick veneer of culture, making me think of a

shoddy paperback mistakenly bound in crushed Levant morocco. I turned my head. Davey was standing there.

He was a well-set-up young fellow, but he had managed to conceal the fact. Rough sandals shod his dirty bare feet. Worn jeans, an ancient military tunic from the Boer War, a grubby sweatshirt, and a huge peace symbol on a string completed his attire. He was, of course, copiously whiskered, and his dull black hair hung to his shoulder blades. However, he carried a proper professorial briefcase —a symbol, I imagine, of his tenure.

"My God!" I said. "How long have you been here?"

"Long enough, you bastards," he replied. "So the two of you have got yourself a time machine, is that it? I damn well knew all that jazz about alchemy was just a cover! Millions are starving. Millions are murdered by imperialistic pigs. And you build *this*. Who financed you? The Pentagon? Dow Chemical? The lousy Rockefellers?"

"Mr. Shagreen's project," I told him coldly, "has been supported by the Hober Murrain Twitchett Memorial Endowment for the Investigation of the Arcane Sciences."

"And by my Uncle Hassan, who is rich as Croesus ever was, I do believe, and kindly too," Mr. Shagreen added.

"And you're going to let this fink here use the thing—which ought to be devoted to the welfare of the people—to make a liar out of me, is that it?" Davey snorted rudely. "I knew some dirty work was going on when I spotted him coming here with that tart you've got working for you. Well, all of you better think again! If anybody goes, it's going to be *me*. I wouldn't trust Piddleweed six weeks away, let alone two hundred years."

Addleweed favored him with a superior smile. "My good Davey," he purred, "you'd really better not. After all, you'd be among English *gentlemen*—your betters, as it were. They'd spot you instantly. Besides, everyone was clean-shaven in those days; your lovely facial fungus would have to go."

"Don't worry about me, you creep!" Davey's features twisted in a snarl. "And I can always grow my beard again."

"Gentlemen—" I said, and the word evoked still another snarl from Davey. "Gentlemen, we have a fascinating experiment before us. Why don't you *both* go, together?"

"Don't be a funny, Grumpole. You think I'd go back there among those dirty fascists with *him?* And leave you here to slam the door on both of us?"

"No, that would never do," said Addleweed.

Something of the sort had indeed been in my mind, even though I was by no means sure that we *could* slam the door. However, now I was finally thinking with the swiftness and efficiency which only long study of magical disciplines can inculcate. "Well, in that case—" I smiled upon them—"allow me to point out that it really doesn't matter which one goes? As Mr. Shagreen has already demonstrated, the speculum follows the time traveler everywhere, and the one left behind can watch his every action and hear his every word. Why don't you flip a coin? Then, to even things up, the loser can take a short exploratory trip into that same century, just so that the other can be sure that everything'll work."

The two of them glared at each other distrustfully; they glared at me and at Shagreen.

"Hey, does that blow my mind!" Miss Kornmulder cried out enthusiastically. "Each of you gets to watch the other guy, and I get to watch the both of you. That's got to be a better show than *Fanny Hill!*"

"I'm afraid dear Willa misunderstands our purposes," remarked Addleweed wryly.

"*She* would!" growled Davey.

"I'll flip the coin!" offered Miss Kornmulder, in no way put down.

"The hell you will, you stupid bitch!" Davey almost spat at her. "I'll flip the frigging coin!" He fished a quarter from his pocket. "But only if the one of us who's proven wrong agrees to admit it publicly, resign from the faculty, and get the hell away from Murrain."

After only a moment's hesitation, Addleweed nodded his agreement.

"Okay," Davey sneered. "You want to call it, fink?"

"Heads," said Addleweed.

Davey sent the coin tumbling over and over in the air. It landed on the carpet at my feet. None of us touched it. We all stared down at it.

"It's tails!" I announced, and Davey crowed in triumph.

Angrily, Miss Kornmulder stamped her dainty foot, but Addleweed, though obviously crestfallen, took it in surprisingly good part. He shrugged. "If we're lucky," he remarked, "maybe a recruiting party'll pick him up. Wouldn't he look fine with a Brown Bess musket on his shoulder and all that hair powdered and tucked into an eel skin?"

I moved in swiftly. "Now that we have that settled, my dear sirs,"

I said with unction, "why don't we go our several ways till after dinner and then meet here again? That will enable you to find suitable attire, which will of course be essential, and it'll give Professor Davey a chance to shave."

"Yeah?" grunted Davey. "And come back to an empty office, with both you and Shagreen denying everything?"

Again, Addleweed and his enemy agreed. "I'm afraid that's the way of it, Grumpole," he declared. "Why don't we stay right here? Willa knows somebody in the drama department rather well—"

Miss Kornmulder simpered.

"—and I'm sure he'll furnish her the costumes. Neither of us should be too hard to fit. And we can have dinner sent up to us from some Chinese or Italian restaurant. We'll have a jolly little picnic and then set forth. As I'm making the first trip, I'll choose to visit Samuel Taylor Coleridge, whom I do not hold in very high regard, but whom I have always wished I could have met simply because he did write one or two good essays."

"Well, I can't wait here with you," said Miss Kornmulder. "If I'm going to work on Jody to crack open that backstage wardrobe, it's going to have to be in person and right away. Jody's a real feelum, smellum boy. My voice over the phone wouldn't crease him."

Mr. Shagreen frowned at her jealously, but I frowned at him, and he made no active protest. Neither did Addleweed or Davey; clearly there was no other way to go about it.

She blew a kiss at Shagreen, called out, "Save me some shrimp chow mein, beddy-boy!" and took her leave.

Professor Davey was already on the phone ordering an Italian dinner from a restaurant near the campus, and it was delivered to us— minestrone, green salad, veal scallopini, pasta, and two bottles of red wine to wash it down with—in less than twenty minutes

I shall never forget that strange meal. Addleweed's table manners were precise and picky. Davey's were deliberately abominable. Addleweed, between bites, speculated on the nature of the incident from which the song had started. Widdecombe, or Widecombe on Mere, he pointed out, was in Devon, more than a hundred miles from Marlow. If there had indeed been a fair at Widdecombe, coinciding with the summer solstice, certainly no Buckinghamshire gentleman would reach it, however hard-riding he might be, unless it lasted much, much longer than country fairs were wont to last. Davey, between gulps and belches, told him he was an idiot not to know that,

in the Eighteenth Century, hard-drinking country gentlemen would
—at least when they weren't busy grinding the faces of the poor—
take any wager, however hazardous, if horses were involved, and it
was obvious that Tom Pearce's gray mare must have been a famous
horse indeed.

Halfway through dinner, Willa Kornmulder rejoined us, bringing
her eager, panting Jody with her. Mr. Shagreen prudently had
covered up the speculum again with the paisley shawl, but Jody was
too much absorbed in the Kornmulder anatomy to have noticed it
anyhow. He brought in the two costumes in their mothproof bags
and put them down and congratulated whichever of us were going to
the masquerade, and Willa had a little difficulty in getting him to
leave. Finally, though, he was gone, and she displayed what he had
found us: for Addleweed a fine gray suit of watered silk with silver
buttons, knee breeches and silk stockings, expensive linen, a periwig,
a silver-braided tricorn hat, silver-buckled shoes, a silver-hilted
smallsword; for Davey, the costume of a poor Church of England
clergyman, coat, breeches, stockings, hat all black, no sword at all,
and a rumpled white stock which seemed to advertise a whining ec-
clesiastical humility.

Davey sputtered an obscenity. Addleweed asked him if he was
quoting the great poet Gooeyduck. Miss Kornmulder explained hypo-
critically, "I'm sorry. It was all he had would fit you, Peter." She also
produced a razor and a can of aerosol shaving cream, which Jody
had been kind enough to lend her. Davey turned red, quoted
Gooeyduck at length, then with ill grace accepted the inevitable. He
stormed out of the room, carrying the razor and the costume, and returned fifteen minutes later a different man.

Even without his whiskers, he made a villainous-looking parson;
and Addleweed, who had changed his garments shamelessly in front
of all of us, stared at him in amused astonishment. "Don't tell me!"
he said archly. "Let me guess—the Vicar of Wakefield? No, that
won't do at all. The Vicar of Bray? No, by that time he'd have gone
to his reward. I know—you're the Little Shepherd of Kingdom
Come!" And he roared with laughter.

If he had not had the sword, I'm sure Davey would have attacked
him physically; as it was, we finished up our dinner in a hostile silence broken only by the affectionate murmurings of Mr. Shagreen
and Miss Kornmulder, who were repairing the small rift caused by
the intrusion of young Jody into their affairs.

Finally, Davey thrust back his plate, wiped his hands on his coat-tails, and said, "All right. For Christ's sake, let's get *with* it!"

Addleweed sipped his glass of wine, taunting him deliberately, and I felt impelled to intervene again. "We really should, you know," I told them. "Our experiments must be completed before the janitors arrive."

"Very well." Addleweed arose; he walked up to the speculum. "Turn the thing on," he said.

Hurriedly, I chattered out the Words of Power. *"Time Was!"* announced the brazen head we could not see.

"The year 1797," declared Addleweed, speaking clearly and distinctly. "An isolated farmhouse on Exmoor, between the villages of Porlock and Linton, the house at which Samuel Taylor Coleridge is staying to recuperate. The day is not important, but it must be when he is in—and of course out of sight of anyone."

Even before he finished, the undefined past dissolved, and we were looking at a farmhouse, apparently from around the corner of an outbuilding. Addleweed looked a little apprehensive, but he did not hesitate. He stepped through into the Eighteenth Century, glanced about him when a dog began to howl, and walked straight to the door. A serving woman, perhaps the farmer's daughter, answered his knock. "Good day to you, sir. What brings you here?" she said.

"I'm here to meet the celebrated Mr. Coleridge, my good woman," he replied grandiloquently, "for I have matters to discuss with him, and have come from Porlock for the purpose."

The woman turned her head. "Here's a person from Porlock, Mr. Coleridge," she called out. "He declares he has business with you."

And we heard Coleridge's voice replying, a bit testily, "Well, I suppose I'll have to see him, though he comes at a bad time. Show him in."

The speculum followed Addleweed as he was ushered through into a plainly furnished room, where Coleridge presently appeared, looking slightly disheveled and with reddened eyes, as though only recently awakened. He was unmistakable: the slightly curling, black, untidy hair, the wide mouth, the thin, pale features. But when he spoke, greeting Addleweed, such was his charm that even Davey, for a moment, stopped sneering and muttering imprecations.

Then we were treated to an almost unbelievable performance, for Addleweed introduced himself by his true name, explained that he was visiting in the neighborhood, but that he had come from the new

United States, where he was a man of substance and a trustee of Harvard College.

At that point, Coleridge smiled and remarked pleasantly, "I daresay, sir, that this explains why your attire, though of the finest quality, is some years behind our fashion."

Addleweed, in no way put out, explained that this was so, and that his friends in the vicinity—who by the way had dropped him there by coach and would return for him in possibly an hour—had told him the same thing.

"*An hour!*" howled Davey. "The son of a bitch—taking up an *hour,* when he knows I'm waiting to get our really important job done! Damn him! Isn't there any way we can snake him back here?"

"Oh, dear!" answered Mr. Shagreen unhappily. "I fear there isn't any way, no way at all, indeed—unless perhaps truly you'd like to go yourself, and catch him by the arm, and pull him back by main force? Though even the results of that I cannot prophesy, for lack of intimate experience with the speculum, with the mechanics and the secret movements of it, as it were."

So, during the balance of the hour, poor Davey was forced to contain himself, storming back and forth and quoting Gooeyduck at all and sundry.

Addleweed informed the poet that he was himself a patron of the arts, and at great length he discussed a project whereby he would endow some vast sum to maintain Coleridge and perhaps the Wordsworths too in opulence, provided only that they would cross the sea and take up residence in Massachusetts. Coleridge politely put him off, pleading his health, and giving other reasons. They discussed poets and poetry, politics and letters, until finally it became evident even to Addleweed that his host was getting tired. He stood up, repeated his invitation and his offer, bowed his good-bys, and finally took his leave, saying, "I trust I did not interfere with your labors, Mr. Coleridge?"

"No, no, pray don't concern yourself," replied the poet wearily. "I daresay that I'll recall the other stanzas, sir, when I get back to it."

Addleweed left, the door closed behind him, and slowly he strolled back to the outbuilding. Then he said, "*Enfold me!*" and was with us instantly.

It seemed to me singularly fitting that a Twentieth Century Professor of English Literature should have been the man to happen by and spoil Coleridge's remembrance of *Kubla Khan,* but I deemed it wiser not to comment on it, and Davey missed the point entirely. He did not even speak to Addleweed. He strode up to the speculum, now once more turgid. "Marlow, in Buckinghamshire, goddamn it! on Midsummer's Eve, 1769. In the courtyard of the best inn there, but where nobody can see!"

The stable yard took form before our eyes. There was no living thing in sight. With a final curse, Professor Davey stepped into it, and marched to the inn door, which he threw open. It was a low-ceilinged room, built in Elizabethan times, with huge glowering beams where shadows strove against each other, cast by candles and by the great fireplace where a fowl or two, a leg of lamb, and a vast joint of beef were spitted. Two or three countrymen sat at a table with their tankards, playing draughts; and at a long oaken table near the fire a group of gentry, deep in their cups and surrounded by the bottles with which they had contended, were arguing riotously.

"By God!" roared a booted hunting squire in bottle green. "I tell ye, Joranda *will* be at the Fair—may be there now, for all I know— with all her cov—"

"Hush, Will!" A smaller, older gentleman snapped out the words. "That's for us alone!" He was dressed modestly in brown, but his face, saturnine and hungry and implacable, was enough to strike silence into anyone.

"Well, Gypsy or no, she's a damned pretty witch, she is!" Will grumbled. "But you're right, Sir John, you're right. I'll say no more, but I will be with her tonight, Devil take me if I don't!" And he poured himself almost a pint of port.

In the meantime, the innkeeper, a displaced Irishman by the manner and the sound of him, and probably an ex-sergeant by his look, had greeted Davey favorably enough, asking him how his journey went—for was he not a stranger in these parts?—and would he eat and drink?

"I've dined," Davey grunted. "And wined too. But some sherry might do well to top it off with."

The innkeeper brought him a bottle and a glass and said, "And now there'll be the price of it, your Riverence, if you please."

We saw Davey's cheek redden; we watched him fumble in his pockets angrily; we realized that, in his rage, he'd never thought of money to take with him.

Addleweed chuckled. "Well, well!" he said. "I knew if I could only get him wild enough, he'd foul it up! Do you suppose he'll pop back out of there to borrow a few of old King George's shillings from us?"

But Davey had no intention of retreating.

"Well, sir," remarked the Irishman, "'tis a few pence only, and surely you'll be having that about you?"

"I haven't a goddamned penny on me!" shouted Davey, now tried beyond endurance. "And that's the bloody truth, and make the most of it." And taking up the bottle he began to pour.

The innkeeper reached out a big, hairy hand. "I cannot let you do that without paying, sir. Though you're a man of the cloth, still you are not from hereabouts. We do not know you, sir—" And he made as though to retrieve the bottle.

As I have said, Professor Davey was a well-made young man, with power in his solid body. With a tremendous oath, he brushed the hand aside. He brought the bottle down on the tabletop so hard that sherry spilled. "Damn your black Irish soul!" he roared. "I'll drink this bottle and pay you when I can! Do what you like about it—but if you try, I'll break the thing and ram it up that fat arse of yours!"

"Fantastic!" whispered Addleweed. "He remember to say *arse* instead of *ass.*"

The Irishman, amazed by such behavior from a parson, gave way a step, obviously to recruit his energies. But by this time, the gentlemen across the room had become aware of what was going on. Several of them had risen to their feet so that they might see more clearly. One of them, red-faced, white-haired, and many years older than the rest, exclaimed, "Heigh-ho, me lads! Why, here we have a fighting cockerel of a starveling parson, right enough! Methinks he is a man after my own heart." Taking a coin from his pocket, he called out, "Paddy, my boy, give him what he wants." He tossed the coin. "Tonight, by God, we well may need a chaplain, and he'll be my guest! Pick up your glass and bottle, sir, and join us. I'm Thomas Cobleigh of Cobleigh Manor, hard by. What is your name?"

And Davey, as he walked across to them, gave us over his shoulder a look of utter scorn and pure triumph. He introduced himself. "I'm Peter Davey," he declared, "and it's true I am a stranger." He actually bowed slightly. "At least I am a stranger well received. I thank you, sir."

"By God, I didn't think he had it in him to be courteous," muttered Addleweed.

Davey's host and benefactor now presented his companions: Sir

John Steward, whose wicked eyes were appraising the newcomer calculatingly; Mr. William Brewer; Peter Garney, a lean and leathery man meticulously dressed; Mr. Daniel Whidden, broad-shouldered and beetle-browed; and Mr. Harry Hawke, who—Cobleigh boasted —might be small, but "Damme! He could put a horse at any fence in England—aye, and over it!"

After Davey had proposed a toast to all of them, and they had drunk it, Sir John began to ask him questions: where was he from? and was he staying in the neighborhood? and had serious business of some sort brought him there?

Davey replied that he had spent twelve years in the town of New York, in the American Colonies, but there had been a little difficulty —he smiled at them evilly—involving the wife of a parishioner, and he had felt it wiser to depart.

"Unfrocked you, did they?" Sir John demanded, leaning forward slightly with a new interest.

Davey muttered unintelligibly, conveying the impression that he had indeed been unfrocked. There was a ripple of drunken laughter, and Will Brewer slapped him heartily on the back. Then the questioning resumed, and Davey hinted that he was staying with friends at Medmenham.

"Who?" asked Sir John.

Davey hesitated for a moment only. "At Medmenham Abbey," he replied.

"How on earth did *he* ever hear of the Hell Fire Club?" whispered Addleweed. "Do you suppose he read a book? The idiot! It's lucky for him they don't have telephones!"

I heard Sir Francis was at London?" Sir John's voice suddenly was icy.

"Certain of his friends are staying as his guests, and I am of their number. It was they who suggested I might find good entertainment here, sir, if someone would but introduce me to Tom Pierce."

"Devil take me, that is a trick Bubb Doddington would play!" exclaimed Peter Garney with a neighing laugh.

Davey smiled, but answered neither yes nor no.

"Did he also tell you," asked Sir John, "that Tom Pierce and Sir Francis are rivals in a way? Or that Tom has outdone him very neatly? Aye, there's nothing they do at the Abbey Tom's not done better—or perhaps I should say *worse*. For look you—" He again leaned forward, and his eyes stabbed at Davey like a knife—"at the abbey, it's all playacting, do you see? But what Tom has done at Direwolf Hall no man has dared to do since Dr. Dee—as you shall see, my not-so-reverend friend. We're going there directly, and we shall take you with us, if you will."

"D'you think it wise, Sir John?" grumbled Daniel Whidden. "After all, we do not know this man."

"God rot you, Whidden! Be done with carping at me. You know as well as I there's always a good use for any unfrocked parson at the Hall."

"Aye, aye," said Cobleigh. "Pierce will be glad enough to have him there. But are we going there indeed?"

Here Will Brewer again staggered to his feet. "Damned if we don't!" he shouted. "I tell ye, Joranda's at the fair at Widdicombe, the pretty witch—aye, she and all her tribe! And I shall lie with her tonight, d'you hear? And it'll be Tom Pierce shall fetch us there!"

"I fear you overrate Tom's powers, Will," Sir John said with a sneer. "Nothing can get you to Widdicombe this night!"

"I'll lay a thousand pound on it!" Brewer bellowed.

"Done!" said Sir John. "But how d'you think he'll manage it?"

And Davey looked at both of them, and said, "Perhaps with his gray mare?"

Instantly, there was utter silence in the room, a stillness where even the fire seemed frozen and no man moved. I, standing in my office before the speculum, knew the strangeness of it, and in my bones felt that dark doings would soon be afoot.

But laughter tore the silence into shreds. "Gray mare!" whinnied Peter Garney. "Namesake Davey, I warrant ye'll never see a mare the likes of her!" It seemed to be a joke between the lot of them. Will Brewer roared and chuckled; Whidden and old Tom Cobleigh rumbled and guffawed. Even Sir John Steward smiled secretly. But the Irish innkeeper, and the rustics at their tankards, and the plump, blushing serving maid whom all of them that night had bussed and pinched, these did not laugh at all; instead they seemed to draw into themselves.

Now all the gentlemen were rising; Thomas Cobleigh was tossing money on the table to pay the reckoning. "Sir John and I," said he, "will take Parson Davey here with us in my coach. See that you don't fall off your horses, boys! We'll meet you there."

The stable yard was faintly moonlit, and the coach, its two feeble lamps flickering fitfully, was waiting there, its harness and its leathern springs creaking as the four horses shifted in their traces. Inside, it was completely dark, as though the vehicle, now moving forward, denied permission to all light to enter it. Occasionally, a small shaft of moonlight, slipping by, would be reflected by a golden button, by a sword hilt, by the wild whites of Sir John Stewart's eyes; but usually his voice reached us out of darkness.

He told the history of the hall and of its owners, not leaving out the present tenant, describing it as a cold, towering grimness of gray stone, raised through the generations over and around the ancient walls of Direwolf Priory where, in the Twelfth Century, the abbot and all but seven of his monks had suffered at the stake for having sold their souls to Satan, practicing Black Magic and the like. It was a history of murders and betrayals, plots, cruelties, bitter tears, and unclean deeds, and its narrator seemed very proud of it. "There's been nothing like that at the abbey, I assure you, sir—whatever Dashwood and his friends may say; and since Tom's restored the old friary chapel, and refurnished it, and dedicated it again—well, to-night you'll see!"

The coach turned off the road, clattering at a good stiff trot down a tree-shadowed avenue—and there the hall loomed, vast and ominous. The horsemen, who'd passed by on the road at a drunken gallop and shouting wildly, were already there; and together they knocked at the forbidding door. Two servants opened it, huge, dull-eyed men in a black livery, and beckoned to them silently to follow, and the door closed to behind them. In wall sconces and in chandeliers candles guttered, but there was darkness everywhere. Dark pictures stared from darkness-haunted walls. Dark suits of armor were on silent guard at every turn. They passed through the great hall, where among the roof beams, in a chill updraft, dark banners beat their long-neglected wings. Then one of the servitors unlocked a mighty portal in the wall, and they went down a stone passageway, down worn stone steps, to a final door. The servants threw it open, but did not go in. Sir John leading the way, they filed through.

I saw that they were in the chapel of the friary, long dead, long buried, long forgotten—now brought once more alive. There were no stained glass windows here, no symbols of the Resurrection and the Life, but Christ Crucified hung upside down behind the black stone altar, on which a naked woman lay—a woman young and very beautiful, but with vile eyes. Black tapers burned in their branched candlesticks. High on the dark wall, a hideously horned head glared down, and on a votive table before the altar, a book reposed—a tall, narrow folio bound in alum-tanned pigskin and clasped with iron. And there Tom Pierce stood, wearing the black habit of a monk, its hood thrown back to show his shaven head, and his once-handsome pockmarked, ravaged face. Now he came forward, towering over all of them, and his eyes were terrible pools of emptiness. And it was plain that he too was very, very drunk.

"Brethren," his heavy voice rasped out, "I was told that you would come, a stranger with you. Who is he?"

"Lord Abbot," replied Sir John, with something very like fear in his voice, "he is an unfrocked priest and a friend of Francis Dashwood's and Doddington's, who sent him to us. Peter Davey is his name. He is one of us."

Pierce looked Davey up and down, and through and through. "Belike he is," said he. "Soon enough we'll know."

As the rest advanced, Davey purposely had lagged behind; now he turned his head and, under his breath, spoke to the speculum. "Okay, Addleweed, you fink! Here it is—a lot of drunken slobs with too much money playing Dracula! Next we'll be marching to the stables to meet the mare!"

Then he felt Pierce's eyes on him and rejoined the rest. Will Brewer, his arms around the false monk's shoulders, was telling of his wager and of his determination to be in Widdicomb that night to lie again with Joranda. "She'll have her coven with her," he declared. "More than enough for the whole lot of us! John here still says you can't get us there, but I, by everything unholy, declare you can!"

"A few days since," declared Pierce, "Brother John would have been right indeed. But doors have opened for me. There's much I've learned. Now I have *powers*—" And he laughed mirthlessly as he pronounced the word—"which can take us all to Widdicombe while you blink an eye. Yes, or to the moon did we wish to go there. Or into hell itself!"

He opened the tall book. "Do ye all wish to go?" he asked of them.

They answered that they did.

He asked them once, and twice again, and they gave him the same reply.

"Very well, then," he said. "We'll waste no time with the Mass and all such flummery." He gestured to the girl, who climbed down, and donned a nun's habit lying by the altar. "I shall command the one who'll bear us there!"

Then, carrying the book, he began walking withershins around the pentacle, chanting in a strange and ugly tongue.

My own fears had been mounting. Now I turned to Shagreen. "Those people are not playing!" I exclaimed. "Or if they are, it's a damned dangerous game. Isn't there *some* way to get him out of there?"

"None, none at all, truly," moaned Shagreen.

Clinging to him, Miss Kornmulder quivered with excitement. "Hey!" she chattered. "Talk about your Gothics! This is just the *greatest!*"

Pierce had thrown the black hood forward over his head. His voice was swelling now, and in among the unknown words I began recognizing names—names which never should be thought, let alone cried aloud. His tone had been almost one of pleading. Now it was changed to one of savage, absolute command. Finally he repeated one name three times, so that the chapel echoed and reechoed with his voice, his mouth writhing in a smile so cruel that he no longer appeared human.

The echoes died away, but the name seemed to linger there, over them.

And it was then that Davey spoke to him. "Er—Lord Abbot," he began, "pardon my interrupting, but before the night is too far gone, could I see your gray mare? They tell me she's—"

Abruptly, Tom Pierce turned about. Within the black shroud of his habit, he seemed almost literally to *grow*. *"Gray mare?"* he screamed. "Man, are ye daft? Or are ye as simple as the country folk? It's no horse of this world that'll bear us all to Widdicombe!" He lifted high the open book. *"It is my grimoire!"*

Then once more he cried the name and said in clear English, *"I order you!"* and spoke a Word of Power which I had heard about but never seen in print.

What happened then occurred so swiftly that, later, none of us could quite agree on it. A cloud was there, between them above the pentacle, pitch black and fraught with forces unrestrained—and it had features amorphous in their hideousness and horror, and it had eyes. It filled the chapel instantly. We heard a desperate, pitiful *"Enfol—"* from Davey's lips.

Then suddenly there was an implosion of the air around us

through the speculum—and the material of the speculum was no longer there. The bronze ring stood before us, a vagrant curl of smoke wreathing from it, and the strong smell of brimstone—and through the ring there was nothing but my office to be seen.

It was some time, I assure you, before we could recover enough of our equanimity even to leave the office and lock it up behind us. I, an authority on sorcery, should perhaps not have been affected; instead, I felt as Einstein must have felt when he first read of Hiroshima. What I had seen left me terror-stricken. Poor Addleweed was in a thorough panic, and it was all that we could do eventually to get him changed and on his way. Mr. Shagreen was not so much shocked and horrified as plunged into despair by the destruction of the instrument on which he had lavished so much time and effort. As for Miss Kornmulder, her one regret was that the show ended without the promise of a next installment.

However, ultimately things really worked out for the best. We all agreed that it would be much wiser to keep the happenings of the evening completely to ourselves. Professor Addleweed, knowing now that his theory and not Davey's had been right, decided that he would do the necessary research to prove that dabbling in Black Magic had indeed caused the demise of the Brethren of Direwolf Hall, and I was able to get him a very generous two-year grant from the Hober Murrain Twitchett Memorial Endowment to take him back to England for that purpose—which made life easier for him, because Davey's campus followers were bruiting it about that Addleweed had made away with him.

Not only was Professor Addleweed clearly the winner in the controversy, but scarcely a week after Davey's disappearance, the N.A.A.C.P. revealed, after a careful investigation, that Gooeyduck was actually neither American nor black, but an illegal immigrant from Syria, with an Afro wig, a genuine talent for mimicking accents, and a keen eye for a soft touch.

In his distress, Mr. Shagreen stayed away from my office for three days, solacing himself with Willa Kornmulder, who had asked for leave. Then he returned suddenly, his spirits quite restored. He had received a letter from his *guru,* who had informed him that the Maharajah of Jehazpore, once the greatest of the Native Princes and still the world's richest man, wished to support him in his studies and had offered facilities and rewards beyond his wildest dreams.

"I really do not want to leave you, dear Grumps," he told me fondly. "Indeed I do not, for haven't we had such great fun together? But His Highness thinks that perhaps, with the assistance of the speculum, which I shall make haste to recreate, he can improve the desperate lot of India, for now the poor land is ruled by all sorts of self-seeking politicians and—as he puts it—by the ghost of Mrs. Eleanor Roosevelt, God rest her soul!"

I agreed with him that this was a goal worthy of his talents, and with considerable relief, I must admit, drove them—for Willa Kornmulder was going with him—to the airport. There we parted, she kissing me a moist good-by and telling me a little vaguely that she just couldn't wait to get there and be an *houri*.

Now ten months have passed. Occasionally I have had letters from Shagreen telling me of his progress, and how His Highness had instructed him to take those measures in the past which would bring again the civilized and prosperous days of the British Raj, when the Princes were all secure on their thrones and in their incomes, and how pleased His Highness now was with his efforts, and how he had just been made Grand Vizier, or Prime Minister.

I am really happy for him, for I'm sure it's all quite true. This morning in the paper I read that His Majesty Charles III, the King-Emperor, has proclaimed a Royal Durbar to be held in New Delhi—the first, I understand, in many years.